Night Play

Sherrilyn Kenyon

piatkus

PIATKUS

First published in the US in 2004 by St. Martin's Press, New York
First published in Great Britain in 2005 by Piatkus Books
This paperback edition published in 2011 by Piatkus

A CIP catalogue record for this book
is available from the British Library.

ISBN 978-0-7499- 5530-4

Printed and bound by CPI Group (UK) Ltd, Croydon CR0 4YY

Papers used by Piatkus are from well-managed forests
and other responsible sources.

MIX
Paper from
responsible sources
FSC® C104740

Piatkus
An imprint of
Little, Brown Book Group
100 Victoria Embankment
London EC4Y 0DY

An Hachette UK Company
www.hachette.co.uk

www.piatkus.co.uk

For my husband and sons who are my world. For all my friends who are there through thick and thin: Lo, Janet, Brynna, Tasha, "Nick," Dara, Ret, Cathy, Donna, Chris, Rebecca, and Kim.

To the DH fans all over the globe who make the world of the website and loops thrive and who give me endless hours of smiles—I wish I had space to list all of you by name, but from the bottom of my heart, thank you. For my RBL sisters who are always there and for my readers who make it all worthwhile. I can never, never thank you enough.

To Kim and Nancy for all the hard work you do and for still allowing me to take the DH to the outer limits of my imagination and beyond. And I haven't forgotten either of you, Alethea and Nicole!

Words can never truly express just how much I adore all of you and how much you mean to me.

May God bless and keep you all. Hugs!

NIGHT
Play

Gennisi

Come with me, modern traveler, back to a time that has been shrouded by mystery. Back to an ancient legend that has been mostly forgotten. Or at the very least . . .

Distorted.

We see remnants of it in our advanced world. What present-day mortal doesn't know to fear strange noises in the light of the full moon? To fear the howl of the wolf? The cry of a hawk? To look with caution into the darkest alleys. Not in fear of human predators, but in fear of something else.

Something dark. Dangerous. Something even deadlier than our human counterparts.

But mankind didn't always hold this fear. Indeed, there was a time once, long ago, when humans were humans and animals were animals.

Until the day of the *Allagi*. They say the birth of the Were-Hunters, like most great evils, started out with only the best of intentions.

King Lycaon of Arcadia had no idea that when he wed, his precious, beloved queen wasn't human. His wife held within her a dark secret. She was born to the cursed Apollite race and was destined to die in the heart of her youth . . . at age twenty-seven.

It wasn't until her last birthday when Lycaon watched his beloved die horribly of old age that he realized the two sons she had borne him would follow her to an early grave.

Grief-stricken, he had sought out his priests who all told him there was nothing he could do. Fate was fate.

But Lycaon refused to heed their wisdom. He was a sorcerer and he was determined that no one would steal his sons away from him. Not even the Fates themselves.

And so he set about experimenting with his magic to prolong the lives of his wife's people. Capturing them, he magically spliced their essence with various animals who were known for their strength: bears, panthers, leopards, hawks, lions, tigers, jackals, wolves, and even dragons.

He spent years perfecting his new race, until at last he was sure he'd found the cure for his sons. Blending them with a dragon and a wolf, the strongest of the animals he had experimented with, he imbued them with more strength and magic than any of the others. In truth, he gave of his own power to his sons.

In the end, he received more than he had bargained for. Not only did his sons have longer lives than his wife, they had longer lives than any known species.

With their magical abilities and animal strength, they now lived ten to twelve times longer than any human.

The Fates looked down and saw what the proud king had done. Angry at his interference in their domain, the

Fates decreed that he must kill his sons and all like them.

Lycaon refused.

It was then the Fates sought out their own form of punishment for his hubris. His children and all like them were cursed anew.

"There will never be peace among your children," Clotho, the Fate who spins the threads of life, proclaimed. "They will spend eternity hating and fighting until the day when the last of them breathes no more."

And so it was. Whenever Lycaon blended an animal with a human, he, in fact, made two beings. One being who held an animal's heart and one who held a human heart.

Those who walked as men and who held human hearts were termed Arcadians after Lycaon's people. Those who held animal hearts were termed Katagaria.

The Katagaria were born as animals and lived as animals, yet once they reached puberty, when the magical powers were unlocked by their hormones, they would be able to become human—at least externally. Their animal hearts would always govern their actions.

Likewise, the Arcadians were born as humans and lived as humans until their puberty brought with it their magic and their ability to shift into animal form.

Two sides of a single coin, the two species should have been at peace. Instead, the goddesses sent Discordia to plant mistrust between them. The Arcadians felt themselves superior to their animal cousins. After all, they were humans with human rationality while the Katagaria were only animals who could take human form.

The Katagaria learned quickly that the Arcadians weren't honest about their intentions and would say one thing, then do another.

All throughout time, the two groups have preyed upon each other while each side took the moral high ground. The animals believe the Arcadians are the real threat while the Arcadians believe the Katagaria must be controlled or put down.

It is an endless war.

And as with all wars, there has never been a true victor. There have only been casualties who still suffer from the prejudice and unfounded hatred.

Prologue

New Orleans, Mardi Gras night, 2003

"I'm so sorry, Vane. I swear didn't mean to get us killed like this."

Vane Kattalakis ground his teeth as he fell back from trying to pull himself up. His arms ached from the strain of lifting two hundred pounds of lean muscle up by nothing more than the bones of his wrists. Every time he got close to raising his body up to the limb over his head, his brother started talking, which broke his concentration and caused him to fall back into his hanging position.

He took a deep breath, trying to ignore the severe pain of his wrists. "Don't worry, Fang. I'll get us out of this."

Somehow.

He hoped.

Fang didn't hear him. Instead he continued to apologize for causing their deaths.

Vane strained again against the sharpened cord that held his hands tied together above his head, secured to a thin limb, as he hung precariously from an ancient cypress tree over some of the darkest, nastiest-looking swamp water he'd ever seen. He didn't know what was worse, the thought of losing his hands, his life, or falling into that disgusting gator-infested slime hole.

Honestly, though, he'd rather be dead than touch that stank. Even in the darkness of the Louisiana bayou, he could tell just how putrid and revolting it was.

There was something seriously wrong with anyone who wanted to live out here in this swamp. At last he had confirmation that Talon of the Morrigantes was a first-rank idiot.

His brother, Fang, was tied to an equally thin limb on the opposite side of the tree where they dangled eerily amid swamp gas, snakes, insects, and gators.

With every movement Vane made, the cord cut into the flesh of his wrists. If he didn't get them freed soon, that cord would cut all the way through his tendons and bones, and sever his hands completely.

This was the *timoria,* the punishment, that they were both receiving for the fact that Vane had protected Talon's woman. Because Vane had dared to help the Dark-Hunters, the soulless Daimons who were at war with the Dark-Hunters had attacked Vane's Katagaria wolf pack and slaughtered his beloved sister.

Katagaria were animals who could take human form and they followed one basic law of nature: kill or be killed. If anyone or anything threatened the pack's safety, it was put down.

So Vane, who had caused the Daimon attack, had been sentenced to being beaten and left for dead in the swamp. Fang was with him only because their father had hated both of them since the hour they had been birthed and had feared them since the day their preternatural powers had been unlocked by their pubescent hormones.

More than that, their father hated them for what their mother had done to him.

This had been a once-in-a-lifetime opportunity for their father to be rid of them both without the pack turning on him for the death sentence.

Their father had seized it gleefully.

It would be the last mistake his father ever made.

At least it would be if Vane could get their asses out of this damned swamp without being eaten.

Both of them were in human form and trapped by the thin, silver *metriazo* collars they wore around their necks that sent tiny ionic impulses into their bodies. The collars kept them in human form. Something their enemies thought would make them weaker.

In Fang's case that was true.

In Vane's it wasn't.

Even so, the collar did dampen his ability to wield magic and manipulate the laws of nature. And that was seriously pissing him off.

Like Fang, Vane was dressed only in a pair of blood-ied jeans. His shirt had been ripped off for his beating and his boots taken just for spite. Of course, no one ex-pected them to live. The collars couldn't be removed except by magic—which neither of them could use so long as they wore them—and even if by some miracle they did get down from the tree, there was already a large group of gators who could smell their blood. Gators who were just waiting for them to fall into the swamp and provide the gators with one tasty wolf meal.

"Man," Fang said irritably. "Fury was right. You

should never trust anything that bleeds for five days and doesn't die. I should have listened to you. You told me Petra was a three-wolf humping bitch, but did I listen? No. And now look at us. I swear, if I get out of this, I'm going to kill her."

"Fang!" Vane snapped as his brother continued to rail while Vane tried to manage a few powers even through the painful electrical shocks of the collar. "Could you lay off the Blame Fest and let me concentrate here, otherwise we're going to be hanging from this damned tree for the rest of eternity."

"Well, not for eternity. I figure we only have about half an hour more before the cords cut through our wrists. Speaking of, my wrists really hurt. How about yours?" Fang paused while Vane took a deep breath and felt a tiny movement of the cord coming loose.

He also heard the limb crack.

His heart hammering, Vane looked down to see one massively large gator eyeballing him from the murky depths. Vane would have given anything to have three seconds of his powers to fry that greedy bugger.

Fang didn't seem to notice either threat. "I swear I'm never going to tell you to bite my ass again. Next time you tell me something, I'm going to listen, especially if it concerns a female."

Vane growled. "Then could you start by listening to me when I tell you to shut up?"

"I'm being quiet. I just hate being human. This sucks. How do you stand it?"

"Fang!"

"What?"

Vane rolled his eyes. It was useless. Any time his

brother was in human form, the only part of his body that got any exercise was his mouth. Why couldn't their pack have gagged Fang before they strung him up?

"You know, if we were in wolf form, we could just gnaw our paws off. Of course if we were in wolf form, the cords wouldn't hold us, so—"

"Shut up," Vane snapped again.

"Does the feeling ever come back into your hands after they get all numb like this? This doesn't happen when we're wolves. Does it happen a lot to humans?"

Vane closed his eyes in disgust. So this was how his life would end. Not in some glorious battle against an enemy or his father. Not quietly in his sleep.

No, the last sound he would hear would be Fang bitching.

It figured.

He leaned his head back so that he could see his brother through the darkness. "You know, Fang, let's cast blame for a minute. I am sick and tired of hanging here because of your damned big mouth that decided to tell your latest chew toy about how I guarded a Dark-Hunter's mate. Thanks so much for not knowing when to shut the hell up."

"Yeah, well, how was I to know Petra would run to Father and tell him you were with Sunshine and that that was why the Daimons attacked us? Two-faced bitch. Petra said she wanted to mate with me."

"They all want to mate with you, dickhead, it's the nature of our species."

"Fuck you!"

Vane let out a relieved breath as Fang finally quieted down. His brother's anger should give him about a three-minute reprieve while Fang simmered as he searched for a more creative and articulate comeback.

Lacing his fingers together, Vane lifted his legs up. More pain sliced through his arms as it cut deeper into his human flesh. He only prayed his bones held a little longer without severing.

More blood ran down his forearms as he lifted his legs up toward the branch over his head.

If he could just get them wrapped . . . around . . .

He tapped the wood with his bare foot. The bark was cold and brittle as it scraped against the soft topside of his foot. He cupped his ankle around the wood.

Just a little . . . bit . . .

More.

Fang snarled at him. "You are such an asshole . . ."

Well, so much for creativity.

Vane focused his attention on his own rapid heartbeat and refused to hear Fang's insults.

Upside down, he wrapped one leg around the limb and expelled his breath. Vane growled in relief as the weight was mostly removed from his throbbing, bloodied wrists. He panted from the exertion while Fang continued his unheard tirade.

The limb creaked dangerously.

Vane held his breath again, terrified of moving lest he cause the branch to snap in two and send him plummeting into the putrid, green swamp water below.

Suddenly, the gators thrashed about in the water, then sped away.

"Oh shit," Vane hissed.

That was not a good sign.

There were only two things he knew of that could

make the gators leave. One was if the Dark-Hunter named Talon, who lived in the swamp, returned home and reined them in. But since Talon was off in the French Quarter saving the world and not in the swamp tonight that seemed highly unlikely.

The other, far less appealing option was Daimons—those who were the walking dead, damned to kill in order to sustain their artificially prolonged lives. The only thing they prided themselves on killing more than humans were Were-Hunters. Since the Were-Hunters' lives spanned centuries and they possessed magical abilities, their souls could sustain a Daimon ten times longer than the average human.

Even more impressive, once a Were-Hunter's soul was claimed, his or her magical abilities were absorbed into the Daimons' bodies where they could use those powers against others.

It was a special gift to be a "nubby" treat for the undead.

There was only one reason for the Daimons to be here. Only one way for them to be able to find him and Fang in this isolated swamp where Daimons didn't tread without cause. Someone had offered the two of them up as a sacrifice so that the Daimons would leave their Katagaria pack alone.

And there was no doubt in his mind who had made that call.

"Damn you!" Vane snarled out into the darkness, knowing his father couldn't hear him. But he needed to vent anyway.

"What did I do to you?" Fang asked indignantly. "Besides getting you killed, anyway."

"Not you," Vane said as he struggled to get his other leg up enough so that he could free his hands.

Something leaped up from the swamp into the tree above him.

Vane twisted his body to see the tall, thin Daimon standing just above, looking down at him with an amused gleam in his hungry eyes.

Dressed all in black, the blond Daimon clucked his tongue at him. "You should be happy to see us, wolf. After all, we only want to free you."

"Go to hell!" Vane snarled.

The Daimon laughed.

Fang howled.

Vane looked to see a group of ten Daimons pulling Fang down from the tree. Dammit! His brother was a wolf. He didn't know how to fight them in human form without his magical powers, which he couldn't use so long as Fang wore his collar.

Infuriated, Vane kicked his legs up. The limb broke instantly, sending him straight into the stagnant water below.

Vane held his breath as the putrid, slimy taste of it invaded his head. He tried to kick himself to the surface, but couldn't.

Not that it mattered. Someone grabbed him by the hair and pulled him to the surface.

As soon as his head was above the water, a Daimon sank his fangs into Vane's bare shoulder. Growling in rage, Vane elbowed the Daimon in the ribs and used his own teeth to return the bite.

The Daimon shrieked and released him.

"This one has fight," a female said as she made her

way toward him. "He'll be worth more sustenance than the other."

Vane kicked her legs out from under her before she could grab him. He used her bobbing body as a springboard to get out of the water. Like any good wolf, his legs were strong enough to propel him from the water to one of the cypress knees nearby.

His dark wet hair hung in his face while his body throbbed from the fight and from the beating his pack had given him. Moonlight glinted off his wet, muscled body as he crouched with one hand on the old wooden knee that was silhouetted against the backdrop of the swamp. Dark Spanish moss hung from the trees as the full moon, draped in clouds, reflected eerily in the black velvet waves of the water.

Like the animal he was, Vane watched his enemies closing in around him. He wasn't about to surrender himself or Fang to these bastards. He might not be dead, but he was every bit as damned as they were and even more pissed off at Fate.

Lifting his hands to his mouth, Vane used his teeth to bite through the cord around his wrists and free his hands.

"You'll pay for that," a male Daimon said as he moved toward him.

His hands free, Vane backflipped from the stump, into the water. He dove deep into the murky depths until he could break a piece of wood from a fallen tree that was buried there. He kicked his way back toward the area where Fang was being held down.

He came out of the water just beside his brother to find ten different Daimons feeding from Fang's blood.

He kicked one back, seized another by the neck and plunged his makeshift stake into the Daimon's heart. The creature disintegrated immediately.

The others turned on him.

"Take a number," Vane snarled at them. "There's plenty of this to go around."

The Daimon nearest him laughed. "Your powers are bound."

"Tell it to the undertaker," Vane said as he lunged for him. The Daimon jumped back, but not far enough. Used to fighting humans, the Daimon didn't take into account that Vane was physically able to leap ten times as far.

Vane didn't need his psychic powers. His animal strength was enough to finish this. He stabbed the Daimon and turned to face the others as the Daimon evaporated.

They rushed him at once, but it didn't work. Half of a Daimon's power was the ability to strike without warning and to cause their victim to panic.

That would have worked except that Vane, as a cousin to the Daimons, had been taught that strategy from the cradle. There was nothing about them that made him panic.

All their tactic did was make him dispassionate and determined.

And in the end, that would make him victorious.

Vane ripped through two more with his stake while Fang remained unmoving in the water. He began to panic but forced it down.

Calmness was the only way to win a fight.

One of the Daimons caught him with a blast that sent

him spiraling through the water. Vane collided with a stump and groaned at the pain that exploded down his back.

Out of habit, he lashed back with his own powers only to feel the collar tighten and shock him. He cursed at the new pain, then ignored it.

Getting up, he charged at the two males who were heading for his brother.

"Give up already," one of the Daimons snarled.

"Why don't you?"

The Daimon lunged. Vane ducked under the water and pulled the Daimon's feet out from under him. They fought in the water until Vane caught him in the chest with his stake.

The rest ran off.

Vane stood in the darkness, listening to them splashing away from him. His heart pounded in his ears as he allowed his rage to consume him. Throwing his head back, he let out his wolf's howl, which echoed eerily through the misty bayou.

Inhuman and baleful, it was the kind of sound that would send even the voodoo mavens scurrying for cover.

Now certain the Daimons were gone, Vane raked his wet hair from his eyes as he made his way to Fang, who still hadn't moved.

Vane choked on his grief as he stumbled blindly through the water with only one thought in his mind . . . *Don't be dead.*

Over and over in his mind, he saw his sister's lifeless body. Felt her coldness against his skin. He couldn't lose them both. He couldn't.

It would kill him.

For the first time in his life, he wanted to hear one of Fang's stupid-ass comments.

Anything.

Images flashed through his mind as he remembered his sister's death just the day before at the hands of the Daimons. Unimaginable pain tore through him. Fang had to be alive. He had to.

"Please, God," he breathed as he closed the distance between them. He couldn't lose his brother.

Not like this . . .

Fang's eyes were open, staring unseeingly up at the full moon, which would have allowed them to time-jump out of this swamp had they not both been wearing the collars.

There were open bite wounds all over him.

A deep, profound grief tore through Vane, splintering his heart into pieces.

"C'mon, Fang, don't be dead," he said, his voice breaking as he forced himself not to cry. Instead, he snarled out, "Don't you dare die on me, you asshole."

He pulled his brother to him and discovered that Fang wasn't dead. He was still breathing and shaking uncontrollably. Shallow and raspy, the hollow sound of Fang's breaths was a symphony to Vane's ears.

His tears broke as relief pierced him. He cradled Fang gently in his arms.

"C'mon, Fang," he said in the stillness. "Say something stupid for me."

But Fang didn't speak. He just lay there in complete shock as he shook in Vane's arms.

At least he was alive.

For the moment.

Vane ground his teeth as anger consumed him. He had to get his brother out of here. Had to find someplace safe for both of them.

If there was such a place.

With his rage unleashed, he did the impossible, he tore Fang's collar from his throat with his bare hands. Fang turned instantly into a wolf.

Still, Fang didn't come around. He didn't blink or whine.

Vane swallowed the painful lump in his throat and fought the tears that stung his eyes.

"It's okay, little brother," he whispered to Fang as he picked him up from the foul water. The weight of the brown wolf was excruciating, but Vane didn't care. He paid no attention to his body, which protested carrying Fang.

So long as he had breath in his body, no one would ever hurt anyone Vane cared for again.

And he would bring death to anyone who ever tried.

Chapter 1

Lilac and Lace Boutique on Iberville
The French Quarter
Eight months later

Stunned, Bride McTierney stared at the letter in her hand and blinked. She blinked again.

It couldn't really say what she thought it said.

Could it?

Was it a joke?

But as she read it again for the fourth time, she knew it wasn't. The rotten, cowardly SOB had actually broken up with her via her own FedEx account.

> *Sorry, Bride,*
>
> *But I need a woman more in keeping with my celebrity image. I'm going places and I need the kind of woman at my side who will help me, not hinder me. I'll have your things delivered to your building. Here's some money for a hotel room tonight in case you don't have any vacant rooms.*
>
> *Best,*
> *Taylor*

"You sorry, sycophantic, scum-sucking dog," she snarled as she read it again and pain engulfed her so profoundly that it was all she could do not to burst into tears. Her boyfriend of five years was breaking up with her . . . through a letter that he'd charged to her business account?

"Damn you to hell, you filthy snake!" she snarled.

Normally Bride would sooner cut her own head off than cuss, but this . . . this warranted serious language.

And an ax to her ex-boyfriend's head.

She fought the urge to scream. And the need she felt to get into her SUV, go over to his television station, and pound him into itty-bitty bloody pieces.

Damn him!

A tear rolled down her cheek. Bride wiped it away and sniffed. She wouldn't cry over this. He so wasn't worth it.

Really, he wasn't, and deep inside she wasn't surprised. For the last six months, she'd known this was coming. Had felt it every time Taylor put her on another diet or signed her up for another exercise program.

Not to mention the important dinner party two weeks ago at the Aquarium where he had told her that he didn't want her to join him. "There's no need in you getting all dressed up for something so boring. Really. It's best that I go alone."

She'd known the minute he'd finished speaking that he wouldn't be around much longer.

Still it hurt. Still she ached. How could he do such a thing?

Like this! she thought angrily as she waved the letter around like a lunatic in the middle of her store.

But then she knew. Taylor had never really been happy with her. The only reason he had gone out with her was because her cousin was a manager at a local television station. Taylor had wanted a job there and, like a fool, she had helped him to get it.

Now that he was safely ensconced in his position and his ratings were at the top, he pulled this stunt.

Fine. She didn't need him anyway.

She was better off without him.

But all the arguments in the world didn't ease the bitter, awful pain in her chest that made her want to curl up into a ball and cry until she was spent.

"I won't do it," she said, wiping away another tear. "I won't give him the satisfaction of crying."

Throwing the letter away, she seized her vacuum cleaner with a vengeance. Her little boutique needed cleaning.

You just vacuumed.

She could just vacuum again until the damned carpet was threadbare.

Vane Kattalakis felt like shit. He'd just left Grace Alexander's office where the good—and he used the word with full rancor—psychologist had told him there was nothing in the world that could heal his brother until his brother was willing to heal.

It wasn't what he needed to hear. Psychobabble was for humans, it wasn't for wolves who needed to get their stupid asses out of Dodge before they lost them.

Ever since Vane had crawled out of the swamp with his brother on Mardi Gras night, they had been lying low at Sanctuary, a bar owned by a clan of Katagaria bears who welcomed in all strays, no matter where they came from: human, Daimon, Apollite, Dark-Hunter, Dream-Hunter, or Were-Hunter. So long as you kept the peace and threatened no one, the bears allowed you to stay. And live.

But no matter what the Peltier bears told him, he knew the truth. Both he and Fang were living under a death sentence and there was no place safe for them. They had to get mobile before their father realized they were still alive.

The minute he did, a team of assassins would be sent for them. Vane could take them on, but not if he had to drag a hundred-and-twenty-pound comatose wolf behind him.

He needed Fang awake and alert. Most of all, he needed his brother willing to fight again.

But nothing seemed to reach Fang, who had yet to move out of his bed. Nothing.

"I miss you, Fang," he whispered under his breath as his throat tightened with grief. It was so hard to make it alone in the world. To have no one to talk to. No one to trust.

He wanted his brother and sister back so badly that he would gladly sell his soul for it.

But they were both gone now. There was no one left for him. No one.

Sighing, he tucked his hands in his pockets and turned onto Iberville as he walked through the French Quarter.

He wasn't even sure why he cared anymore anyway. He might as well let his father have him. What difference did it make?

But Vane had spent the whole of his life fighting. It was all he knew or understood.

He couldn't do as Fang and just lie down and wait for death. There had to be something out there that could reach his brother.

Something out there that could make both of them want to live again.

Vane paused as he neared one of those women's shops that were scattered throughout the French Quarter. It was a large redbrick building trimmed in black and burgundy. The entire front of it was made of glass that showed inside where the store was littered with lacy women's things and delicate, feminine tchotchkes.

But it wasn't the merchandise that made him pause.

It was *her*.

The woman he'd thought he would never see again.

Bride.

He'd seen her only once and then only briefly as he guarded Sunshine Runningwolf in Jackson Square while the artist had sold her artwork to tourists. Oblivious to him, Bride had come up to Sunshine and the two of them had talked for a few minutes.

Then Bride had walked out of his life completely. Even though he'd wanted to follow after her, Vane had known better. Humans and wolves didn't mix.

And definitely not wolves who were as screwed up as he was.

So he'd sat idly by even while every molecule of his body had screamed out for him to go after her.

Bride had been the most beautiful woman Vane had ever seen.

She still was.

Her long auburn hair was pulled up into a messy bun on top of her head that left curls of it to caress her porcelain face. She wore a long, black dress that flowed around her body as she jerked a vacuum cleaner across the carpet.

Every animal instinct in his body roared to life as he saw her again. The feeling was primal. Demanding.

Needful.

And it wouldn't listen to reason.

Against his will, he found himself headed toward her. It wasn't until he had opened the burgundy door that he realized she was crying.

Fierce anger tore through him. It was bad enough that his life sucked, the last thing he wanted was to see someone like her cry.

Bride paused her vacuuming and looked up as she heard someone entering her shop. Her breath caught in her throat. Never in her life had she seen a more handsome man.

Never.

At first glance his hair was dark brown, but in reality it was made up of all colors: ash, auburn, black, brown, mahogany, even some blond. She'd never seen hair like that on anyone. Long and wavy, it was pulled back into a sexy ponytail.

Better yet, his white T-shirt was pulled tight over a body that most women only saw in the best magazine ads. It was a body that was meant for sex. Tall and lean, that body begged a woman to caress it just to see if it was as hard and perfect as it appeared.

His handsome features were sharp, chiseled, and he had a day's growth of beard on his face. It was the face of a rebel who didn't cater to current fashions . . . one who lived his life solely on his own terms. It was obvious that no one told this man how to do anything.

He . . . was . . . gorgeous.

Bride couldn't see his eyes for the dark sunglasses he wore, but she sensed his gaze. Felt it like a smoldering touch.

This man was tough. Fierce. And it sent a wave of panic through her.

Why would someone like this be in a shop that specialized in women's accessories?

Surely he wasn't going to rob her?

The vacuum, which she hadn't moved a single millimeter since he'd entered her store, started to whine and smoke in protest. Drawing her breath in sharply, Bride quickly turned it off and fanned the motor with her hand.

"Can I help you?" she asked as she struggled to put it behind her counter.

Heat suffused her cheeks as the motor continued to smoke and spit. It added a not-so-pleasant odor of burning dust to the potpourri-scented candles she used.

She smiled lamely at the devastatingly hot god who stood so nonchalantly in her store. "Sorry about that."

Vane closed his eyes as he savored the melodic Southern lilt of her voice. It reached deep inside him, making his whole body burn for her. He was swollen with need and desire.

Swollen with a feral urge to take what he wanted, damn all consequences.

But she was scared of him. His animal half sensed it. And that was the last thing his human half wanted.

Reaching up, he pulled the sunglasses off and offered her a small smile. "Hi."

It didn't help. If anything, the sight of his eyes made her even more nervous.

Damn.

Bride was stunned. She wouldn't have thought he could ever become better looking, but with that devilish grin, he did.

Worse, the intense, feral look of that languid hazel-green gaze made her shivery and hot. Never in her life had she seen a man even one-tenth as good-looking as this one.

"Hi," she said back, feeling like nine kinds of stupid.

His gaze finally left her and went around the store to her various displays.

"I'm looking for a present," he said in that deeply hypnotic voice. She could have listened to him speak for hours, and for some reason she couldn't explain, she wanted to hear him say her name.

Bride cleared her throat and put those moronic thoughts away as she came out from behind her counter. If her cute ex couldn't stomach her looks, why would a god like this one give a rat's bottom about her?

So she decided to calm down before she embarrassed herself with him. "Who is it for?"

"Someone very special."

"Your girlfriend?"

His gaze came back to hers and made her tremble even more. He shook his head slightly. "I could never be so lucky," he said, his tone low, beguiling.

What an odd thing for him to say. She couldn't imagine this guy having trouble getting any woman he wanted. Who on earth would say no to *that*?

On second thought, she hoped she never met a woman that attractive. If she did, she would be morally obligated to run her over in her car.

"How much are you wanting to spend?"

He shrugged. "Money doesn't mean anything to me."

Bride blinked at that. Gorgeous and loaded. Man, some woman out there was lucky.

"Okay. We have some necklaces. Those are always a nice gift."

Vane followed her over to an alcove against the far wall where she had a mirror set up, with a multitude of beaded chokers and earrings that were on cardboard stands around it.

The scent of her made him hard and hot. It was all he could do not to dip his head down to her shoulder and just inhale her scent until he was drunk with it. He focused his gaze on the bare, pale skin of her neck . . .

He licked his lips as he imagined what she would taste like. What it would feel like to have her lush curves pressed up against his body. To have her lips swollen from his kisses, her eyes dark and dreamy from passion as she looked up at him while he took her.

Even worse, he could sense her own desire and it whetted his appetites even more.

"Which is your favorite?" he asked, even though he already knew the answer.

There was a black Victorian choker that had her scent all over it. It was obvious she had tried it on recently.

"This one," she said, reaching for it.

His cock hardened even more as her fingers brushed the black onyx stones. He wanted nothing more than to run his hand down her extended arm, to skim his palm over her soft, pale skin until he reached her hand. A hand he would love to nibble.

"Would you try it on for me?"

Bride trembled at the deep tone of his voice. What was it about him that made her so nervous?

But then she knew. He was intensely masculine and being under his direct scrutiny was as excruciating as it was disconcerting.

She tried to put the necklace on, but her hands shook so badly that she couldn't fasten it.

"May I help?" he asked.

She swallowed and nodded.

His warm hands touched hers, making her even more jittery. She looked in the mirror, catching sight of those hazel-green eyes that stared at her with a heat that made her both shiver and burn.

He was without a doubt the best-looking man to ever live and breathe and here he was touching her. It was enough to make her faint!

He deftly fastened the necklace. His fingers lingered at her neck for a minute before he met her gaze in the mirror and stepped back.

"Beautiful," he murmured huskily, only he wasn't looking at the necklace. He was staring into the reflection of her eyes. "I'll take it."

Torn between relief and sadness, Bride looked away quickly as she reached to take it off. In truth, she loved this necklace and hated to see it go. She'd bought it for the store, but had wanted to keep it for herself.

But why bother? It was a six-hundred-dollar handmade work of art. She didn't have anywhere to wear it. It would be a waste, and the pragmatic Irishwoman in her wouldn't allow her to be so foolish.

Pulling it off, she swallowed the new lump in her throat and headed for the register.

Vane watched her intently. She was even sadder than before. Gods, how he wanted nothing more than to have her smile at him. What did a human male say to a human female to make her happy?

She-wolves didn't really smile, not like humans did. Their smiles were more devious, seductive. Inviting. His people didn't smile when they were happy.

They had sex when they were happy and that, to him, was the biggest benefit to being an animal—rather than a human. Humans had rules about intimacy that he had never fully understood.

She placed the necklace in a large white box with a cotton pad in the bottom. "Would you like it gift-wrapped?"

He nodded.

Carefully, she removed the price tag, set it next to the register, then pulled out a small piece of paper that had been pre-cut to the size of the box. Without looking up at him, she quickly wrapped the box and rang up his sale.

"Six hundred and twenty-three dollars and eighty-four cents, please."

Still she didn't look at him. Instead her gaze was focused on the ground near his feet.

Vane felt a strange urge to dip down until his face was in her line of sight. He refrained as he pulled his wallet out and handed her his American Express card.

It was laughable, really, that a wolf had a human credit card. But then, this was the twenty-first century and those who didn't blend quickly found themselves exterminated. Unlike many others of his kind, he had investments and property. Hell, he even had a personal banker.

Bride took the card and ran it through her computer terminal.

"You work here alone?" he asked, and quickly learned that was inappropriate since her fear returned with a scent so strong it almost made him curse out loud.

"No."

She was lying to him. He could smell it.

Good going, jackass. Humans. He'd never understand them. But then, they were weak, especially their females.

She handed him the receipt.

Aggravated at himself for making her even more uncomfortable, he signed his name and handed it back to her.

She compared his signature to his card and frowned. "Katta . . ."

"Kattalakis," he said. "It's Greek."

Her eyes lighted up just a bit as she returned the card to him. "That's very different. You must have a hard time spelling it for people."

"Yeah."

She tucked the receipt into her drawer, then placed the wrapped box in a small bag with corded handles. "Thanks," she said quietly, setting it on the counter in front of him. "Have a nice day, Mr. Kattalakis."

He nodded and headed for the door, his heart even heavier than before, because he had failed to make her happy.

"Wait!" she said as he touched the knob. "You left your necklace."

Vane looked back at her one last time, knowing he would never see her again. She was so beautiful there with large, amber eyes set in the pale face of a goddess. There was something about her that reminded him of a Rubens angel. She was ethereal and lovely.

And far too fragile for an animal.

"No," he said quietly. "I left it with the woman I wanted to have it."

Bride felt her jaw go slack as his words hung in the air between them. "I can't take this."

He opened the door and headed out into the street.

Grabbing the bag from the counter, Bride ran after him. He was heading quickly down toward the center of the Quarter and it took her some serious rushing to catch up to him.

She took hold of his arm, amazed at the tautness of his biceps as she pulled him to a stop. Breathless, she looked up at him and those beguiling hazel-green eyes.

"I can't take this," she said again, giving the bag to him. "It's way too much."

He refused to take it. "I want you to have it."

There was so much unfathomable sincerity in those words that she couldn't do anything more than gape at him. "Why?"

"Because beautiful women deserve beautiful things."

No one unrelated to her had ever said anything so kind. Today more than any other, she needed to hear it. She'd never thought any man would ever think of her that way. And to hear it from this gorgeous stranger meant the world to her.

Those words reached so deep inside her that . . . that . . .

She burst into tears.

Vane stood there feeling completely at a loss. What was this? Wolves didn't cry. A she-wolf might tear out a man's throat for pissing her off, but she never cried and especially not when someone had complimented her.

"I'm sorry," he said, completely confused by what he'd done wrong. "I thought it would make you happy. I didn't mean to hurt your feelings."

She cried even more.

What was he supposed to do now? He looked around him, but there was no one to ask.

Screw the human in him. He didn't comprehend that part of himself, either. Instead, he listened to the animal part that only knew instinctively how to take care of someone when they were hurt.

He scooped her up into his arms and carried her back toward her store. Animals always did better in their native environment so it only stood to reason that a human might, as well. It was easier to cope with familiar things around.

She latched on to his neck as he carried her and wept even harder. Her hot tears raised chills on his skin and he ached for her.

How could he make this better?

Bride hated herself for breaking down like this. What the hell was wrong with her? Worse, he was carrying her!

Carrying her! And he wasn't complaining that she was fat and heavy, or grunting from the strain of it. She'd jokingly asked Taylor to carry her over the threshold when they had moved in together and he had laughed, then asked her if she was trying to give him a hernia.

Later that night, Taylor had agreed to do it only if she bought him a forklift for it.

And yet here this total stranger carried her with ease down the street. For the first time in her life, she almost felt petite.

But she wasn't that delusional. Bride McTierney hadn't been petite since she was six months old.

He opened her door, stepped inside, then closed it with his boot heel. Without breaking stride, he took her to the tall stool behind her register. He sat her down with care, then untucked his white T-shirt and used the end of it to blot her eyes.

"Ow!" she said as he almost poked her right eye out. It was a good thing she didn't wear contacts or she'd be blind.

He looked contrite. "Sorry."

"No," she said, looking up at him through her tears.

"I'm the one who needs to apologize. I didn't mean to have a nervous breakdown on you."

"Is that what this is?"

Was he serious? He definitely appeared so.

She drew in a ragged breath and wiped her eyes with her hands. "No, this is me being stupid. I'm so sorry."

He offered her a small, seductive grin. "It's okay. Really. I think."

Bride stared at him in disbelief. Why was this man in her store being so kind to her? It didn't make sense.

Was this a dream?

Trying to regain some of her dignity, she pulled his credit slip from the register box. "Here," she said, handing it to him.

"Why are you giving me this?"

"Oh, come on. No one buys a necklace this expensive for a complete stranger."

Again he didn't take it. Instead, he reached inside the bag and took out the box. She watched as he unwrapped it, then placed the choker around her neck again. The contrast between his hot hands and the cool beads made her shiver.

He laced his fingers through the tendrils of her hair while gazing at her like she was some delectable dessert that he was dying to taste.

No one had ever given her such a hot look before. It wasn't natural for a man this handsome to look at her like that.

"It belongs on you. No other woman could do it justice."

Tears welled in her eyes, but she blinked them back before he called the psycho ward on her. The heat of his hand against her neck was searing. "What? Did you lose a bet or something?"

"No."

"Then why are you being so nice to me?"

He cocked his head as if puzzled by her question. "Do I need a reason?"

"Yes."

Vane was completely baffled. Humans needed a reason to be nice to each other? No wonder his kind avoided them.

"I don't know what to say," he admitted. "I didn't know there were rules for giving gifts or for trying to make someone feel better. You looked so sad as I walked by that I only wanted to make you smile."

He took a deep breath and handed her the credit slip. "Keep the necklace, please. It looks good on you, and I have no one else to give it to. I'm sure my brother wouldn't want it. He'd probably shove it someplace real uncomfortable if I gave it to him. And if he didn't, that would scare me even more."

Finally, she laughed. The sound lightened his heart instantly.

"Is that a smile?" he asked.

She nodded and sniffed delicately before she laughed again.

Returning her smile, Vane reached out and cupped her cool cheek. She was so beautiful when she laughed. Her dark amber eyes sparkled. Before he could stop himself, he leaned down and kissed the tears from her lashes.

Bride couldn't breathe as she felt the heat of his lips against her skin. No man had ever treated her like this. Not even Taylor, whom she had hoped to marry.

She inhaled the warm scent of Vane's skin. It was tinged with some sort of aftershave and a rich, masculine scent.

God, it felt so good to be held right now when her whole life was falling apart.

Before she realized what she was doing, she had her arms wrapped around his lean waist and had laid her head against his strong chest. His heart pounded heavily under her ear. She felt strangely safe here. Warm. Most of all, she felt desirable. As if maybe she weren't a total loser, after all.

He didn't protest her hold. Instead, he held her there with his hand still on her face while his thumb gently stroked her cheekbone. He leaned down and placed a chaste kiss on the top of her head.

Heat flooded her. A deep-seated need tore through her body. It was one she didn't understand.

In all her life, Bride McTierney had never done anything other than what she was supposed to. She'd graduated high school and lived at home with her parents while she went to Tulane, where she had seldom dated and had spent more nights than not in the library.

After graduation, she'd gotten a job as a manager at the mall until her grandmother had died and left her the building that now housed her shop. And here she had worked every day without fail. No matter how sick or tired she was.

Bride had never taken a step on the wild side. Fear and responsibility had ruled her life from the moment of her birth.

Yet here she sat, holding a complete stranger in her

arms. A gorgeous stranger who had been kinder to her than anyone else.

And she wanted to taste him. To know just once what it was like to actually kiss a man who looked like this.

Lifting her head, she looked up at him and trembled with a deep-seated desire she didn't comprehend. But she felt it all the way through her.

Don't . . .

She squelched the voice of reason, reached up and pulled the band from his hair. Freed, those long dark strands framed the face of heaven.

The heat of his hazel-green eyes scorched her. He dipped his head down until his lips hovered dangerously close to hers, as if he were asking her permission.

Breathless, she closed the distance and laid her lips against his. He growled deep in his throat like some animal before his kiss turned hungry, passionate.

Bride was thrilled and amazed by his reaction. No man had ever seemed to enjoy kissing her as much as this one did. His strong hands cupped her head as he ravished her mouth as if he were starving for her and her alone.

Vane pulled her to him as the animal inside him roared to life. It wanted her with a desperation that bordered on madness. He could taste her own passion on his tongue. Hear her heart beating in rapid time to his.

Most of all, he could smell her desire and he wanted more. The animal inside him wouldn't be satisfied until it tasted her fully.

In his world, sex had no emotional meaning. It was a biological act between two creatures to ease a female's fertile time and a male's urges. If the two wolves weren't mates, then there was no chance of pregnancy, nor was there any form of sexually transmitted diseases between them.

If Bride were one of his people, he'd already have her naked on the floor.

But she wasn't a she-wolf . . .

Human females were different. He'd never made love to one of them and he wasn't sure how she would react if he took her the way he would one of their females. Her kind was very frail in comparison.

In all honesty, he didn't know why he was so hot for her now. It wasn't normal. Not once in all the centuries he had lived had he ever even contemplated taking a human lover.

But this one . . .

He couldn't stop himself. Every instinct he possessed demanded he take her.

His wolf's soul wanted to taste her. It wanted to breathe her in and let her softness ease the loneliness that had filled his heart these past months while he grieved for his sister and brother.

Just for one moment, he wanted to feel unalone again.

Bride shivered as Vane left her lips and trailed his kisses to her throat where he nibbled the sensitive skin there. His whiskers gently scraped her skin, making her burn even more as her breasts tightened with need. Good grief, he was so innately masculine. So incredibly hot. And every lick he delivered to her skin made her stomach contract.

This was so out of character for her. She didn't usually neck with men she knew like this. Never mind a perfect stranger.

And yet she didn't want to push him away. Just once in her life, she wanted something out of the ordinary. Deep inside she knew Vane would be spectacular.

Terrified of what she was about to do, she took a deep breath and braced herself for his rejection.

"Would you make love to me?"

Instead of the laughter she expected, he pulled back from nibbling her throat to look at the open windows of her shop. "You don't mind?"

Heat exploded across her face as she realized it was dark outside and anyone passing by on the street had a perfect view of the two of them necking like horny teenagers.

"Hold on," she said, scooting out of his arms to lock her door, flip her Open sign around to say Closed, and dim the lights.

She wished she still had an apartment to take him to, but maybe this was better. If they left here together, she would most likely chicken out, which would be the smart thing to do.

Or he might change his mind.

No, she wanted to do this. She wanted him.

Taking his hand, she led him through her shop, toward the door to the back room.

As she opened the door, he pulled her to a stop.

Bride looked back to see him staring into the dressing room that was to her right. A wicked grin spread across his face.

Walking backward, he led her into the room and shut the curtains.

"What are you doing?" she asked.

He pulled his T-shirt off, over his head.

Oh, dear heaven! Bride couldn't breathe as she got her first look at his bared chest. She'd known he had a great body, but this . . .

It exceeded anything from her dreams. His broad shoulders tapered to a washboard stomach that could do enough laundry for an entire nation. Forget six-pack, this man had eight, and they rippled with every breath he took. His entire torso was lightly covered by hair, making him look even more masculine and raw.

There were several deep scars that curved around his left shoulder and biceps, and one that looked strangely like an animal bite of some kind.

It was all she could do not to drool.

Or faint.

Really, no mere mortal woman should be in the presence of someone this fine and not need oxygen.

He opened the button on his jeans, then pulled her back into his arms.

"Don't be afraid," he whispered. "I'll be gentle."

But that wasn't what she was afraid of. What she feared was his reaction when he saw what she looked like naked. Good grief, he didn't have an ounce of fat on him and here she was a good, solid size eighteen.

He was going to run screaming for the door any minute.

Instead, he reached up and pulled her hair down around her shoulders. Running his hands through it, he pulled her lips to his so that he could ravage her mouth again.

She moaned in bliss. This man certainly knew how to use his tongue to his advantage. She could have kissed him all day.

Bride ran her hands over the lean muscles of his chest, amazed at how good they felt. She flicked her fingertips over and around his hardened nipples, delighting in the deep moan she heard from him.

He moved to unbutton her dress.

"It's darker in the back room," she said.

"Why would I want it darker?"

She shrugged. Taylor had always insisted on absolute darkness whenever they made love.

She shivered as he unbuttoned her dress and dropped it to the ground. She expected him to pull away.

He didn't. He still wore that hot, hungry look as he stared at her in her underwear. Thank goodness it actually matched and it wasn't her old stuff.

Vane had never been more unsure of himself than he was at this moment. He cupped her face in his hands and kissed her carefully, afraid he might hurt her. Ever since he'd hit puberty, he'd heard stories of wolves who had killed human partners accidentally while mating with them.

Human bones lacked the density of his kind. Their skin bruised much more easily.

Carefully, he pressed her back against the wall so that he could feel every inch of her lush curves against his hardness. The smell of her perfume and skin intoxicated him. It was all he could do not to howl in triumph.

He nibbled his way from her delicate mouth, down her jaw, while he reached behind her and unhooked her bra. He heard her sharp intake of breath as her breasts were freed. They were a lush bounty. Pale and swollen, they overflowed his hands. He'd never seen anything more beautiful. She laced her hands in his hair while he dipped his head down to suckle her.

Closing his eyes, he groaned in pleasure as he ran his tongue around her puckered nipple.

He hadn't touched a female in almost a year—a record for him. But since the night his sister had died, his life had shot from bad to worse and there hadn't been anyone who appealed to him.

Not to mention that memories of Bride the one time he had seen her in the Square had haunted him. Midnight fantasies of him taking her in every position known. Of him exploring every single inch of her succulent body.

He'd spent hours damning himself for not leaving Sunshine to her own devices and following after this woman.

Protecting Sunshine had cost him everything, and for what? For a damned Dark-Hunter's happiness?

No good deed goes unpunished.

It was Fury's favorite saying. A rogue wolf, Fury was as unreliable and selfish as any, but there were times when the wolf was amazingly astute.

But now as Vane held Bride in his arms and felt her soft, tender body against his, he felt a strange sense of comfort that had eluded him all these past months.

It didn't erase the pain he felt at the loss of his siblings, but it lightened it.

And that alone made her priceless to him.

Bride couldn't think straight as she watched Vane savoring her breasts. He looked as if he were tasting divinity. Her body burned in rich desire. He was spectacular.

His eyes were hooded and dark. She stared at his back in the mirror and wondered at the scars that marred his smooth, tanned flesh. She touched the ridges of them while he moved from her right to her left breast.

What had happened to him to cause so many scars? She'd never seen anything like it. Some of the scars were obviously claw and bite marks that looked like he had been mauled by some kind of wild animal. One in particular was deep and large. It went down his shoulder blade, up under his arm.

There was something so deadly about him and yet he held her with a gentle touch. He ran his hand down her stomach, burning a trail over her skin.

Her eyes half-closed, she watched him in the mirror as he dipped his tanned hand under the elastic of her black panties and touched her intimately.

Bride groaned at the sensation of his long, tapered fingers separating the tender folds of her body so that he could caress her. At the sight of his hand playing there in the mirror as he gently sank his fingers deep inside her.

She moaned at the sight and feel of him.

It was so odd to be able to see him from so many different angles. To see herself being loved by him.

She should be embarrassed and yet she wasn't. She didn't even feel self-conscious. If anything, she felt strangely empowered by it.

A man like this so hungry for her.

It was unimaginable.

Vane kissed his way down her stomach. Moving his hand, he actually pulled her underwear off with his teeth. He removed her sandals, taking time to rub the arches of her feet before he tossed them over his shoulder.

He crouched on the floor in front of her, looking up with a hot, devouring, intense stare. He still wore his jeans and boots while she was completely naked.

Vane couldn't breathe as he watched her. There was still a tinge of fear in her, but it was overshadowed by her desire.

He wanted to pull her to him roughly and take her like the animal he was. He wanted to show her how his people mated, forcefully and with dominance.

But he didn't want to scare her. Most of all, he didn't want to hurt her.

She was so vulnerable.

A she-wolf would take human form for the mating. She would walk seductively around the available males, making them crazy with lust until they were ready to kill each other to have her.

Sometimes they did.

There was always a battle for the female. Then she would pick whichever male had impressed her most with his beauty and skill. Usually it was the victor who mated with her, but not always. Vane's first lover had claimed him even though he had lost the fight because she had liked the passion he had shown while trying to win her.

Once her choice was made, the she-wolf would remove her clothes and offer herself to her champion. The male would pin her down and spend the rest of the night showing her just how much stamina and power he had. The female would spend the night testing him. She would try to throw him off or out of her and it was his duty to make sure she didn't. If he tired before morning or before she was fully sated, another male would be brought in.

It was the greatest shame not to please a she-wolf, to have to call out for a second.

Vane had never been shamed.

And he had never taken a woman like Bride. One who wasn't biting and clawing at him as she demanded he please her. Something inside him relished the rarity of this.

The gentleness.

In a life where violence and territory and blood wars reigned, it was nice to have a reprieve. A tender lover's touch.

The human side of him craved this.

It craved her.

Bride bit her bottom lip as Vane nudged her legs apart. His breath scorched her thighs. He closed his eyes and laid his head against her thigh as if he were savoring just being with her. The tenderness of that action brought a lump to her throat.

She ran her fingers down his stubbled cheek, letting the manly feel warm her even more. He nipped her fingers playfully.

She smiled down at him until he nudged her legs farther apart and took her into his mouth. Bride hissed in pleasure as her legs went weak.

It was all she could do not to fall. He devoured her. There was no other word for it. He licked and teased until her head spun, and when she came for him, it was forceful and deep. Bride cried out as her body was turned inside out by his touch.

Vane growled at the sound of her pleasure, at the taste of it. Like all males of his kind, he took pride in her orgasm. There was nothing sweeter than hearing the screams of a lover climaxing. Nothing sweeter than knowing a male could fulfill the female.

He kissed his way up her body slowly until he was again on his feet. She looked up at him with awe shining bright in the amber depths of her eyes. He took her hand into his and led it to his throbbing erection.

Bride swallowed as she sank her hand deep into the denim. His short, crisp hairs teased her fingers as she found what she sought. He growled deep in his throat like a wild animal as she wrapped her hand around the hard length of him. The man was huge and he was already wet and straining.

Cupping her face, he kissed her passionately while she stroked him. Her body thrummed with heat at the thought of having his hard cock deep inside her.

He pulled away from her, then quickly jerked his boots off. Bride held her breath as he reached for his fly and unzipped it.

She watched in a passion-numbed daze as he slid his pants down and she caught her first sight of him in all his glory.

Commando!

There was nothing sexier than a man who dared to wear nothing under his clothes. Then again, there was nothing sexier than the man in front of her.

He was bold and commanding. Wild. And he made her shiver uncontrollably.

Tossing his pants into the corner, he moved her away from the wall. Bride was thankful her dressing

room was larger than most. It had been designed to ac-
commodate women with baby strollers or toddlers.
And it gave them plenty of room to maneuver.

Vane moved around to her back. She stared at him
in the mirror. He was a full head taller than she was and
the sideways, hungry grin on his face undid her.

"You are so beautiful," he said, his voice deep and
hungry.

She'd never felt that way. Normally, she avoided
looking at herself in mirrors. But there was something
terribly erotic about seeing the two of them reflected in
the three mirrored walls.

He brushed her hair from her neck, then nibbled the
sensitive flesh there. He slid his tongue around the
beads of the necklace.

His hands cupped her breasts before he trailed one
hand back to the dark auburn triangle of hair between
her legs.

Somehow, he lowered them slowly, in unison, to the
floor. She wasn't really sure how he did it without breaking his hold. The man was incredibly strong. She leaned
back against him where his body was hot and prickly.
Masculine.

His tongue swirled around her ear, then plunged
deep inside at the same time he entered her from behind. Bride cried out in pleasure at the sensation of
him filling her.

He lifted his head so that he could watch her face as
he thrust himself even deeper.

Bride couldn't speak or think as pleasure over-
whelmed her. All she could do was watch him make

love to her. Watch his hand pleasure her in time to his forceful thrusts.

Vane growled again at the feel of her wet, welcoming body. Her body was much softer than a she-wolf's. Born fighters, they were hard-muscled and tough. A she-wolf would be trying to bite him. She would be clawing his arm, demanding he give her more satisfaction. Demanding he move faster and harder until she came again.

But not Bride.

She didn't make any demands as he took his time, with slow and easy strokes. She didn't try to throw him out. Instead, she leaned back against his chest and made the most incredible sounds of pleasure with every stroke his body delivered to hers. She completely surrendered herself to him.

The trust it took for her to do that . . .

He'd never known anything like it.

He'd spent so many months dreaming of what she would be like in his arms. Now he knew.

She was divine. She reached over her head to sink her hand in his hair so that she could hold him close. "Oh, Vane," she breathed, nuzzling her cheek against his.

He felt his powers growing as he kissed her cheek, and he quickened his fingers. She jerked and moaned in response to him. He felt himself growing even larger. The wolf in him was snarling in satisfaction.

It howled at the feel of her hot, wet body wrapped around his. And as always, it gave his magical powers a surge. Sex always charged his species, making them stronger.

More dangerous.

She covered his hand with hers. The sight of her spread out while he thrust into her made his heart pound even harder. His powers shivered through his body, sparking and dancing until he was raw from it.

Bride couldn't breathe from the intensity of her pleasure. This was the most incredible encounter of her life. He was so thick and hard inside her. So commanding. And oddly enough, he felt as if he were getting bigger. He filled her to capacity, but it wasn't uncomfortable in the least.

And when she came this time, it was even more forceful than the last. She screamed out with such satisfaction that it made her hoarse. Weak. Her body shook uncontrollably as he continued to give her even more.

"That's it, baby," he whispered to her. "Come for me."

And she did. In a way she had never orgasmed before. It was so primal and powerful she wasn't even sure how she survived it. Oh mercy! How could anything feel so wonderful?

Every stroke he continued to give her only made her orgasm more. Made her entire body sensitive. This had to be the longest climax of her life!

Vane kept a tight grip on her as he felt his own pleasure mounting. He quickened his strokes as he neared the peak.

Bride turned her face into his and laid the sweetest kiss imaginable on his lips. It sent him careening over the edge.

He wrapped her in his arms as he released himself

deep inside her body. Unlike a human, he wouldn't be finished quickly with this. His orgasm would last for several minutes.

Holding her tight, he used his powers to heighten her pleasure and to hide the time he stayed inside her while his body spent itself. He leaned his head against her neck and just reveled in her scent. Reveled in her.

He buried himself deep, then gently rocked her in his arms while he let his release and an unfounded sense of peace and comfort wash through him.

Vane couldn't take his eyes off Bride as his body finally relaxed. Slowly. Peacefully.

He held her in his lap and watched the slight smile that still hovered on the edges of her lips. This woman was a goddess. Pure and simple. Lush and full, she was everything a man could ever desire.

"That was incredible," she breathed, reaching up to run her fingers along his jaw.

"Yes, it was," he breathed gently, still amazed at what he had felt inside a human female.

Maybe Acheron had been right after all. Maybe there was more human in him than he thought. It was the only reason he could think of for why he felt the way he did right now.

A phone rang from outside the dressing room.

She jumped in his arms, then checked her wristwatch. "Oh no," she breathed. "That's probably Tabitha. I'm supposed to meet her and her sister for dinner tonight."

Vane sighed. For some reason he couldn't name, he didn't want to let her go. Didn't want her to leave his side.

If she were one of his people, she wouldn't even think about leaving until dawn.

But she wasn't.

And wanting to stay here was crazy. He was a wolf under a death sentence and she was a human.

What they had shared had been exceptional, but it was time he put her out of his thoughts.

Forever.

Kissing her cheek, he withdrew from her and got up to dress.

Bride felt a bit awkward as Vane handed her her clothes. He didn't ask her for her number or for anything else as he pulled on his pants and boots.

Did he regret what they had done?

She wanted to ask him for his number, but her pride wouldn't let her. Maybe she was being stupid, but given Taylor's actions she didn't want to risk another dent to her ego tonight.

Vane buttoned her dress, then pulled his shirt on over his head. "Is your car nearby?" he asked.

"It's parked in the back, but I was just going to walk over to the restaurant. It's only a few blocks away."

He brushed her hair with his fingers. There was an air of sudden sadness to him. "Would you like me walk with you?"

She nodded.

He held the curtain open for her. She ducked out and turned to watch while he tucked his T-shirt into his jeans. He raked his hand through his hair to settle it back into place.

All the playfulness was gone from him now. There was something almost predatorial about him.

He went to wait outside while she set the alarm and locked the door.

She felt even more awkward as she straightened to smile at him outside her store. The air was a bit chilly, but he didn't seem to notice. He draped an arm around her shoulders as they headed toward Tabitha's favorite restaurant, Acme Oyster House.

They didn't speak while they walked. Bride wanted to, but what did a woman say to a guy who had just given her the best sex of her life?

A guy she didn't know.

A guy she would most likely never see again.

Oh, how she hated this. This was the first time in her life she'd ever had a one-night stand. It was disconcerting to have been so intimate with a complete stranger.

He slowed as they neared the restaurant.

Bride peeked in the large, painted window. She'd been right, her friends were already there and she saw Tabitha dialing a cell phone. No doubt Tabitha had been the one calling, and if Bride didn't go in soon, she would start to worry.

"Well," she said, pulling away from Vane. "I guess this is where we say goodbye."

He nodded and offered her a kind smile. "Thank you, Bride."

"No," she said, touching her necklace that he had given her. "Thank you."

He kissed her hand, then turned, tucked his hands inside his pockets, and walked slowly down the street toward Bourbon. Her heart heavy, she watched that deadly masculine swagger.

"Bride?"

She turned to see Mina Devereaux standing in the open doorway. "You okay?" she asked.

Nodding, Bride forced herself to go inside. Mina led her to a table near the window where her sister, Tabitha, was seated.

"Hey, Bride," Tabitha said in greeting as she unwrapped a cracker. "You okay? You look a little distracted."

"I don't know," Bride said as she took a seat across the table from Tabitha. "I've had the strangest day of my life and I think I may have just made the biggest mistake of all time."

Only she wasn't sure if the mistake was sleeping with someone she didn't know or letting him leave her.

Chapter 2

His heart heavy with regret, Vane made his way through the French Quarter down to 688 Ursulines Avenue where the bar Sanctuary stood on the corner. The redbrick building had saloon-type doors with a sign outside that featured a dark motorcycle silhouetted by a full moon on a hill.

A tourist attraction, the biker bar was crowded as always with natives and tourists. There were already several motorcycles lined up on the sidewalk outside that belonged to the local biker gang who called themselves the Vieux-Doo Dogs. The first time he'd seen the gruff bikers enter the building, Vane had laughed. The biker humans had no idea that Sanctuary wasn't just a place for them. It was one of the very rare true havens for his kind.

All over the world and in various time periods, certain Were-Hunter families had established places like this one where Katagaria members could hide out while running from their enemies. But of all the known animal havens, Mama Bear Peltier's Sanctuary was the most respected and renowned. Mostly because hers was one of the few establishments that welcomed Dark-Hunters, Apollites, Daimons, and gods equally. So long as you came in peace, you were allowed to leave with all body parts intact.

As the Sanctuary slogan went: *Don't bite me and I won't bite you.*

Anyone who breached that one rule was quickly sacrificed by one of Mama Peltier's eleven sons or her exceptionally large mate. It was a well-known fact that Papa Bear Peltier played with no one but Mama Bear.

Though Mama and her boys were bears in their native form, they welcomed all Katagaria branches: lions and tigers and hawks and wolves. There wasn't a single known group that didn't have at least one member hiding here.

Hell, there was even a drakos, and as a rule the dragons seldom made the twenty-first century their home. Due to their size, dragons had a tendency to live out their lives in past times where a smaller human population and open fields made it easier for them to hide.

The Peltiers even had an Arcadian Sentinel who watched over the place and that was the greatest feat of all. Arcadians were the Were-Hunters who had human hearts and they were mortal enemies to the Katagaria, who had animal hearts. In fact, the two species had been at war with each other for thousands of years.

The Arcadians were supposedly the kinder branch of Vane's people, but his experience said that was wishful thinking on their part. He'd much sooner trust a Katagaria with an animal heart than an Arcadian with a human heart any day.

At least the animals attacked you openly. They weren't nearly as treacherous as a human.

But then, no Katagaria female had ever held him the way Bride had. None had ever made him feel this strange protectiveness that wanted nothing more than to go back to the restaurant where he'd left her, take her into his arms and carry her home with him.

It didn't make a bit of sense.

He strode through the saloon doors to find Dev Peltier sitting on a tall barstool at the entrance. Dev was one of Mama Bear's quadruplets. Even though they were identical in looks, each of the quads had a very distinct personality and carriage.

Dev was easygoing and slow to anger. He exuded an air of powerful grace and moved methodically like most bears—as if he had all the time in the world. But Vane knew the bear could be damned near as quick to move as any wolf. The first time he had seen Dev lunge at his younger brother Serre in a play fight, he'd developed a healthy respect for the bear's abilities.

Tonight, Dev wore a black T-shirt that didn't quite cover up the Artemis bow mark on his biceps that he had as a goof on the Daimons and Apollites who occasionally ventured inside the bar. He was playing five-card draw with Rudy, one of the human employees who had no idea that half the "people" in the bar were really animals walking on two legs.

Rudy had straight black hair pulled back into a ponytail, and a rough face that showed every sign of how hard the ex-con's life had been. He had a full black beard and every inch of exposed skin was covered with some kind of colorful tattoo.

The man was truly grimy and, unlike the Were-Hunters who made this their home, he wasn't attractive. In fact, that was the easiest way to tell the humans from the animals. Since Vane's people valued beauty above all else, it was rare to find an unattractive Were-Hunter.

Like his brothers', Dev's curly blond hair fell all the way down his back. As always, he wore it loose. He had on a pair of tight, faded jeans and black boots.

Dev acknowledged him with a tilt of his head. "Hey, wolf, you okay?"

Vane shrugged as he neared them. "Just tired."

"Maybe you should cop a nap at the house," Dev said as he reached for two more cards.

Peltier House was adjacent to the bar. It was there that they could assume their animal forms without fear of discovery. The Peltiers had more alarm systems than Fort Knox and at least two members of the family were on guard at all times against any intruder, human or otherwise.

"It's all right," Vane said. He earned his keep and Fang's. The last thing he wanted was for anyone to accuse him of taking charity from the Bear clan, so he worked an average of ten hours a day, every day, for the Peltiers. "I told Nicolette I'd relieve Cherise at the bar tonight."

"Yeah," Rudy said as he took a drag on his cigarette, then adjusted his cards. "Cherise is dying to go home early. Nick is going to take her to Antoine's for her birthday."

Vane had forgotten it was the human's birthday. For some reason, those were special to humans. Probably because they had so few of them.

Vane excused himself and headed toward the bar. He passed the tables where Wren, a rare white leopard Katagaria, was clearing them. Marvin the monkey (the only animal at Sanctuary that couldn't take human form) sat on the leopard's shoulder and held tight to Wren's blond hair.

Those two had a strange relationship. Much like Vane and Fang, Wren had come to the Peltiers as an exile. He kept to himself and seldom spoke to anyone other than Marvin. Even so, there was something lethal about the leopard's eyes that told everyone to leave him alone if they valued their lives.

Wren looked up at Vane as he passed the tables Wren was cleaning, but said nothing.

"Hey, Vane!" Cherise Gautier said, her face beaming as she caught sight of him. She was a beautiful blond woman in her early forties. Her ever-ready smile and warm heart could win over just about anyone. "You okay, honey? You look tired."

It still amazed him just how intuitive Cherise was for a human. Vane lifted the back section of the bar's countertop and let himself into the serving area. "I'm fine," he said, even though he didn't feel that way.

He felt as if something were missing. As if he should go back to Bride.

How stupid was that?

"You sure?" she asked.

He could sense her concern. And that made him extremely uncomfortable. No one other than his brother and sister had ever given a damn about him.

Cherise was a strange human.

She flipped the white towel she'd been cleaning the bar with over her shoulder. "You know, my son is your age . . ."

Vane fought the urge to laugh at that. Nick Gautier was twenty-six in human years while Vane was four hundred and sixty. But of course, Cherise had no idea of Vane's true age. Any more than she knew her son was working for the Dark-Hunters, who were all immortal vampire slayers.

"And I know how you guys burn yourselves out. You need to take better care of yourself, sweetie. I swear you haven't had a day off since Mama hired you. Why don't you take the night off for once and go have some fun?"

"It's all right," he said quietly as he took the towel from her shoulder. "I've got it. Besides, Rudy said it was your birthday."

She blew him a raspberry. "I'm too old for birthdays. I'd rather see you enjoy your youth while you still have it."

"Yeah," Kyle Peltier, the youngest of the bears, said as he joined them from the back room with a large rack of clean glasses. Just Nick's age, Kyle was barely out of puberty since Were-Hunters didn't mature until their twenties. "Why don't you enjoy the six seconds you have left of your youth, Vane?"

Vane flipped him off, then urged Cherise toward her purse. "Go home, Cherise."

"But—"

"Go," Vane growled, "and have a good birthday."

She sighed, then patted him on the arm. "All right." She grabbed her sweater and purse from under the bar.

"I'll punch you out," Kyle said, lifting the bar counter for her so that she could step out.

"Thanks."

Vane started pulling the glasses out of the rack and putting them away while Kyle went to help Wren bus the tables.

Colt Theodorakopolus sauntered up to the bar. The Ursulan Arcadian stood even in height with Vane, who felt an instant dislike for the were-bear. Though, to be honest, Colt seemed decent enough. His mother's mate had been killed while his mother was pregnant with him. Knowing she would die as soon as her cub was born, she'd come to Sanctuary and begged the Peltiers to raise her son for her.

To Vane's knowledge, Colt had never met another Arcadian bear member. As a Sentinel, Colt should have one side of his face covered by Sentinel markings—strange, geometric designs that appeared as a birthmark once the Sentinel reached maturity. But Colt, like many Sentinels who lived outside of their clans or in seclusion, chose to hide them, along with his powers.

No one knew how powerful Colt was until they crossed him. Then it was too late.

A hiding Sentinel was a most dangerous thing.

Unlike the other bears, Colt had short black hair and looked remarkably clean-cut.

"Give me whisky," Colt said to Vane. "And hold the human hair."

Vane nodded at the phrase that meant Colt wanted the hard liquor that would completely inebriate a human with one shot. Since their kind had a higher metabolism, they could handle a lot more alcohol.

He poured a large shot glass, then placed it on the bar in front of Colt. The instant he pulled his hand back, he felt a strange burning sensation.

Hissing, Vane blew across his palm. He moved to one of the bar lamps to see what he'd done to it.

As he looked, a strange scrolling design seared itself onto his skin.

"Oh shit," he breathed as he saw it take form.

Colt ducked under the bar and came up behind him. His jaw went slack. "You're mated?" he asked incredulously. "Who's the lucky she-wolf?"

Vane couldn't breathe as he saw the marking. How could this be?

"It's impossible."

Colt laughed. "Yeah, right, you sound like Serre when he got mated. Trust me, it happens to the best of us."

"No," Vane said, meeting the bear's gaze. "She's human. I'm a wolf. I can't be mated to a human. It's not possible."

The color faded from Colt's face as the full impact of Vane's situation hit him. "You unlucky bastard. It's not often that an Arcadian mates to a human, but it does happen."

"I'm not Arcadian," Vane snarled. There was nothing human in him. Nothing.

Colt grabbed his hand and held it up to Vane's line of sight. "Argue with this all you want to. But face it, Vane. Your three weeks are ticking. Either you claim the human or you'll live out the rest of your life without ever feeling another female's touch."

. . .

"Ow!" Bride snapped as her hand started burning. She pressed it up against her glass of water.

"What's wrong?" Mina asked as she picked out another oyster to eat.

"I don't know," Bride said. "My hand just started hurting."

Tabitha touched Bride's plate. "Nothing's hot. Did you cut your hand on an oyster shell?"

"No," Bride said, pulling her hand back to look at it. There was a beautiful design on her palm. It reminded her of some ancient Greek design. "What on earth?"

Mina frowned as she looked at it. "Did you get a henna tattoo?"

"No. I didn't do anything. I swear. It wasn't there five seconds ago."

Tabitha leaned over to look at it. "How weird," she said. "And coming from me, that means something."

That was very true. Tabitha Devereaux was the epitome of odd.

"You've never seen anything like this?" Bride asked Tabitha.

"Nope. Maybe we're all delusional. Maybe it's like Plato's theory and there's nothing there but skin. Maybe we're just seeing what we want to see."

Mina snorted as she poured Tabasco sauce on her oyster. "Just because you live in a constant state of insanity, Tabby, doesn't mean the rest of us do."

Bride laughed at them.

She traced the design on her palm and wondered what on earth could have placed it there.

. . .

Colt gave Vane a hard stare. "Look, I know you can't stand me. But I've got your back. Go see your woman and I'll cover here in the bar."

"I don't need you to—"

"Stop being so damned stubborn," Colt said from between clenched teeth. "You have a mate out there, Vane, and whether you're Arcadian or Katagaria, you know the one law that governs us all. Your mate's safety comes above all else."

Colt was right and Vane knew it. The animal inside him was already straining at the human half of him. It wanted its mate. It demanded it.

Normally the human and animal parts of himself coexisted in a delicate balance. Hormones and stress could easily disturb that balance, and then he became truly dangerous. If the animal took control of him . . .

Many of his kind, both male and female, lost themselves to that animal half. Unable to handle it, they went mad from it and became ruthless slayers who killed anything or anyone who crossed them. It was similar to a rabies infection and there was no cure for it.

That was why the Arcadians had Sentinels. Their job was to track and kill those who couldn't control their animal soul. Slayers. Of course, the Arcadians as a rule were rather liberal when applying the term "slayer" to one of his people. Pretty much any Katagari who crossed their path was usually classified as a slayer . . . with or without evidence.

"Go, Vane," Colt said, urging him toward the door.

The bear was right. There was no use fighting his nature. It was a battle he could never win.

He handed Colt the towel and quickly left the bar.

Out on the street, Vane made sure no one could see him and then flashed himself into wolf form. Unlike his brother, he was a solid white timber wolf. He was also bigger, weighing in at one hundred and forty pounds.

It was why his pack mates had feared him most in his animal state. As powerful as they were, he was more so. And he didn't follow rank the way the others did.

Animal he might be, but at the end of the day even though he denied it, he had enough human in him to refuse to follow anyone docilely.

He was a born alpha and everyone around him knew it.

Vane sprinted through the streets of New Orleans, careful to stay to the shadows of the darkening evening. He'd learned long ago that humans had a tendency to make him out to be a large dog if they saw him, but still the last thing he needed was a dogcatcher after him.

He had a long history of animal-control encounters. None of which had ever been good for the humans.

It didn't take him long to return to Iberville and the Acme Oyster House where he'd left Bride. Rising up on his hind legs to stand against the glass, he peered inside to see her seated with two other women.

One had dark auburn hair and a ragged scar down the side of her face. If not for the ghastly mark, she would have been exceptionally attractive. The other one was a very pretty brunette who shared similar features.

However, neither of the skinny women appealed to him.

Only Bride did. The sight of her cut through him intensely, making him ache with need. She might claim to be human, but there was more magic in her smile than his entire wolf pack possessed.

She was absolutely beguiling and those lips did the most amazing things to his body.

To his heart . . .

The three women were talking and laughing while they finished a platter of oysters. None of them seemed to notice anything different about Bride.

Maybe she wasn't his mate, after all.

But that was a futile thought. The mark only appeared after a Were-Hunter had had sex with his mate, and usually within a short time frame. Vane hadn't been with any other woman for months now.

There was no one else it could be.

Her hand markings should match his exactly—they were emblems that showed his parental lineage and could only be read by another of his kind.

But then again maybe it was different because Bride was human. What if the mating mark wasn't binding on a human female?

He went cold with that thought.

He would be screwed. Literally.

The only hope he would ever have for a family rested in his ability to claim his mate.

But she must be willing . . .

Bride and her friends got up and headed out of the restaurant. Vane crouched low as he tried to decide what to do.

"I'm telling you, Bride," the brunette said as she led the way out into the street, "our sister Tia can hex anyone. Say the word and we'll turn Taylor into a eunuch."

Bride laughed at that. "Don't tempt me."

The scarred redhead stopped as she caught sight of him in the shadows. "Hey there, big boy," she said kindly, holding her hand out for him to sniff. "Want Tabby to scratch you behind your ears?"

"Tabitha!" the other woman snapped. "Leave the strays alone. I swear, one day you're going to get rabies."

"He doesn't have rabies," Bride said.

"See," the one called Tabitha said. "And the daughter of the vet should know."

Bride held her hand out to him.

Vane went to her immediately and sniffed her hand. Her scent went through him, piercing and hot, along with images of what she'd looked like in complete surrender to him. The sounds of her pleasure . . .

Nosing her fingers, he forced her to open them so that he could see his worst fears confirmed.

She was marked.

Damn.

What was he going to do now?

"He likes you, Bride."

Tabitha had no idea just how true her words were.

"I think he likes her leftovers," Mina said with a laugh.

Bride knelt down while she stroked his ears. She cupped his head and examined him carefully. "I think he's a wolf."

"A wolf?" Tabitha asked. "Are you nuts? How did a

wolf get in the city? Besides, he's way too big for a wolf."

"You are a big boy, aren't you?" Bride said as Vane nuzzled her face. She looked up at her friend. "Contrary to popular opinion, Tabby, wolves are the largest of the canines. But I think he might be some kind of mixed blood."

If she only knew . . .

She stood up and started off with her friends.

Vane followed. In wolf form, it was compulsory. His human half had very little control now. He could still understand and listen, but his animal ruled him in this state.

So long as he was in his current body, he was feral and lethal.

Bride had the strangest feeling down her spine. She paused and looked back over her shoulder to find the white wolf following behind her. She could swear his eyes were an exact match for Vane's hazel green, and the way he looked at her . . .

At them . . .

It was as if he understood exactly what they were saying and doing.

It was really weird.

Tabitha and Mina walked her back to her shop.

"You sure you don't want to spend the night over at my place?" Mina asked. "I can easily kick my guy out."

"Or my apartment," Tabitha offered. "I have no guy to kick out, and since my twin absconded with my dog and Allison wanted to find a saner, safer bunkmate, I have all the room in the world."

"I thought Marla was living with you now?" Mina asked.

"Nah," Tabitha said. "Her stuff is there, but she's been spending all her time at her boyfriend's house. I never see her anymore."

Bride smiled at their kindness. "It's okay, guys. I have to get used to being alone again. Really. I just want to curl up with a good book and put him out of my mind."

But what disturbed her most was that all she had to do was think of Vane and all thoughts of Taylor went flying out of her head.

Maybe her "encounter" with him had been a good thing after all.

"Hey, just keep dreaming about the guy you met," Tabitha said, winking at her.

Bride frowned at that spooky coincidence. Of course, Tabitha claimed to be able to read minds. At times such as this, Bride could almost believe that.

"Yeah," Mina concurred. "Maybe he might pass back by."

Bride sighed wistfully. "I have a feeling I've seen the last of Mr. Bodacious."

Mina gave her a sisterly hug. "Call me if you need me."

"I will. Thanks."

Tabitha hugged her too and patted her on the back. "Remember, if you need Taylor's kneecaps broken, I have just the tire iron and I won't ever tell the media who put me up to it."

Bride laughed, grateful for her friends and their kindness to her in her hour of need. "You're such a nut."

"I'm serious, though. You change your mind, speed dial the number. I can be at his place in under twenty minutes."

"Ha!" Mina said. "With your driving? You'd be there in less than ten and that's with a flat tire going against traffic."

Bride shook her head at their teasing as she pulled her keys from her pocket and opened the door on the side of her building that led to the courtyard and the wrought-iron stairs in the back. Her store took up the entire bottom floor of the building, but the upper three floors had been made into apartments by her grandmother. The stairs back here led to each of the apartments above. There was one more tiny studio apartment in the back near the garage that used to be a barn back in the days before New Orleans was paved.

Up until Taylor had talked her into living with him, she had lived in the biggest apartment on the top floor. Now all the apartments were rented except for the one studio out back. It was so small that she had never felt right about taking money for it. Instead, Bride used it for storage.

Now it was going to be home sweet home for a while.

She wanted to cry again, but she refused. If the worst thing that ever happened to her was Taylor leaving her, then she was truly blessed.

Still, it did hurt. Deeply.

As Mina and Tabitha walked off, the wolf came forward to stare up at her.

"You are beautiful, aren't you?" she asked, reaching down to stroke his ears again.

He licked her hand before he rubbed himself against her legs much like a cat might.

"C'mon," she said, indicating the courtyard with a nod of her head. "I don't really want to be alone tonight and you look like you might appreciate somewhere warm and dry to sleep."

He padded inside the gate while she locked the door and made her way over to the renovated stable/apartment.

Her heart heavy, Bride was grateful that she had this one tiny place left, otherwise she would be in a hotel room tonight. Or worse, her parents' house. She loved them dearly, but she wasn't in the mood to answer their questions or see the look of disappointment on her mother's face as she lamented the fact that if Bride didn't get married, she'd never have any more grandchildren.

At least here in her own place she had some comfort. Maybe.

She opened the door and switched on the lights. Luckily, the water and electricity for this apartment was turned on since it ran off the same line that provided the water and electricity for her store.

The wolf hesitated as he looked around the three hundred square feet of boxes and artwork.

"Oh," she said playfully, "you feeling picky, huh?"

If she didn't know better, she would swear he shook his head no before he came in and started nosing around her boxes.

After locking the door, Bride went to the dusty desk and dropped her keys on top of it. Then she pulled the cover from the couch and coughed as she unearthed a dust bunny farm of death.

"I really hate you, Taylor," she said quietly as she sniffed. "I hope you choke on your skinny new girl-friend's thong."

As if he sensed her sadness, the wolf came over and rubbed against her side. Bride sank down to the floor to pull him into a tight hug.

The wolf didn't complain at all as she let her tears fall into his snowy fur. He sat there quietly with his head on her shoulder as pain flooded her.

How could she have been so stupid as to think for a minute that she loved Taylor? Why had she given him so much of her life and time when he'd only been us-ing her?

Was she really so desperate for love that she would lie to herself about him?

"I just wanted someone to love me for me," she whispered to the wolf. "Is that so wrong?"

Vane couldn't breathe as Bride held him in a death grip and her words tore through him. Worse, he under-stood exactly what she meant. Rejected by everyone except his brother and sister, he knew that the only thing that had saved him from being the omega wolf in his pack had been his willingness to kill anyone who tried to make him or Fang a scapegoat.

Every time they had tried to pick on them, Vane had fought back, and with maturity, he'd grown to such a size that no one dared challenge him again.

Not even his father.

How could anyone hurt Bride like this? His heart pounded wildly as the wolf in him craved blood from the man who made her cry.

He didn't understand what kind of man could voluntarily let her go. Once his kind mated, it was eternal. Unbreakable.

And now that he had confirmation that she was in fact his predestined mate, he was honor bound to protect her until she either finished their mating ritual by accepting him or they parted ways.

The latter wouldn't affect her at all. But as a wolf, he would never be able to have sex with another female so long as Bride lived.

That was completely unacceptable to him. Vane Kattalakis wasn't meant for enforced celibacy. The idea of spending the next few decades impotent was enough to make him do someone damage.

But how could a human ever accept an animal as her mate?

Damn the Fates for this. They were evil bitches who lived for no other purpose than to make others suffer.

The phone rang. Bride released him and went to answer it while Vane nosed around the small, cramped room. It was a dismal place.

"Hey, Tabby." Bride pulled a sheet away from a table and sent a box falling.

Vane yelped and dodged away from it.

Bride patted his head, then moved the box. "You didn't have to do that, you know?" He could sense she was a bit irritated at her friend, but underneath she seemed pleased. "Okay, I'm coming to let you in."

Bride hung up the phone, then grabbed her keys and

opened her door. Vane followed her outside to the street where she opened the wrought-iron door to let Tabitha, who stood on the other side with a wheeled cart loaded with bags, into the courtyard.

"Good grief!" Bride said as she saw bags. "What did you do?"

Tabitha shrugged. "Creature comforts every woman should have." She handed a six-pack of Corona Light beer over to Bride, then wheeled her cart inside.

Bride locked the door and followed Tabitha.

Vane trailed behind them.

Once they were inside the small apartment, Tabitha smiled down at him. "I had a feeling you'd still be here."

She pulled a bone out of the top sack and unwrapped it.

He grimaced inwardly as she set it down on the ground. There was no way in hell he was going to chew on that.

His gaze went to Bride. She was the only chew toy that interested him.

Bride stood with her hands on her hips. "Tabitha—"

"Don't, Bride. As a recent member of the I-Ain't-Got-No-Man-and-Don't-Ever-Want-Another-One Club, I know the last thing you need is to be alone tonight." She pulled a set of silk sheets out of the sack.

"What are these?"

"I told you, creature comforts. We have everything in here. Krispy Kreme doughnuts, beer, soda, creme horns, potato chips, dip, and enough hunk-filled DVDs to sink the *Titanic*. It's time for a hunk fest of men who can't break your heart." Tabitha handed her a small bag.

Bride shook her head. "Thank you, Tabby. I really appreciate this."

"No prob."

Vane sat back as Tabitha hooked up the TV and VCR while Bride opened up boxes that held plates and silverware.

"I'm glad I kept all this," Bride said as she dusted off a crate and set it up like a coffee table in front of the TV. "Taylor didn't want all my things mixed in with his. I should have known then, shouldn't I?"

It was all Vane could do to stay in wolf form. He wanted to soothe her so much, but didn't dare. Especially not with Tabitha present.

"Don't think about it, hon," Tabitha said as she popped the sealed top off the beer with her bare hand and handed it to Bride. "We never see the signs we don't want to see. You know? Look on the bright side, at least your guy didn't leave you because you were nuts."

"You're not nuts."

Tabitha gave a disbelieving laugh at that. "Yeah, right. Amanda aside, only fruits and nuts come out of my family tree. But hey, at least we're entertaining."

Bride gave her a chiding stare. "Does Mina know you say that?"

"Mina? She's a bigger loon than I am. Have you seen her collection of ancient vampire-killing kits? I swear she's the one who made that anonymous bid at Sotheby's for that turn-of-the-century vampire-slaying kit."

Tabitha placed an entire doughnut into her mouth and swallowed it whole.

Bride wrinkled her nose at the action. "Please tell me how you stay so skinny eating the way you do. I barely eat half a Pop-Tart and I gain thirty pounds. I swear I've seen you eat more tonight than I eat in an entire week."

Tabitha licked the sugar from her fingers. "You sound like Amanda."

"Why would she say that? You guys are twins and she's every bit as twiggy as you are."

"Yeah, but she's a good fifteen pounds heavier than I am and she hates me for it. I don't know why you guys complain, at least you two have boobs. I have the body of a twelve-year-old boy."

Bride scoffed. "Any time you want, I'll trade you."

Vane growled at that. The last thing he wanted was a skinny mate. There was nothing wrong with Bride, and if he were in human form, he'd show her exactly what those lush curves did to him.

Unfortunately, he needed her girlfriend to leave first.

"Is something wrong, boy?" Tabitha asked as she came over to him.

He trotted over to Bride.

Tabitha gaped at him. "Well, I've just been dissed by Benji. Jeez. I think you've picked up a lifelong friend here, Bride. Just wait until he finds out your dad is the if-you-love-them-neuter-them king."

Vane cringed in spite of himself.

They wouldn't dare . . .

"Shush, Tabby, you'll scare him." She looked down at him as she stroked his chin. "But you're right, he hasn't been fixed."

And he damned well wasn't going to be, either.

"Maybe I should take him over to Dad's tomorrow and have him look him over."

"You going to keep him, then?" Tabitha asked.

Bride lifted his head so that she could look him directly in the eyes. "What do you think, Mr. Wolf? You want to stay with me for a little while?"

She had *no* idea. If he had his way, he would be a permanent addition.

Chapter 3

Vane stood outside the bathroom in human form while Bride took a shower. Tabitha had left a short time ago after threatening one last time to hunt down Bride's ex and hurt him.

If Vane ever laid hands on the bastard, there wouldn't be enough left of him for Tabitha to bother with. Not that he should feel that way. After all, if Bride hadn't been on the outs with the man, she wouldn't have been his tonight.

And he might never have known that she was his mate.

But that was human rationale and human rationale had no place in his animal world.

"I'm not human," he breathed, feeling the profound pain of that statement. At least he wasn't *fully* human.

No one, not even him, was really sure what he was.

He was a cursed hybrid who belonged to no real group. Half Arcadian, half Katagaria, Vane had been born in the native form of a wolf pup only to find his native form changed to human once he hit puberty.

He flinched as he recalled the day he'd changed over. The terror of it. The fear. The confusion. All of his life, he'd existed solely as a wolf, and then for a few months, against his will, he'd been locked inside a human body and unable to transform back into a wolf at all. His new body had been alien to him. He hadn't known how to eat as a man, how to survive or to cope. Even walking had been difficult at first. He'd been assailed by human emotions and feelings. Human sensations.

Worst of all, he'd been weak. Helpless.

Nothing had ever been more degrading to him than to realize he couldn't fight back. That he was completely reliant on his brother for survival.

Every night he'd prayed that come the morning he would be an animal again, and every morning he awoke to the horror that he was a man.

If not for Fang and Anya, his pack would have killed him. Luckily, his brother and sister had shielded him from the others and had helped him hide the fact that he was no longer a pure wolf.

For centuries he had hidden from everyone, even himself, the fact that after his puberty he held a human heart.

How could such a change even be possible?

Yet here he was: a living contradiction. A living impossibility.

And he was mated to a regular human.

Vane clenched his marked hand. He couldn't hide the truth of his physical being from the Fates. They had known what he was and they had sought to bind him to a human woman.

Why?

Life as a hybrid was hard enough. The last thing he wanted was to father children who would be even more outcast than he was.

Would they be human or Were-Hunter?

And all those arguments telling him why he couldn't mate with Bride didn't amount to anything when the human heart inside him craved the woman on the other side of that closed door.

Even now he could imagine what she must look like in there, naked. The water sliding against her pale skin as her hands slid over her body, soaping her thighs, her . . .

The wolf in him demanded he kick it down and claim her.

The man in him just wanted to hold her close and protect her.

He'd never been so torn. So confused.

So damned horny!

Vane trailed his hand over the cool silk pajamas that Bride had pulled out of one of her boxes and left on the chair beside the door. They held her unique scent of strawberry potpourri and woman. He lifted the top and inhaled the richness of her as his groin burned and strained.

It was all he could do to not go to her in the shower and take her again. But it wouldn't accomplish anything other than to terrify her.

She was human and knew nothing of his world. She knew nothing of him.

A wave of hopelessness consumed him. He didn't know how to court a human female. Not to mention that his being mated to her didn't really affect her at all.

She could leave him and live a nice, normal life with another man. She could fall in love with anyone and bear that man's children.

Leaving her to that end would be the decent thing to do. By the very laws that governed his people, he couldn't force her to take him as her mate. His own parents were proof of that. For three weeks his father had kept his mother chained against her will. He'd brutally tried to force her into accepting a Katagari male as her mate.

No amount of violence had worked.

His Arcadian mother had refused, even after she'd learned she was pregnant. To her, all of the Katagaria were animals who should be slaughtered without compassion. Vicious even by Katagaria standards, his father had never tried to show her any other side of himself.

Then again, his father had never had a more tender side. Markus was violent at best, lethal at worst. Vane and Fang both bore enough scars inside and out to prove that.

So the three-week window of mating opportunity had closed for his parents and left both of them frigid and sterile. Since then his parents had lived in open warfare with each other's people.

And with their own children.

"Don't look at me with that bitch's eyes, whelp. I'll rip your throat out." In fact, his father had spent the whole of Vane's life trying not to look at him.

The one time Vane had met his mother, she had made her own position clear.

"My base form is human and that alone is why you

and your Katagari brother are alive. I couldn't bring myself to kill you as helpless puppies even though I know I should have. But now that you're grown, I have no such compunctions. All of you are savage animals to me and if I ever see you again I will kill you as such."

Honestly, he couldn't blame her for that, given what his father had done to her. He had never expected kindness from others and so far he hadn't been disappointed.

Except with the bear clan. He still didn't understand their tolerance of him and Fang. Especially Fang, who couldn't protect the bears or work for his keep.

Why would they take them in when their own wolf clan would kill them if they found them?

Vane let out a deep breath as the reality came crashing down on him. He was living under a death sentence with no pack to help protect or raise his young. No pack to shelter his mate. He couldn't expose Bride to the danger that was a daily part of his life.

No matter what the Fates decreed, he couldn't have a human mate. Bride would never accept him and his world. She didn't belong to it any more than his mother had belonged with his father.

They were different species.

His job was strictly to protect her until his mark was gone. Then she would free and he . . .

"I'll be a fucking eunuch," he growled under his breath, hating the very idea of it.

But what else was there?

Keep her in chains like his father had done his mother? Beat her into submission?

None of that would work. Besides, Bride was his

mate. He couldn't find it in him to hurt her in any way. Unlike his father, he understood what "protective" meant.

Vane had spent his entire life guarding Anya and Fang. Taking their pack's and their father's abuse for them. He wasn't about to hurt the one person the Fates had designated for him.

He heard Bride turning off the water. Flashing back to wolf form, he forced himself not to go into the room where he would meet temptation.

But then, he didn't have to. Bride came out a few seconds later with a towel wrapped around her.

He ground his teeth at the sight of her standing there with the damp towel clinging to every curve of that damp, voluptuous body. Worse, the towel was too small and left a large gap of succulent flesh bared to his gaze.

She dropped the towel to the floor.

It was all he could do not to whine, especially when she bent over to sort through a box of clothes for her underwear.

Bride started at a strange sound from her new pet. Turning, she saw the wolf staring at her with an intensity that was extremely wild and disturbing.

A tremor of fear went through her. "You're not going to attack me, are you, boy?"

He came over to her with his tail wagging. He jumped up unexpectedly and licked her cheek, then bounded back to the other side of the room.

Well, that was weird.

Frowning, she grabbed her panties and pulled them on, then quickly dressed in her pajamas. They were a bit tight, which was why they were in storage. Her

mother had given her a whole new wardrobe two years
ago when she had gone on a liquid protein diet that had
caused her to drop twenty-five pounds. It had worked,
but within a year every ounce of the weight had come
back plus another ten pounds.

Bride sighed and put the matter out of her mind.
Screw Taylor and his diets. Like her mother and grandmother before her, she was destined to be a round Irishwoman, and no amount of anything would ever change
the fact that she was chromosomally damaged.

"I should have been born in the fifties when it was
fashionable to be pudgy."

Sighing, she went over to the couch to sleep. The wolf
came over to her and stuck his nose close to her own.

"Sorry, kid," she said, patting his head. "No room
for you tonight. Tomorrow we'll get a real bed, okay?"

He nuzzled her face.

"You are good company, aren't you?" He seemed
to like it best when she stroked him just under his chin.
He closed his eyes and wagged his tail as she gently
scratched him there. "So what am I going to name you?"

She thought it over, but only one name hovered in
her mind . . .

"Don't be stupid," she said to herself. It would be
ridiculous to name him after a one-night stand.

And yet . . .

"Would you mind being called Vane?"

He opened his eyes at that and licked her chin.

"Okay then, you'll be Vane Two. Vane for short,
though."

Bride reached over her head to turn off the lamp,
then snuggled down to sleep.

Vane sat in the dark, watching her quietly. He couldn't believe what she was going to call his wolf form. If he didn't know better . . .

But no, she didn't have any sort of psychic powers. Maybe she had just liked his name.

He waited for her to fall sound asleep before he changed to human form again and made sure all her doors and windows were locked. Once he was certain she'd be okay for a bit, he flashed from her apartment back to his room at Sanctuary.

It was pitch-black here, too. He opened the door and headed to the next room, where Fang was staying. As he'd been since the night Vane had brought him here, his brother was in wolf form, lying comatose on the bed.

Vane sighed wearily as he crossed the room.

"C'mon, Fang," he said, moving to the bed. "Snap out of this. I miss you, little brother, and I could really use someone to talk to right now. I have one serious problem on my hands."

But it was useless. The Daimons had taken more than his brother's blood. They had stolen his spirit.

The shame of what had happened to Fang was more than the wolf could face. Vane understood that. He'd felt it himself when he'd found out he was human.

There was nothing worse than being attacked and not being able to fight back. He flinched as memories assailed him.

The first time he'd turned human had been in the middle of a fight with an angry boar. The beast had stabbed him so badly that he still felt a pain in his ribs if he moved the wrong way. One minute, he'd been a wolf, and the next he'd been on his back while the boar bit, clawed, and tusked him.

Had Fang not come along . . .

"Get up, little brother," he whispered. "You can't keep living like this."

Fang didn't acknowledge him at all.

Vane ran his hand over his brother's dark brown fur, then turned to leave him there.

In the hallway outside, he passed Aimee Peltier. In human form, she held a bowl of beef soup in her hands as she came from the direction of the stairs.

The only daughter of the bear clan, she was a tall, thin blonde with an exceptionally beautiful face. Her brothers had a full-time job keeping the human men from coming on to her whenever she helped out in the bar that was attached to the house.

It was a job they all took very seriously.

"Is he eating?" Vane asked her.

"Sometimes," she said quietly. "I got a little soup in him at lunch so I was hoping he might take some more tonight."

She'd been a godsend to him. Aimee alone seemed to be able to reach Fang. His brother seemed somehow more alert whenever she was near.

"Thanks. I really appreciate your watching over him for me." In fact, she spent a great deal of time with Fang. It was enough to make him wonder, but Fang hadn't moved out of his bed once since the night Vane had brought him here.

She nodded.

"Aimee?" he asked as she started past him.

She turned.

"Never mind. It was a stupid thought." There wasn't anything between his brother and the she-bear. How could there be?

Vane continued on his way down the hall, to the stairs.

He made his way downstairs, across the foyer, and into the small antechamber where a door connected Peltier House to the Sanctuary bar next door.

It opened into the bar's kitchen where two Were-Hunters, Jasyn Kallinos and Wren, were guarding it innocuously from the human kitchen staff, who had no idea why no one but a select few could pass through the doorway to the other side. It was mostly because those of the bear clan who had young kept their cubs on the top floor of Peltier House. Occasionally, one of the cubs would escape their nurse and roll down the stairs.

The last thing the Peltiers needed was for someone to call animal control on them for the unlicensed zoo that made their house a home.

Of course the idea of a human coming in and finding a wolf, panthers, lions, tigers, and bears asleep in their various beds was rather amusing to Vane. Or better yet, the dragon who slept coiled up in the attic. Someone really should keep a camera handy. Just in case.

Vane inclined his head toward Jasyn, a tall, blond Were-Hawk who was one of the deadlier inhabitants of the house. The price on Jasyn's head made a mockery of Vane's death sentence. Mostly because, unlike Jasyn, Vane only killed when he had to. True to his animal predatorial heart, Jasyn was in it for the thrill of the kill.

Jasyn lived to stalk and to maim.

As Vane neared the swinging door that led out to the bar area, it was slung back. Kyle Peltier came running through it in human form like a bat out of hell.

Vane stepped back out of the way.

Remi Peltier, one of the identical quads with long curly blond hair, tackled Kyle to the floor just in front of Vane's feet and started slugging his younger brother. Kyle tried to fend him off, but it was impossible. Remi was a much older, stronger bear who loved to fight.

Vane grabbed Remi and pulled him away before he hurt the cub. "What are you doing?"

"I'm killing Gilligan," Remi snarled, trying to get past Vane to grab Kyle again.

"I happen to like the song," Kyle said defensively, wiping at the blood on his lips as he moved to stand behind an unamused Jasyn.

Wren handed the cub a towel to blot his face.

Remi curled his lips. "Yeah, but we don't just play that damned song for the hell of it, you idiot. Half the friggin' clientele ran for the door."

Mama Bear came in from the Peltier House side to see Kyle bleeding.

"What on earth?" she asked, taking him by the shoulders so that she could examine his split lip. "*Mon ange,* what happened?"

All maturity left Kyle as he faced his mother. He even let a portion of his short blond hair fall into his blue eyes. "Remi attacked me."

Remi twisted his arm out of Vane's grasp. "He played 'Sweet Home Alabama' on the jukebox, *maman.*"

Nicolette rolled her eyes at her youngest cub. "Kyle,

you know we only play that when the Dark-Hunter Acheron comes through our doors as a courtesy alert to our clientele. What were you thinking?"

Vane stifled a laugh. Acheron Parthenopaeus was the leader of the Dark-Hunters. He was a man of many dichotomies and unbelievable power, and most everyone Vane knew was scared shitless of him. Whenever he entered the bar, most Weres, and all Daimons headed for the door. Especially if they had something to hide.

Kyle gave her a sullen look. "That it's a good song, *maman,* and I wanted to hear it."

Remi rushed for Kyle's throat, but Vane pulled him back.

"He's too stupid to live," Remi snarled. "I think we should cut his throat and save ourselves the heartache."

Wren gave a rare laugh while Jasyn went stone-faced.

The human staff stayed wisely out of it, and went about their business as if nothing were happening. But then they were used to the brothers and their constant bickering among themselves.

Nicolette growled at her older son. "We were all stupid at his age, Remi. Even you." She patted Kyle on the arm and urged him toward the door to Peltier House. "You'd best stay away from the bar for the rest of the night, *cher.* Papa and your brothers will need time to cool their tempers."

Kyle nodded, then looked back at his brother and stuck his tongue out.

Remi made a bear sound that caused every human in the kitchen to stare.

The look on Mama's face said there would be hell to

pay once she had her older cub out of the sight and earshot of the humans.

"I think you'd best head back to the bar, Remi," Vane said, letting him go.

"Fine," Remi snarled. "Do us all a favor, *maman.* Eat your young."

This time it was Jasyn who laughed, then sobered the instant Nicolette gave him a gimlet glare.

Shaking her head, she told the kitchen staff to go back to work.

Vane started for the bar.

"Vane, *mon cher,* wait."

He looked back at her.

She moved to stand by his side. "Thank you for saving Kyle. Remi has never learned to govern that temper of his. There are times I fear he never will."

"It's all right. He reminds me a lot of Fang. When he's not comatose anyway."

She looked down, then frowned. Lifting his hand, she stared at his marked palm. "You're mated?"

He balled his hand into a fist. "It happened earlier tonight."

Her jaw went slack before she pulled him back into her house. She shut the door, then faced him. "Who?"

"A human."

She cursed in French. "Oh, *cher,*" she breathed. "What are you going to do?"

Vane shrugged. "There's nothing to be done. I'll guard her for the duration, then leave her to her life."

She gave him a puzzled stare. "Why would you damn yourself to so many years with no woman or mate? If you let her go, you may well never mate again."

Vane started to leave, but she pulled him to a stop.

"What should I do, Nicolette?" he asked, using her real name instead of *Mama*, which most called her. "I'm a living example of why we need to breed within our own species. The last thing I want is to spread my disease to another generation."

She looked appalled by his words. "You are not diseased."

"No? Then what would you call it?"

"You are blessed, as Colt is."

He gaped incredulously at her words. That was one word he would never have applied to himself. "Blessed?"

"Oui," she said sincerely. "Unlike the rest of us, you know what it's like for the other side. You've been both animal and human. I'll never know what it's like to be human. But you do."

"I'm not human."

She shrugged. "Whatever you say, *cher*. But I know other Arcadians who have mated with humans. If you wish I could have them come talk to you."

"To what purpose? Were they mixed blood like me?"

"Non."

"Then what are they going to tell me? If my mate bears children, will they be human or wolf? Will they change base forms at puberty? How do I explain to a human mate that *I* don't know what our children will be?"

"But you are Arcadian."

He hated the fact that Nicolette, Acheron, and Colt could see what he'd been able to hide from others. He didn't know how they were able to detect him, but it seriously pissed him off. Even his own father hadn't known he was an Arcadian.

Of course it helped that his father barely looked at him.

"Am I Arcadian?" he asked, lowering his voice to an angry whisper. "I don't feel the human side the way Colt does. How can I have been a wolf pup and then convert to human during puberty? How is that even possible?"

She shook her head. "*Je ne sais pas,* Vane. There is much in this world I don't understand. There are very few mixed bloods, you know that. Most humans who are brought in as mates are sterile. Maybe yours is, too."

That gave him some degree of hope, but he wasn't foolish enough to grasp it. His life had never been an easy one. Every time he had reached out for something he wanted, he'd been slapped down viciously.

It was hard to be optimistic in a life where optimism had never been rewarded positively.

"It's a chance I can't take," he said quietly, even though a part of him wanted that chance with a desperation that frightened him. "I refuse to screw up her life."

Nicolette stepped back from him. "Very well. That's something that's completely up to you, but if you change your mind—"

"I won't."

"Fine. Why don't you take the next few weeks and stay with your mate while she is marked? We'll take care of Fang in the meantime."

Did he dare trust that offer?

"Are you sure?"

"*Oui, cher.* You can trust some animals, even bears. I promise you, your brother is safe here, but your mate, she's not safe alone while she carries your scent on her."

Nicolette was right. If, as he suspected, his pack was looking for them, their scouts might find his scent around Bride. She would carry it as long as she bore his mark, and a trained Were-Hunter would be able to sniff her out.

There was no telling what his enemies might do to her.

"Thank you, Nicolette. I owe you."

"I know. Now go and be with your human while you can."

Vane nodded, then flashed back to Bride's side.

She was still asleep on her couch. Lying on her back, she looked extremely uncomfortable. Her legs were bunched up and she had one arm over her head while the other dangled off into nothingness.

Tenderness flooded him as he remembered the way she had looked as she came for him. The sight of her face in the mirror as he held her.

She was a passionate woman. One he ached to taste again and again. Against his common sense, he reached out and touched her soft cheek.

Her eyes fluttered open and she gasped.

Bride sat up with a hiss as she thought she saw Vane standing over her.

"Vane?"

The wolf padded around the couch to sit beside her.

Confused, she looked around, then gave a nervous laugh. "Boy, am I hallucinating or what? Oh yeah. Looney Tunes, here I come."

Shaking her head, she lay back down and tried to go back to sleep, but as she did, she could swear she smelled Vane's scent on her skin.

For two days, Vane stayed in wolf form as he watched over Bride, but with every minute of it, he felt as if he were being brutally tortured. His natural instinct was to claim her.

If she were a she-wolf, he would be inside her even now, showing her his prowess and authority.

The beast inside him demanded the courtship. The human in him . . .

It scared him most of all. Neither part was listening to his cool, calm rationale. Not that he really had any of that where she was concerned. Around her, he had a raging hormonal surge so profound it made a tsunami look like a toddler's wave pool.

His need to touch her was becoming so ferocious that he was even afraid to be with her now.

A few minutes ago, in wolf form, he'd run out the door to try and get a grip on himself before he returned to her shop for more torment. Every time she moved, it made his blood heat. The sound of her voice, the lick she gave her long, graceful fingers as she flipped through the pages of her magazines, it was all torture for him.

It was killing him.

You wish.

Really, he was beginning to. Death had to be preferable to this. Where were the assassin wolves when he needed them? Yeah, pain. That was the answer. Nothing like severe pain to curb his sexual appetites.

Think of something else.

Vane had to get his mind off Bride and her body. More importantly, off what he wanted to do to and with her body.

Determined to try, he stopped in front of a small store on Royal Street. It was a doll shop, of all things. He didn't really know why he was here except one of the dolls in the window reminded him of the one Bride had in a box by her TV.

"Well, don't just stand outside, young man, come on in."

A tiny old woman stood in the doorway. Her hair was gray, but her eyes were sharp and intelligent.

"It's okay, I was just looking," Vane said.

And then he caught a scent of something strange. A fissure of power in the air that was even stronger than that of a Were-Hunter.

Acheron?

The old woman smiled at him. "Come inside, wolf. There's someone I think you want to talk to."

She held the door open as he entered the small, dark shop, lined with shelves and cases of custom-made dolls. Without a word, she led him behind the counter and through a set of heavy burgundy curtains.

Vane drew up short as he saw the strangest sight of his entire four hundred years of life.

The mighty Dark-Hunter Acheron Parthenopaeus sat on the floor of the back room with his legs crossed as he played dolls with his demon companion and a human infant.

Vane couldn't move as he watched the infant girl sitting on Ash's bent, leather-clad knee while the Dark-Hunter held her there with one large hand on her belly. Dressed in a frilly pink pinafore and black Mary Janes, she was beautiful, with short, dark auburn curls and a plump, angelic face.

Ash held a male doll in his right hand while the little girl chewed on the head of a red-haired Barbie that looked strangely like the Greek goddess Artemis, who had created and ruled the Dark-Hunters. The demon sat in front of them holding a blond doll. The demon herself had black hair with a red stripe in it that matched Ash's hair perfectly.

"See, I knew baby Marissa was quality people," the demon said to Ash. "Look how she eating the head off the redheaded Artemis doll. Simi needs to teach her to belch fire, then introduce her to the real heifer-goddess herself."

Ash laughed. "I don't think so, Sim. Marissa isn't quite ready for that, are you, sweetie?"

The little girl reached up and placed a wet hand to Ash's chin as she laughed at him. Ash playfully nipped at her hand while the demon took his doll and made it dance with hers.

"I think my doll needs a pair of horneys, *akri*," the demon said to Ash. "You think Liza will make me a demon doll like me?"

Horns appeared instantly on the doll's head, along with red and black hair.

The demon squealed in delight. "Oh, thank you,

akri. It's a Simi doll!" Cocking her head, the demon looked at the little girl in Ash's lap. "You know, Marissa is a cutie baby, but she be even prettier with horneys too."

"No, Sim, I don't think Amanda or Kyrian would appreciate getting their daughter back with a pair of horns on her head."

"Yeah, but she look so . . . so . . . deprived without them. I could make them really pretty. Maybe pink to go with her dress?"

"That's okay, Simi."

The demon pouted. "Oh pooh, you no fun, *akri*." She held up the male doll. "See this, Marissa? Okay, now here's what happens when he make Barbie mad. She gets her barbecue sauce and she eats him."

Ash quickly took the doll from Simi's hand before she could place it in her open mouth. "No, no, Simi. You're allergic to rubber."

"I am?"

"Don't you remember how sick you got when you ate those tires off the truck that made you mad?"

The demon looked really disappointed. "Oh. Is that what made me ill? I thought it was because the heifer-goddess was there."

Ash placed a quick kiss to the top of the baby's head, then handed her to Simi. "Watch Marissa for a few minutes and don't eat her or let her eat anything."

"No worry, *akri*. I would never eat baby Marissa. I know how much you would miss her if I did."

Ash gave the demon an affectionate hug before he got up and sauntered over to Vane. Tall and lean, Ash was the epitome of a young man in the prime of his life. There weren't many people taller than Vane, but Ash was one of them.

And it wasn't just his height that was intimidating. There was something primal and powerful about the Dark-Hunter. Something that even the animal in Vane feared.

Even so, they had known each other for centuries. In fact, Ash had been the one who had helped Vane to find his mother. To this day, Vane wasn't sure why the Dark-Hunter had helped him.

But then, no one understood Acheron Parthenopaeus.

"You know, it's not nice to spy on people, wolf."

Vane snorted at that. "As if anyone could ever spy on you." He looked back at the demon and little girl. "I never pegged you for a babysitter."

Ash glanced down at Vane's hand, then met him with a level gaze. There was something extremely disconcerting about Ash's liquid silver eyes that swirled with mystical power and ancient knowledge. "I never pegged you for a coward."

Anger sizzled through Vane at the insult. He lunged at Ash, only to have the Atlantean spin out of his reach.

"Don't." That single word carried enough command to give Vane pause.

Ash looked over his shoulder to the old woman who was still standing in the opening of the curtains. "Liza, would you fetch Vane a cup of tea, please?"

"I don't drink tea."

"Liza?"

"I'll be right back with it." The old woman went out into the shop.

"I don't drink tea," Vane reiterated.

"You'll drink hers and you'll like it."

Vane's gaze darkened again. "I'm not one of your Dark-Hunters, Acheron. I don't dance to your command."

"Neither do they. But that's neither here nor there, is it?" Ash cocked his head as if he were listening to something that only the Atlantean could hear. "You're seeking answers."

"I don't need anything from a Dark-Hunter. Ever."

Ash let out a slow, deep breath. "I'm sorry about Anya, Vane, but it was meant to be."

Vane curled his lip at the offer of sympathy; his heart was still broken over her loss. "Don't talk to me about fate, Dark-Hunter. I've had it with that subject."

To his amazement, Ash agreed. "I know the feeling. But it doesn't change what's going on inside you, does it?"

He cut a glare at Ash. "What do you know about it?"

"Everything." Ash crossed his arms over his chest as he watched him with a gaze that set Vane on edge. "Life would be so easy if we had all the answers, wouldn't it? Will your pack come for you? Will Fang be normal again? Will Bride ever accept you as her mate?"

Vane went cold at his words. "How do you know about Bride?"

He didn't answer. "You know, humans are amazing in their capacity to love. Don't sell either one of you short because you're afraid of what *might* happen. Instead, maybe you should focus on what *will* happen if you leave her."

That was easy for him to say. He wasn't the one being hunted. "What do you know about fear?"

"Enough to teach a lifetime course on it." Ash looked past him to see the infant standing up beside the demon on wobbly little legs that were still learning how to support the baby's weight. "She's beautiful, isn't she?"

Vane shrugged. He was far from an expert on what made a human child beautiful.

"Hard to believe that if Kyrian hadn't had faith in Amanda and in their future together, she would never have existed at all. No one would have heard the beauty of her little laugh or seen the preciousness of her smile . . . Think about it, Vane. An accountant who only wanted a normal life and a Dark-Hunter who thought love was a fable. If Kyrian had walked away, he would still be living alone as a Dark-Hunter. And Amanda, had she managed to survive the Apollite and Daimon who were out to steal her powers, would probably be married to someone else by now."

"Would they have been happy?" Vane wasn't sure why he asked that question.

Ash shrugged. "Maybe, maybe not. But look at their baby. She's going to grow up the daughter of a sorceress and a Dark-Hunter. She will know things about this world that few people ever do. For that matter, she already does. Now imagine if she never existed. What would the world have lost without her?"

"What has it gained with her?"

Ash didn't hesitate to answer. "It has gained a truly beautiful soul who will grow up to help anyone who needs it. In a world full of malice, she will never do harm. And two souls who have never known love now have each other."

Vane scoffed at that. "Have you ever thought about writing romance novels, Ash? That might wash in fiction, but let me tell you about the real world. That little girl will grow up, have her heart broken, and be used by people out to take advantage of her."

"And her parents will tear the heart out of anyone who tries it. Life is a gamble, Vane. It's harsh and painful most of the time, and it's not for the timid. Spoils go to the victor, not to the one who doesn't even show up for the battle."

"What are you saying?"

"I think you already know. Will Bride have a better life without you? Who's to say? Maybe there is some human out there who can appreciate her. But will he ever appreciate her as much as you do?"

No. Vane knew it deep in his heart. Her tender touch was priceless to him. "What if I get her killed?"

"Death is inevitable for humans. She will die someday. But the real question is, will she ever live?" Ash started away, then paused. "Will you?"

Vane stood there in silence as he thought over what Ash had said.

Liza returned with the tea and Vane thanked her before he tasted it.

Much to his dismay, Ash was right. It was good stuff and he did like it.

Ash picked the baby up and turned back toward him. "You know, there's always the possibility that Bride might not accept you. Meet her as a man, Vane. Give her what your father never gave your mother. Let her see the man and the animal and then let her decide for herself."

"And if she leaves me?"

"Is that what you fear most?"

Vane looked away. Damn Ash for his sagacity. No, his worst fear was that she would accept him and that he wouldn't be able to keep her safe from his enemies.

"All you can ever really do, Vane, is give it your all and trust that everything will work out."

"Do you really trust the Fates?"

Ash's answer surprised him. "Not at all. They make mistakes just like everyone else. But in the end, you have to believe in something." Ash cuddled the baby to his chest. "So what will you choose?"

Ash's question hung in Vane's mind as he made his way back to Bride's shop. He didn't know what choice to make and Ash hadn't really helped.

In wolf form, he nosed his way in the door of her boutique. Since he'd moved in with her, Bride had made it a habit to leave the shop door ajar any time he left.

As if she knew he'd be back.

She'd also made him a comfortable pallet behind her counter so that he could lie quietly and watch her while she worked. And he did like to watch her, especially when she interacted with other people. There was a kindness to her that others he'd known lacked.

He particularly liked to watch her with Tabitha. The two of them were extremely amusing. At least when they weren't discussing how much every member of his gender, with the exception of their fathers, sucked.

He half-expected Tabitha to attempt to neuter him just because he was male.

Right now, Bride sat on her wooden stool beside her register as she finished eating half of a deli sandwich.

"There you are," she said, smiling at him. "I was wondering what happened to you."

She held out the other half of her sandwich and let him eat it from her hand. Vane finished it off, then placed his head in her lap. She stroked his ears and the tenderness of it shattered him.

Maybe Ash was right. Didn't he owe it to both of them to at least give her a choice?

Vane Kattalakis had never allowed fear to govern him. But then, he had never lost anyone he loved until eight months ago.

In one night, he had lost everything.

Gods, he was so tired of being alone. So tired of not trusting anyone.

Of having no one to laugh with.

Maybe Bride was his future.

Maybe he would try this and see.

But how?

What did humans do to court each other?

Bride sat on her stool as she cleaned up after her lunch and tossed the garbage in the trash can. The last two days had been horrible as she put her tiny apartment in order and did her best to forget Taylor and his cruelty. Except the rat bastard had yet to return her stuff.

"Please don't make me have to go and get it," she said as she reviewed a catalogue for new merchandise by her register.

If she did, she was taking Tabitha with her just for the sake of vengeance.

And if Tabitha happened to bring a tire iron . . . well, it wasn't as if Bride could keep her from it. It was a free country, after all. And if the tire iron ended up falling against Taylor's kneecaps a time or two or three . . . dozen, well, accidents did happen.

Relishing the thought, she reached down and petted her wolf behind his ears and felt instantly better.

Over the last two days, Vane had become her constant companion. He sat even now behind the register at her feet, completely content just to be with her. If only she could find a man so loyal.

The door to her shop opened.

She looked up to see Taylor coming inside. Her heart stopped. He was tall and good-looking in that phony TV sort of way. He wore a pair of khakis and a black Ralph Lauren polo shirt.

He strode into the store like he owned it. Like he hadn't carelessly broken her heart just a few days ago.

"Hi, Bride," he said with that perfect capped-tooth smile of his. "Are you alone?"

Her wolf started to growl.

"Hi, Taylor," she said, reaching down to touch and soothe her companion. "Except for my pet, yeah."

"Pet?" He peeped over the counter to look at Vane, who was now on his feet with his ears laid back.

Taylor stepped back. "That's a hell of a pet you have there. Did your dad give him to you?"

"What do you want?" she asked. "I know you didn't just come to shoot the breeze with me."

"I've, um, I've got your stuff outside and wanted to know what to do with it."

She looked outside to see a small moving van parked behind Taylor's red Alfa Romeo. "You were supposed to have it here two days ago."

He made a disgusted sound at her. "Yeah, well I've been busy. You know, I actually have a life."

She rolled her eyes at him as anger took hold. "You know, I do, too."

"Yeah," he said with a laugh. "Eating bonbons and watching TV is so time-consuming."

She gave him a reproachful glare. "You are such a jerk. What did I ever see in you?"

He held his arms out as if he were presenting himself to her and smiled. "Same thing every woman sees in me, babe. Face it, we both know you'll never have another guy who looks as good as me interested in you."

Vane leaped at him.

"No!" Bride snapped, but it was too late. The wolf had already latched on to Taylor's arm.

Taylor screamed out in pain.

She grabbed the wolf and pulled him back. Vane strained against her, barking and snarling ferociously as he finally let go of Taylor's arm.

She pulled him into the back room and locked him up.

Taylor held his bleeding arm to his side. "That's it. Consider yourself sued."

"Don't even try it," she said, her own temper snapping as she came back to where he was standing. "You were on my property. I'll tell the police you were threatening me."

"Yeah, right, who would ever believe that?"

"Any anchor person at the other two stations who hate you as much as I do."

His face went pale.

"Yeah, Taylor," she said evilly. "Remember who all the little fat chick knows in this town. I'm the last person you want to screw with."

He turned on his heel and went outside.

Bride followed him and heard him yell at the movers, "Just dump her shit on the street."

"Don't you dare!"

"Do it," he snarled at the men.

To her instant chagrin, the movers opened the back of their truck and started putting boxes on the curb.

Bride was aghast. "I'll pay you three hundred dollars to take it to my apartment around back."

The movers passed a look to each other, then nodded and headed for her gate.

"I'll double whatever she offers you to leave her stuff on the street like the trash that it is."

They set the boxes back on the curb.

"You unbelievable bastard!"

He opened his mouth to respond, then closed it as a motorcycle came roaring toward them.

Bride frowned as the rider jumped the curb in front of the Alfa and parked it right outside her shop. The instant the rider removed his helmet, her heart pounded.

It was Vane—and not the furry one.

Dressed in a black leather jacket and faded jeans, he looked good enough to eat.

And his rugged handsomeness made a mockery of Taylor's pretty-boy features.

Taylor stared at them as Bride closed the distance between them. Vane put the kickstand down, then slung a long, masculine leg over the bike. In one fluid move, he pulled her against him and kissed her like something out of a movie.

"Hi, Bride," he breathed against her lips.

She smiled up at him. "Hi."

"Who the hell is this?" Taylor asked.

Vane gave him a once-over that said he didn't think much of Taylor. "I'm her lover, who the hell are you?"

Bride bit her lip as happiness tore through her. She could kiss him again for that.

"I'm her boyfriend."

"Ah," Vane said. "You're the skank dickhead." He looked back at Bride. "I thought you threw this loser out."

She smiled even wider before she cast an evil glare at Taylor. "I did, but he came back . . . begging."

Vane looked over her shoulder at the movers, who were quickly piling her furniture and boxes on the sidewalk. "What are they doing?"

She drew a ragged breath at Taylor's cruelty. "Taylor is paying them to leave my stuff on the street like trash. Whatever I try to pay them to take it to my apartment, he's going to double it."

Vane looked less than pleased by that. "Really?" He lifted his chin. "Hey, guys?"

They paused to look at Vane.

"Ten thousand dollars to take her stuff inside and put it wherever she wants it."

The tallest of them laughed. "Yeah, right. You got it on you?"

Vane left her side. He pulled his cell phone off his belt and handed it to the man. "Press one and it rings Wachovia. Ask for Leslie Daniels, she's the bank president, and give her your bank and account information. She'll wire it instantly into your account, or to Western Union if you prefer."

The man looked skeptical, but did as Vane asked. As soon as he asked for Leslie, his eyes bulged.

He looked at the rest of the movers and then went to the truck to pull out his checkbook.

Vane winked at her.

A few minutes later, the mover came back and returned the phone to Vane. "She wants to talk to you to make sure you're Mr. Kattalakis."

Vane took the phone. "Hey, Les, it's me . . . Yeah, I know." While he listened, he passed an angry glare at Taylor. "Tell you what. Make it fifteen thousand for them. They seem like damn decent men . . . Yeah, okay. I'll talk to you later." He hung up the phone and looked at the movers.

The one in charge offered him a nod of admiration. "Okay, guys, you heard Mr. Kattalakis. Be careful with the lady's stuff and put it wherever she wants it."

Vane passed what could only be called a shit-eating grin toward Taylor. "You feel like doubling it now?"

Taylor started toward them, but the feral look on Vane's face made him take a step back.

Taylor raked them with a disgusted curl of his lip. "You're welcome to the fat bitch."

Before she could blink, Vane had Taylor thrown

across the hood of his car and his hand wrapped around his throat.

Bride ran to them while Vane beat Taylor's head against the hood.

"Vane, stop, please! Someone will call the cops."

Snarling, Vane let him go. "You *ever* insult Bride again, I swear I'll rip your throat out and feed you to the gators in the swamp. You understand me?"

"You're crazy. I'm swearing out a warrant for you."

Vane smiled tauntingly. "Please try it. All I have to do is press two on my phone for my attorney. I'll slap you with so many suits for so many years, your grand-kids will be the ones who go to court."

Crawling off the hood of the car, Taylor narrowed his eyes, but he clearly knew he'd been outmaneu-vered. His breathing ragged, he grabbed open his car door, got in and squealed off.

"Hey, lady?" the mover asked. "Whenever you're ready to show us where to put this stuff, please let us know."

Bride left Vane long enough to open the gate and show them to her studio in the back. When she came back, she found Vane leaning against the side of her building, looking at the moving van.

Her heart pounded. "Thank you," she said quietly. "I'm really glad you came by when you did."

He reached to toy with an idle curl she had lying on her shoulder. "Me, too."

"I, um . . . I'll have to make payments to you for the movers."

"Don't worry about it. It's a gift."

"Vane—"

"Don't worry about it," he insisted. "I told you, money has no real value to me."

How much money would he have to have to be able to say that about fifteen thousand dollars? And why would a guy this rich be hanging out with her?

"Well, it has value to me and I don't want to be obligated to you for anything."

"You're not obligated to me, Bride. Ever."

"No, I have to pay you back."

"Then have dinner with me and we'll call it even."

She shook her head at him. "That's no way to pay you back."

"Sure it is."

She opened her mouth to respond, then remembered her other Vane. "Oh no, I have to go get my wolf. He'll be beside himself!"

Vane went pale at her words, but she didn't notice since she was already headed back into her store.

He looked around to make sure the movers couldn't see him, then flashed himself back into the closet in the back room as a wolf.

He had barely made it before she opened the door.

"There you are, boy," she said, kneeling down to pet him. "I'm so sorry I had to put you in here. You okay?"

He nuzzled her gently.

She gave him a tight hug and then stood up. "C'mon, baby, I have someone I want you to meet."

Vane ground his teeth at her words. How on earth could he meet himself? He was powerful, but that was beyond even his abilities.

Instead, he bolted for the half-open door and kept running until he was sure she was out of sight.

Bride went running after her wolf.

"Vane!" she called, rushing to the door. She couldn't see a trace of him anywhere.

"You called?"

She jumped, then turned to see the human Vane behind her. "No, my wolf—"

"Is named Vane?"

She opened her mouth as her face heated. "It's a long story."

He just smiled at her.

Oh Lord, how did she get herself into these predicaments?

"Well, I wouldn't worry about him. I'm sure he'll come back."

"I hope so. I've gotten kind of attached to him."

Vane's heart sank. That was the last thing he wanted her to tell him. But in truth, he'd gotten attached to her, too. Something that was lunacy.

He dropped his hand from her hair even though what he really wanted to do was pull her into his arms and kiss those lips. Both parts of him wanted nothing more than to strip their clothes off and rub himself against her. To feel her soft skin sliding against his. Taste her flesh with his tongue . . .

Bride swallowed at the look on his face. He stared at her as if she were a cake he was about to devour.

No man had ever given her such a hungry, needful look. She was paralyzed by it.

"Hey, lady?"

She jumped at the mover's call. "Yeah?"

"Where do you want us to put the bed?"

She looked up at Vane. "I'll be back, okay?"

He nodded. She left his side and felt his hot, heavy stare on her the whole way as she went to the movers.

Vane struggled to breathe as he watched her walk away from him. That woman had the best-looking ass he'd ever seen. And he loved and hated the way she wore her hair up. Tendrils of it hung down, grazing her neck, making him want to lick every inch of that tantalizing flesh.

Did all wolves feel like this with their mates? Or was it something about Bride?

He didn't know for sure.

But he was now human with her.

God help them both.

Chapter 4

Not once in her entire existence had Bride ever felt more awkward. What did a woman say to a man who had bailed her out of one of the worst moments of her life?

"Thank you" was so inadequate for what she felt for him. He was truly a hero to her.

She left the apartment and headed back toward her store while the movers continued to unload her belongings.

At first she didn't see Vane anywhere. Had he left?

His motorcycle still stood where he'd parked it.

Frowning, she looked inside the store and found him browsing through a rack of slinky dresses that had come in earlier that morning.

He paused at a snazzy black number that had caught her attention. It was made of heavy silk with a halter top that would look great on someone built like Tabitha. She'd ordered them on impulse because she knew instinctively that the dress would really set off the beaded choker Vane had bought for her.

She'd originally planned on displaying the two items together.

Bride opened the door and headed toward him. "Would you like to try one on?" she asked playfully.

He laughed at that. His entire face lightened and his green eyes sparkled. Gracious, no man should be so handsome.

"I don't think I have the cleavage to pull it off and it'd probably make my ass really flat."

She laughed.

He pulled the largest one out and held it up to her. "You on the other hand . . . beautiful."

"Oh no," she said, smoothing the cool silk with her hand. "It's too clingy for me. Besides, I don't like anything that shows off my upper arms."

He looked confused by her words. "Why?"

She shrugged. "I don't know. It makes me really self-conscious."

He looked at the dress, then at her, as if he were imagining her in it. "Yeah, you're probably right. Too many guys would ogle you, then I'd have to hurt them."

He was serious. Amazed by that, Bride arched her brows as she took the dress from him and returned it to the rack.

Vane watched her closely as her scent wrapped around him. The thought of her in that dress . . .

He was so aroused by her that it was all he could do to stand here and not leap. He stared at the bared flesh of her neck, wanting to press his lips there and taste that delectable skin.

In the wild, he wouldn't have hesitated to pull her to him and kiss her until she begged him for mercy. But the humans he'd seen didn't behave that way. There were protocols to courtship that he wasn't sure about.

She turned toward him.

Vane looked away, afraid she could sense how badly he wanted her. How uncertain he was.

In his realm, a timid wolf was a dead one. In the human realm . . .

Did timid win or lose?

Damn, he should have paid more attention.

"So how about that dinner?" he asked, trying the middle ground between timid and forceful. "Want me to give you a couple of hours to get the movers straightened out and then come back?"

She bit her lip. "I don't know."

"Please?"

She nodded, then blushed prettily.

For some reason he couldn't explain, he felt like howling in triumph. He reached for the dress on the rack and pulled the skirt of it out. "Would you wear this?" he asked hopefully.

Bride looked at it doubtfully, but the expression on his face made her reach out for it. He'd been so nice to her so far . . .

"Only if you swear you won't laugh at me in it."

His look seared her. "I would never laugh at you."

She swallowed at the fierce tremor that went through her at the deep sincerity of his words. He really was too sexy for his own good. "Okay. What time will you be back?"

He checked the time on his cell phone. "Six?"

"It's a date."

The satisfied look on his face sent an unfamiliar

thrill through her. *Bride, don't. The last thing you need is to have your heart broken by Mr. Bodacious.*

Maybe he would be different.

Or maybe he'll be worse.

She wouldn't know unless she took a chance.

Breathing in deeply, she took the dress from his hands. Bride McTierney had never been a timid woman. Occasionally she'd been stupid, such as when she'd let Taylor use her, but never cowardly.

Bride met life head-on and she wasn't going to be afraid with Vane. "Six o'clock," she repeated.

"I'll see you shortly," Vane said. He bent down and laid an extremely chaste kiss on her cheek.

Even so, it warmed her every bit as much as a full-blown caress. Bride watched as he made his way out of her store.

Outside, he actually paused to look back at her and smile before he put his sunglasses on.

Hissing at the splendid sight of him, she watched as he started the bike, then rode it off the sidewalk, into the street.

"Oh please, Vane," she whispered under her breath. "Don't break my heart, too."

Bride took the dress to the dressing room and did her best not to remember how fine Vane had looked naked in here. How good he had felt inside her. The look of supreme satisfaction on his face as he rocked her gently in his arms.

She hung the dress up and went to find accessories for it. She didn't know where he was going to take her, but she was going to look her best if it killed her.

· · ·

Vane made his way back to the doll store where he'd left Ash.

He had a date.

With Bride.

Panic was already setting in. What on earth did humans do on a date besides have sex?

He'd seen humans in the bar interact with each other, but those encounters had been similar to what wolves did. Someone would come in, look around, find the partner they wanted to claim, and take them home to screw them. Dev had told him from the very first night that that wasn't the way the human world normally worked. That some things at Sanctuary were different.

The other, more subdued humans who came in were already dating or married to each other. They usually seemed to be having a good time . . . unless they were fighting. But Vane had never paid very much attention to them.

He didn't know anything about trying to make a human actually "like" him. He'd spent the last four hundred years of his life either killing those who threatened his siblings or trying to scare the rest away.

What would make Bride fall in love with him enough so that she would agree to be his mate?

After parking his bike on a side street, he went back to Liza's for some help.

Vane hesitated as he entered the front room where two women were browsing the doll collection while talking to Liza. One of the women was an exact copy of Tabitha, except she didn't have the scar on her face.

She must be Kyrian Hunter's wife, Amanda. Vane had crossed paths with the ex-Dark-Hunter from time to time, but had never met his wife. Marissa was in Amanda's arms, playing with her mother's hair. The other woman, a short brunette, he knew well. She was Dr. Grace Alexander, the human psychologist who kept telling him nothing would help his brother until Fang was ready to be helped. Grace held her son in her arms while Amanda stopped mid-sentence.

All three women turned to stare at Vane, who hesitated just inside the door.

"He's in back still," Liza said, as if she knew who he was looking for.

"Thanks."

He heard Liza explain who and what he was to Amanda as he headed toward the back room.

Vane passed through the curtains to find the demon gone and Kyrian, Nick Gautier, and Julian Alexander talking to Ash.

He knew Nick from the number of times the young human had come into Sanctuary to see his mother, Cherise. Nick was strange, but since he served the Dark-Hunters and they loved his mother, the bears treated him like another one of their cubs. Kyrian was slightly taller than Julian, with blond hair that was a shade darker. Even though they were mostly human, the two men possessed enough authority and skill that Vane respected them.

"What's up, wolf?" Ash asked as he reclined against

a worktable that was littered with doll parts and fabrics. Ash had his butt resting on it, with his legs stretched out before him and his hands braced on either side of his long, lean body.

Nick, Julian, and Kyrian stood in a semicircle between him and Ash.

Vane hesitated. He didn't relish the idea of a public consultation, but since two of the men were married to modern-day women and Nick was known to date a lot, maybe they could help him out.

"I need dating advice. Fast."

Ash arched a single brow at that. "I'm useless. I've never been on one."

The three human men turned to gape at him.

"What?" Ash asked them defensively.

Nick started laughing. "Oh man, this is priceless. Don't tell me the great Acheron is a virgin?"

Ash gave him a droll look. "Yeah, Nick. I'm lily-white."

"How did you get through life without a date?" Kyrian asked Ash.

"It wasn't an issue back then," Ash said curtly.

"Yeah, well, it's a serious issue to me," Vane said, nearing them. "Julian, how did you meet your wife?"

Julian shrugged. "My brother the sex god cursed me into a book for two thousand years. Grace got drunk on her birthday and summoned me out of it."

Vane rolled his eyes. "That's useless. Kyrian? What about you?"

"I woke up handcuffed to Amanda."

Vane could work with that. "So I need to get a set of handcuffs?"

"Not on a first date," Ash said with a smirk. "You'll scare her to death if you handcuff her."

Kyrian scoffed. "It worked for me on a first date."

Ash gave him a bored stare. "And so did having an insane Daimon out to kill the two of you. But I don't think Vane wants to go that route."

"So what do you wolves do to date?" Nick asked.

"We don't date," Vane said. "When a woman is in season, we fight for her and then she picks who mounts her."

Nick gaped. "Are you kidding? You don't have to buy her dinner? You mean you don't even have to talk to her?" He turned to Acheron. "Dayam, Ash, make me a wolf."

"You wouldn't like being a wolf, Nick," Ash said. "You'd have to eat raw meat and sleep outside."

Nick shrugged. "That sounds like a typical Mardi Gras to me."

"What else?" Vane asked them, interrupting Nick's recitation of his Mardi Gras habits. "What did you guys do when you were human?"

Kyrian thought about it before he answered. "Well, in our day," he said, glancing at Julian, "we took women to chariot races and plays."

"Oh jeez," Nick said. "You guys are pathetic. Chariot race, my ass." He stepped forward and draped an arm around Vane's shoulders. "All right, listen to me, wolf. You get some cool clothes and impress her with a lot of cash. You need to take her somewhere good to eat. There's a place down on Chartres where you can get a two-for-one dinner—"

"Nicky!"

They all turned to look at Amanda, who stood between the curtains, glaring at them.

"What?" Nick asked.

"Don't you dare tell him how to date." Amanda came over and handed her daughter to Kyrian. "Have you ever noticed that Mr. Suave here seldom dates a woman twice? There's a reason for that."

Grace clucked her tongue at the men as she joined them. "I swear, we should make all of them take a rudimentary dating course. It's a wonder any of you got married."

Julian offered his wife a devilish grin. "I didn't hear you complain when—"

She covered his mouth with her hand, then placed her son in his arms. "You two go home before you get into any more trouble."

"And you," Amanda said to Ash, "are old enough and wise enough to know better."

"I didn't do anything," Ash said, but there was a gleam in his silvery eyes that belied his denial.

"Yeah, right." Amanda shooed him toward the door.

Ash sauntered out as if greatly amused by the women.

Nick started out after him, but Amanda grabbed his arm.

"You wait here."

"Why?" Nick asked.

Amanda pulled a set of car keys out of his shirt pocket. "Because you are going to loan Vane your car tonight."

"Like hell. Since when can a wolf drive a Jag?"

Grace looked at Vane. "Can you drive?"

"Yes."

"It's settled, then," Grace said. She turned back to Nick. "Take the Jag to the car wash and for heaven's sake clean the McDonald's Happy Meal boxes out of it."

"Hey," Nick said, his face offended. "That's a low blow. Those boxes are collectibles."

Grace ignored him. "What time is your date?" she asked Vane.

"Six."

Amanda handed the keys to Nick. "Okay, Nick, have the car at the house by five-thirty."

"But, but—"

"No buts, just do it."

They forced Nick out the door, then turned to face Vane with hands on their hips.

It was a good thing Vane wasn't a goose. Even so, he felt thoroughly cooked when two women looked at him like that. He had a distinct feeling he was in for it.

"All right. You want to date a human?" Amanda asked.

He nodded.

"Then come with us and listen well."

Bride checked her watch. It was six on the nose and there was no sign of Vane.

"He'll be here," she told herself as she checked her hair and makeup again in the mirror while trying not to see anything below her chin.

If she did, she'd want to change clothes, and it had

taken her a long time to get up the nerve to wear the low-cut, revealing dress Vane had liked. She opened the front door of her apartment only to find no sign of either Vane. Her wolf hadn't been back since he'd run off on her.

She hoped that wasn't a bad sign.

"Get a grip," she said to herself. She hadn't been this nervous in years.

But then she hadn't been this crazy over a man . . .

Ever.

Someone beeped a horn in front of her gate.

Bride frowned at the silver Jaguar that was idling there. Was that Vane's car? She grabbed her purse, locked the door, and crossed the courtyard to see a man in the driver's seat she didn't recognize.

"Can I help you?" she asked as she drew near.

Around her own age, the man was extremely good-looking, with about a day's growth of beard on his face. Dressed in a tacky blue Hawaiian shirt, he had dark brown hair and a charming grin.

"Are you Bride?" he asked.

"Yes."

He got out of the car and pulled his sunglasses off to show her a set of beautiful blue eyes. "Nick Gautier," he said, holding his hand out to her. "I'm your chauffeur, sort of."

"My chauffeur?"

"Yeah, Vane got tied up, and they told me to get my butt over here and make sure you got to the restaurant on time with no waiting. He said he'd meet you there."

Nick walked to the passenger side of the car and opened the door for her.

Bride got in and adjusted her dress while Nick came around to the other side.

"Do you work for Vane?" she asked as he slammed his door shut.

Nick laughed out loud. "Nah. But I've learned not to argue with my boss's wife. She might look all nice and sweet, but she's a nasty thing when you get her riled. Amanda said for me to do this, so here I am not making her angry."

He threw the car in reverse and almost gave her whiplash as he spun it around and stomped on the accelerator.

Bride suddenly had second thoughts about being in the car with Nick. He was an odd man.

Who couldn't drive.

He drove them a few blocks over to Royal Street, which was now open for traffic, and pulled up in front of Brennan's Restaurant.

Bride expected Nick to get out again and open the door for her, but he didn't.

"He said he'd meet you inside as soon as he could."

"Okay." She let herself out.

Nick took off, tires squealing, the minute she was on the sidewalk.

Okay . . . he must have had something else to do.

Bride adjusted her beaded shawl around her bare shoulders and glanced about, hoping for a sign of Vane.

There wasn't one.

Gathering her failing courage, she opened the door and went inside. A young woman dressed in a white blouse and black skirt was at the maître d' stand. "May I help you?"

"Um, yes. I was supposed to meet someone here for dinner. Vane Kattalakis."

The girl looked over her ledger. "I'm sorry, we don't have a reservation for anyone by that name."

Bride's heart sank. "Are you sure?"

The woman turned the ledger to face her. "It's with a *K*, right?"

Bride scanned the names. Her stomach tightened even more when she spotted a familiar name.

Taylor Winthrop.

She wanted to die right there in the foyer. Brennan's was her favorite restaurant and Taylor had refused to bring her here. He'd always said it was too pricey for him and that he couldn't see spending that kind of money on a single meal.

What he'd meant was that he didn't want to spend it on *her*.

She was a fool.

"Thank you," Bride said, stepping away. She balled her hands up in her shawl as she debated what she should do.

All of a sudden, she felt like she was fifteen again, waiting for her prom date to show.

He never had.

He'd found someone else to take and hadn't even bothered to tell her. She'd learned about it the next day from a friend. And when Tabitha had found out, she'd put liquid heat in the guy's jockstrap and a poison-ivy potion in his underwear.

Bride loved Tabitha to this day for that.

But there was no Tabitha here tonight to make it better. Surely Vane wouldn't be so cruel.

Would he?

Had this all been some kind of set-up?

No. He'd be here.

Her stomach in knots, she waited a full ten minutes before the door opened. Bride turned, hoping to see Vane. Instead, it was Taylor with a tall, black-haired woman. She wasn't overly pretty, but the woman had the body of a brick house.

Taylor pulled up short the instant he saw her.

Bride derived a small, evil bit of satisfaction to see that he had a black eye from his earlier encounter with Vane.

He raked her with a sneer. "Meeting your parents here, Bride?"

"No," she said. "I'm waiting for my date."

He leaned over and whispered something in the woman's ear. She looked at Bride and laughed.

At that moment, Bride felt so small that it was all she could do not to run from the restaurant. But she refused to give him the satisfaction.

A male maître d' approached from the back of the restaurant. "May I help you, sir?"

"Yes, we have a reservation for two for Taylor Winthrop. And make sure you give us a romantic, secluded table."

The maître d' checked his name off the list and nodded. "It'll be just a few minutes, Mr. Winthrop."

Taylor passed the man a tip. The maître d' turned to her. "May I help you, madam?"

She felt her face heat up. "There was a mix-up with our reservations. I'm just waiting for my date to arrive."

The man nodded again while Taylor laughed at her.

"That's what happens when you date losers," he said to the woman with him.

Bride's first instinct was to return the insult, but in truth she felt sorry for Taylor's trophy date. The poor woman had no idea what a snake she was dining with.

She just hoped the woman never found out.

Bride pulled her shawl up higher over her shoulders and felt three times more self-conscious. Of course, it didn't help that Taylor and his date kept looking over at her, whispering and then laughing.

She wanted to die.

Just as she was about to leave, the door finally opened and in came Vane.

He was devastating. Dressed in a black Armani suit, he had left his black shirt open at the collar, showing off the powerful tendons of his tanned neck. The ebony color really brought out the green of his eyes. His dark, wavy hair hung loose, and his face was freshly shaved.

He'd never looked more dangerous. More appealing.

Sexier.

Bride heard Taylor's date suck her breath in sharply at the sight of him.

She half-expected Vane to look at the woman. He didn't. He had eyes only for her.

He made his way straight to her side, placing his large warm hands on her shoulders and kissing her lightly on the cheek. She melted instantly as she inhaled the masculine scent of him and his aftershave.

It was all she could do not to purr.

"Why are you waiting at the door?" he asked as he pulled back slightly.

"We don't have reservations."

Vane scowled at her. "I never have reservations. I don't need them." He took her hand and led her over to the counter.

The maître d' appeared instantly. "Mr. Kattalakis," he said, smiling. "It's so good to see you again."

"Hi, Henri," Vane said, placing his arm around Bride's waist. "Is my table ready?"

The smile faded as Henri's gaze went to Bride. He turned instantly contrite. "Oh, I didn't realize she was your date. She said . . ." He turned to Bride. "Madam, please accept my deepest apologies that you were kept waiting. Was it Tiffany who left you standing here unseated? She's new, but I will have her instantly reprimanded for it."

"It's okay," she said, smiling happily at Vane as her heart pounded with relief.

"You sure?" Vane asked.

"Yes. It wasn't her fault."

Henri breathed a sigh of relief. "I will still have a word with her and this will never happen again. I promise you."

The woman with Taylor huffed loudly. "Why do they get a table without waiting, Taylor? He's not on TV."

Vane turned toward them with a penetrating glower that shut both of them up immediately.

"Please follow me," Henri said. "We have your terrace table waiting."

Bride looked over her shoulder at Vane as Henri led them through the restaurant. "How do you get such great service?"

"It's good to be king," he said with a shrug as he

tucked his hands in his pockets. "Money talks and a lot of money sings and dances."

Yeah, but still . . .

They were led to a corner table upstairs that overlooked the beautiful courtyard below. It had a breathtaking view of the flowering fauna. Henri held a chair out for Bride, who scooted into it.

Vane pulled out his wallet and handed several hundred-dollar bills to Henri. "Do me a favor. That guy downstairs . . . Taylor. Give him the worst table in the house."

Henri's eyes danced with amusement. "For you, Mr. Kattalakis, anything."

Vane took his seat as Henri walked off.

"That was so bad of you," she said with a coy smile.

"Do you want me to take it back?"

"Hardly. I was merely pointing out that it was bad."

"What can I say? I'm just a big bad wolf." Vane took her hand in his and laid a sweet, endearing kiss to her palm where that strange mark was. It was kind of odd that he didn't seem to notice it. "You look good enough to eat."

Heat exploded across her face. "Thank you. You look pretty scrumptious yourself."

"I'm sorry I was late," he said, pulling a single red rose out of his jacket and handing it to her. "It took them a little longer to get my suit ready than they thought it would."

"You bought a new suit for our date?"

"Well, yeah. I'm not really a suit kind of guy. I'm more of a natural beast."

Two waiters came up to the table dressed in black jackets and ties. One was an older, distinguished-looking gentleman, and by his short stature, accent, and coloring, Bride would take him for a Cajun. The other was a younger man in his early twenties.

"Mr. Kattalakis," the older one greeted. "How nice to see you with company for a change."

Vane gave her a hot, searing look. "Yeah, it is nice, isn't it?"

"Would you like your usual wine?" the waiter asked.

"Sure."

They looked at Bride.

"Evian, please."

"You want some wine?" Vane asked.

"No, water's fine. Really."

He frowned while the waiters went to get their drinks.

Bride picked up her menu and noticed that Vane didn't bother looking at his. "Just how often do you come here?"

He shrugged. "A couple of times a week. They have a really good breakfast and I've become addicted to their Bananas Foster. What about you? Do you ever come here?"

She squelched the pain she felt at the thought of Taylor and his date, and Taylor's refusal to bring her here. "I haven't in a long time, but yeah, I love their food."

Vane looked relieved by that.

Bride tried to read the menu, but it was hard since he didn't take his eyes off her. There was something extremely animalistic and powerful about the way he treated her. The way he watched her.

It was flattering and, at the same time, almost scary.

She glanced up at him. "What?"

"What?" he asked back.

"Why are you staring at me?"

"I can't help it. I keep expecting you to not be real."

His words floored her.

The waiters came back with their drinks. "Are you ready to order now?"

Bride set her menu down. "I'll have the Brennan salad with no cheese, please."

He wrote it down.

"And?" Vane asked.

Bride looked up at him. "And what?"

"What else are you eating?"

"Just the salad."

Vane frowned at that. "Bernie," he said to the waiter. "Could you please give us a minute?"

"Sure, Mr. Kattalakis. Take your time."

Vane waited until they were gone before he leaned forward. "I know you're hungry, Bride. What did you eat for lunch? Half a deli sandwich?"

His question surprised her. "How did you know that?"

"It was a guess since I can hear your stomach rumbling."

She put her hand over her stomach. "I didn't realize I was so obnoxious."

He growled at her. Bride shifted nervously at the sound that wasn't quite human.

"Look, Bride," he said, his voice deep and resonant. "I'm going to be honest with you. I don't know what I'm doing tonight, okay? I've never had a date before and I was told that women liked to be taken out some-place nice to eat. Grace and Amanda said that I should be myself and not try to impress you. So here we are at my favorite restaurant, but if you don't like it here, we can go someplace else and eat something you want."

Bride's eyes teared up at his words and what they meant. "You asked someone how to date me?"

He let out a sigh and glanced down at his clenched hands. "Great. Now I've made you sad again. I'm sorry. This was a really bad idea. I'll just take you home and you can forget that you ever laid eyes on me."

She reached out and took his hand into hers. "Okay, since we're being honest with each other. I don't know what I'm doing, either. A week ago, I knew what I wanted. I was a fairly successful business owner, dating a guy I stupidly thought I loved and one I planned on marrying someday.

"In one afternoon, my entire life shattered and then all of a sudden this great guy comes along like some mythical knight in shining armor. He's gorgeous, loaded, and says all the right things to me. He makes me feel like I can fly, and every time he shows up, he makes everything better. I'm not used to this, okay? And I'm not used to being with a guy who is so incredibly sexy that he makes me feel like the booby prize."

"I think you're beautiful, Bride."

"See!" she said, gesturing toward him. "There you go being perfect again. I think you need your head examined."

He looked extremely offended by that.

Bride pulled back and sat up straight. "Okay, let's try this again." She held her hand out to him. "Hi, I'm Bride McTierney. Pleased to meet you."

His expression said he thought she was the one who

needed her head examined. He took her hand into his. "Hi, I'm Vane Kattalakis and I'm starving. Would you like to have dinner with me, Bride?"

"Yes, Vane. I would."

He smiled at her. "Okay, so now is this the part where we share sex stories?"

Bride burst out laughing—so loudly that several people nearby turned to stare at her. Covering her mouth, she looked at him. "What?"

"That's what Nick said you should do to get to know a woman."

"Nick?" she asked in disbelief. "The tacky-shirt-wearing, I-can't-drive-my-way-out-of-a-paper-sack Nick?"

Vane's eyes turned dark. Dangerous. "Did he offend you when he picked you up? Say the word and I'll kill him."

"No, but if I were you, I don't think I'd take dating advice from him."

"Why? He gets women all the time."

"Yeah, but does he ever keep any of them?"

"Well . . . no."

"Then don't take his advice."

"Okay." Vane motioned for the waiters who were waiting nearby. "You want to share the chateaubriand Bouquetière with me? Since it's supposed to serve two they get kind of scared when I wolf it down by myself."

She bit back a smile at his words. "I would love it."

Vane looked up as Bernie returned. "We'll start with two Crêpes Barbaras for appetizers, then the chateaubriand Bouquetière."

"Very good, Mr. Kattalakis. Very good."

Vane handed them the menus, then leaned forward. "And make sure to save room for the dessert."

"I don't know if I can hold it, but I'll try. If you want a woman who can eat all that, you need to date my friend Tabitha."

He took her hand into his again and massaged it as if it were unspeakably precious. "I don't want to date Tabitha," he said, laying her hand against his smooth cheek. "I only want to be with you."

Bride had never felt like this in her whole life. She felt so desirable around him. So feminine.

He somehow even managed to make her feel petite.

"So how is it a guy like you has never had a date before?"

Vane took a drink of wine as he thought about how to answer her question. He didn't want to lie to her, but he couldn't exactly tell her that he was a wolf who had grown up living in the woods, sleeping in dens with other wolves.

That might scare her a bit.

"I grew up in a commune of sorts."

She seemed nervous now and reminded him of a cornered rabbit. "What kind of commune? You're not one of those religious nuts who's going to kidnap and brainwash me for my money, are you?"

Vane shook his head. This woman got the strangest ideas. "No. Definitely not. I just grew up in a way most people don't. What about you?"

"I grew up here. Both my parents are vets. They met in grad school and got married when they graduated. There's really not much to tell. I had a very normal, average life."

Vane tried to imagine such a thing. In his world, where they could command magic, the elements, and even time itself, normal didn't really factor in. In a way, he envied Bride her human world where the impossible wasn't reality. "That must have been nice."

"It was." She took a sip of her water. "So what do your parents do?"

"Think up creative ways to kill each other." Vane cringed as that flew out of his mouth. He was so used to saying it that he didn't think about it until he'd heard himself say it.

"No, really."

Vane looked away uncomfortably.

Bride's jaw went slack as she realized he wasn't kidding. "Why would they do that?"

Vane actually squirmed a bit before he answered. "It's a long story. My mother ran off not long after I was born and my father wants me dead, so here I am . . . With you."

She didn't know what to think of that. "This . . . um . . . this family insanity, it's not hereditary, is it?"

"It doesn't appear to be," he said seriously. "But if it creeps up on me, feel free to shoot me."

She wasn't sure if he meant that or not. So, suddenly grateful that they were in a public place, she decided to change the subject to something a little safer. "How do you have so much money? After what you just said, I don't think your parents gave it to you, did they?"

"No. I make investments. Sometimes I sell artifacts."

Now that sounded interesting. "What kind of artifacts?"

He shrugged. "This and that."

The waiters brought their appetizers. Bride sat back and watched as Vane set about eating. He looked regal and refined as he ate in the traditional European manner.

"You know, for someone who grew up in a commune, you have impeccable manners."

A deep, dark sadness came over him. "My sister taught me. She said . . . well, she felt that people should eat as people and not animals."

Bride heard his voice break as he spoke of his sister. It was obvious that his sister meant a lot to him. "Where is she now?"

His sadness increased tenfold as he swallowed. The pain in his eyes was so profound that it made her ache for him. "She died a few months ago."

"Oh, Vane, I'm so sorry."

"Yeah, me, too." He cleared his throat.

Her heart breaking for him, Bride reached out and brushed her fingers against his cheek to offer him comfort. He turned his face into her arm and kissed the inside of her wrist.

The look in his feral eyes made her quiver.

"You're so soft," he breathed, then kissed her hand and moved slightly away from her. "If I keep smelling you, we might make a spectacle here tonight."

"What kind of spectacle?"

"I just might toss you over my shoulder and carry you out of here so that I can ravish you again."

She laughed at the thought. "Would you really?"

She saw the raw, ragged truth in his eyes. "I would if you'd let me."

Bride retreated to her side of the table and they

spent the rest of the meal in idle, safe chitchat. Vane was witty and warm. A rare treat.

Once they had polished off dinner and dessert, they made their way back downstairs where she saw Taylor and his date sitting outside the kitchen door. Neither one of them looked pleased.

"You are so bad, Vane," she said again, laughing at the sight of them.

"Hey, that's kind compared to what I want to do to him. At least this way, he's still breathing."

Henri bid them good night as they left and headed back toward her home.

"Do you mind walking?" she asked him. "It's really nice out tonight."

"Walking doesn't bother me."

She took his hand and led him toward Iberville.

Vane watched the way the moonlight played in the tendrils of her auburn hair and reflected off the beaded choker he'd bought her. Her dress set her curves off to perfection and the halter top reminded him just how easy it would be to slide his hand inside it and cup her breast gently in his palm.

His groin tightened. Over and over he remembered what she had felt like. How warm and tender her caresses had been.

He craved that now. The wolf in him was howling for a taste of her.

Bride was a bit nervous from Vane's intense stare. There was something animalistic about it. Devouring.

There were times when she was with him that she felt like prey to his predatorial nature.

They didn't speak much as they walked back to her apartment. At the gate, she called for her wolf.

"You don't think they picked him up, do you?"

"No," Vane said. "I'm sure he's okay. He's probably out enjoying himself tonight."

"You think so?"

He grinned wickedly. "Yes, I do."

She sighed. "I hope so. I'd hate to have anything bad happen to him."

He followed her to her apartment door. Bride opened it, then hesitated.

Vane dipped his head down to the crook of her neck where he inhaled her scent. He rested his warm hands on her shoulders. "I want to be inside you again, Bride." He lifted his head up and cocked it in a way that reminded her of the wolf Vane. "Would you take me in?"

Bride was uncertain. She wanted him too, but what kind of relationship was this?

She started laughing uncontrollably.

Vane frowned at her. "What's so funny?"

"I'm sorry, I just heard this horrible cliché in my head of 'Will you still respect me in the morning?'"

He looked baffled. "Humans don't respect each other after they have sex?"

"You know, when you say things like that, you sound like an alien from outer space."

"I feel like an alien from outer space. A lot."

What an odd thing for him to say. "How long did you live in that commune of yours?"

"All my life. Up until eight months ago."

"Oh, my God. Really?"

He nodded.

No wonder he didn't know how to date. She couldn't imagine living isolated from the world.

He brushed his hand over her shoulder. "Since then I've been staying with . . . friends who own the Sanctuary bar on Ursulines. They've taught me a lot about how people behave, but Amanda said that you wouldn't appreciate my using the lines and moves that the men in the bar use to pick up the women they meet there."

Bride tried not to focus on how warm his hand was on her bare skin. How good his caress felt. It sent chills all the way through her, straight to her breasts, which hardened, aching for his touch. "Amanda who?"

"Hunter."

Bride started at the name. "Tabitha's twin sister?"

He nodded.

Good grief, what a small world. But if he knew Amanda, that was a relief. Amanda, unlike her twin sister, wasn't a lunatic and didn't, as a rule, hang out with psychos. If Amanda had really helped Vane, then he was most likely safe.

"You said no one dated in your commune. What did you do when you found a woman you liked?"

He looked a bit frustrated. " 'Like' doesn't have the same meaning where I come from as it does to you. We didn't really 'like' anyone. If you were attracted to someone, you slept together and then moved on. We didn't get our emotions tangled with our bodies the way you do."

"How is that possible? It's human nature."

Vane sighed. It might be human nature, but it wasn't animal nature. "We just thought differently."

She stiffened indignantly. "So you think nothing of

sleeping with me and then moving on to the next woman?"

Shit!

"No. That's not what I meant." He toyed with a curl that was brushing her bare shoulder. "I want to be with you, Bride. Only you. I want you to accept me."

"Why?"

"Because I need you."

"Why?"

Vane ground his teeth. How could he explain to her the feral yearning inside him to claim his mate? This infectious insanity that wouldn't rest until they were joined.

He'd never understood what had driven his father to attack his mother. Now he did. Every part of him simmered for her. It was feverish and raw and he wasn't sure how to control it.

How did a wolf mate with a human?

"I'm scaring you," he said as he smelled her fear. "I'm sorry. I'll leave you alone now."

He started away from her.

Bride took his hand. She was being stupid and she knew it. Vane had done nothing to hurt her. He'd gone out of his way to make her happy and to be kind.

What was she so afraid of?

The mere fact that he was willing to just walk away told her he would never do her harm.

Before she could stop herself, she pulled his lips down to hers and kissed him soundly.

Every hormone in her body sizzled at the taste of him. He crushed her against him, holding her in those steely arms she remembered so well.

He was overwhelmingly masculine.

His breathing ragged, he pulled back from her. "Tell me to go, Bride, and I will."

She stared up at him in the moonlight and saw the sincerity of those hazel eyes. "Stay with me, Vane."

His smile made her knees weak as he threw his head back and let out an eerie howl.

Before she could move, he picked her up and carried her through the door of her apartment.

"You were right. They're not dead."

Markus Kattalakis looked up from the bonfire where his wolf pack was gathered around as fury grabbed hold of him. For the last two months, his pack had been out in the backwoods of Nebraska, tending their young and biding their time until the pups would be old enough to jump time periods under the light of a full moon.

"What?" he asked his second in command, Stefan.

"Your senses were correct about Vane and Fang. I shifted to Sanctuary myself and saw Fang there."

"Why didn't you kill him?"

"He wasn't alone. One of the bears was with him. Their female cub. It appears the Peltiers have made them welcome. I can't strike at either of them while they are there. Not unless you wish a feud with the Peltiers."

Markus curled his lip at the news. It was tempting. But wolves and bears . . .

It had been a long time since Katagaria clan had fought clan. To engage the bears, who were renowned for maintaining one of the few Were-Hunter sanctuaries, was suicide. If the bears and their miscreants didn't kill his clan, others would. The Peltiers were respected by all.

To take them on would be to break their one and only cardinal rule.

Damn.

"For once you showed good judgment," he said to Stefan. Damn it, though. He needed those two killed. He should have sent someone sooner, but he kept hoping that he was wrong. That the Daimons he had sent for Vane and Fang would return with news of their deaths.

He'd hoped the Daimons had merely absconded with Vane's and Fang's powers. He should have known he wouldn't be so lucky.

"You will have to catch them outside the perimeters of Sanctuary. Take a patrol and—"

"Father, you can't."

Markus turned to see his youngest adopted daughter, Matarina, standing behind him. Barely fifty years old, she looked to be no older than a human teenager. She was young, and hopelessly devoted to the two half-human sons he had once fathered on his Arcadian mate.

Matarina would never believe that Vane and Fang posed a threat to their pack.

Only he knew, and he intended to keep it that way.

"They have to die."

"Why?" she asked, moving forward. "Because of Anya? That was an accident. I know Vane would never have allowed her to die. He loved—"

"Enough!" Markus roared. "You know nothing of it, child. Nothing. They were charged with seeing her pups safely home and instead they let them die. I will not allow such abominations to live while Anya and her pups lie in their grave."

By the look in her eyes, he could tell she knew he was lying. Revenge for Anya was only one of several reasons he needed Vane and Fang dead. So long as Anya had lived, he'd had partial control over his two werewolf sons.

With her death they would be uncontrollable. Unstoppable. Zeus have mercy on them all if Vane ever came home.

He turned back to Stefan. "Take a tessera and go finish their death sentence. Kill anyone or anything who tries to stop you."

"And the Peltiers?"

"Only if necessary and never on their home ground. If you kill one, hide it, but don't hesitate to do whatever is necessary to finish this."

Stefan inclined his head before leaving to follow Markus's orders.

Markus took a deep breath, but it didn't help him relax. Every animal instinct he possessed told him that sooner or later Vane would be back to exact revenge on them all.

He was, after all, his mother's son.

Chapter 5

Vane laid her carefully on the bed. He was extremely glad tonight that he'd paid the movers to set up her furniture. It was going to make this a lot easier than trying to share that old couch with her.

He pulled the pins from her auburn hair and let it fall down around her round face. She had such a delicate, beautiful face. Placing his cheek against hers, he inhaled her fragrant scent.

She pulled the jacket from him while he savored the softness of her body under his.

She tossed his jacket to the floor, then ran her hands down his back. Vane drew his breath in sharply as intense pleasure consumed him. He knew why he hated being human. If he dared use his powers, they would both be naked in an instant and he could feel every inch of her. Flesh to flesh.

But that would most likely terrify her.

So instead, he leashed his powers and shielded his body marks from her, especially his palm. For once in his life, he would be with a woman not as a wolf or a warrior.

He would spend tonight with Bride as a man.

Bride savored the feel of Vane pressing down on her as he pulled her shoes and then her pantyhose off with consummate skill. His muscles rippled under her hands while her tongue danced with his.

Ummmm . . . this man knew how to kiss like nobody's business.

She would never get tired of the way he tasted. It was raw and decadent. Desirable and hot.

He held himself up on his arms while she slowly unbuttoned his shirt to reveal, inch by inch, that lean, strong chest. She untucked the silk to let it fall open while she ran her hands over the tanned flesh. She raked her fingers carefully through the masculine hairs that dappled his chest and abdomen, then ran them over his lean ribs.

His kiss deepened and she felt his heart pounding under her hands. He nipped at her lips, rubbing his body against hers in a way that heightened and teased her to incredible arousal.

Bride looked up at him and saw the unadulterated hunger on his face. How could a man like this want her so badly?

Part of her told her to have more confidence in herself, but it wasn't a lack of self-esteem that made this so hard to believe. She was a realist. Men who looked like Vane didn't date women who looked like her. They just didn't.

Not even Taylor was this scrumptious and he had

only been using her. She didn't want to be hurt again. Not like that and especially not by Vane.

Relax, Bride.

Vane pulled back. "Are you okay?"

"I'm just trying to figure out what you see in me," she admitted.

"I see a beautiful woman," he said earnestly, dipping down to nibble the sensitive skin below her ear. "Whose kind heart shines in her eyes and whose spirit is boundless." He pulled back so that he could stare down into her eyes. "The way you stood up to Taylor this afternoon . . ." His half-smile made her heart pound. "You wouldn't ever let anyone get the better of you, would you?"

"I try not to."

He rolled over onto his back and pulled her across him. The dark tenderness on his face wrapped around her heart and squeezed it tight. "Most of all, I like the fact that you share yourself with me. That I don't have to prove my strength to you. I don't have to hurt or be hurt to lie with you."

There was a note in his voice that told her just how important that was to him.

What an odd thing to say to a woman.

Just what kind of commune did he come from? It definitely sounded like one of those weird ones where people were made to do all kinds of strange things to belong to it.

She ran her hand over the rough smoothness of his face. "There's something inside you that scares me, Vane. Are you sure you're normal?"

He gave a light laugh at that. "I don't know what

normal is. But I would never hurt you, Bride." His eyes burned her with his sincerity. "Never."

He pulled her lips to his, then moved his hands around her neck to undo the top of her dress and her necklace. He placed her necklace on the box by the bed, then played gently with her breasts. His rough palms scraped her nipples, making them tight and heavy, and sending pleasure through her entire body.

Bride wanted to melt into him. No man had ever made her feel the way he did.

Vane could barely breathe from the emotions warring inside him. He should let her go. He had no business mating with anyone. And yet he couldn't keep himself from her. Tonight he could very well father children with her. It was the first time in his adult life that that was a concern.

In the back of his mind, he could imagine her with his baby. See her suckling it with love in her eyes . . .

How could he let her go?

How could he even think it?

The Fates had decreed that they should be united. Who was he to argue against the goddesses?

Vane had spent his entire life fighting. Why should he not fight for this? Just once, didn't he deserve someone to love him?

What if she never does?

Just as his mother had never loved his father.

The question hung heavy in his heart. What if he didn't win her over by the end of his three weeks?

No, it wasn't an option. He would win her and he would keep her.

Holding on to that thought, he took her hand and led it to his chest so that she could feel his heart beating. Unable to stand being without her, he opened his pants and freed himself.

Bride gasped as he shifted his hips and filled her unexpectedly. Mmm, he was so thick and hard inside her. So commanding.

Biting her lip, she looked down at him as he lifted his hips and drove himself deep inside her.

No man had ever been so impatient to be with her. It made her feel strangely powerful. Desirable.

The look of pleasure on his face seared her heart. It made her ache for him. Still inside her, he unzipped the back of her dress and pulled it over her head.

Completely naked, she looked down at him. His shirt was open, but still on his body. He'd only slid his pants down enough so that he could take her.

She lifted one of his hands from her breast and kissed his scarred knuckles while she rode him slow and easy.

He stared up at her with his mouth slightly parted, his eyes dark and hooded. His expression showed her just how much he savored her body. Her touch.

That made her soar most of all.

He placed his hands on her hips and held her still as he took over the thrusting. Bride was amazed at the strength it took for him to do that.

But she didn't mind ceding control over to him as he quickened his deep, penetrating strokes. Each one went through her, hot and bittersweet. She leaned forward onto her arms, letting her hair fall over them as her body throbbed and ached for more of him.

Her pleasure built until she cried out from sweet release.

Vane watched her face as she climaxed in his arms. Joy tore through him at the sight of her, at the warm sweetness of her body cradling his. He claimed her lips and moved even faster, wanting his own moment of perfection.

Closing his eyes, he found it. He pulled back from her lips to growl deep in his throat as his body exploded into bliss.

Still joined with her, he pulled her down onto his chest and held her quietly while their hearts pounded in time and his body continued to orgasm for several minutes. He ran his hands over her back, delighting in the tranquility of this moment.

It was the only peace his violent life had ever known. There was no fear here with her. No terror that she had the powers to unmask his human heart and kill him for it.

There was only them.

Bride didn't move for the longest time. She lay on his chest, savoring the strength of his arms holding her.

She nuzzled her face against his chest, then kissed his nipple before she pulled away.

As she started to move from the bed, he tugged lightly at her arm to stop her. "Where are you going?"

"I was going to clean up."

"Why? I'm far from finished with you."

She laughed until she realized he wasn't kidding. He quickly pulled his shirt off and tossed it toward his jacket. His pants, shoes, and socks quickly followed.

Before she could protest, he had picked her up and

placed her back on the bed. He nudged her legs apart with his knees, then slid his hips and groin between them.

Bride groaned at the sensation of him lying on top of her. He was already growing hard again.

He took his time exploring her mouth, nibbling her lips, and tasting her, until she thought she would pass out from his gentle exploration.

They stayed like that for the rest of the night. Skin to skin, body to body. Bride had never experienced anything like it. Vane had more stamina than anyone she'd ever heard of. By dawn, she was exhausted and fell asleep nestled in his arms.

He slept quietly spooned up behind her with one leg nestled between her thighs.

This was heaven. And for the first time in a long while, she felt a sense of belonging. Of acceptance. Vane didn't care that she wasn't skinny. He didn't mind that they were on a rickety old bed in a tiny apartment.

He seemed happy just to be with her.

And that was the nicest part of all this.

Vane lay there quietly, listening to Bride's soft snore as she slept in his arms. Her scent permeated his head. There was nothing he treasured more than her scent mingled with his. Than the feeling of her in his arms.

He was sore and exhausted. And he loved every bit of it. He looked down at her hand and withdrew his magic so that his mark was visible, too.

Mates.

He pressed his markings to hers and laced their fingers together. They would have to make love with their hands joined in this fashion in order to complete their mating ritual.

Bride would have to accept him.

And he would have to open himself up to her.

In the early light of dawn, that wasn't as frightening to him as it should have been.

Closing his eyes, he let sleep wash over him, and for the first time in months he wasn't racked with nightmares. He only felt the peace of his mate nestled up against him.

But what would happen once his mate found out he wasn't the man he pretended to be?

Could she ever accept the wolf that lived inside him?

He didn't know, but he promised himself that he would be honest with her. Once she was awake, he would come clean with everything.

He only hoped that being honest with her wouldn't cause him to lose her forever.

Bride got up fifteen minutes past the time to open her store. As she pulled away from Vane, his arm tightened around her for just a second before he woke up.

Those deep hazel-green eyes opened, then squinted against the bright light of the morning sun coming in through the windows.

"What time is it?" he asked, his voice deep and hoarse.

"Quarter after ten."

He rubbed his hand over his face and groaned.

Bride bit back a smile at that. "Not a morning person?"

"No," he said gruffly, rolling over onto his back. He slung a long arm over his eyes to block out the light.

Bride had to take a deep breath at the image he presented lying naked in her bed. The blankets were twisted over his body, barely covering those long, manly legs. His chest was completely bare, showing off the muscles of his abdomen, pecs, and arms. His dark whiskers added an almost deadly masculinity to his face, which was crowned by his long, wayward hair.

Good grief, he was spectacular.

He moved the arm over the top of his face to peep at her with one eye. "We've only been asleep for four hours, why are you up?"

She pulled her pink bathrobe on without getting up from the bed. "I have to work."

He reached out his hand to sink it deep into her hair. "Do you ever take a day off?"

"Only if I make plans with Tabitha in advance for either her or one of her staff to come over and cover for me. And of course I'm closed on Sundays. Other than that, no."

She kissed his hand, then pulled his arm away. He let it fall back to the bed without making any further comments.

Getting up, she left him in bed and went to shower.

Vane lay quietly as he listened to the water come on in the other room. His entire body ached from last night's exertions, but he reveled that the pain of it didn't come from his back, chest, and arms having been clawed. He'd had too much fun with Bride last night and fun was something that was sorely missing from his life.

He grimaced at the brightness of the morning light. He really hated mornings.

Forcing himself up, he pulled on his pants and zipped them, but left the button undone as he wandered into the kitchen area. Bride liked to eat two pieces of toast with marmalade in the morning.

While the bread toasted, he sliced her grapefruit for her and sprinkled a spoonful of sugar over it, then poured her a glass of orange juice.

He was putting the marmalade on the toast when she came out of the bathroom and stopped to stare at him.

"What?" he asked, puzzled by the deep scowl on her face.

"Is that your breakfast?"

Vane made a face. "Not hardly. I was going to fry some bacon for me."

"Then how did you know I liked to eat that?"

Vane paused as he realized that the man Vane wouldn't know what the wolf Vane knew. Clearing his throat, he shrugged. "I opened the fridge and saw the marmalade and grapefruit. Most people only eat those for breakfast so I figured you wouldn't mind them."

She seemed to accept that as she pulled the towel from her hair and draped it over her chair. "Thank you," she said, placing a kiss on his cheek.

Vane closed his eyes as his body hardened instantly. Without thought, he pulled her into his arms for a much more satisfying kiss. He trailed his lips over to her neck as he opened the front of her robe and pulled her naked body against his.

Bride moaned at the feel of his cool, hard body against hers. She ran her hand over the flexing muscles of his back and felt the scars he had there. His whiskered chin and cheek scraped gently against her skin.

"If you keep this up, I'll never get my store opened."

"Keep it closed and stay with me."

She cradled his head in her hands while his tongue played gently in the hollow of her throat. "I can't."

He pulled back. "I know. I was only hoping." He released her, then tied her robe closed. "Eat your breakfast."

Bride sat down at her small bistro-style table as he returned to the stove to make his bacon. She nibbled on the toast and watched him. "You have serious guts to fry bacon without a shirt on. Aren't you afraid it'll splatter?"

He shrugged. "It doesn't really hurt."

She frowned as she traced the various scars with her gaze. "How did you get so many scars, Vane?"

Vane debated how to answer her. She wasn't ready for the truth—that they were battle scars from four hundred years of being pursued by Arcadians who thought he was a Katagari Slayer. For that matter, they thought any Katagari male was a Slayer. That he had been forced to fight his own pack to keep his brother safe. That some of them were from the she-wolves he'd been with.

Some were from beatings.

"I haven't had an easy life, Bride," he said quietly as he turned the bacon over in the pan. He turned around to look at her. "I've never had anything I didn't have to pay for with blood and bone. Until you."

Bride sat perfectly still as that green gaze held her transfixed. There was something about his open expression that reached out to her. He was laying himself bare to her, she sensed it.

God, it would be so easy to love this man. He asked her for nothing and he was so incredibly giving. This moment felt surreal to her. She'd never known anyone like him.

This is too easy.

That niggling voice in the back of her head reared its ugly head. Nothing was perfect. Nothing was this easy.

There had to be more to him than what she saw.

What if there isn't?

What if he really was just as he appeared? She couldn't see any deception. Maybe it was because there wasn't any.

"Thank you for last night, Vane," she said.

He inclined his head to her, then went back to his bacon. He removed it from the pan and placed it on a plate, then turned off her stove and brought his plate to the table.

"You want some?" he asked.

Bride took two crispy strips while he got himself a glass of juice. There was something so intimate about sharing breakfast with him. She didn't know what it was, but in five years of dating Taylor, she'd never experienced a feeling like this. It was wonderful.

She ate quickly, then got up.

"I've got it," Vane said as she reached for her dishes. "You get ready and I'll clean up."

"You really are too good to be true," she said, kissing the top of his head before she darted to her makeshift wardrobe closet.

Vane tried not to watch her dress, but he couldn't stop himself. He was aroused just by seeing her pull on her underwear and dress.

Cocking his head, he realized she never wore pants. She always wore flowing dresses in dark earth tones or black. She slid her feet into a pair of flats and brushed her hair. Then she coiled it into that familiar messy bun.

Vane was enchanted by her actions. There were so many details involved in her morning routine. Such as the way she put on her makeup and then powdered it down. The precise movements it took to put on mascara and lipstick.

He loved watching the way she artistically dressed herself and styled her hair.

Bride paused as she lined her eyes to look at him in the mirror. "Something wrong?"

He shook his head. "I'm just thinking I'm glad I'm not female. I can't imagine putting on all that every day."

She smiled at him and his heart thundered.

As soon as she finished, she scooped her keys up and headed for the door. "Will you lock up?" she asked him.

Vane nodded.

She blew him a kiss, then left him alone in her apartment. Outside, he could hear her calling for the wolf as she made her way to her store.

He cringed at that. "I'm going to have to tell her."

The longer he put it off, the harder it would be.

"Okay. I'm going to do it."

After he showered.

And dressed.

And cleaned.

An hour later, while Bride was dusting in her store, she felt the hair on the back of her neck rise.

She turned around expecting to see someone behind her.

No one was there.

She rubbed her neck and glanced about. Still, the feeling was there. It was almost evil.

How weird was that?

Frowning, she went to look out the store windows. There wasn't anyone out there.

"Bride?"

She screamed and whirled about to find Vane coming from the back room.

He quickened his steps to reach her side. "You okay?"

Bride laughed nervously at her childishness. "I'm sorry. I didn't hear you come in the back door. You just startled me."

"You sure that's all it was?"

"Yes," she said, taking a deep breath.

Vane was dressed in his black slacks and shirt. He must have left his jacket in her apartment. Stepping back from her, he had an odd look of discomfort about him.

Oh Lord, here it comes . . .

"You need to get back to your life, huh?" she asked, trying to be brave while inside she struggled not to cry.

"What life?" He looked confused by her question. "What are you talking about?"

"Isn't this the part where you tell me we had fun and you break up with me?"

He looked even more confused. "Is that what I'm supposed to do?"

"Well, no. I mean, I don't know. Isn't that where you were heading?"

He shook his head. "No. I was just going to tell you that I . . ." Vane's voice trailed off as he looked past her, to the door.

Bride turned to see two women entering the store.

Vane stepped back while she greeted them. They began to browse, but their eyes kept returning to Vane, who moved to stand near her counter.

Bride busied herself rearranging a necklace display. She could tell Vane wanted to talk to her, but when those two customers left, three more came in.

Vane watched while Bride showed her merchandise to the women. He really wanted to get this over with, yet the last thing he needed was an audience when he told her that he was a werewolf.

More customers came in.

Oh, this was getting bad.

He could use his powers to make the women leave, but he didn't want to interfere with her business.

"I'm going to wait outside for a bit," he said to her while she rang up a sale.

"Are you okay?" she asked.

"Fine," he said. "I'll be out in the back."

He headed into the storeroom, then out the back door that led to the courtyard.

Damn.

"It's okay," he breathed. He would have plenty of time to talk to her later. He just wanted to get this over with as soon as possible.

"Vane."

A cold shiver went down his spine as he heard the low, gravelly voice inside his head.

He stiffened and went to the gate to see a sight that

made his entire body go cold. Coming up Iberville was one of the last animals he expected to see.

It was Fury in human form.

Equal in height to Vane, Fury had shoulder-length blond hair and eyes that were one shade darker than turquoise. He wore his hair pulled back in a ponytail and tight blue jeans with a long-sleeved black shirt.

The wolf approached him with a deadly, carefully measured stride. Power and strength bled from every molecule of his body. This was one of the few wolves Vane had never sought to fight.

Not that he didn't think he couldn't take Fury. He was sure he could, but Fury wasn't the kind of wolf who fought fair. He was much more likely to tear your throat out while you were sleeping.

There was an amused glint in the wolf's eyes as he stopped by Vane's side and glanced to where Bride stood inside her store.

"You're being careless, *adelfos*."

"We're not brothers, Fury. What the hell are you doing here?"

His smile turned crooked, evil. "I wanted to warn you that your father knows you and Fang are alive. I was one of the ones chosen to kill you two."

Vane went rigid.

"Relax," Fury said. "If I wanted you dead, I would have attacked by now."

"Why haven't you?"

"I owe you, remember?"

It was true. He had saved Fury's life back when the wolf had first joined their pack. "You waited a long time to pay up."

He shrugged. "Yeah, well, some things take time."

"I don't understand why you're breaking from the pack to help me."

A sinister smile curved his lips. "Because it'll piss off the old man. I hate him, he hates you, so I guess that makes you my new best friend."

That was news to Vane. "Why do you hate him?"

"I have my reasons and they're all mine and not for public consumption."

"Then why have you stayed in the pack all these centuries?"

"Again, I have my reasons."

Yeah, Fury was an odd creature. "If they ever find out you've told me, they'll kill you."

The wolf shrugged nonchalantly. "We all die sometime." Fury's brow lifted as Bride came around the corner, then reversed directions as more customers neared her boutique. He sniffed the air. His eyes widened. "You're mated."

Vane grabbed him by the throat and shoved him back against the building.

"Easy, Vane," Fury said. There was no fear in the beast. Only amusement and honesty. "I won't hurt your mate, but Stefan and the others will."

Vane didn't doubt it. Stefan would give up both testicles to have a way to hurt him. "Who hunts?"

"Me, Stefan, Aloysius, and Petra."

Vane cursed. Every one of them had a personal ax to grind against him, especially Petra, who hated him because he had shunned her when she tried to mate with him, and then he'd come between her and Fang. If they ever learned of Bride, they would kill her without hesitation—just to cut him. And that was if they were kind. The males of his pack would do much worse than that if they found her.

Whenever a mated male broke from the pack, the pack struck back by punishing the female mate.

Vane would kill anyone who did that to Bride. Anyone.

"You gonna move that hand off my throat now or do I have to hurt you first?"

Vane debated, then released him.

"Obliged," Fury said as he straightened his shirt with a tug.

"Look," Fury said, his tone deadly serious. "I never had a problem with either you or Fang, you know that. Honestly, you were the only two strati I could ever stand. I figure you guys have had a hard enough time losing Anya. You don't need this shit just because your father's afraid you're going to take over his pack."

Vane cursed. "I couldn't care less about the pack."

"I know. Believe it or not, I hate injustice as much as you do. The last thing I want to see is the only two decent wolves in the pack killed."

Those were unexpected words. But then, Fury had kept himself away from others in the pack much the way Vane had. The wolf had confided in no one. Trusted no one.

Fury started away from him.

"Fury, wait."

He looked at him, his brow arched.

"Thanks for letting me know."

Fury inclined his head.

In that moment, he felt a strange kinship with the

wolf. Not to mention the fact that he now owed Fury, and Vane always paid his debts in full. "Where are you off to?"

Fury shrugged. "I don't know. I guess I'm a lone wolf." He howled low. "Clichéd as hell, isn't it?"

The wolf really was crazy.

Vane looked back at Bride through the windows of her store and a thought struck him.

"Can I trust you, Fury?"

"No," he answered honestly. "I'm a wolf and I'm always going to do what's best for me. Why?"

Vane hesitated, but in the end, he had no choice except to make a pact with the wolf. "Because I need help for the next couple of weeks. I can't be in two places at once."

"Wow," Fury breathed in disbelief. "I never thought I'd live to see the day Vane Kattalakis ever asked another living soul for help."

He ignored the sarcasm. "If you help me until Bride is either free or fully mated to me, I'll make sure you never have to hunt for another pack again."

Fury didn't say anything.

"I know what it's like to be alone, Fury," Vane said, his voice betraying his own pain at being left to his own defenses. "You help me and I'll swear brotherhood to you."

That wasn't something ever taken lightly. To take a blood oath of loyalty was almost as major a commitment as mating. It was an unbreakable oath. Fury had no one else on this earth. His family were all dead and he had come to them as a scared, callow youth.

Fury glanced away before he nodded. "All right, Vane. I'll do it."

Vane let out a slow breath as he held his hand out to Fury. For some reason, he felt as if he had just made a bargain with Lucifer.

Fury hesitated, then shook his hand. "So what do you need me to do?"

Vane saw that Bride was headed back toward them. "For now, I need you to pretend to be me as a wolf. I've been posing as Bride's pet to guard her, and now that I'm in human form, I could really use a wolf around so as not to raise her suspicions." Especially since he didn't dare tell her the truth about himself until he found some way to throw the hunters off his trail.

Fury laughed at that. "Damn good thing we're both white timbers, huh?"

"Yeah. Now could you take your wolf form?"

Fury stepped out of Bride's line of view and flashed into the wolf. Two seconds later, he lifted his leg near Vane's foot.

"Do it, Fury, and I'll neuter your rank ass."

He could hear Fury laughing in his head. *"Oh,"* Fury said in his head. *"By the way, I forgot to tell you that the others know Fang is at Sanctuary."*

Vane went cold all over again. "What?"

"Yeah. Your father told them to not attack him so long as the bears were present. But the minute he's alone . . ."

"Watch Bride."

"Wha—"

Vane flashed instantly to Sanctuary.

Fury sat on the street, completely confused by what he should do.

"Vane?"

He didn't answer.

Aw shit. As a wolf he had no way to tell Bride where Vane had gone, and the last thing he wanted to deal with was a distraught human female who couldn't find her mate.

This wasn't right.

Flashing to human form, Fury quickly picked his clothes up off the street and dressed. Unlike Vane, his strength was physical, not magical. He could wield magic, but nowhere near as precisely as Vane. If he tried to put his clothes on with his powers, he'd have about a fifty-fifty shot at them ending up on him in the right order and in the right place. So rather than have his sock end up as a shirt, he pulled them on while praying no one happened by to catch him bare-assed on the street corner.

By the time Bride came around the corner, he had everything on except his shoes.

She drew up short as she caught sight of him pulling on his boot.

"Pebble in my shoe," he explained lamely. Lying wasn't his forte, either.

"Both shoes?" she asked.

"Freaky, huh?"

She gave him a strange look before she scanned the yard behind him.

"If you're looking for Vane, he's not here."

"You know him?"

"Uh, yeah."

She gave him a penetrating stare. "And you are?"

"Fury."

"Fury?"

"Yeah, I know. My mom was on crack when she named me."

By the look on her face he could tell he probably should keep his mouth shut.

"Uh-huh," Bride said, taking a step away from him.

Fury took a step forward. She was panicking now, he could smell it. "Really, it's okay. I'm not going to hurt you. Vane told me to keep an eye on you till he gets back."

"Where did he go?"

Fury panicked at the question. Damn humans for their inquisitive natures. Various lies went through his head, but all of them would probably get Vane into trouble so he settled on the one least likely to offend her. "He went to piss."

Yeah, that was stupid, he realized as soon as her face turned red.

"Where did you come from?"

Like he could answer that. If he told her he had teleported himself from Nebraska down to New Orleans an hour ago she'd run for the cops.

He pointed down the street. "That way."

She was even more nervous than before.

Fury offered her a grin he hoped wasn't too ominous. He wasn't used to trying to make people unafraid of him. Normally he reveled in making humans wet themselves in terror.

This was a weird change of pace for him.

"Really," he said, "I swear I'm safe."

"And I should believe you, why?"

He paused before he gave her an answer he hoped would soothe her. "I'm Vane's brother and he would kick my ass if I hurt you."

Bride stared at the strange, oddly handsome man in front of her. In spite of his words, there was an air of ominous danger about him. He looked like the kind of person who could cut someone's throat and then laugh about it. "You don't look like Vane."

"I know," he said. "I take after our mother and he takes after our dad."

"Uh-huh."

He sighed and set his boots down on the ground. "Look, I basically suck at social skills, okay? Just pretend I'm not here until Vane gets back. I'll watch you, you ignore me, and we'll get along fine. Sound good to you?"

She wasn't sure. Something about him made her want to run inside and lock the door. Could she trust him?

"Hey, Bride? Can I get some help?"

She looked toward the entrance of her store where one of her regular customers stood with a dress in her hands. "Sure, Teresa. I'll be right there," she said, moving away from the odd man in front of her.

He pulled his boots on, then followed in her wake.

"What are you doing?" she asked as he trailed her into her store.

"Keeping an eye on you. Just ignore me."

It was hard to ignore someone who was so much taller and scarier than she was.

"How long has Vane been gone?" she asked him as she walked across her boutique.

"I don't know, he must have had to go real bad. Might be a bladder thing. I'm not sure."

She gaped at him.

He looked extremely uncomfortable. "I'm just going to shut up now and stand here looking tough. That's what I'm best at."

He did and she had to agree. When silent, Fury was quite intimidating. She had to give the man credit, he definitely knew his forte.

Vane materialized in Peltier House, just outside of Fang's door. He stood perfectly still, listening.

Sensing.

There was no disturbance. No scent of anyone else. No sensation of feelings probing the psychic plane for him or Fang.

Everything appeared completely normal.

Relaxing, he pushed open the door to find Fang just as Vane had left him. Alone in his bed.

Vane walked slowly into the room, just to make sure Fang was okay.

He went to the far side of the bed. Fang didn't move or twitch. His throat went tight. Fang didn't appear to be breathing.

"Oh God, no," he said, choking in panic.

Vane grabbed his brother, who instantly yelped and growled.

He tightened his hold on Fang's fur. "Damn you, you bastard!" he snarled angrily. "You die on me and I swear I'll tear your throat out."

Fang nipped at him until Vane released him. His

brother settled back down in the bed into his comatose state.

"Fang, listen. Dad knows we're here and he's sending a squad after us. C'mon, wolf, talk to me."

He didn't. Fang just lay there staring into space.

"C'mon, Fang, this isn't fair to me. I don't know what to do to help you. I miss Anya too . . ."—he tried to make Fang look at him—"and I miss *you*."

Still, his brother didn't respond to him.

Vane wanted to choke him for his obstinacy.

It was then he felt a strange ripple in the air around him. He glanced over his shoulder to find Stefan standing there with a smug sneer on his face.

Without a second thought, Vane attacked.

Chapter 6

Vane caught Stefan about the waist and the two of them went bursting through the hard oak door, into the hallway.

Aimee Peltier jumped away from them and started screaming for help while Vane pulled Stefan up from the floor and slugged him hard and furiously.

Instead of attacking, Stefan changed to wolf form and ran for the stairs. Vane started after him. But before Stefan could head down them, Wren, who was bounding up them in human form, caught the wolf by the neck and hauled him back into the hallway.

Stefan snarled, trying to bite Wren. The leopard held him with an ease of strength that gave Vane pause. He'd had no idea the young, quiet Katagari was so strong.

Vane stood back, breathing raggedly, as Nicolette came out of her room at the end of the hallway.

Aimee ran to her mother while Wren maintained his grip on the snarling wolf.

"What is going on here?" Nicolette asked.

Vane gestured toward the wolf. "He was in Fang's room."

Stefan switched to human form, flashed into his clothes, then pushed Wren away from him.

Wren barely moved a step away and the look on his face promised Armageddon if Stefan touched him again.

That harsh look succeeded in calming Stefan a degree as he took a step away from the leopard. "I wasn't doing anything. I was only checking on them to see if they were really here." Stefan curled his lip at Vane. "Vane attacked *me*."

Stefan turned back toward Nicolette with an expression that was almost respectful. "I thought it was against the rules of Sanctuary for anyone to attack without provocation."

Vane narrowed his eyes as understanding dawned. He realized only too late that this had been a set-up.

Stefan was smarter than Vane had given him credit for.

"Vane?" Nicolette looked at him. "Is what he says true? Did you attack him?"

"He was coming to kill Fang. You know he was."

"But did he attack him?"

Vane stiffened as he glared at Stefan. "He would have had I not stopped him."

"Did he attack first, or did you?" Nicolette insisted.

Vane's anger snapped out of control. "What are you? A fucking lawyer?"

"Watch your tone, Vane," Nicolette warned harshly. "I am the supreme law here and you know it."

Vane apologized even though it stuck tight in his craw to do so.

Wren gave him a sympathetic look that said he too would like to rip into Stefan. His whole body was coiled for it, but he stayed put.

Nicolette lifted her chin in acceptance of Vane's apology. "Now tell me the truth. Who attacked first?"

Vane wanted to lie, but Nicolette would sense it and that would only make matters worse. "I did."

She closed her eyes as if that pained her. When she opened them, her expression told him how much she regretted what she was about to say. "Then I have no choice except to banish you, Vane. I'm sorry."

Stefan's eyes gleamed.

At that moment, Vane hated all of them equally. So this was what it came down to. He was punished for protecting his brother.

So be it. It wasn't the first time this had happened. At least Nicolette didn't take a whip to him as punishment.

"Fine," he said between clenched teeth.

Vane headed into Fang's room to collect his brother, only to discover Aimee Peltier rushing to cut him off. She slammed the door closed, then ran to block him from the bed.

He tried to step around her, but she wouldn't let him.

"Vane, listen to me. *Maman* is only angry. Give her time—"

"No, Aimee," Vane said in a low, deadly tone as he fought not to take his anger out on her. "I knew the rules and I broke them. Your mother will never forgive that and you know it."

Aimee held her arms out as he tried to step past her. "Leave Fang here," she insisted. "You and I and even *maman* know what Stefan is doing. I will make sure that Fang is never left alone. I will stay with him myself every moment of the day and night. No one will hurt him so long as he resides in Sanctuary."

Her offer confused him. He didn't understand why the bear female would care what happened to them. "Why?"

Her pale eyes were soft and kind as she looked up at him and dropped her arms back to her sides. "Because no one should be hurt like the two of you were. What they did was cruel and unnecessary. It was a human punishment, not an animal one. I have lost brothers and I know firsthand the pain you feel in your heart for your Anya. I will not let Fang die, I swear it."

She glanced down to his hand where his mark was hidden, then she looked to the door behind him as if she were afraid someone might overhear her. She lowered her voice. "You have another to protect now. The last thing you need is Fang with you in this state. Go and guard her. You can call me anytime, day or night, to check on your brother."

Vane pulled her into his arms and hugged her kindly. "Thank you, Aimee."

She patted him on the back. "Anytime. Now go, and I hope you kick the shit out of that wolf outside."

He laughed halfheartedly before he let go of her and went back to the hallway.

Stefan arched a challenging brow at him, goading Vane to hurt him.

But he wasn't that stupid.

Vane would hurt him all right, but it wouldn't be on Nicolette's property.

Instead, Vane turned toward Nicolette to make sure Stefan understood what he intended to do. "Fang broke no rules. Is he safe to stay?"

Nicolette nodded, then passed a meaningful glare at Stefan, who cursed. "He is under our protection and we will make certain no harm befalls him."

The look on Stefan's face was priceless. And it told him one thing. This was far from over.

Bring it on.

Vane headed for the stairs.

"This isn't over," Stefan growled.

"I know the cliché," Vane said wearily as he paused to look back at the wolf. "It won't end until one of us is dead." He gave Stefan a taunting smirk. "And for the record, it won't be me."

Stefan growled low in his throat, but wisely kept his distance.

As Vane started for the front door, Stefan tried to follow.

Wren stopped him. "Rules of Sanctuary," he said quietly. "Vane gets a head start and if you try to follow, you'll be limping . . . Permanently."

Vane tried to decide what he should do. Part of him was terrified of going anywhere near Bride lest he lead Stefan and the others straight to her. The other part of him was terrified of leaving her alone.

Especially with Fury there.

There was no way she could defend herself against any of them.

He cringed as he remembered the scars on his mother's face and neck that she had received from fighting his father and his tessera. Tessaras were small groups of wolves sent out as soldiers or scouts. They usually killed anything they came in contact with.

And he would kill anyone who touched his Bride. No one would ever cause her harm. Even if she rejected him, she was still his mate, and he would spend the rest of her life making sure she had anything she needed.

As for Fang, he was safe under the protection of the bears. Vane had no doubt of that.

But Bride . . .

What should he do? He wished he could remove the mark from both their hands. Of all the times to find a mate, this wasn't one of them.

If she were Katagaria, he'd only have to wait for her to decide to finish their union. Very few Katagaria females refused their mates. If they did, the male would remain completely impotent until the female died. The female on the other hand would be free to take as many lovers as she liked, but she would never be able to breed children with them.

That was why the males took great care to please their females and to woo them during the three-week mating period.

Although his knowledge of humans was limited, he didn't think Bride would approve of him flashing himself naked in her bed and then offering himself and his eternal loyalty to her.

It might even scare her.

Not that he should even be thinking of mating with her anyway. He had no idea what kind of children they would produce. What would she do if she birthed a puppy?

At least his human mother had held enough decency not to kill them as pups. She'd cast them off on their father and vanished.

But then, his mother had been Arcadian. She knew and understood what his father had been. And she hated his father for it to this day. She hated all of them for it.

Not that any of this mattered. Vane had to go back and get Fury away from Bride. The wolf was unpredictable at best and deadly precise at worst.

Vane flashed himself into her shop, taking care to choose the closet in the back room where he doubted she would be. It wouldn't do to frighten her.

He let himself out and went to the back courtyard where he found Fury outside the door in human form.

"What are you doing?" Vane growled. He'd never intended Fury to be human around her.

"Leaving?"

Before Vane could respond, Fury flashed into wolf form.

Bride came into the courtyard a second later.

Vane cursed as he was forced to zap Fury's clothes into invisibility to keep her from seeing them.

"Oh good, you're back," she said with a smile as she closed the door to her shop. "I thought you had fallen in."

Vane frowned. "Fallen in what?"

"Your brother said you went to the restroom."

He was even more confused. "My brother?"

"Fury." Bride looked around. "Where did he go? He was just here guarding the back door while I locked up for a few minutes for lunch."

"Go with it, Vane," Fury said in his head. *"I couldn't think of anything better."*

He glared at Fury. *"And just why were you in human form around her to begin with, Fury? You were supposed to be a wolf."*

"I panicked. Besides, I wanted to meet her."

"Why?"

The wolf refused to answer him. *"You know, if I hadn't turned human, she would have thought you ran off on her without saying goodbye. I can't exactly speak to her as a wolf, not without her freaking out on both of us."*

"Vane?" Bride asked. "Are you okay?"

Vane narrowed his eyes even more. "Fury had to leave." *And he better stay gone as a man if he wants to keep breathing.*

Fury growled low in his throat.

"Oh," She looked down and smiled at Fury. "There you are, sweetie. I was worried about you."

Fury leaped up to put his paws against her breasts and lick her face.

"Yo, down," Vane snapped, forcing the wolf back. "There'll be none of that."

"I don't mind," Bride said charitably.

Fury wagged his tail and smiled wickedly, then tried to look up Bride's dress.

Vane caught him quickly by the neck. *"Stop!"* he

snarled mentally to Fury. *"Or I'll rip your head off."*

Bride frowned at them. "Don't you like my wolf?"

"Yeah," Vane said, patting him roughly on the head. "He's my new best friend."

"I'm your only friend, dickhead."

Vane balled his fist in the wolf's fur as a warning to him. "You know you have to be firm with wolves. Let them know who the alpha is."

"Your father?"

Vane smacked Fury's head.

"Ow!"

"Yeah," Bride said. "That's what my father says about all canines."

"Your father?"

She nodded. "He's Dr. McTierney, the leading expert in Louisiana on dog care. He's a vet over in Slidell. You might have seen his commercials. 'If you love your pet, neuter or spay.' He leads that whole campaign."

"Really," he said, grinning at Fury. "Maybe we should make an appointment."

"Yeah, right. Try it and die."

Vane clenched his fists as he tried to hide his anger from Bride. He was only one step away from choking the wolf in front of her.

Bride frowned as she glanced at Fury. "Strange . . ." She reached for his back paw. "I don't remember him having a brown patch there."

Vane bit back a curse as he realized Fury wasn't an identical match for him. Damn, she was observant.

"Maybe you just didn't notice it before," he said, trying to distract her.

"Maybe."

Bride led them across the back courtyard. She opened the door to her apartment and let the wolf in. She paused in the doorway.

Vane leaned his hand against the doorframe above her head and smiled at her. "You're nervous," he said quietly. "Why?"

"I'm just not sure what you're still doing here."

"I'm talking to you."

She laughed at that. "You know, I don't exactly have a manual of etiquette on what to do when a gorgeous guy drops into my life one day, gives me an expensive necklace I've been dying for, then we have the best sex of my life, and you vanish. Then pop back in when I need a hero and pay more money than those movers probably make in six months just to help me out. You take me out for a great dinner and then spend an entire night making my head spin. I don't know where to go from here."

"I have to say this is a first for me, too." He reached out and let his fingers rub against the lock of hair lying against her cheek. "What can I say? You're irresistible to me," he breathed.

It was hard to stay sane and rational when he looked at her like that. As if he were starving for a taste of her.

"And you're even more nervous." He sighed, then stepped back.

"I'm sorry," she said quietly. "It's not you. Really. I'm just not used to things like this happening to me."

"Neither am I." He dipped his head and kissed her. He savored her taste until he remembered that they had an audience.

Opening his eyes, he saw Fury staring at them inquisitively.

He hated that wolf. Reluctantly, Vane pulled back. "Why don't you close the store for an hour and take a real lunch with me?"

Bride hesitated, then nodded. Lunch with him would be wonderful. "I think I will. I have some leftover spaghetti in the fridge. We could walk to a store a block away and get some wine to go with it."

He looked rather uncomfortable with her suggestion as he scanned the yard outside. Was he looking for his brother?

"That would be nice," he said, but his body language belied the nonchalant tone.

For the first time in her life, Bride had a truly radical idea. She checked her watch. It was almost two-thirty and no one had come into her store for the last half an hour. Friday afternoons were traditionally slow for her . . .

"Tell you what," she said before she chickened out. "Why don't I close up early?"

His gaze heated with interest. "Can you do that?"

She nodded. "Give me a few minutes to do paperwork?"

"Take your time. I'm all yours."

The look in his eyes told her *exactly* what he meant by that.

Bride bit her lip at his invitation. How often did a woman hear that out of the mouth of a man who looked like this one?

Bride returned to her shop and quickly counted

down her register. She did her paperwork while Vane browsed through her shelves.

It was hard to focus on sorting receipts while he was there, distracting her. He had his back to her as he looked through her drawers of rings. He had the nicest rump that had ever graced a man's backside. Worse, she could see his face reflected in the mirror.

And he could be hers . . .

Swallowing, she forced herself to fill out the bank deposit slip. He came up behind her as she was putting everything in the large zippered envelope. Bracing his arms on each side of her, he bent down and took a deep breath in her hair as if he were savoring her.

"Have you any idea what you do to me, Bride?"

"No," she answered honestly.

Vane stood there, his heart pounding wildly. His body hard and aching.

His presence here was madness. He had covered his scent before he appeared here, but Stefan and the others were damned good at what they did.

It wouldn't be long before they found him.

Of course, so long as Bride bore his mark, she bore his scent, and even if he left her, they were just as likely to pick up that and appear to her as they were to find him.

More so in fact, since Bride didn't know to hide herself.

He was desperate for a taste of her and he knew she wouldn't deny him. But he couldn't take her again. Not unless she understood the full impact of that decision.

And the inherent dangers.

He shouldn't be here, in human form. But unlike Fury, his stronger incarnation was that of human. It was how he could protect her best.

It also made him even more vulnerable to her.

Leaning over, he brushed the exposed skin of her neck with his lips. "I wish you were mine," he breathed, inhaling the warm scent of her skin.

Bride couldn't breathe as she heard the deep, growling tone of his voice.

She felt like this was some kind of strange dream. How could this be real? She leaned back against Vane's chest so that she could look up at him.

The look on his face seared her.

A playful smile lightened the intensity of his stare. "We took things too fast, didn't we?"

She nodded.

"I'm sorry for that. When I see something I want, I have a bad tendency to take it first and then think later about whether or not I should have."

He moved away from her and headed for her door. "C'mon," he said, indicating the door with his head. "I'll escort you to the bank and we'll get the wine."

She slid off her stool and followed after him. Outside, there was a hint of a chill in the air. And an aura of danger around Vane. She had the feeling that he was paying way too much attention to the streets around them. Every time someone came near, he watched them intently as if expecting them to leap at them.

She made her deposit and then let him choose their wine after they crossed the street and entered a package store on Canal Street. When she tried to pay for it, she could have sworn he growled like an animal at her.

"I've got it," he said.

"You know, I can take care of myself."

He smiled at that as he took the wine from the clerk. "I know. Where I come from the only thing deadlier than a man is a woman. Believe me, I have a healthy respect for what a pissed-off woman can do."

Was he talking about the commune again? For some reason she didn't think so. "Where do you come from?"

"I was born in England."

Bride paused at that, surprised. But then, Vane had a habit of constantly surprising her. "Really?"

"Aye, luv," he said in a perfect English accent. "Born and bred."

She smiled. "You do that well."

He opened the door of the package store for her without comment.

"Funny," she said, entering the store. "I never really thought of Englishwomen as particularly vicious."

He snorted at that. "Yeah well, you never met my mother. She makes Attila the Hun look like a fluffy bunny."

There was a lot of anger and hurt in his tone and face as he said that. His mother must truly not have much of a maternal instinct.

"Do you ever see her?"

He shook his head. "She made it clear a long time ago that she wasn't interested in having any sort of relationship with me."

Bride wrapped her arm around his and gave a light squeeze. "I'm sorry."

He covered her hand with his. "Don't be. My kind don't have mothers like—"

Bride paused in the street. "Your kind?"

Vane stood there in shock at what had slipped out of his mouth. Damn. Bride was a lot easier to talk to than she should be. He was used to being on his guard around people.

"Lone wolves," he said, stupidly borrowing Fury's term.

"Ahh, so you're one of those macho I-don't-need-no-tenderness types."

He used to be, but after spending time with Bride . . .

What he felt for this woman scared the shit out of him.

"Something like that."

Bride nodded as she started back toward her shop. "So it's just you and your brother, then?"

"Yeah," he said, his throat tight as he remembered his sister. "It's just us. What about you?"

"My parents live in Kenner. I have a sister in Atlanta who I get to see a couple of times a year, and my older brother works for a firm in the business district."

"Are you close to them?"

"Oh yeah. Closer than I want to be sometimes. They still think they should all run my life for me."

He smiled. That was how Anya used to feel about him and Fang. It brought a bittersweet pain to his chest. "You must be the youngest."

"You know it. I swear, my mother still cuts my meat for me every time I go home."

He was unable to imagine a doting mother like that. It

must have been nice to know such love. "Don't knock it."

"Most days I don't." Bride frowned up at him. "Why do you keep doing that?"

"Doing what?"

"Scanning the street like you're afraid someone is going to jump out at us."

Vane rubbed the back of his neck in nervousness. He had to give her credit, she really was observant. Especially for a human.

The last thing he could tell her was that he did in fact fear just that.

If Stefan or the others ever tracked him down . . .

He didn't want to think about the consequences.

"I don't suppose I could talk you into closing your store for a couple of weeks and taking off to some exotic island with me, could I?"

She laughed at him. "Good one."

Yeah. Little did she know, he was quite serious. Part of him was tempted to kidnap her, but after what had happened between his parents, he knew better than to chance it.

Four hundred years later, his mother was still emotionally scarred over his father's kidnapping her against her will. He didn't want to destroy Bride's kindness. Her open smile. God help her, she trusted people, and that was so rare that he would do anything to keep her that way.

She opened the door to her yard and led him to her apartment where Fury was waiting for them.

Rushing toward them, Fury went straight for Vane's groin to rack him in typical dog fashion. "Get down," he snapped, brushing the wolf aside.

"He likes you."

Likes annoying me. "Yeah, I noticed."

Bride frowned as she walked over to the stereo, which was blasting the old Troggs song "Wild Thing."

"How strange," she said, turning it off. "I didn't leave the stereo on."

Vane tightened his grip on Fury's neck.

"That hurts, Vane. Let go."

He did so reluctantly. *"What else did you do?"*

"Nothing, really. I just watched some TV, went through her CDs . . . she has some really good shit . . . and made some coffee."

"Fury, you weren't supposed to move in!"

"You said watch her, that implies moving in."

He reached for Fury, who darted over to Bride.

"Maybe you have a ghost," Vane said. "It is New Orleans, after all."

"You're not funny," she said.

She took the wine from him and headed to the small kitchenette where she set it by her two-cup coffeepot. She pulled the carafe out and looked at it. "What on earth is going on here?"

"What?"

She met Vane's gaze. "Did you make coffee this morning?"

"Oops," Fury said. *"I kind of poofed that in. I probably should have poofed it out once I was finished."*

"You think?"

"Be nice to me, man. I don't have to stay here."

"And I don't really have to let you live, either."

"Are you okay?" Bride asked as she replaced the carafe.

Vane smiled and forced his stern expression to relax. "I'm fine."

"This coffee is fresh." She looked down at Fury, then shook her head. "No way. That's just stupid."

"What?"

"Nothing. I won't even say it for fear of being put away for the rest of my life."

She put the wine in the freezer to stay cold while she opened the cabinets and pulled out a saucepan and boiler.

Without thinking, Vane went to the tiny pantry to get the spaghetti sauce. For some reason, she loved putting it on everything.

"How did you know to go there?" she asked.

Vane cringed. Damn, he shouldn't have known where she kept it. "It seemed the most likely place."

She appeared to accept that.

Fury jumped up and pushed him into Bride. Vane sucked his breath in sharply as their bodies collided and he felt her lush curves against him.

She looked up, her lips parted from her gasp of surprise.

"Sorry," he said, his heart pounding. "The dog hit me."

"I'm not a dog."

"You're going to be dog food if you don't stop."

"Oh c'mon, you idiot. She's your mate. Move on her."

"I can't force her. Believe me, it's something I will not do."

To his surprise, Fury cocked his head and stared up

at him. *"You know, I think I just learned to respect you for that. You're a good wolf, Vane. Now hand me your shirt and let me outside."*

"Do what?" Vane was so stunned that he spoke out loud.

"What?" Bride asked.

"Nothing," he said, wondering at what point tonight she was going to decide he was completely mental.

"Trust me," Fury said. *"I'll use your scent to lead the others far away from here. Hell, by the time I get through with Stefan, he'll be chasing his tail in circles."*

Vane was impressed. It was a good thought. *"Can I trust you not to lead him here?"*

"Yeah, you can."

What an uncharacteristic response for Fury. Vane looked at him as he debated whether or not he could trust him.

In the end, he had no choice.

Fury went to scratch at the door.

"I'll let him out," Vane said, heading to the wolf.

"Thanks," Bride said as she pulled out the leftover angel hair pasta.

Vane followed the wolf into the back courtyard. He pulled off his shirt, then conjured up a fresh one while Fury flashed into human form to take it.

"Put some clothes on, Fury. I'm going blind here."

"Shut up," Fury snapped. "I'm not as talented as you are with my powers and I'm not staying human long enough to care. I just wanted to tell you to be careful. She seems like a nice enough woman, for a human. Be a damned shame to see something happen to her."

"I know."

A car pulled up to the gate.

Fury stepped into the shadows and vanished. Vane didn't move as he watched the car pull in. It was the stripper who lived in one of the upstairs apartments.

Relieved it was a friendly car, he went back inside to find Bride spooning the sauce into her pan.

He had to find some way to get her to agree to leave with him until they could safely part company.

Vane watched her and felt something very peculiar. In his world no one cooked for him. He either ate it raw or bought it in human form, then cooked it himself.

No one had ever made food for him before except when he paid them to do it. This was almost homey. Not that he understood what homey was.

Maybe it was this strange feeling in his stomach. The pull inside that urged him to touch her even when he shouldn't.

"Bride?" he asked, moving closer to her. "Do you believe in the impossible?"

She pulled a bag of salad from her fridge. "Impossible how?"

"I don't know. Fairies? Leprechauns? Wolves who can turn into humans?"

She laughed. "Ahh, the loup-garou. You're not buying into local legends, are you?"

He shrugged as his heart shrank. It was too much to hope that she would be anything other than a typical human.

"Although," she said, making his heart lighten. "I do

have a friend who chases vampires after dark. She's nuts, but we love her."

Damn.

"Yeah," he breathed. "Tabitha is a bit out there, isn't she?"

Bride stood stock-still. "How did you know she—"

"Everyone in New Orleans knows the resident vampire slayer," he said quickly. "Tabitha Devereaux has been around a long time."

Bride laughed. "I'll have to tell her she's a legend. It'll please her to no end."

Vane turned back toward her. "But what about you? You don't believe in weird things, do you?"

"Not really. The scariest thing I've ever seen is my accountant in April."

Outwardly, he smiled at that, inwardly he shriveled. She would never be open to his world. To the reality that sometimes the people she passed on the street weren't really people at all. That they were the worst sort of predators.

Let her have her delusions. It would be cruel to take them away from her. And for what purpose? So that he could show her a world where the two of them would be perpetually hunted?

Where their children would be outcasts?

No, that wouldn't be fair to her. He didn't need a mate, and he damned sure didn't need children.

"You okay?" she asked as she set out two plates.

"Yeah, fine."

He just hoped they both stayed fine until the mark vanished from their hands.

. . .

It didn't take Fury long to find Stefan and the others who were in human form on Bourbon Street while they tried to recapture Vane's scent.

The three of them were outside a bar, sniffing patrons who came and went.

As always, he was struck by the beauty of his people, but then, it was to be expected. In their world, ugly or different was quickly rejected or killed—usually the latter. Animals had no mercy on anyone or anything.

Not even the animals who fooled themselves into believing they were mostly human. He'd been with Arcadians long enough to see for himself that when they said they were human, they were deluding themselves.

Just as humans did.

There was nothing humane about humanity. At the end of the day, they were all animals with only survival instincts.

It was dog-eat-dog. And Fury knew more about that principle than he cared to recall.

Stefan whirled about as he caught Fury's scent.

"Well, well," Fury said, gifting him with a smirk. "I've been standing here long enough that I could have killed all of you before you even sensed me. You're getting old, Stefan."

"Is that a challenge?"

Fury raked him with an amused stare. He fully intended to challenge the older wolf and kill him one day.

Right now, however, he wasn't in the mood.

"Don't make me hurt you, Stefan. You can prance

around like an alpha all you want, but we both know who holds your leash."

Stefan grabbed for him, but Fury twirled out of his grasp.

"Don't, old wolf. I don't want to embarrass you."

"What do you want, Fury?" Petra snapped.

Fury gave her a full-fledged grin. Out of the group, she was the one who hated Vane the most. For years the she-wolf had wanted to mate with him, and when he had refused, she had moved on to Fang. She had stalked Vane to distraction. Since he was the oldest of their leader's children, the natural assumption would be that Vane would one day inherit the pack. Even though his father hated him, Vane was without a doubt the strongest of them all.

Only Fury knew why. Vane wasn't Katagaria and the rest of them were too stupid to realize it.

He had smelled it on Vane the moment they met. That twang that came only from human genes. A so-called human heart. More than that, the scent came from the most elite of the Arcadians. Vane wasn't just an Arcadian. He wasn't just a Sentinel.

He was an Aristos. A rare breed who had the ability to wield magic effortlessly. In the Arcadian realm, the Aristi were considered gods and were guarded zealously by werewolves who would gladly die for them.

It was why he, himself, hated Vane.

But patience was a virtue. Not just to humans, but especially to animals.

Petra sniffed, then frowned. She came closer until she buried her nose against Fury's shirt.

"Vane," she breathed. "You caught him?"

"Where's his hide?" Stefan asked immediately.

Fury gave Stefan a hooded glare. "You're all pathetic. Haven't any of you ever learned that half the fun of the kill is running it to ground?"

Petra cocked her head. "Meaning?"

"I know where Vane is. But it's not enough to kill your enemy. First you screw with his head."

Chapter 7

Bride pushed the salad around on her plate as she tried not to stare at Vane. There was something so compelling about him. It was also disconcerting to be around someone so lean and muscular. At least with Taylor, he'd been skinnier than her, but he didn't work out, and had love handles of his own.

There wasn't an ounce of excess on Vane's entire body. Her face flamed as she remembered just how great that man looked naked.

"Are you okay?" he asked.

"Fine."

"Why aren't you eating?"

She shrugged. "I guess I'm not hungry after all."

He took the fork from her hand and twirled the spaghetti around the tines, then held it up for her.

"I'm not a baby, Vane."

"I know." His hot look scorched her. "Eat for me, Bride," he said in a low, commanding tone. "I don't want you to go hungry. There's nothing good about starving."

From the tone of his voice, she could tell he spoke from experience. "You've been hungry?"

"Take a bite and I'll answer."

"I'm not a child."

"Believe me, I know." He wagged the fork for her.

She shook her head at his serious play, then opened her mouth.

He carefully placed the fork inside so that she could close her mouth around it before he slid the fork back out.

Bride chewed while he twirled the fork in her pasta. "Yes, I've gone hungry. My parents weren't nurturing or caring like yours. As soon as a male is old enough, they throw him out and he either learns to . . . to survive or he dies."

Vane's heart twisted as he remembered his youth. The pain and constant hunger. He'd almost died more times than he could count that first year on his own. Until he hit puberty, he'd been a wolf cub. Virtually overnight, he had become human. His magical powers had been new to him and he'd been stuck in human form when he needed to be a wolf.

Unused to being human, he couldn't track or kill prey. He'd been blitzed with unfamiliar feelings and emotions that wolves didn't have. Worst of all, his senses were dulled in human form. Humans might see better in daylight, but they couldn't hear as clearly, move as quickly, or smell their enemies around them. They didn't have the physical strength to fight bare-handed against other predators and animals for food and protection.

Nor could they kill as easily. They were consumed by guilt, horrified by bloodshed.

But like Darwin had written, it was survival of the fittest, and so Vane had learned how to survive. Eventually. He'd learned to take his blows and bites without surrendering to the agony of his wounds.

At the end of the first year of his adulthood, he had returned to his pack angry and controlled. A human who knew what it meant to be a wolf. A human who was determined to control the part of himself that he loathed.

He'd also returned home with more power than any of them had dared dream.

Still, he wouldn't have made it had Fang not saved him. In the beginning, it had been Fang who had killed for both of them so that they could eat. Fang who protected him and watched over his human state while Vane had to relearn even the simplest of tasks. When others would have abandoned him, Fang had stayed by his side.

That was why he would always protect his brother, no matter the cost.

"It must have been hard," Bride said, bringing him back to the present.

Back to her.

Vane fed her another bite. "You get used to it."

She looked at him as if she understood the sentiment. "It's amazing what you can get used to, isn't it?"

"How do you mean?"

"Just that sometimes we let other people treat us wrongly because we want to be loved and accepted so badly that we'd do anything for it. It hurts when you know that no matter how much you try, how much you want it, they can't love or accept you as you are. Then you hate all that time you wasted trying to please them and wonder what about you is so awful that they couldn't at least pretend to love you."

He saw red at her words and the hurt that glimmered in her amber eyes. "Taylor is an idiot."

Bride widened her eyes at the deep, growling intensity of his voice.

Vane set the fork aside and placed his hand on her cheek. He studied her face and stroked her skin with his fingers. "You are the most beautiful woman I have ever seen and there is nothing about you I would ever seek to change."

It felt so good to hear him say that, but she didn't delude herself for a minute. She'd always been the chubby little girl who didn't want to wear a bathing suit in public. The one who pretended to have her period at parties so that no one would mock her for her weight.

How many times had she watched the skinny little *putas* come into her shop, to try on the slinky dresses she sold but could never wear?

Just once in her life, she wished she could wear one of Tabitha's more outrageous outfits and not watch a guy's eyes drift immediately away from her as he sought out someone more desirable.

"You keep talking like that, Vane, and I might be forced to keep you."

"You keep looking at me like that, and I just might let you."

She shivered at his words. "You're too good to be real. There's this voice in the back of my head that keeps telling me I need to run before it's too late. You're a serial killer, aren't you?"

He blinked, then frowned. "What?"

"You're like that guy in *The Silence of the Lambs*. You know, the one who is making a woman suit who's being charming so that he can seduce and kidnap a woman for her skin."

He actually looked aghast at her words, even offended. Which meant he was either innocent or a great actor.

"You're going to throw me naked into a pit and make me drench myself in baby lotion, aren't you?"

He did laugh at that. "You live in New Orleans, where they can't even dig a grave. So tell me where I'm going to find this pit?"

"It's an aboveground pit."

"Hardly secretive."

"But possible," she insisted.

He shook his head. "You don't give up, do you?"

"Look, I'm a realist and I just had my heart ripped out. I don't want to be involved with anyone right now. You've been so kind to me and I don't know why. It's just that things like this don't happen in real life. Prince Charming doesn't come to the rescue all the time. Most of the time, he's too busy with perfect freakin' Cinderella and her teeny-tiny perfect feet to even notice the rest of us."

She could tell he was irritated at her.

Sighing, he reached for a glass.

Bride frowned as she caught a glimpse of his palm and the strange markings there. Markings that hadn't been there last night or she would have seen them.

Her heart stopped beating.

Reaching out, she pulled his hand into hers and stared at it.

Vane cursed inwardly as he realized he had forgotten to mask his marking when he flashed into her store-room. Part of him wanted to jerk his hand free, the other part couldn't move as she compared their palms.

"You burned me?"

"No," he said, offended that she would think such a thing.

She was panicking. He could smell her fear.

"I didn't hurt you, Bride, I swear."

She didn't believe him. "Get out!"

Oh, this was bad. He didn't know how to convince her. She got up and grabbed her broom from the corner.

"Out!" she shouted, brandishing it at him.

"Bride!"

She wouldn't listen. "Get out or I'll . . . I'll call the police!"

Vane bit back a curse. This wasn't going the way he needed it to. But maybe it was going the way it should.

At least he couldn't be tempted by a woman who hated him and thought him insane.

Dodging out the door, he stood there while he heard her lock it tight.

"Bride," he said, staring at her through the glass. "Please let me in."

She closed the blinds on him.

Vane leaned his head against the cool glass and let the war inside him shred his control. The animal part of him wanted her, regardless of reason.

The human part knew it would be better to let her go.

Unfortunately, when the two halves of him warred like this, more times than not, the animal won.

That was usually for the best.

This time it wouldn't be. Sighing, he looked around to make sure he was alone and flashed to wolf form. He just hoped Fury didn't come back as a wolf and blow his cover.

Bride might accept one wolf at her door, but two . . . that was pushing it.

Bride stood in the center of her room, clutching her broom. She was shaking in terror. She thought about calling her parents, but didn't want to scare them. They lived far enough out that by the time they got here she might be dead.

She thought about calling the police, but what would she tell them? That a good-looking guy was eating with her, making her all hot and bothered, and then he flashed his hand at her and she freaked?

It wasn't like Vane had done anything wrong. The police couldn't arrest him unless he did something to hurt her.

Tabitha . . .

She swallowed at the thought of calling her friend. If there was one thing Tabitha knew, it was self-defense, and the woman was armed to the teeth.

Bride ran to her cell phone and quickly dialed Tabitha's store. Luckily she was in.

"Tabby," she said, scanning the windows around her to see if Vane was trying to break in. "Please come over. I think my new boyfriend is going to kill me. Really kill me, as in hide-my-body-in-the-woods dead."

"What?"

"I'll explain when you get here. I'm scared, Tab. Really, really scared."

"Okay. Stay on the phone with me while I head over. Hey, Marla," Tabitha called to her store manager. "Take over the shop for a while. I have an emergency. Call the cell if you need me."

Bride sighed, only partially relieved. Tabitha's store on Bourbon Street was just a few blocks over from her house. It wouldn't take Tabitha more than ten or fifteen minutes to get here on foot.

"Is he still there?" Tabitha asked.

"I don't know. I threw him out and locked the door and I'm having these horrible flashbacks from bad movies where the demon people break through the windows to grab me."

"He's not a zombie, is he?"

She rolled her eyes at Tabitha's suggestion. For most people that would be an attempt at humor. Tabitha was serious. "Hardly."

"Is your wolf with you?"

"No," Bride said, her chest tight. "He went out and I haven't let him back in yet. Oh God, you don't think he'd hurt my wolf? Do you?"

"Don't worry. I'm sure the wolf can handle itself."

Bride could tell by Tabitha's breathlessness that her friend was running now. God love her. Tabitha was the best in a crisis. Everyone should have a friend like her.

There was nothing Tabitha wouldn't do for a friend or her family.

"You still there?" Tabitha asked.

"Yes."

Bride chatted with her the whole time about nothing while she checked outside to see if Vane was still there.

He wasn't.

After a few minutes, she heard her wolf growling outside the door.

"Shh," Tabitha said over the phone. "It's just me, boy."

"You here already?"

"Yeah," she said. "Hang up and open the door."

Bride did. To her relief, it was just the wolf and Tabitha outside.

"It looks clear," Tabitha said as the wolf ran into the apartment. "He must have left."

Bride took a deep breath in relief, but she still locked the door tight. "I've never been more terrified, Tabby. It was awful."

Tabitha scanned the apartment. "What happened?" she asked as she opened doors and looked out windows.

"I don't know. We were having a late lunch and everything was great until I saw this . . ." She held her palm up for Tabitha to see the strange tattoo mark on her palm. "He had one identical to it on his palm."

"You're kidding."

"No, and the weirdest part is that I don't know how I got it. Remember when we were eating and it just appeared?"

Tabitha took Bride's hand into hers and studied the tattoo.

"He branded me or something, didn't he?" Bride asked. "He's placed his mark on me and now he's going to kill me. I knew it was too good to be true."

Tabitha shook her head. "Honestly, I can't answer that. There haven't been any murders like this in the state, I know that much."

And Tabitha would. She made it a habit through a friend of hers in the police department to stay on top of all murder investigations.

"So what do you think?"

Tabitha held her hand closer to her face. "It looks Greek in origin. Tell you what, let's make a break for my sister's house. We can ask her husband what he thinks."

"Which sister?"

"The twin one." Tabitha released her hand.

Bride balked at the thought of going to Amanda. "Amanda knows my psycho boyfriend-turned-serial-killer. She even set us up on our date!"

Tabitha made a disgusted sound. "Figures. Mandy has always been a rotten judge of character. Jeez! Never let her set you up with any guy."

"I thought that's what they say about you, Tabby?"

Tabitha ignored her. "You know, it might be a good idea for you to pack a bag and camp out at Amanda's at least for tonight, until we find out more about your serial-killer friend. If he does know Amanda, then he knows enough to leave her alone."

Bride didn't argue. In all honesty, she didn't want to be home alone even with her wolf to guard her. If Vane really was psychotic, he could kill her pet and then her.

"Okay, give me a sec."

Tabitha petted the wolf while Bride grabbed a change of clothes, her makeup, and something to sleep in.

Vane lowered his head as he watched Bride packing. He was relieved at her actions and Tabitha's suggestion. Kyrian lived in a house that not even Vane could break into. It was protected against not just human criminals, but otherworldly intruders as well.

There, the rest of his pack couldn't trespass unless Kyrian allowed it, and the former Dark-Hunter knew better than to let a pack of Were-Hunters in.

He nuzzled Tabitha's leg, grateful she wasn't a complete lunatic.

In no time, Bride was packed. She turned off the lights and opened the door.

They tried to leave him behind, but Vane refused.

"Let him come," Tabitha said as Bride tried to drag him away from Bride's SUV.

"Yeah, but doesn't your sister have Terminator now?"

"She does, but he's friendly enough with other dogs. It's vampires he hates."

Bride didn't comment on that. Instead, she let the wolf into the back seat of her Jeep Cherokee. She put her bag in beside him, then got in and waited for Tabitha to jump in. They pulled out of the drive and Bride's heart stopped as she caught sight of Vane's motorcycle outside her shop.

"What is it?" Tabitha asked.

She pointed toward the motorcycle. "He's still here."

"Gun it," Tabitha said as she pulled out her Glock and checked its magazine.

"Oh, good grief, Tabitha. You can't shoot him."

"Trust me, I can." Tabitha touched the scar on her face. "Now go before he finds us."

Bride did as she said.

It didn't take long to reach Amanda and Kyrian's antebellum mansion in the Garden District. The Greek-revival house was one of the best preserved in the state. It was also one of the largest.

Bride pulled into the driveway and paused in front of the massive iron gates that had to be opened from inside.

Tabitha used her cell phone to call Amanda.

"Why not just buzz the house?" Bride asked.

"Because Kyrian can be a dickhead about letting me in sometimes."

Bride frowned. "Why?"

"I tried to kill him once and he hasn't gotten over it. I swear, that man can hold a grudge like nobody's business." She paused. "Hey Mandy, it's me. We're out here in the driveway. Could you buzz us in?" She winked at Bride. "It's me and Bride McTierney . . . yeah, okay."

The gates opened. "Thanks, sis. See you in a minute."

They drove up the driveway and Bride whistled low. She'd never been inside the gates before, but everyone in town knew about this house.

It was even more beautiful up close than it had been from the street.

They drove up the semicircular driveway to the front door, which swung open the instant they stopped. Amanda Hunter stepped out, holding her infant daughter on her hip.

The baby girl started bouncing the second she saw Tabitha. "Mama, mama, mama!" the baby cried in her infant gibberish, reaching for Tabitha, who scooped her up and hugged her.

Before Tabitha's face had been scarred, the only way to tell the two women apart had been their wardrobes. While Tabitha preferred a goth chic look, Amanda was mainstream to the extreme. She wore a pair of black slacks and a thin, dark green cashmere sweater.

"What brings you two here?" Amanda asked.

"She has a psycho chasing her," Tabitha said while Bride let her wolf out of the car and grabbed her bag.

Amanda looked at her with concern. "Are you okay, Bride?"

Bride held on to her wolf. "I think so. I'm really sorry to impose."

"No, not at all," Amanda said as she neared Bride. "I know how much my sisters love you. I'd hate to see any-thing happen to you." Amanda froze as she caught sight of the wolf with her and frowned.

"Do you mind that I brought him?" Bride asked. "Tabitha said it would be okay."

Still frowning, Amanda looked at Tabitha. "Okay . . ."

Amanda held her hand out to the wolf who went im-mediately over to her. "You probably want to go inside, don't you, boy?"

The wolf moved back to Bride's side.

"Or not," Amanda said. "Well now, why don't we all go inside and find out some more about this lunatic who's after Bride?"

They followed Amanda into the house. Bride pulled up short, a bit intimidated by the size of the place and the pristine collection of antiques that looked like they belonged in a museum. She'd never seen anything like it.

But the oddest part was that the antiques were balanced out by contemporary furniture such as the plush black couches and an expensive entertainment system.

Not to mention strange vampire bric-a-brac. They even had a coffin-shaped coffee table.

How very odd . . .

A gorgeous blond man entered the room from the hallway to the right and cursed the instant he saw Tabitha in the foyer.

"Love you, too, Kyr," Tabitha said with an open, friendly smile.

He took a deep breath that said he would need patience to deal with Tabitha. "Kill any vampires lately?" he asked.

"Apparently not, you're still breathing, huh?" Tabitha clucked her tongue at Amanda. "When's Geritol here gonna drop dead from old age, anyway?"

Kyrian narrowed his eyes at his sister-in-law before he looked at his wife. "You know, I always thought I had faced evil incarnate. And then I met your sister. She makes a total mockery of all known malevolent forces."

"Would you two stop?" Amanda said to them. "We have company, and speaking of evil incarnate. Why don't you go face it in the nursery and change your daughter's diaper?"

"Anything to get her out of Tabitha's clutches before she corrupts her. It's even worth facing the toxic waste."

Tabitha snorted at that. "Go on, little Marissa, and make sure you do something really nasty to Daddy when he changes you, okay?"

The baby laughed as Tabitha handed her over to her father.

Kyrian started for the stairs, then stopped as he caught sight of the wolf sitting quietly behind Bride.

"Is that who I think it is?" Amanda asked him.

Kyrian cocked his head. "Yeah, I think so."

Bride's heart stopped. "You know his owner?"

Kyrian looked a bit uneasy with her question. "He doesn't really have an owner per se. How did you end up with him?"

"He turned up at my house and I took him in."

Kyrian and Amanda exchanged a puzzled look. "He let you?"

"Well, yeah."

Tabitha opened her mouth as if she understood what they were thinking. "Oh, dear Lord, don't tell me he's one of your cockamamie friends."

"They're better than yours," Kyrian snapped. "At least mine aren't insane."

"Yeah, right. They're just . . ." Tabitha snapped her mouth shut, then passed a fake smile to Bride. "You want to show him your hand? I'm sure he's going to know all about your mysterious serial killer."

Bride hesitated. "He knows serial killers?"

"He knows lots of truly unsavory people."

"And Tabitha leads off that list."

"Kyrian!" Amanda snapped.

Tabitha crossed her arms over her chest and shrugged nonchalantly. "It's okay, Mandy. Let him pick. At least I'm not the one with the receding hairline."

His face suddenly ashen, Kyrian ran his hand along his hairline.

"You're not going bald," Amanda snapped, then she turned to her sister. "Would you stop picking on my husband?"

"Geritol started it."

Bride wasn't sure what to think of them now. This had to be the weirdest house she'd ever been inside. "Maybe I should have called the police."

"Nah," Tabitha said in a blasé tone. "No doubt your serial killer would kill them, too. Show him your hand."

Slightly hesitant, Bride moved forward to do so. "Have you ever seen anything like it?"

Kyrian nodded.

She swallowed in fear. "Am I going to die?"

"No," he said, locking gazes with her. "It's not a death symbol."

Bride let out a relieved breath. "What is it, then?"

He cringed a bit before he responded. "That I really can't tell you. But I can promise you this, whoever has a matching mark would sooner kill himself than see you hurt."

Bride closed her hand. "That's what Vane said."

Kyrian's gaze went to the wolf. "Well, you can trust him. Now if you'll excuse me, I have a diaper with my name on it."

"Is that all you're going to tell her?" Tabitha asked as he left them.

"It's all I *can* tell her," Kyrian said meaningfully, heading up the stairs.

Tabitha huffed. "Well, aren't you Mr. Information?"

"Tabby," Amanda said, taking her arm and pulling her toward the couches. "Leave him alone." She smiled graciously at Bride. "Can I get you anything to eat or drink?"

"No, thanks. I'm okay. At least as okay as I can be given the weirdness of this day."

Bride sat down on the couch in front of the windows while her wolf dashed up the stairs after Kyrian.

"Oh no." She got up to go after him.

"It's okay," Amanda said, stopping her as she rounded the coffin coffee table. "Let him go. Kyrian will bring him back down in a few minutes."

"Are you sure it's okay?"

Amanda nodded.

Kyrian had just finished changing Marissa's diaper when he felt a Were-Hunter presence outside his door. "Is that you, Vane?"

Vane pushed open the nursery door. "Thanks for not ratting me out down there."

Kyrian tossed the dirty diaper into the pail and picked Marissa up. She slapped a wet palm against his face before she squeezed his cheek playfully. "No problem. So what's up with the two of you?"

"I don't know. She's the human I was asking you how to date."

"I figured as much when I saw her. You should have told us it was Bride."

Vane sighed in frustration as he ignored that. "How do you tell a human what you are? How did Amanda react when she found out you were a Dark-Hunter?"

"She handled it with remarkable grace and dignity. Of course, it helps that her twin sister is certifiable. So, all things considered, I was the lesser of two evils."

Vane gave him a droll look.

"Does Bride have any loons in her family?" Kyrian asked him.

"Not that I know of."

"Then you're screwed."

"You have *no* idea," Vane said under his breath. "My pack knows I'm in New Orleans. They've already called out a tessera for me."

Kyrian felt for the wolf. He'd been in a similar situation and it was hard to be true to your preternatural nature while your heart was entangled with a human. "You want to leave her here?"

Vane looked at the baby in Kyrian's arms and a part of him ached at the sight. He'd never really thought about having children before he'd found Bride. And in truth it was strange to see the former Dark-Hunter playing daddy.

What would it be like to hold his own child?

In the back of his mind, he could see a small daughter with red hair and pale skin . . . like her mother.

"I can't endanger your family," Vane said quietly.

"I might be mortal now, but I'm still capable of fighting."

Vane shook his head. "No you're not. Neither is your wife. My people live their lives commanding magic and the forces of nature. You've never fought the Katagaria before and you have no idea what they're capable of."

Kyrian shifted his daughter in his arms as she started fussing. "So what are you going to do?"

"I don't know." And honestly, he was getting tired of not knowing. A year ago, Vane had known exactly who and what he was.

Exactly how to live his life and how to kill anyone who threatened it.

Ever since the night Anya had died, he'd been lost.

It wasn't until that evening in Bride's shop that he'd felt something other than despair.

Now he didn't know what he felt.

"Kyrian!"

Both men jumped at Amanda's call from downstairs. Kyrian clutched his daughter as they ran for the steps.

Vane was halfway down the curving stairs when he saw something that made his body run cold.

Jasyn Kallinos, one of the Katagaria hawks who was living temporarily at Sanctuary, was in the foyer in human form, bleeding. Amanda stood with her hand on the doorknob. From where she had *invited* him in.

Vane jumped over the banister and landed on the black-and-white marbled floor in a crouch just before Jasyn. Coming to his feet, he ignored Bride's gasp of alarm.

"What happened?" Vane asked.

"Those fucking wolves attacked us." His breathing ragged, Jasyn met Vane's gaze and the horror there singed him. "They killed Fang."

Chapter 8

Vane couldn't breathe as Jasyn's words echoed in his head. Fang dead?

No! It couldn't be. His brother couldn't be gone. He couldn't. Fang was all he had left and he had sworn to see his brother whole again.

He howled from the pain that skidded through his heart and sent him reeling. How could this have happened? How could they have gotten to Fang?

Jasyn held his hand over his bleeding shoulder as he panted from pain. "We tried to save him, Vane. We did everything we could."

Vane glared at him as he fought back tears of anger and agony.

And now he would do everything he could to make sure the wolves paid for this. Rage simmered deep in his soul. There was no power on this earth that could shelter them now.

No quarter that would keep them safe from his wrath.

He would have all of them, including his father.

His vision darkening, Vane headed for the door only to find Kyrian in front of him. He handed his daughter off to his wife. "Where do you think you're going?"

"To kill them."

Kyrian braced himself as if he knew he was about to have to fight him. "You can't."

"Watch me." Vane tried to flash out of the house only to find he couldn't. "What the hell?"

"I'm not going to let you commit suicide," Amanda said sternly. She handed her daughter to her sister, then came forward to stand beside her husband. "We won't let you do this."

Vane was tempted to blast the binding spell back at her, but didn't want to hurt her. She had no idea what she was dealing with and didn't know how easily he could rupture her powers while leaving his pristine. "You're not as strong as you think you are, Amanda. Release my powers."

"No. Revenge isn't the answer."

"Revenge is the only answer," Jasyn said from behind him. "Let him go."

Something strange went through Vane at that. A weird fissure . . .

He turned to look at Jasyn.

The man behind him looked like the Katagari hawk. He was the same height and build.

But he was bleeding . . .

He was *wounded*.

Vane paused as those facts registered in his mind. For the Katagaria, it was almost impossible to maintain their human form while injured. Only the strongest of the strong could do it. And usually it was done only when they had no choice except to blend in with the human realm or endanger themselves by discovery. To maintain human form under those circumstances bled off powers and drained their strength, both physical and magical. It made them extremely vulnerable to attack and death.

Why would Jasyn do such a thing?

Even under the best of circumstances, Jasyn hated taking human form. For that matter, Jasyn hated everyone and everything. Why would the bears send him with this news?

Why would Jasyn come?

Vane narrowed his eyes as a bad feeling came over him. "Who are you?"

The "hawk" stared blankly at him. "You know who I am."

"Kyrian, protect the women," Vane snarled as he seized his powers from Amanda.

Amanda cried out, but Vane didn't hesitate as he realized what he was facing.

"Alastor," he snarled, curling his lip at the demon.

The demon laughed. "You are a smart one, wolf."

Tabitha began reciting a banishing spell in Latin. The demon threw out his hand and blasted her through the far wall.

Vane caught him about the middle and tried to slam him into the doorframe of the foyer. Before he could do it, the demon vanished and left him to barrel into it with his shoulder.

Vane growled angrily in frustration and pain as his entire shoulder ached.

Without pausing, he conjured his cell phone and called Sanctuary.

"Nicolette," he said as soon as Mama Bear answered the phone. "Is Fang still alive?"

"Of course, *cher*. I am in the room with him and Aimee right now."

"Are you sure?" he asked, thinking only of his brother and his fear of leaving Kyrian and the women unprotected.

"*Oui*. I am touching him and he is alive and relatively well."

Vane sank to his knees in relief.

Fang was alive.

"Guard him," he said in a low, ragged tone. "Someone has called out Alastor."

The bear started cursing in French.

"Don't worry," she said at last. "No one will bring harm to your brother. If the demon shows up here, it will be the last mistake of his life."

Vane heard her order her daughter to fetch two of the nastier inhabitants of Sanctuary to guard Fang. "*Merci,* Nicolette."

He hung up the phone to see Amanda kneeling by her sister who was sitting up now, rubbing her head.

Tabitha wiped the blood from her nose as she cursed under her breath. "I really hate demons," she muttered sullenly.

Vane reached out with his powers and healed her and the wall.

Tabitha's eyes widened before she pushed herself to her feet.

"Are you okay, Tabby?" Amanda asked as she looked from her sister to her now-repaired wall.

Tabitha nodded.

Vane rose slowly. His gaze went to Bride, who sat on the couch watching him.

"Did I hurt you, Amanda?" Vane asked without taking his eyes off his mate.

"It wasn't exactly comfortable," Amanda said. "You could have warned me before you yanked."

"I'm sorry. There wasn't time."

"What just happened?" Bride asked quietly. She sat on the couch as if she were in a daze. "What is going on here?"

Vane exchanged an uncomfortable look with Amanda and Kyrian. How was he going to explain this to her?

Kyrian picked up his daughter, who didn't seem the least bit concerned about the fact that a demon had just visited them. Then again, she had played dolls with one earlier. To Marissa such things were probably every-other-day occurrences.

Kyrian went to Amanda and Tabitha. "I think we should go to the kitchen and put some ice on Tabby's hard head."

"Lay off me, Geritol, or you're going to need some ice for your groin," Tabitha said as she led the way toward the kitchen.

Vane waited until he was alone with Bride.

This had to be the most awkward moment of his entire life. He didn't even know where to begin. But at least she wasn't afraid of him at the moment.

That was something, anyway.

Bride sat there in stunned disbelief as she tried to make sense of . . . of . . . She didn't even know what to call it.

She wasn't sure what she had just seen. Everything

had happened way too fast. The knock on the door, followed by a bleeding man who had just vanished into nothingness.

She felt bewildered, and in the back of her mind, she thought she might be on the *Scare Tactics* show. *Candid Camera*? Did they even do *Candid Camera* anymore?

Maybe this was some other new reality show.

How to Make You Lose Your Mind in One Afternoon.

Her thoughts rambled as she struggled to come to grips with these bizarre events.

"Kyrian said you weren't a psycho serial killer." That sounded stupid even to her, but she didn't know what else to say to him.

"No," he said quietly as he came to stand in front of her. "But I'm not human, exactly."

Tabitha's angry voice echoed from the kitchen. "What do you mean, he's a friggin' dog?"

They both turned as Tabitha rushed into the room.

"You're a dog?" she asked Vane.

"Wolf," Vane corrected.

Bride got up and put the couch between herself and Vane. This wasn't real.

No. This was a dream. She'd hit her head. Something.

"Jeez," Tabitha sneered. "I should have known it that night you were outside the restaurant. I thought you looked too smart for the average beastie."

Kyrian came into the room and tried to pull Tabitha back to the kitchen.

Tabitha shrugged off his hand. "Bride needs me. She's not used to you loons."

"I need to go home," Bride said as a strange lucidity came over her. It was as if her mind were rejecting everything she'd heard.

Vane a dog . . .

Yeah, right. Well, most men were dogs, but that was only figuratively speaking.

No. This was some weird dream. Vane had drugged her during lunch and she was now hallucinating. Whenever she woke up, she was definitely calling the cops on him.

She moved to the door only to have Vane materialize in front of her. "You can't leave."

"Oh, yes I can," she snapped angrily. "This is my bad psychotic delusion and I can do anything I want to in it. Just watch. I'm going to turn into a bird now . . ."

Okay, she didn't.

Bride waited for a full minute. "Why am I not a bird? I want to be a bird."

"Because you're not dreaming," Vane said, placing his hands on her arms. "This is real, Bride. In a very fucked-up sort of way."

"No, no, no," she insisted. "This isn't real. I reject it all. I have—" Bride stopped mid-sentence as she looked past Kyrian to see his daughter. Marissa was crawling into the room. The baby stopped near the couch, and sat up, laughing.

She held her tiny arm out and her sippee cup on the coffin-shaped coffee table flew into her outstretched hand. "Rissa, cup, Daddy," she said happily even though the baby was too young to speak.

"Yeah," Bride said while Marissa sipped her juice and Kyrian picked his daughter up from the floor. "I am definitely one oar short on the boat."

She started past Vane only to have him pull her to a stop.

"Please, Bride, you have to listen because your life is in danger, but not from me."

She looked into those magnetic hazel-green eyes and wondered if his image was part of her hallucination, too.

Maybe none of this had ever happened. Maybe she was still in bed with Taylor and all this had been one very long, odd dream.

She shook her head at Vane. "I can't accept what I've just seen. It's not possible."

He held up his palm with the same tattoo as hers. "I don't know how to help you accept this. The unbelievable has been part of my life since the moment I was born. I . . ."

Vane sighed, dropped his hands from her arms and pulled his cell phone out again and dialed it.

He was making a call? Now?

Yeah, why not? That made as much sense as the rest of this.

What had she eaten for dinner? It must have been a doozy. She better make a note not to eat it again.

Vane's gaze stayed on her. "Acheron, I need a favor from you. I don't care what it costs. I'm at Kyrian's house with my mate and I need you here to guard her for me until she's freed."

"Mate?" she repeated. "As in 'friend'?"

"As in 'wife,'" Tabitha said.

Bride gaped. "I'm not married."

Vane hung up the phone. "No, you're not, Bride." He cupped her cheek with one warm hand and gave her a look of sad longing. "No one is going to make you do anything you don't want to do, okay?"

He stroked her cheekbone with his thumb. "Stay here, where things are mostly normal and where you'll be safe for the next two weeks, and I won't bother you ever again. I swear it. Just be safe for me."

It was hard to be afraid of a man who looked at her the way Vane did just now. With that sincerity burning deep in his gaze. With such a look of yearning and need.

She was uncertain.

Scared.

"What are you?" she asked.

He looked down, took a deep breath, then lifted his head up.

Bride gasped as she saw that one-half of his face was covered with a deep red tattoo similar to the one on her palm.

"I'm human," he said in a tormented tone. "And I'm not." He dropped his hand to her shoulder. "I never knew softness," he breathed. "Not until the moment you touched me in your store. My life is violent and dangerous. It's dark and twisted and no place for someone like you. I have more people wanting me dead than I can count. They will stop at nothing, and you . . ." He ground his teeth before he spoke again. "You'll never want again for anything in your life. I swear it on what little bit of human soul I have left."

He stepped back and headed for the door. "Take care of her for me, Kyrian."

Then he was gone.

Bride felt drained by his sudden absence, and for reasons unknown, her heart ached.

She looked over at Tabitha, who had tears in her eyes. "Dog or no dog," Tabitha said. "That was . . ." She rushed to Bride's side and urged her toward the door. "Don't let him leave, Bride. Go get him."

She didn't have to say those words; Bride was already headed for the door.

"Vane!" she called, looking for him.

There was no sign of him anyplace.

"Vane!" she tried again, even louder this time.

Only the damp, cool air answered her.

Her heart breaking, she stepped back into the house and collided with Tabitha. "I can't believe I let him go."

"I can't believe the idiot went."

Bride panicked as she heard that voice. It wasn't Tabitha's. It was the demon's.

In the blink of an eye, everything went black.

Vane walked down the street away from Kyrian's house, doing his best to ignore Bride's call. His heart was breaking into pieces at the thought of losing her.

He had done the right thing. He'd let her go. So why did it hurt so much?

And it did hurt. It ached and burned deep inside his heart until he was sure he couldn't bear it.

It was for the best.

She was human and he . . .

He was the wolf who loved her. Vane cursed at the

reality of that statement. He wanted desperately to deny it and he couldn't. She was everything to him.

There was nothing about her he would change. He loved the way she looked at him as if he were crazy. The way she hummed quietly to herself while she dusted her shelves. The way she always made sure to split her food with him.

The way she felt in his arms as she came for him, and the sound of her breathless voice as she said his name while in the throes of her orgasms.

Hell, he even liked the way she hogged the covers.

"Oh, fuck this," he snarled. He wasn't going to just let her go.

He loved her and he wasn't going to just up and leave. Not without a fight and not without at least telling her.

He turned and headed back toward the house.

"Vane! Come quick."

He paused at Kyrian's deep voice. At the urgency he heard in the former Dark-Hunter's tone.

Flashing back to the house, Vane materialized in the foyer to find Kyrian there with his daughter and Tabitha. Bride was nowhere to be seen.

A bad feeling consumed him. "Where's Bride?"

"The demon took her," Tabitha said.

The animal inside him snapped and snarled with vengeance. He reached out and found nothing in the air. No scent, no trace.

It didn't matter. Alastor had taken his mate.

Vane would find her, and when he did, there would be one less demon in the universe.

. . .

Bride wanted to scream, but couldn't. Her vocal cords seemed to be paralyzed.

Sight came back to her so suddenly that it hurt her eyes.

She blinked to find herself inside what appeared to be an old cabin or house of some sort. It was long and narrow with an old-fashioned fire blazing out in the open with no fireplace or real confinement.

"Don't be afraid," the demon said, releasing her.

He stepped around her. Instead of the good-looking blond he had been earlier, he was now hideous. His skin was a deep, dark purple shade and he had flaming red hair and eyes.

His feet were twisted and looked more like over-grown clubs. He limped as he walked toward the door and opened it.

"Bryani!" he called out, then he looked back at her and sniffed like an animal. His large teeth were too big for his mouth, and when he spoke he lisped. "No one is going to hurt you, *bobbin*."

Bride was getting seriously tired of people telling her that. "Where am I?"

He wiped at his nose. "Don't worry yourself, *bobbin*. You're safe here."

"I was safe where I was." Sort of, anyway.

What kind of screwed-up delusion was this? If she was going to lose her mind, she much preferred losing it with Vane than with an ugly monster thing who could barely speak.

The demon stepped back to make way for a beautiful

woman who reminded Bride of a young Grace Kelly, only this woman had three vicious scars on her face and neck that made a mockery of Tabitha's.

Underneath the scars, the woman bore a red tattoo very similar in design to Vane's.

She looked to be no older than her mid-twenties and yet the woman carried herself with the bearing of a regal queen. She entered the room as if she owned it and dared anyone to question her authority.

Blond braids were wrapped around her head in an elegant design that was held in place by a gold circlet decorated with what appeared to be very large diamonds, rubies, and sapphires.

Bride frowned at the woman's clothes. She wore what appeared to be something out of an episode of *Xena*. It was gold body armor that covered her torso, but left her arms bare, except for gold arm- and wristbands. Her vibrant red and dark green plaid skirt was voluminous and many-layered.

Most impressive, the woman had a sword, bow, and quiver of arrows strapped to her back.

Oh yeah, Bride was definitely nuts, she decided. Her mind had snapped completely. Maybe she was even dead.

Right now, she was game for just about any explanation.

Grace Kelly, or Bryani as the demon had called her, scrutinized Bride. "Has he hurt you, child?"

Bride looked at the demon. "Define 'hurt'? I mean, I didn't really want to be brought here, wherever *here* is."

"Not Alastor," Bryani snapped in an accent unlike

anything Bride had ever heard. "The other one. The bastard wolf. Did he hurt you?"

Bride was twice as confused. "You mean my pet wolf or my boyfriend who thinks he's a wolf?"

Bryani grabbed her hand and held it up to her face. "The one whose hand matches yours. Did he rape you?"

"No," Bride said emphatically as she wrested her arm from the woman's grasp. "He didn't do anything."

Bryani let out a relieved breath, then nodded at the demon. "You got to her in time. Thank you, Alastor."

The demon inclined his head to Bryani. "We are done now." He vanished instantly and left them alone.

Bryani didn't seem the least bit concerned by the oddity of that action.

She held her hand out to Bride. "Come, child. I would have you at the hall where we can all protect you while you bear the mating mark."

Her first instinct was to pull away, but Bride forced herself to take the woman's hand. What the hell? She'd already lost her mind. The least she could do was see where this psychotic episode was going to take her.

Hopefully it would be someplace nicer and warmer than this spartan room.

Bride laughed at the thought. "Have you ever seen that episode of *Buffy* where Sarah Michelle Gellar flashes between the insane asylum and her life in Sunnydale as the Slayer?"

Bryani cocked her head. "What is Buffy? Is she a Lykos too or another kind of Katagaria?"

Bride was a bit miffed that her conjured escort had no idea who Buffy was. "Never mind. Obviously this is my Sunnydale version and I'll be waking up real soon in my padded cell."

Bryani released her as they left the room behind.

Bride followed her out of the hut only to find herself in the middle of what appeared to be a green valley with mountains rising up around them. It was lovely, albeit rather cold for her taste.

How she had gotten here, she had no idea. This wasn't New Orleans, which was where she'd been five minutes ago.

Even odder, everyone around her was dressed in ancient clothing and spoke a language she couldn't even begin to understand.

And every person near them paused to stare as they walked past. Silence settled instantly. Eerily. The women at the makeshift well. Those who were carrying baskets and chatting. Even the children stopped playing.

But it was the men who captured Bride's attention, especially since every one of them stopped and turned to stare at her as if she were their target or prey.

She realized that with the exception of the demon, every person in this village was literally a gorgeous, stunning specimen of human physiology. This was definitely a dream or delusion of some kind.

Not even Chippendales had this much bodacious muscle. And never mind the women. They were the epitome of why Bride refused to buy fashion magazines. If she didn't know better, she'd think she'd fallen down the rabbit hole of Hollywood extras.

Bride followed Bryani into a large wooden building that reminded her of something out of a low-budget

King Arthur movie. Made of wattle and daub, it was spartan inside except for the large fire blazing in the center of the hall, surrounded by long tables and wooden benches. Something that looked like dried weeds and herbs were scattered over the earthen floor.

As soon as Bride entered, she found herself surrounded by gorgeous men, some of whom actually sniffed her.

"Excuse me?" she said, brushing them away. "This is my fantasy and I'd rather you not do that."

A tall blond man cocked his head in a way that reminded her of a canine. He directed a cutting glare at Bryani. "Why would you bring a Katagari whore here?"

Bryani pulled Bride away from the men and put herself between them. "She is not a whore. She's a terrified human female who doesn't understand what has happened to her. She thinks herself mad."

The blond man laughed. "I think we should send her back to her mate the way the Katagaria send our mates back to us." He took a step toward them.

Bryani pulled the sword off her back and angled it at him. "Don't make me slay you, Arnulf. I brought her here for protection."

"Then you made a mistake."

Bryani was aghast. "We are *human*."

"Aye," he agreed, sliding a dangerous smirk toward Bride. "And I quest for vengeance same as you, my princess. My mate lies dead from their abuse of her. I say we return it upon their females tenfold."

As the men started forward, a howl rang out.

Everyone froze.

Bride turned to see the door behind her open. An old man stepped through it. His hair was white and he wore a beard that reminded her of an old ZZ Top video. By his side was a large brown timber wolf.

Like Bryani, half of the old man's face was covered with an eerie green tattoo. "What goes here?"

"We beseech moral restitution," Arnulf said. "Your daughter has brought a Katagari mate into our pack. *We* want her."

The old man raked a censoring gaze over Bride, then looked to Bryani.

"I had to, Father," Bryani said as she lowered her sword. "There was no other way."

The old man ordered the others to leave them.

The men did so reluctantly. But before they left, some howled like animals. Others looked back with expressions that promised they intended to renew this discussion.

For the first time, Bride was scared. Something wasn't right about this "fantasy."

If she didn't know better, she'd swear it was real. But it couldn't be.

Could it?

Once they were alone, the old man led them toward the farthest table in the room; it stood high on a dais. Two chairs that looked like large, hand-carved thrones capped with wolfheads stood behind the table. "What are you thinking, Bry?" he asked her escort.

"I wanted to protect her, Father. Is that not what a Sentinel does? Are we not to protect the world from the Katagaria animals?"

He looked aggravated by her words. "But *she* is mated to one."

"They have not joined themselves. She is only marked. If we keep her here until the mark is gone, then she will be free of him."

The old man shook his head while his wolf came over to sniff at Bride.

Bride stared at it, wondering if it would stay a wolf or become something else.

"Why not just kill her mate?" the old man asked.

Bryani looked away.

The old man let out a tired breath. "I told you to kill them centuries ago, daughter."

Anger flared in her eyes. "I tried to kill him, remember? He grew too strong."

The old man made a disgusted sound in the back of his throat. "She is yours to guard. I will rally the others, and this time when he comes to us, we will finish what was started."

Bryani nodded, then motioned for Bride to follow her. She led her past the thrones, down a narrow corridor in back that led to a set of rooms off the hall.

The place was spartan for the most part, but it did have some interesting comforts, such as a large, padded bed and furs, and twenty-first-century novels.

Bride picked up Kinley MacGregor's *A Dark Champion* and laughed. Oh yeah, good dream here. "Could you please conjure me a Coke?" she asked Bryani. "I'm feeling the need for one."

"Nay, I cannot. That would require my going forward in time to retrieve one and my powers for that were taken from me." Her tone was angry and bitter. "It is why I had to conjure the demon to fetch you."

"Who took your powers?"

"My mate." Bryani spat the words. "He stole much from me, but have no fear. His son will not violate you. I will see to it."

Bride returned the book to the small stack on the nightstand. "You know, none of that makes a bit of sense to me."

Bryani put her hands on her hips as she faced her. "Then how about this? The so-called man who took you, Vane, is a wolf I was forced against my will to give birth to over four hundred years ago. And if I could, I would kill him for you."

"Excuse me?"

Bryani ignored her as she explained herself. "Like many women, when I was young, I was stupid. On my first venture out with my Sentinel patrol to hunt the Katagaria wolves, I was captured by our enemies, who thought it would be great fun to take turns raping me."

Bride felt sick from hearing Bryani's story. A wave of sympathetic ache consumed her.

This poor woman. She couldn't imagine anything worse.

And she was Vane's mother . . .

Her lips curled, Bryani shook her head. "But the Fates are often cruel and I, like you, found myself mated to one of those animals who had hurt me. Vane's father kept me captive for weeks as he abused me more, trying to make me accept him as my mate. They can't, you know. Acceptance is strictly in our hands. Not theirs."

This couldn't be real. No. Bride was dreaming, though why she was dreaming this, she had no idea. "You don't look like Vane."

Pure, unadulterated hatred glowed in Bryani's hazel eyes. "He looks like his filthy father."

Bride frowned as she remembered Fury saying that to her. Ah, her mind was replaying it in her delusion. Made sense.

Sort of.

But why would she make up so tragic a tale? Bride had never been the kind of person to wish ill on anyone, least of all Vane's mother.

Could this be real?

Was that possible?

Bride moved toward the blond woman and took her hands in hers to study her palms. "You don't have a mark."

"Nay. If the mating isn't consummated within three weeks, the mark fades and we as women are free to go our own way. The men are left impotent for the duration of our lives."

Bride frowned up at her. Bryani was really tall. "You left his father impotent?"

An evil glint came into Bryani's hazel-green eyes. "I left him more than that. Once my children were born, I took my three human children and left my three puppies with him, then gelded the bastard for what he'd done to me. I'm sure not a day passes where he doesn't wish he'd killed me when he had the chance."

Bride cringed at the thought. "Why am I dreaming this?" she asked. "I don't understand this nightmare."

Bryani shook her head. "This is real, Bride. I know in the human world things such as what I describe don't happen. But you must believe me. There are things that reside alongside you in the everyday world that you never realize are there."

One second Bryani was standing in front of Bride and in the next, the woman was a huge white timber wolf that bore a terrifying resemblance to her adopted pet.

Bride staggered back.

No, this wasn't real. This wasn't.

"I want to go home," she said out loud. "I have to wake up. Please, God, let me wake up!"

Vane pulled out of his trance as he realized where his mate was.

Bride was in his mother's homeland. A place where he had sworn to never return. He'd only been there once. Long ago when he had bartered with Acheron Parthenopaeus to help him find his birth mother.

To this day, Vane didn't know why he'd wanted to find her. Maybe it was all the years of living with a father who hated him and he wanted to see if there was any chance his mother might tolerate him.

Or maybe because he had become human, he thought she might accept him.

Instead, she had tried to kill him.

"I curse the day I bore you."

Her words still resonated deep inside him and now she had struck the final blow. She had set loose a demon to take his mate. No Were-Hunter could remove a human from their time period without the human's permission. Only demons and gods were exempt from that rule.

But why? Why would his mother have taken Bride back to Dark Age Britain? He didn't trust his mother. Her hatred of him and his father was too great.

Vane trusted no humans.

No, Bride was his responsibility, and the last thing she needed was to be left alone with an Arcadian pack in the past where he'd been born.

He would have to go and claim her and bring her back to her home.

Only this time, he didn't have any backup. He was going in alone.

He only hoped that he survived the encounter. Otherwise, Bride just might find herself trapped in the past for eternity.

Chapter 9

As the hours ticked by slowly while Bride was confined to her tiny room, she learned one thing.

This wasn't a dream.

She didn't know how it was real, but she had no choice except to come to terms with the fact that this wasn't the asylum episode of *Buffy,* or a delusion. All of these people were real and they had the worst-tasting food she'd ever tried to eat.

No wonder they were all so damned skinny.

Her tray of barely touched food was set on the nightstand with the books. Bride paced the room while listening to the people in the hall debate what they should do to her.

This was getting scarier by the minute.

Suddenly she sensed a movement behind her. Bride spun around to find a man standing there who reminded her of Vane. He had the same multicolored dark hair and green eyes, and his face was eerily similar. Clean shaven, he wore his hair longer than Vane and was dressed in ancient leather and mail armor pieces. Like Bryani, he had a sword strapped to his back.

He watched her in a manner that was definitely reminiscent of a wild animal examining its prey.

"Who are you?" she asked him.

He didn't speak. Instead, he moved closer so that he could take her hand into his and look at her marked palm. Hatred blazed in his eyes.

Before she could blink, she found herself somehow taken from her room into the center of the hall where the angriest group of people on the planet were found. She felt like the only hot rock in a nest of vipers.

Their loud voices increased tenfold in volume when she appeared.

"Dare!" The shout rang out from the old man. "Why have you brought her here?"

The Vane lookalike cast a malevolent look at Bride. "I call for a *timoria* against her mate."

Agreement echoed from the crowd.

"Nay," Bryani said as she pushed her way through the crowd to reach them.

"What's the matter, Mother?" Dare asked as he turned toward Bryani. "Have your feelings for the animals who prey upon us changed?"

"You know better."

"Then let us give back to them what they have given to us."

Bryani pulled her sword on her son. "I took a Sentinel's oath to protect—"

"A Katagari whore?" Dare asked, interrupting her. He pushed Bride toward Bryani. "She reeks of their scent. I say we settle this once and for all."

A cheer rang out.

Bride shook with terror.

"Father?" Bryani said to the old man. "Is this the way it's to be?"

The old man took his time scanning the crowd before he faced his daughter. "You should have consulted me before you brought her here, Bryani. You seek protection for our enemies when there is not a family among us who hasn't been torn apart by the Katagaria. Gods of Olympus, look what they have done to our own family. I have lost your mother's sanity and all my children save you to them. You barely returned from their clutches and then only because you managed to fight them off. Now you beg clemency for one of them? Have they driven you completely mad, too, daughter?"

He passed a less than sympathetic gaze to Bride. "We shall put the *timoria* to a vote. Who among you says aye?"

The roar was so loud that Bride had to cover her ears.

"Who says nay?"

"I do," Bryani said, but she was a lone voice in the crowd.

The old man gripped his staff and took a deep breath. "It is decided, then. Prepare the human for the *timoria*."

Bride had a really bad feeling the *timoria* wasn't a good thing, especially when three women came forward to drag her off.

"What's happening?" she asked the women who grabbed her. "What's a *timoria*?"

"I'm so sorry, Bride," Bryani said before she was pulled away. "Please forgive me."

Forgive her for what?

"Excuse me?" Bride snapped hysterically as she tried to pry the women's hands off her. It was useless. "Would you please tell me what the hell is going on here?"

The tallest of the women turned on her with a snarl. "For mating with a Katagari, there is only one punishment. You will be given to the unmated men of our clan."

"Given to them how?"

The look on the woman's face said it all. They intended to rape her.

Bride screamed and fought them with everything she had.

Vane took a minute to get his bearings as he arrived in ancient Britain. Time-travel always disoriented him. It took a lot of power to time-jump.

He also had to be careful now. If he sent out probes to locate Bride, they could be intercepted by his mother or her people. Not that he feared them. But he didn't want to go to war without an army.

In this time period, his mother's people ruled. His grandfather was the *regis* of one of the most powerful wolf clans and it was said that good old Gramps had killed more Katagaria than any other Sentinel in their history.

Vane took a deep breath as he scoped out the village on the other side of the hedge where he was crouched. They would be expecting him.

Sort of.

Vane heard something rustling in the forest behind

him. Spinning around, he expected it to be a wild animal or one of his mother's people.

It wasn't.

It was Fury.

Vane couldn't have been more stunned if he'd found his mother right in front of him. At least that would have made sense. Fury's presence made none whatsoever.

The wolf flashed instantly to human form and gaped in all his naked horror at Vane, who quickly averted his gaze.

"What the hell are you doing here?" they asked each other simultaneously.

"Put some clothes on me," Fury said, snarling the words as he cupped himself with his hands.

Rather than go blind, Vane quickly obliged and dressed the wolf in black jeans and a T-shirt. "Why are you here, Fury?"

He spoke between clenched teeth. "I'm doing what I told you I was doing. I'm leading the tessera away from you and Bride, only here you are while they are over there." Fury pointed angrily at a hill not far away. "You're supposed to be in New Orleans, you moron, not Britain."

Suspicious of Fury, Vane frowned. "Why did you bring the tessera here?"

Fury gave him a sinister glare. "Because this was the easiest way I knew of to eliminate them all at once. I can't do it alone and I thought Bryani would get her rocks off hacking one of Markus's tesseras into pieces."

Vane was even more confused and suspicious than before. "You know about Bryani?"

Fury rolled his eyes. "Yeah, I do. She gleefully ran me through and left me for dead several centuries back. Wanna see the scars?"

Vane caught the scent of Stefan coming closer to them.

Fury grabbed him by the arm and hauled him toward a copse of trees. "Look, we're in serious danger here. The Arcadians hate us with a passion."

"I know."

"No you don't," Fury said, his tone gravely earnest. "You really don't know how much they would pay to have both of us for breakfast. We have to get you out of here."

Vane wrested his arm free. "Bride is in that village and I'm not going anywhere unless she's with me."

Fury cursed. "How long has she been there?"

"I don't know, since I just arrived. Time doesn't flow the same way in both time periods, you know that."

"All right, we have to get her immediately and pray that she hasn't been there long."

"Why do you think I'm here?"

Fury didn't seem to hear him. "Okay, think, think, think." He looked up at Vane. "Do you have any ideas?"

"I'm going in there and get my mate."

"Bryani will have a dampening spell to curtail your powers."

Vane laughed. "Let her try."

"God, you have balls," he said respectfully under his breath. "What the hell? You can't live forever. Just promise me that if something goes wrong, you'll kill me rather than leave me to them."

There was such growling sincerity in that request that it took Vane aback. What had they done to Fury?

"Swear to me, Vane."

"I swear."

Before Fury could say anything more, Stefan, Aloysius, and Petra broke through the woods in wolf form. Their heads down, the wolves circled them, snarling and snapping.

"Shit!" Fury growled as the wolves hunkered down, preparing to strike.

A scream rang out from the village.

Vane didn't hesitate. Grabbing Fury, he flashed them out just as Stefan was about to reach them.

Bride dug her heels into the ground and bit one of the women holding her. The woman growled and slapped her. Bride bit her again.

Be damned if she was going to let them tie her down! She might not be Tabitha, but she could bite and pull hair with the best of them.

One of the men came forward to wrap his hand around Bride's neck.

"Let . . . her . . . go." Vane's steely voice echoed as he enunciated each word slowly.

Bride's eyes filled with tears as she heard the most blessed sound on the planet. She looked to her right to see Vane in human form, standing there without a weapon, and with her white wolf by his side.

Why wasn't he armed?

The men closest to Vane attacked en masse. Stunned,

she watched as he twirled around and kicked and punched them to the ground. He moved so fast that she could barely see him.

Then Vane vanished, only to reappear by her side. The women turned on him. Vane sent one flying backward, into the crowd, while he ducked and tripped the second one. The third one, he flipped head over heels onto the ground.

Forget Hollywood, they had nothing on Vane's speed and agility.

As Vane untied her hands, she could hear the wolf fighting and snarling.

Bride threw her arms around his shoulders the instant she was free and held him close while the women tried to reach them, only to recoil off what appeared to be an invisible wall of some sort.

"Fury," Vane called.

The wolf came running to their side. The man chasing him also rebounded off the wall.

Fury materialized into a naked man and laughed evilly at their pursuers.

Bride was completely stunned by the appearance of Vane's naked brother who, she had to admit, had a great body.

Oh, good grief, was no one what they appeared?

Vane snapped his fingers, and clothes appeared on Fury.

Dare cursed at them. "I thought you said you killed Fury, Mother."

Fury raked Dare with a sneer of repugnance. "Oh, she tried her best, little brother. But animals are remarkable survivors." He looked at Bryani. "Aren't we, Mother?"

Dare started for Fury, only to find himself slung backward by nothing.

In fact, every man who tried to reach Bride, Fury, or Vane found himself thrown to the ground.

"What is this?" Dare snarled, striking the invisible wall with his sword.

Fury laughed again. "This is your worst nightmare, *adelfos*. Meet the eldest of our litter." He gestured toward Vane. "Vane's powers make a mockery of everyone's here, even Grandfather's." He glanced at Bryani. "You were right, Mom. The blending of Arcadian and Katagaria blood did produce a sorcerer of unparalleled power. It just wasn't me. Sorry."

Vane's heart pounded as he listened and understood. Fury really was his brother. But that wasn't important to him at the moment, only Bride's safety was.

One of the Arcadian men came at Vane's back. He spun about and blasted him away from them. "You're lucky I'm not the animal you think I am," he growled at the Arcadians. "But if you ever come near my mate again, I will be."

Dare laughed cruelly. "Fine, take your woman. The full moon isn't for another three weeks and that gives us plenty of time to hunt you down and kill you. You have to sleep sometime. Then you'll be ours."

Fury shook his head. "You didn't hear a word I said about Vane, did you? It's such a pity I wasn't the one born with his power. I'd have killed all of you if I were. But I guess he's a better man than I am."

Vane smiled coldly at his "human" brother. Dare looked much like Fang when Fang was human. It was a pity that their parents' hatred of each other had come to this. That it had bred and poisoned a whole new generation.

But then, Vane had never thought to coexist with his Arcadian kin. They had thrown him out and written him off centuries ago.

Vane smiled evilly at Dare. "Unlike you, little brother, I don't need no stinking moon to time-jump."

And in one blink, Vane, Bride, and Fury were back in New Orleans, safely inside Kyrian's house.

"I think I need a Tylenol . . . jug," Bride said as she staggered away from Vane and sat down on the nearest couch. "And a lot of vodka to wash it down."

Kyrian, Amanda, and Tabitha came running into the room.

"That was quick," Tabitha said. "Damn, Vane, you don't mess around, do you?"

Vane ignored Tabitha's question as he knelt in front of Bride. "Are you okay?"

"I don't know," she answered honestly as she stared at him in numbed hysteria. "My boyfriend is a dog, his mother's psychotic, and I just nearly missed being the main attraction in some low-budget porn flick, complete with bad costuming and food. I mean, what is this? 'Welcome to the family, you now get to sleep with all my brothers, and I do mean *all* my brothers, cousins, friends, hell, everyone'? You know, most in-laws just bring over a casserole, not a four-hundred-year-old vendetta."

It was so good to be able to rant, but a part of her was still terrified. Nothing felt secure to her now. Nothing.

"Am I safe, Vane? Or is someone else going to poof into the living room and grab me and take me who knows where? I don't want to see Barney the real dinosaur with the naked cavemen chasing him! I don't want to see anything except my normal life here in New Orleans."

Vane cupped her face in his hands. On some level, his touch comforted her. "You're safe, Bride. I'm not going to let anyone else grab you. I swear it."

"And I can believe that, why?"

"Because I give you my word."

"Well, that just settles it all, huh?" Bride shook her head. "After this, I can't wait to meet your father. I'll bet he's just a barrel full of laughs." She stared at Vane as the horror of the last few hours washed through her. "Any other freaky family traditions I need to know about? Bones hidden in the backyard? Crazy aunts? Fleas?"

She looked over at Fury. "I don't have to sleep with him now, do I?"

Tabitha arched both her brows at that. "What kind of place did she go to? Sounds like it could be fun."

"Wanna go?" Fury asked. "I can take you there."

"Fury," Vane snapped. "You have enough to answer for already. Don't mess with the humans."

"Or Tabitha, either," Kyrian said.

Amanda elbowed him in the stomach.

"What?" Kyrian asked innocently.

Vane sat back on his heels and looked at Kyrian and Amanda over his shoulder. "I've got a shield on the house that should keep them out. Notice I said *should*. I have no idea what else the demon is capable of, especially if Amanda invites him into the house again."

"Nothing."

Bride looked up at the sound of a new deeply masculine voice. Now this was without a doubt the last person she expected to see here.

Though why she was surprised, she couldn't imagine. At the rate things were happening, for all she knew the woman who rang up her groceries at the supermarket might very well be a were-snake or zombie.

Why not?

"Ash?" Bride asked, recognizing the extremely tall, and incredibly sexy, addition to the room.

At six feet eight, decked out in black leather and possessing an aura that could only be defined as pure sexual attraction, Ash Parthenopaeus was a hard man to miss.

"You know Acheron?" Vane asked her.

"Yeah, he comes into the shop every few months with a cute, albeit odd girlfriend who practically buys the whole place out." Bride looked back at Ash. "You're one of these weirdos, too, huh?"

"Guilty," Ash said, offering her a charming smile.

"Great," Bride breathed. "Anyone else I need to know about?"

The room's occupants looked around sheepishly.

Vane stood up and faced Ash. "What do you know about Alastor?"

"That he's leashed. Your mother bargained with him to kidnap the mates of you, Fury, and Fang. It's a one-way ticket. He took Bride to your mother and there's nothing she can do to negotiate with him anymore."

"Are you sure about that?"

Ash folded his arms over his chest. "I can put my personal guarantee on it."

"Then he'll be back whenever Fang mates?" Fury asked.

"Yes," Ash said. "And to answer your next question, yes again. He'll come for your mate, too."

Fury cursed.

"Sorry," Ash said. "But look on the bright side; your mother puts the 'fun' in dysfunctional."

"You're not amusing, Ash," Vane said. "I thought you were going to protect Bride for me."

"I had intended to, but didn't have time. Even I can't be in two places at once."

"Pity," Vane said. "If you knew about Alastor, couldn't you have told me about it before this?"

"You haven't exactly been talking to me these last few months, Vane. Besides, it's not wise to interfere with the order of fate."

"I hate it when you start that fate crap. This is me, Acheron, not one of your friggin' Dark-Hunters. I know what you are and I know what you can do. Damn you for playing with us."

Fire snapped in Acheron's eyes. "I'm not playing with you, wolf, and you better pray I never do."

By the look on Vane's face, Bride could tell he wanted to strike out at Ash, but knew better than to try.

"What else do you know that you're not telling me?" Vane asked him.

"Tons of stuff. The ultimate fate of the world. The next president. If the Saints will win this weekend. Hell, I even know the lottery numbers for tonight."

"Really?" Tabitha asked, perking up. "Want to share? Come on, Ash, I need the Powerball numbers. Please. Please, please share! I'll even let Simi eat all the popcorn if you tell me."

Ash snorted, then turned toward Kyrian, Amanda, and Tabitha. "I think Vane needs some time alone with his brother and mate to talk."

Tabitha whined. "Ash, give me those numbers!"

He looked at Tabitha drolly. "Six."

Tabitha held up her hands and motioned to him for more. "And?"

"There's definitely a six somewhere in the winning numbers."

"Oh, you suck, big time," Tabitha said, pouting for a second before she shrugged it off good-naturedly. "Well, now that we know Ash really is cruel and Vane isn't a serial killer, I guess I better get back to my store." She paused by Ash's side. "We still on for the movie Friday night?"

Ash nodded. "I'll be there, same as always."

"Cool, see you then." Tabitha made a quick exit.

Kyrian stared at him with his mouth agape. "You're dating Tabitha?"

Ash gave him a crooked grin. "No, but I find her highly entertaining. She screams the most fascinating things at the movie screen and eats more popcorn than Simi. I have to say, Tabby is definitely one of my favorite people."

"You're a sick man, Ash," Kyrian said as he headed for the back of the house.

"I think you're wonderful," Amanda said before she reached up and pulled his head down toward hers. She kissed Ash on the cheek. Releasing him, she turned in the direction Kyrian had headed off and raised her voice. "And my husband will be sleeping in the guest room for the next couple of nights."

The baby started crying upstairs.

"I've got her," Ash said, vanishing instantly.

Amanda paused by the couch. "I'll be in the kitchen if anyone needs anything."

"Sure," Bride said. "You going to just poof out of here, too, Amanda?"

"I don't have that ability." She touched Bride's hand comfortingly. "I know how you feel, Bride. I really do. Like you, I thought my sister was a screaming loon, and have found out over the last couple of years that she is strangely wise. Just take deep breaths and believe in the impossible." She offered an encouraging smile to them, then left them alone.

"Well," Fury said as he rubbed the back of his neck. "I guess this is where you give me the heave-ho and I head out. You guys have a nice life."

"Wait," Vane said, standing up. "You really didn't betray me, did you?"

"No. I only planned on betraying Stefan and his group to the Arcadians. It was a moral imperative that I screwed with their heads, not yours." He watched Vane warily. "I'll be honest though, Vane. I hate you and you piss me off to no end. You always have."

"Why? What did I ever do to you?"

"You have no idea," Fury said, his expression cold and angry. "Mom wasn't always that nutcase you met. At least she wasn't to me."

Fury met Bride's gaze. "I'm really sorry for what she

did to you, Bride. But you have to understand what the Katagaria took from them. After she was kidnapped by my father, they sent all their strati out to find her. While they were gone from the village, another Katagaria pack came in and slaughtered every child they could find. They raped and murdered most of the women. Those who survived only did so because they fought them off, and most of them, like our grandmother, were never right again. That's why you didn't see that many women in the town."

Fury sighed and turned back to Vane. "You don't know about our Arcadian half. Since the first birthing of our kind, there has been an Aristo in mother's family in every generation. Her older brother, who was killed when she was taken, was one of them. Our grandfather was another. When she returned with me, Dare, and Star, they thought I would be one, too. I had a strange scent to me that they assumed was the power."

"But you're not Arcadian."

Fury shook his head. "I was the yin to your yang. I was a human child, then when I hit puberty, my base form changed to that of the wolf."

Vane winced. He understood his brother a lot better than he cared to. "I'm sorry."

"Oh, you've no idea. You think you had it hard? At least Anya and Fang stayed by you. Protected you. I tried to hide, but the minute Dare found out what I'd become, he told Mom. She went, pardon the bad pun, medieval on my ass."

Vane didn't expect anything less. His father would have done the same to him had he ever learned the truth. "She's a Sentinel. It's her job to kill the Katagaria."

"Yeah, I know. I was too young to fight her off. She attacked me with a vengeance unimaginable and tore me to shreds." Fury paused and flinched, as if the memory were hard for him even now. "I lay bleeding for days as I tried to hide from her and the others. You want to know why I can't command magic worth a damn? No one ever taught me. Markus, for all his shortcomings, at least made sure the three of you were trained after you returned from your year of survival. For a hundred years, I was totally alone. I didn't dare enter a Katagaria den for fear of them smelling the Arcadian scent on me. The only thing I've ever learned to pull off well is camouflaging my scent. For all you know, I could be lying to you now."

Vane stared at him, hard. Dangerously. "You're not."

"How do you know?"

"Ash wouldn't have left you here with me if you were."

Fury scoffed at that. "You put too much faith in a Dark-Hunter who could care less about our kind."

"No I don't. I put a lot of faith in a man who has never been anything other than a friend to me." Vane crossed his arms over his chest. "So why did you come to our den?"

"Same reason you sought out Mom. I wanted to know what the rest of my family was like. I had every intention of telling you who I was, but as soon as I saw how much Markus disdained you and Fang, I figured it would be a mistake."

"You could have told *us*. We would have welcomed you."

"And again, I remind you that Dare, my litter mate

who was my best friend, had already betrayed me. He delivered me up to our mother in chains. I was raised believing that animals are unreliable and unpredictable. But you know what? Animals only kill for two reasons: to protect and to eat. Humans kill for many, many more reasons. In spite of what they think, we're not nearly as dangerous as they are. But you know that, don't you?"

Vane nodded.

Fury sighed and stepped back. "Well, you guys have a nice life or whatever."

"Where are you going?" Vane asked.

Fury shrugged. "Wherever."

"So that's it?" Vane asked. "You're just going to introduce yourself to me as my brother and hit the road?"

"What else is there? You don't want me around. You damn sure don't need me."

Vane frowned at that. Didn't Fury have any idea . . .

No, he didn't. The only family he had ever known had betrayed him. Little wonder his brother hated him. At least he, Fang, and Anya had banded together through any and all threats and obstacles.

Fury had been alone for centuries. He'd always stood back in the pack and never talked to anyone. While other strati formed inner circles of friends and allies, Fury had always remained solitary. For that matter, he had seldom fought to claim a she-wolf.

It must have been awful for him to know they were kin and to never breathe a word of it. How often had Fury watched the three of them laughing together? Seen them huddled together as family against the rest of the pack, while knowing he should have been included in their group?

For that omission of friendship, Vane would feel eternally guilty. He should have sensed the bloodline that bound them together.

Fury really was good at hiding his scent.

"You're my brother, Fury," Vane said sincerely. "Family means something to me. If you know nothing else about me, you should know that."

"Since when am I family?"

"Since the minute we were born and since the second you came to me to warn me about Stefan." Vane held his hand out to him. "I don't need an oath to be bound to you, little brother. We're family."

Fury hesitated, then placed his hand in Vane's. Vane pulled him forward and hugged him.

Bride's throat tightened at the look of pain on Fury's face. It was obvious he had never expected Vane's reaction or his acceptance.

"I won't betray you, Fury," Vane said. "Ever. And if Fang ever comes out, he won't either."

Fury stepped back and nodded.

"And if you walk out that door," Vane said between clenched teeth, "I might have to maim you for it."

Fury laughed. "Okay. I'm here for a while, I guess." He cleared his throat and took a step backward. "You two probably want to talk now. I'll go be in the kitchen with Amanda."

Vane waited until they were completely alone before he turned back to Bride. "Hell of a day, huh?"

Bride sat back on the couch and took a deep breath to help her cope with all the odd events of the last twenty-four hours. "Yeah, oh yeah. We got flying babies, wolf-brothers, psycho moms, serial-killer boyfriends, vampire-killing friends, and I'm not even sure what else."

This was so beyond her ability to cope. "Am I insane?" she asked him. "Really, be honest."

"I wish it were that easy. I wish I could say yes so that you could have Grace fix you, but no, you're not crazy."

She was afraid of that. The question now was, what should she do?

"So let me see if I got everything straight from your mother. This"—she turned her hand over to show the mark—"means that we are somehow meant to be husband and wife. But if I refuse you, you spend the rest of your life impotent and alone? But I, on the other hand, am free to live my life however I see fit?"

He nodded.

"It really sucks to be you, doesn't it?"

Vane looked away as a muscle worked in his jaw. "I don't expect you to accept me, Bride. I never did. I mean, I hoped for about an hour or two, but I'm not stupid and I don't live in the world of . . . well, okay, I do live in a world of fantasy, but I've never deluded myself."

He knelt on the floor before her, took her hand in his and kissed her palm. Oh, he was so tender with her. So kind. She curled her fingers against his warm, whiskered cheek.

How could she leave a man like this?

He's not human.

Not fully, anyway. And he lived in a terrifying world of magic and mystery and scary monsters capable of all manner of cruelty.

"What do you want, Vane?" she asked, desperate to know. "Be honest with me. Do you want me simply because of this?" She held her palm out to him. "Or do you want *me*? I mean, you don't really know me, do you? Nor do I know you. I know you're a great guy in a pinch and that you have a family that makes the Addamses look normal. But I don't know the real you."

He took her hand from his face and held it in his callused one, staring up at her with those piercing hazel-green eyes. "The truth is, I don't know. I've never wanted any female the way I want you, Bride. But I honestly don't know if it's the mark or not. I don't."

At least he had told her the truth. That was definitely one thing in his favor. He'd never once lied to her.

"How long do I have to make a decision on this?" she asked.

"Two weeks. Roughly. Barring any further demon or mother interference."

"Then how about we try and act normal?" She burst out laughing at the ludicrousness of that statement. Yeah, they were just Jack and Jill Average climbing the hill to hell. She only hoped Jack didn't break his crown or that she went tumbling after.

Bride sobered. "Okay, at least we can pretend to be normal. Let me see the real *you* in all your strangeness so that I know what I have to look forward to and then I'll decide if I can handle it all without going totally insane."

He looked stunned by her suggestion. "You're not just running away from me?"

"I probably should and I can't imagine why I'm even considering this. But I do like what I know about you,

Vane, and I guess everyone has problems. Not as profound as yours, mind you, but at least with you, when I tell people that my boyfriend is a dog, it's not just a figure of speech."

He chuckled at that.

Bride squeezed his hand. "So give me your worst, wolf. I'll give you mine, and at the end of two weeks, we'll see where we are."

Vane couldn't believe her. She was too good to be true. In all honesty, he had expected her to scream at him and run out the door, calling all of them loons.

But she was giving him a chance.

And that was something he hadn't had in a very long time . . . Hope.

Joy burst through him at the thought that she might actually stay with him. "There's so much I have to tell you."

She cringed. "You're not going to suck my blood, are you?"

Damn. She would pick that one thing to fear. Well, it was pointless now to keep anything from her. Better he lay it all out for her than she get pissed because he withheld something from her. As his mate, she deserved to have her questions answered. "I don't have to, no."

She looked at him suspiciously. "What do you mean, you don't have to?"

"My people aren't vampires, but there are two parts to a mating ritual. First is you accept me as your mate."

"How do I do that? Is it like a wedding?"

"To my people it is. Only we do it naked."

Her jaw dropped. "With witnesses? Forget it!"

"No," he said, laughing at her outrage. She was beautiful whenever her cheeks colored. It made her amber eyes glow. "It'll be just us. I lie on my back, we join our marks together, and you take me into your body, then we make our verbal pledges to each other."

She tilted her head as if she were less than sure about his honesty. "That works?"

He nodded. "It's magic."

"Okay, I guess, and then what's the next part?"

"The next is optional and can be done or not done whenever we choose. It's where I combine my life force to yours."

"Why would you do that?"

"Because you're human, and if we don't you'll die in less than a hundred years, while I still have another four to five hundred years left before my old age kicks in."

Bride was completely stupefied as she recalled Bryani's words. At the time she had attributed them to either her insanity or Bryani's. Apparently, it was true, just like the rest of this madness. "You really are four hundred years old?"

"Four hundred and sixty to be exact."

She breathed in slow and easy at that. Dear Lord, what would it be like to live so long? How much could a person see in all that time?

It was mind-boggling.

But more than that came a frightening realization. One that made her heart clench as a horrible panicked grief swept through her. "I would seriously outlive everyone I know," she breathed. "Tabitha, my brother and sister, my cousins. Everyone would be long gone before I even grew old?"

He took a deep breath and nodded. "It's not easy, but you would have me and my family and friends." His expression lightened as if a thought had occurred to him. "Sunshine Runningwolf. You know her, she's immortal."

Bride was shocked by that. She'd known Sunshine for years. "Sunshine's immortal?"

"Yes."

"Get out! Since when?"

"Always. Both she and her husband are."

Wow! Who knew the woman who sold her the art Bride had hanging in her store and her little apartment was immortal?

She paused at that thought. Now wait a second . . . that wasn't fair!

"Why can't we be immortal?"

Vane shrugged nonchalantly. "Because my people aren't. We have long lives, but they are finite." His grip tightened on her hands. "There are some drawbacks, though. If you decide to bond with me, I will have to take your blood and you will have to take mine. A blood exchange is the only way to do it. Secondly, if one of us dies, we both do."

She went pale. That was a scary thought.

Well, then again, compared to other things in Vane's world, that was probably one of the more minor concerns.

"But you don't have to, Bride," he hastened to assure her. "Both decisions are yours alone to make."

She took a deep breath as she considered all of it. This was one helluva commitment Vane was asking from her. It took "until death we do part" to a whole new level.

But as she looked at him still kneeling on the floor, she couldn't help but wonder how bad life with this man could be. He was considerate and giving. A rarity in her world.

It was worth a two-week shot, at any rate.

"Okay," she said slowly. "Now for my part of this. If we do mate, I want a human wedding. My parents won't understand anything less than that and I'm not sure if I want to tell them about all this."

"That's fine."

"That means you're going to have to meet my parents, Vane."

"Okay. They can't be as scary as mine."

"Well, they're not homicidal as a rule, but they are protective of me."

"I love them already."

Bride gave a nervous laugh at his small, playful grin. "You know, I always thought I would meet some guy and date him for a year or two and then have him go down on his knee somewhere romantic to ask me to marry him. I never dreamed this would be my engagement." She toyed with a lock of his hair. "I guess life is never what we want it to be, is it?"

Vane cringed inwardly at her words. He'd never meant to alter her life so horrendously. He'd only wanted to touch her for a moment.

To have her touch him.

Maybe this was cruel, and yet his heart didn't want him to leave. It only wanted her.

Both the animal and the man in him craved nothing more than to be touched by this woman.

"I'll do anything to make you happy, Bride."

Bride tightened her grip in his hair. In that moment, she felt as though she might actually love this man. At least she knew that she could.

But she had been burned and she didn't know Vane very well. She only had two weeks to learn about him. What she knew so far was terrifying . . . and wonderful.

She only hoped he wouldn't lie or deceive her. If he showed her the real Vane and that man-wolf was honest, then she could accept him.

Her worst fear was that at the end of the two weeks, she would mate with him and he would become the psychotic, harsh animal his mother spoke of.

What would she do then?

Taylor had been wonderful in the beginning of their relationship. He'd even bought her chocolates for their first Valentine's Day.

Over time, he'd become a total ass. Would Vane do the same?

And four hundred years . . . that was a really long time to spend with someone.

Not if you love them.

Maybe that was true.

The least she could do was try. And hope.

"So where do we go from here?" she asked him.

"I have to find someplace to keep you so that if I have to leave you, you'll be safe."

"And my store?"

"I'll get someone to run it for you."

That sounded just a little too easy. "How?"

"I'll ask Acheron for another favor. They have humans who help the Dark-Hunters. They run a lot of the local businesses here in New Orleans and I'm sure they can send one of them over there to keep the shop open for you. The greatest benefit is if one of my people comes calling, they'll know how to handle them."

"All right, then. Let's begin our hand-fasting and see how this will all work."

Vane stood up and held his hand out to her.

Bride hesitated. She had never feared the future before, but she did now.

Taking a deep breath for courage, she placed her hand in his and let him pull her to her feet.

She expected him to lead her to the kitchen. Instead, he flashed her into the nursery.

"You know," she said, feeling light-headed from their "trip." "Feet work well."

Vane laughed. "You said you wanted me to be myself. I prefer the flash-mode of transportation. It's a lot quicker."

Ash sat in an old-fashioned white wooden chair, rocking the baby who was snoozing in his lap while he watched them curiously. He held a half-empty bottle of milk between his legs while the baby, dressed in a pink jumper, sucked on her tiny fist in the shelter of his arms. There was something so incongruous about that image that Bride couldn't help but stare.

A man decked out in black leather and chains with long red and black hair and a dagger earring in his left ear definitely didn't look like someone who should relish caring for an infant. And yet there he sat in the frilly pink room peacefully cradling the baby. Ash ought to look completely out of place and yet he seemed at home here.

"I've already called Jessica Adams to take over the boutique," Ash whispered to them. "She just needs to know where the paperwork is, where the keys to the store are kept, and what bank to make the deposits in."

"Damn, you're good," Vane said.

Ash gave a cocky grin. "The absolute best."

Vane shifted his weight. "Then you know—"

"Here's the address." Ash held his hand up and a business card magically appeared between his first two fingers. He handed the card over to Vane, who stepped forward to take it. "You'll be safe there. Trust me, he's more paranoid than an Apollite commune. Nothing is going to get into his place."

Vane looked down at the name on the card and froze. "Will he be all right with us there?"

Ash shrugged. "His house is big enough. Just try to stay out of his way." He looked past Vane and offered Bride a smile. "He's a bit hard on the nerves, Bride, but Valerius is a good man so long as you don't mention Kyrian's name to him. He'll make sure nothing happens to you."

"Valerius?" she asked.

Vane let out a slow breath, then turned to face her. "He's a vampire with serious attitude."

Chapter 10

When Bride told Vane to do his worst and to let her see the real man . . . er, wolf . . . she'd had no idea just what she was letting herself in for.

He seldom did anything normal and she was beginning to appreciate how much effort he'd used to stay in the "normal" world for her when he'd pretended to be her wolf.

After leaving Ash, they'd gone downstairs to gather up Fury. One minute she'd been telling Amanda that she'd call her and the next, they were inside another house.

"I really wish you'd give me some warning before you do that," she said to Vane as she looked around to get her bearings.

They were in a huge living room that was twice as large as the one in Kyrian's home. The whole house was completely dark and tomblike. Sterile. Cold. The room had expensive, hand-carved mahogany paneling and was filled with more antiques than Bride had ever seen in one place before. Not to mention the marble floor with its intricate Roman-style pattern. It was like touring a European castle. Or a mansion. Everything she could see bled good aristocratic breeding and taste.

Unlike Kyrian's house, there was nothing modern or comfortable here. No stuffed sofas, no television, no obvious phones or computers. Nothing. Even the books lining the exquisite bookshelves appeared to be leatherbound antiques. The sofa was obviously from the Georgian era and had very little padding underneath the burgundy fabric.

But the strangest thing of all was the statuary. Statues of two women who appeared to be nude Roman nymphs flanked the winding staircase. The fact that they were antiques wasn't what was odd, it was the bright red pasties that covered their stone-white nipples.

"What in the world?" she asked.

Fury burst out laughing as he saw them.

"Jeez, Vane, call before you drop in. You're lucky I didn't shoot your ass."

Bride turned to see a tall, darkly handsome man enter the room. He had shoulder-length black hair, sharp dark brown eyes, and about three days' worth of beard.

Dressed in a loud orange Hawaiian shirt and ripped jeans, he carried himself like a man who knew he could kill anyone who came near him.

"Is he the vampire?" Bride asked in a low tone.

"No," Vane said as he looked at the man in disbelief. "He's Mafia. Otto, what the hell are you doing here? Dressed like that? What the hell happened to your clothes? You look like you're morphing into Nick Gautier."

"Suffering in eternal damnation," Otto said, scratching at his beard as he neared them. "They transferred my ass over here, against my wishes I might add, to serve Dickhead Rex because he has to have someone who speaks Latin *and* Italian. God forbid the man have a normal plebeian Squire who just speaks English. Oh no, we must have one with *breeding*." Otto sounded much like Alfred Hitchcock with that last word.

"So why are you dressed like Nick?" Vane asked.

"Just to piss him off. It's truly the only thing that keeps me sane around here."

Vane burst out laughing. "Let me guess, you the red pasties man?"

"Oh, hell yeah. I can't wait till he gets up and freaks over that one." Otto deepened his already low baritone voice and added in an accent that was almost Italian but not quite, "Do not touch nor even breathe upon the statuary, Squire. Unlike you, it's priceless." His voice went back to normal. "Nah, priceless will be his face when he sees it tonight."

This time it was Fury who laughed. "I don't know you," he said, walking toward Otto with his hand extended, "but I can already tell we're going to be friends. Fury Kattalakis."

"Otto Carvalletti." He shook Fury's hand, then looked back and forth between the two wolves. "You two related?"

"Brothers," Vane said.

"Cool," Otto said, turning toward Bride with a charming smile. "You must be Bride." He took her hand as well and she noted he had a black spiderweb tattoo over the back of his knuckles. "Welcome to the madness that is our world, my lady, though personally, I think you're insane for wanting to be here."

Otto kissed her hand and bowed low before her. The action elicited a deep growl from Vane which Otto chose to ignore. "By the way, Bride, you can relax. I am technically human, though my multitude of siblings would deny it. And barring the pasties, I'm really not some sicko. When you meet my boss, you'll fully understand why I have to rattle his cage."

Otto headed for the stairs. "If one of you good wolves would howl, I could do the whole 'the children of the night, what music they make' speech." He looked back at them when neither Vane nor Fury howled. "Or not. Okay, mental note to self that the wolves have no sense of humor or have never read *Dracula* or seen one of the movies. No problem. Follow me and I'll show you to your rooms. One quick rundown of the rules. We try to be as quiet as possible in the daylight so as not to wake Count Penicula."

"Penicula?" Bride asked.

"My pet insult for Valerius. Much like the good Roman general who owns this house, it's a combination of penis and Dracula."

Bride would have laughed, but had a feeling it would only encourage Otto to be bad.

They followed Otto up the stairs.

"When did you get so chatty, Carvalletti?" Vane asked. "I always thought you were a man of few words."

"I normally am, but I've been locked in this mansion

for so long now that I'm going stir-crazy. I'm thinking I should have stayed up in Alaska. Hell, I've even been talking to Nick just to break the monotony."

Otto paused on the stairs to look at them. "Valerius isn't a Dark-Hunter, he's a life-sucking Daimon out to bleed me dry. No wonder his last Squire quit. I keep putting in for a transfer and my father keeps telling me to be a man and take my assignment with dignity. I swear, that man better not get feeble or I'm locking him up in the worst retirement home I can find."

"Dog, and I thought I had issues with my parents," Fury said from behind Bride. "Mine just want to kill me and put me out of my misery, not add to it."

"Yeah," Otto said from the top of the stairs. "You're lucky. I wish mine *would* kill me."

Otto led them down a hallway while Vane leaned over and spoke in her ear. "Don't let Otto's current bizarreness fool you. He was valedictorian at Princeton."

She gaped.

"And I had a brain until this place killed it. You try dealing with Valerius and Nick and you too will find yourself regressing into infancy in a matter of days. But whatever you do, don't tell Master Valerius that I ever stepped foot onto Princeton soil. He thinks I dropped out of the Barbizon School of Modeling."

Bride laughed, then looked at Vane. "So this is the world you're bringing me into? No offense, but these people are really nuts. We have a Princeton graduate who dresses like Don Ho putting pasties on statues, a brother-in-law who's a dog—"

"Yeah, but don't forget, Tabitha came with you," Vane

reminded her. "You have your own share of nutcases."

She held her hands up in surrender. "Okay, but that's only one nut I came with."

"And your dad neuters for a living," Fury said from behind them. "I think that's the sickest thing I've ever heard of."

"Want to go visit my parents, Fury?" Bride asked.

"I'll pass."

Otto opened a door that led to a huge bedroom with the most elaborate antique canopied bed Bride had ever seen. Deep blue velvet curtains hung around the hand-carved cherubs and angels that decorated the ancient wood. "This is magnificent."

"Valerius insists on the best. You two can bunk in here, and I'll take dog-boy farther down the hallway."

"Hey!" Fury snapped indignantly.

"Relax," Otto said. "It's not like I'm making you sleep in the garage or anything."

The two of them left Bride and Vane alone in the room.

"So here we are," Bride said, unsure of herself.

Vane pulled her close. "It's weird not to have to hide myself from you."

"So what all can you do?"

"Just about anything. I can travel through time in any direction. I could flash us from here to Paris or anywhere else you'd like to visit."

Bride considered that. She could have anything, but there was only one thing that would make her really happy. "Can you make me thin?"

Vane looked less than pleased. "I could."

"Do it."

He frowned at her as if the request completely baffled him. "Why?"

"Because I've always wanted to be one of those tiny little women and I never have been."

He moved to stand behind her so that he could pull her against him and hold her close. "I don't want you skinny, Bride. I like you as you are." His breath tickled her neck as he spoke and sent heat all over her. "My people have a saying. Meat is for the man, the bone is for the dog."

"Yeah, but you're both."

"And when given a choice between ribs and steak, I go for top choice every time."

Bride hissed as he placed his lips against her neck and nibbled her. She closed her eyes and inhaled the warm, masculine scent of him. He felt so good holding her. It made her weak and breathless.

"Is this all there is between us, Vane? Just sex?"

He laid his cheek against hers in such a loving gesture that it tore through her heart. "No, Bride. Sex is just the physical demonstration of what I feel for you." He took her hand and led it to his heart where she felt it pounding against her palm. "No one has ever touched me like you do. You're like a whisper. Gentle, soft. Soothing. In my world, the people only shout and scream. But you . . . you're my haven."

She shivered at his poetic words. "God, you're good."

"It's not a line, Bride. I may be human, but I'm also an animal and the animal in me doesn't lie or deceive.

I never thought that part of me would be tamed, but it is now. It doesn't want to lash out at anyone. It just wants you."

How could a woman say no to that?

Bride gasped as her clothes vanished. "Vane?"

Before she could get his name out, they were both lying naked in the bed, under the covers.

"That's some talent you have there," she said as he nuzzled her neck.

"You've no idea," he breathed in her ear before he licked it.

Bride's head swirled at the ecstasy of his touch. For once he didn't waste any time with her. He slid himself inside her with one forceful thrust.

They moaned in unison.

Bride looked up into the raw pleasure on his face. This wasn't playtime to him, he was most serious about taking her.

She slid her hands over his back, feeling his muscles ripple as he thrust into her, strong and powerful. He was the wolf and he was hungry. His green eyes devoured her.

Vane couldn't think straight as he felt her softness under him. The animal in him wanted complete possession. It wanted to mate and to dominate.

The man in him wanted her tenderness. Her heart.

Most of all, he wanted to spend the rest of his life staring into her amber eyes. They were dark now with passion. Her lips were slightly parted as she panted with pleasure.

Vane claimed that mouth. He growled at the taste of her. At the sensation of her tongue against his while he thrust himself deep inside her over and over again.

Famished for her, he forced himself to be easy with her body. To remember that she was human and frail.

He would die if he ever hurt her.

But oh, the feel of her hands on his back. The way she clutched at his ass. She didn't just screw him. She made love to him. And that meant more to him than anything else.

Even if he were immortal, he would never feel anything better than her long, smooth legs entwined with his.

Bride was breathless as Vane devoured her. No man had ever made love to her like this . . . as if he couldn't get enough of her. As if he were desperate to be inside her body.

There was so much power and strength in the arms wrapped around her. Arms that held her tenderly. Carefully.

Every forceful stroke pounded pleasure through her.

"I love the way your hands feel on me," he breathed raggedly as she cupped his rear. "And I love being able to take you like this."

"Like what?"

"Face-to-face," he said, punctuating each word with a deep, lush stroke. "So that I can feel your breasts on my chest. See your expression when you come for me."

He kissed her then. It was masterful and devouring. Fulfilling.

Bride was completely swept away by him. By the intense pleasure of him so thick and full inside her. The way he felt sliding against her body.

Vane let his powers flow through both of them. There was no longer any need to harness them or mask them. He let their passion fuel his powers, charging them to their highest level.

The sensation of it went through him like lightning, heightening every aspect of her flesh against his.

He knew the minute she felt the swell of his powers. She threw her head back in ultimate ecstasy. Her breathing ragged, she met him stroke for stroke.

And when she came, he had to shield her scream with his powers to keep the others from knowing what they were doing.

He smiled at the sight of her lost in the throes of her orgasm. At the feeling of her hands on his back as she gripped him tight.

Then Vane let himself join her. He growled as he released himself inside her. He lay on top of her, panting while his body continued to shiver and spasm.

All the while she played with his hair and held him close.

"That was incredible," Bride breathed. Then she frowned. "You do get bigger toward the end, don't you?"

"Yes," he said, nibbling her lips, "and I can't pull out of you for a few more minutes without hurting you."

Bride could still feel his body quivering. "Why do you do that and how did you keep me—"

"I used a time spell so that you weren't aware of how long it took me to finish." He hissed as another wave of orgasm went through him.

Vane half-expected her to be repulsed. She wasn't.

Instead, she cradled his head to her and toyed with his hair until he was completely spent.

When he was finally finished, he slid himself out of her and collapsed by her side.

She turned to face him. "So this is what you're really like?"

Vane nodded and waited for his heart to stop pounding. She draped herself over his chest and kissed his right nipple. He growled as she gave a light, playful lick to it.

"If you keep doing that, we'll be in this bed for the rest of the day."

Bride scoffed. "I know you men. You'll need at least a few hours to . . ." Her voice trailed off as she felt him hardening against her thigh.

"I'm not human, Bride. Sex invigorates us. It doesn't make us tired."

She lifted the sheet to see the truth of that statement. He was already hard again. "So I can play with you as much as I like?"

"Um-hmmm. I'm all yours, pet."

Biting her lip, Bride slid her hand down to cup him gently and to explore the entire length of him. Since Taylor had never made love to her with the lights on or in daylight, she'd never really had a chance to examine a guy up close before.

He bent one leg up and said nothing while she gently learned every nuance of his body.

Vane watched her closely while he played with the tendrils of her hair. He'd never had a woman so curious about him. She-wolves didn't care what a male looked like so long as he could please her. Once the act was over, their females pushed them away and left. There was no sharing of bodies. No care given to caress and to love. To nurture.

That was what he cherished most about Bride.

Her fingers tenderly examined him. She carefully massaged his sac and his cock. Chills spread over him. His outstretched leg actually twitched.

Bride giggled as she continued to stroke him. "Like that, do you?"

"Yes," he said raggedly as he felt his cock harden even more.

She looked up at him, then did the unimaginable. She took him into her mouth.

Vane threw his head back and buried his hand in her hair as pleasure racked him. He locked his jaw to keep from howling as she licked and teased him from the base to the tip. She slid him deep into her mouth as she sucked and played.

He cupped her face in his hands while his entire body burned. The unselfishness of this act . . .

He hadn't known such a thing existed. A Katagari female would sooner die than touch a male like this. It was the male's job to satisfy the female, not the other way around.

Bride groaned deep in her throat as she tasted the very essence of Vane. She looked up to see him watching her, his eyes hooded with pleasure and disbelief. It was a heady combination.

He looked as if she were showing him heaven. He brushed the hair back from her face, then stroked her cheekbone with his thumb while she tongued the underside of him.

She felt the air around them literally sizzle. She paused at the sound.

"It's okay," Vane said breathlessly. "It's just my powers surging. They do that sometimes."

She returned to him.

Vane ground his teeth as his pleasure built to an unbelievable high. Any second, he was going to come again. Afraid of hurting Bride, he pulled her away from him an instant before his body exploded.

It wasn't the only thing. Every lightbulb in the room shattered with the force of it as his powers played havoc in the room.

He covered himself with the blanket and used his hand to help his body as it orgasmed.

He felt Bride's hand on his. Opening his eyes, he watched as she took him into her hand and gently milked him until his body was completely drained.

"You didn't have to pull me away, Vane," she said after a few minutes.

"I double in size when I come, Bride. I didn't want to see you get hurt by it."

She pulled her hand away from him and kissed his lips.

Vane held her close to him, cherishing this novel moment with her.

She pulled back to look at the shattered bulbs. "I hope our host isn't too—" She broke off as he repaired every bulb with his powers.

"That is some talent you have there."

He smiled wickedly at her. "I prefer yours."

She was confused by that. "I don't have any talent."

"Yes you do. That mouth of yours is definitely magic."

"Mmm," she said, kissing him again. "But it only works for you."

"Good."

Bride pulled back as she realized something. "Wait a minute. You can't ever cheat on me, can you?"

He shook his head. "Without you, I'm a total eunuch. My powers would lessen, too. Once sex is taken away from us, we have no way to recharge our energy. Eventually we lose all our magic."

"Then how is your father the leader of your pack if he can't wield magic?"

He frowned. "How did you know my father was our leader?"

"I heard the medieval people talking about it."

Vane took a long, deep breath before he explained it to her. "He became the pack's leader before I was born. The only reason he's still in charge is that he's extremely strong physically as a wolf and he makes deals with the Daimons for magic."

"Daimons?"

"Vampires. Unlike your television and movies, the real vampires don't thrive on human blood, they thrive on human souls. If they take the soul of a Were-Hunter or a psychic human they can then absorb their powers. Daimons who are truly powerful are able to share that power with someone else. My father routinely makes sacrifices to them so that they'll leave his pack alone and siphon off a bit of their magic to him."

"Sacrifices?"

He sighed as if the thought pained him. "He pretends someone has betrayed the pack and singles them out to be left for the Daimons. My brother Fang and I were the last sacrifices he made. I knew he'd send assassins out to kill us once the Daimons didn't return to share power with him."

She couldn't imagine anything worse than that. His father had sacrificed him to die. His mother hated him and would gladly kill him, too.

Her poor wolf. No wonder he had come to her.

"Oh Vane, I'm so sorry."

"It's okay. I'm only surprised my father waited so long to set us up. I think the only reason he didn't do it sooner was that for all his faults, he loved my sister, Anya, more than anything, and she loved us. So long as she lived, I don't think he wanted to hurt her by killing us. But the instant she died . . ."

"He came after you?"

He nodded.

She pulled his head to her breasts and held him there, wanting to make it all better, knowing she couldn't. But at least Vane seemed to be at peace with the past and with his parents and their unreasoning hatred of him. His strength amazed her. She didn't know of any other man who could have had his past and his pain and be so compassionate and loving.

"What was it like in your commune?" she asked, wondering what other scars he hid with such dignity.

"I don't know. We live like animals. We stay mostly in wolf form unless we head into the cities for something."

"Like food?"

"Or sex. Sex is much more enjoyable as a human than as a wolf. There's a lot more stimulation, especially for our females."

That was something she didn't want to consider. She didn't like thinking about Vane with anyone else. But at least she didn't have the fear of him cheating on her. There was much to be said for that. Her own sister was currently going through a divorce over that very thing.

"So you pretty much live out your lives as wolves?" she asked.

He nodded. "For the Katagaria it's really easy since the wolf is their base form. It's what they default to whenever they rest or are hurt."

"But you're Arcadian."

She could tell by the way he stiffened that it bothered him. "Yeah. So for me, it was unrelenting torture to maintain a wolf form. One of the reasons I'm so strong magically is that I had to learn to channel my powers so that I could remain a wolf while I was fighting, injured, or sleeping. Things that I should do as a human."

"And the tattoo on your face?"

"It's more like a birthmark." He let out a deep breath and it reappeared on his face.

Bride traced the scrolling pattern that was oddly beautiful.

"Sentinels are Arcadian guardians," he explained. "Once an Arcadian is finished with puberty, the Fates choose who they think is strong enough to guard the world from the Slayers or animals who are out to prey on Arcadians and humankind."

She winced as she understood what he was telling her. "So you were living with wolves when you became human and then you became their worst enemy."

"Yes."

Her heart ached for him. "You must have been terrified. Why didn't you leave?"

"I probably should have, but I was young and frightened. I knew nothing about the Arcadians and even less about humans. Remember, I was a wolf as a child. Our young are never allowed near real humans. I had no idea how to conduct myself or interact with your world. That was why I made a bargain with Acheron to take me into the past to meet my mother. I thought if I told her I was no longer an animal, she would help me adjust."

"But she didn't."

"No. She called me a liar and drove me away."

She could kill Bryani for that. What kind of mother would be so cruel? But then, cruelty existed everywhere in the world even though it shouldn't. "Meanwhile Fury was going through the same thing in reverse."

"Yes."

She didn't know which of them had it worse. It was probably Fury. Unlike Vane, he hadn't had a brother and sister to accept him. "So you went back to your pack after you met Bryani?"

He nodded. "It was all I knew and I couldn't ask Fang and Anya to leave because of me. I figured if my father killed me, at least they would still have a home and be protected."

"And no one ever knew the truth about your base form changing?"

"Just Fang and Anya, and apparently Fury. I should have known when he came to us. But he always kept to himself. Stefan and the others tried to turn him into an omega, but he wouldn't have it. What he lacks in magic, he makes up for in brute strength and willingness to kill anyone who crosses him."

Bride paused, her hand in his hair as she tried to understand his world. "Omega?"

Vane kissed her stomach. "In every pack, there's a scapegoat that the other wolves pick on. It's always a male and he is called the omega wolf."

"That's awful."

He lifted himself up to stare down at her. "It's nature and we're animals. You said you wanted to know me and so I'm answering all your questions about my world, gruesome though things can be."

Bride tried to imagine the Vane she knew being cold and merciless. It was hard when he looked at her with such love and desire in his eyes. "Did you ever pick on the omega?"

He shook his head. "I usually came between the omega and the others. It's why the pack hates me. Fang always thought I was an idiot to bother."

Her heart soared at that. He was a good man, even when he was a wolf. She shouldn't have doubted him. "I don't think you're an idiot. I think you're wonderful."

He kissed her for that.

Someone knocked on the door.

"Hey, Vane," Otto said from the other side. "I meant to tell you two that dinner's in an hour, so if you guys wish to eat with Valerius, be in the drawing room promptly or he'll have a major meltdown."

"Does he want us to dress for dinner?" Vane asked loudly.

"Of course he does, but I'll be wearing Bermuda shorts and a T-shirt."

Vane chuckled. "He's going to kill you, Otto."

"I wish. See you guys later." She heard Otto's footsteps receding down the hallway.

Bride lay back in bed, amazed to realize she wasn't the least bit body-conscious around Vane. She should be, given how ripped he was. But she wasn't.

It was so strange to be with a man who was so accepting of her, faults and all. He didn't try to alter anything about her. It was a great change of pace.

She laid her hand against his whiskered cheek and drank in the sight of his lean, languid handsomeness.

But in the back of her mind was that awful voice that kept whispering "All good things must come to an end."

"Do you believe in eternal love, Vane?"

He nodded. "When you live for hundreds of years, you see all kinds of things."

"How does someone know the difference between that and infatuation?"

He sat up between her legs, then pulled her into his lap to cuddle. "I don't think there is a difference. I think infatuation is like a garden. If tended and cared for, it grows into love. If neglected or abused it dies. The only way to have eternal love is to never let your heart forget what it's like to live without it."

His wisdom stunned her. Bride pulled back to stare incredulously at him. "That is profound, especially coming from a man."

"It was what Anya always said." The sadness in his eyes made her heart clench.

"I wish I could have met her. She sounds like she was a wonderful woman."

"She was."

Bride frowned as an idea struck her. "Can't you go into the past and visit her? Or better yet, save her?"

He placed her head under his chin and stroked her arm. "In theory, yes. But we're not supposed to. Time is a very delicate object and it's not something that should be tampered with lightly. As for saving her, no. The Fates have a nasty way of dealing with anyone who trespasses on their territory. Once a life is ended, they tend to get really upset at anyone who thwarts them."

"You sound like you've made that mistake."

"I haven't. But I know someone who did."

"Fang?"

"No, and I won't betray this person by naming them. Destiny is destiny and no mortal should fight it."

"But how do we know what our destiny is? Am I to be with you or not?"

"I don't know, Bride. The only one I know who could answer that is Ash and he won't."

She found that hard to believe. "Ash is what, all of twenty-one?"

"No. He's eleven thousand years old and is wiser than anyone I've ever known. There's nothing, past, present, or future, he doesn't know. The only problem is he won't share that knowledge. It seriously pisses me off most of the time. He has this tendency to say that we make our future by our decisions, but he knows what we're going to decide before we decide it so why he won't tell us is beyond me."

"Because you learn from your mistakes," she said as she realized the reason. "And if you choose wrongly and it turns out badly, you can't blame him for it because he told you what to do. Likewise, if it turns out well, you can take credit for making the right decision on your own. Good or bad, it's our life to do with as we see fit. Jeez, that little booger *is* smart."

Vane laughed at her words. "He's not little, but the rest is true enough."

She waited for him to ask her what her decision would be regarding them, but he didn't.

Instead, he held her in his arms, as if purely content with this moment. Part of Bride was content as well, but another part of her was scared. What would be the right thing to do?

She wanted to stay with him, but where? She wasn't a wolf to live out in the wild and he wasn't the kind of man to be content owning a store in the French Quarter.

At the end of the day, Vane was wild and untamable. He wasn't just a man. He was a guardian.

And a wolf.

She pulled back to stare up at him. All she wanted was to keep him like this forever.

But could she really tame this man? And did she really, truly, want to spend the rest of her life looking back over her shoulder in fear that his parents or brother Dare would be coming for them or their children?

It was a scary proposition.

And the clock was ticking for them. In a few short days she would have to make a decision that could either make them supremely happy, utterly miserable, or . . .

It could kill them both.

Chapter 11

An hour later Bride made her way downstairs alone. Vane had "created" a very pretty dark emerald velvet dress for her to dine in. He had left her at Valerius's with Fury while he went to Sanctuary to see if one of the Were-Hunters there would either give him word of Fang or perhaps rescind his banishment long enough for him to check on his brother.

Bride smoothed her hair nervously as she came down the stairs. She wasn't sure what to expect from a vampire who hunted Daimons. Unlike Tabitha, she'd never met one before. And it would have helped if Otto hadn't departed the house shortly after Vane.

As she left the stairs, she noted the pasties were gone from the statues. She smiled in spite of herself.

She entered the elegant drawing room to find a tall, black-haired man standing with his back to her as he gazed out the bay windows into the rear courtyard. His stance was rigid, unyielding. He wore his hair pulled back into a perfect ponytail and was dressed in an obviously expensive, tailor-made black silk suit.

He cocked his head as if he sensed her presence.

As he turned around, she paused.

He was an incredibly handsome man. Black eyes stared out of a face that had been carefully sculpted by the right kind of genes. He had a long, aquiline nose and lips that were set in a firm line that was unyielding and harsh. He was, without a doubt, the most intense person Bride had ever met.

No wonder Otto gave him such a hard time. It was obvious this man had no sense of humor and took everything very seriously.

"You must be Bride," he said in that odd Italian accent that Otto had pegged perfectly. "I am Valerius Magnus. Welcome to my home."

With his regal bearing, she felt a momentary impulse to curtsy before him.

"Thank you for letting us stay here."

He inclined his head with the stiff formality of royalty.

"Please," he said, indicating a black velvet-covered armchair. "Be seated. Dinner will be placed promptly on the table in five minutes. I shall have a servant bring you your wine while we wait."

Bride had never been more self-conscious in her life than she was walking across the room to sit in that chair. This vampire did seem ancient and powerful.

Most of all, he was good manners and patrician breeding incarnate.

Valerius moved to an intercom where he pressed a button and did in fact, order her wine.

Once finished, he returned to her side. "I apologize that my house wasn't in order when you arrived."

She looked around the perfectly kept room. "How so?"

"The statuary," he said with only a slight curling of his lip. "You may rest assured that Tony Manero has been properly castigated for his actions." She heard him mutter under his breath, "It's a pity that in this day and age it's illegal to beat your servants."

"Tony Manero?" she asked, amazed a man like Valerius would know the pop culture character from *Saturday Night Fever*.

"Otto," he said disdainfully. "I still can't believe the Council sent him to me. I asked them for an Italian Squire, not an *eye*-talian."

Bride burst out laughing. She couldn't help herself. Oh, Valerius had a sense of humor all right. It was just a very dry one.

His face softened a degree at the sound of her laughter, and at that moment, Bride suspected Valerius wasn't as cold and formal as he appeared. That a secret part of him actually liked sharing laughter, but that his icy demeanor kept it all but alien from him.

Fury flashed into the room, just in front of them. Like her, he was still fidgeting with his clothes, which were a bit rumpled.

"Damn," Fury said under his breath. "One day I'm going to master this shit if it kills me." He looked up and blushed as if he weren't aware he'd already arrived. "Sorry I'm late." He cleared his throat and straightened up.

Valerius arched a regal brow at the Were-Hunter.

"You must be Val," Fury said, extending his hand.

"Valerius," he corrected with an arctic glare. He

looked with derision at Fury's hand and made no move to take it.

Fury lifted his arm and sniffed at his armpit. "What? I bathed." Shaking his head, Fury tucked both his hands into his pockets. "Otto's right. Someone needs to take that stick out of your ass and beat you with it."

Bride covered her mouth to keep herself from laughing at something Valerius obviously didn't find funny. He might like to laugh, but not at himself.

"Excuse me?" Valerius growled, taking a step forward.

"Wine for the lady?"

Bride turned to see an older man dressed in a black coat and tie, entering with a crystal goblet of red wine for her.

Valerius seemed to get himself under control. "Thank you, Gilbert," he said, reverting back to his pompous superiority.

The servant inclined his head. "Would your lordship care for another glass for your new guest?"

Bride could tell that Valerius would rather toss Fury out on his rump, but good manners dictated otherwise. "Yes. But bring it in a bowl."

The servant left to complete his new errand.

"Actually," Fury said, "Bride, I can't really hang here with him looking at me like he's afraid I'm going to piss on his rugs or something. You want to join me for a burger?"

Yes, she did, but there was something about Valerius that said he was wounded by Fury's words. It didn't make sense. Yet there was definitely a degree of hurt hidden in those midnight eyes.

"I think I'll stay."

"Okay, your boredom." Fury flashed out of the room.

"You don't have to stay, Bride," Valerius said quietly. "I'll call for the car and security if you wish to leave."

"No, it's okay, really."

She could have sworn that the air in the room went up at least thirty degrees. Better still, Valerius seemed to relax somewhat over the course of the next two hours. He actually became a bit human.

Bride discovered an extremely funny side to Valerius's views of the modern-day world. She got a full tour of the house and gardens as well as fascinating insights into how Roman royalty lived.

"So this was you?" she asked as they stood outside in his atrium. She was in front of a marble statue of a Roman general in full military regalia. There was no denying the similarity in the facial features between the statue and the man beside her.

"No," he said, his tone chilly for the first time in hours. "He was my grandfather and he was the greatest general of his day." There was pride in his voice, but it was edged by something that sounded strangely close to shame.

"He beat back the Greeks and reclaimed Rome for our people. Indeed, he was the one who destroyed the Macedonian threat and who single-handedly annihilated the greatest Greek general who had ever lived . . . Kyrian of Thrace." Real hatred gleamed in his eyes, but she wasn't sure who it was meant for. His grandfather or Kyrian.

"You mean Kyrian Hunter?" she asked. "The guy with the minivan who lives a few blocks over?"

Valerius's eyes sparked at that. "He's driving a mini-van?" There was no mistaking the humor in his tone.

"Well, yeah. I saw it parked out in front of his house and I know from Tabitha that Amanda drives a Camry."

He didn't say anything else for a few minutes and Bride had no clue as to his mood.

So she gazed up at his grandfather, who commanded attention even centuries later. "You look a lot like him."

"I know and I was expected to follow in his grand footsteps."

"Did you?"

This time there was no mistaking the shame in his eyes before he averted his gaze from her. "When my grandfather died, there were parades for a full week of people who mourned his passage." He lifted his brandy up to his grandfather in a silent salute.

Still, she saw through his façade. "You didn't care for him?"

Valerius looked surprised by her words. "I be-grudged him every breath he took," he said quietly, then changed the subject to discuss his recent move from Washington, DC, to the den of iniquity that most people fondly called New Orleans.

As they headed back toward the house, Vane flashed in beside her.

Bride's heart warmed instantly at his presence.

"Sorry it took so long," Vane said before he kissed her on the cheek. His scent surrounded her, making her heart pound at his presence. It was good to have him back with her.

"They let you see him?"

He nodded.

"Is he any better?" Valerius asked, surprising her with the depth of sincere concern that she heard in his voice. While they had dined, he had told her about the night the Daimons had attacked Vane's pack and how he, Acheron, Vane, and Fang had fought them off.

Most of all, Valerius had told her how the two wolves had reacted at the death of their beloved sister.

How the last sight he'd had of Vane was him carrying his sister's body away for burial.

"No," Vane said with a sigh. "He's still comatose."

"My apologies." Valerius took a step back and inclined his head to them. "Since you are here now, I shall take my leave to attend my duties."

Valerius took three steps, then paused and turned back toward them. "By the way, Vane, you have a most charming mate. It would indeed be a pity for the world to lose such a treasure as she. My sword is ever yours to command and my house is here for you so long as she needs protection."

He turned with an imperious whirl and quickly left them alone.

Bride didn't know which of them was more stunned by Valerius's noble declaration.

"What did you do to him?" Vane asked her.

"Nothing. We just had dinner and toured the house and grounds."

He shook his head in disbelief. "See, you really are magic." He picked her hand up and placed a sweet kiss on her knuckles that made her stomach quiver. Placing her hand in the crook of his arm, "You look lovely tonight," he said, then made a single long-stemmed rose appear out of nowhere.

Bride took it from him and smelled it. "If you're trying to seduce me, Vane, you're a bit late. At this point, I'm pretty much a sure thing for you."

He laughed. "In my world the only thing that I'm ever sure about is that someone is most likely lurking in the next shadow to try and kill me."

She stopped and frowned. "You're not kidding, are you?"

"I wish I were. It's what makes being with you so frightening to me. I can't shake the feeling that I'm going to lose you somehow."

She placed a finger over his lips. "Don't talk like that. Have faith."

"All right," he said, kissing her finger. "Tell me, what would you like to do tonight?"

She shrugged. "I don't care as long as I'm with you."

"You are easy, aren't you?"

"Shh," she said, holding her finger up to her lips. "Don't let anyone else know."

He smiled. "Tell you what. I haven't eaten yet. Want to go grab some beignets and then take a carriage ride around the Garden District with me?"

Bride's eyes actually teared up at his offer. She'd lived in New Orleans all her life and had never taken a carriage ride before. They were terribly expensive. Her father had always thought they were a waste of money for someone who lived in New Orleans, and as a teenager, she couldn't afford the one hundred fifty dollars.

As for Taylor . . .

He'd been too concerned that someone would see

him and laugh at a "respectable" anchorman doing something so childish.

"I would love to."

"Good." He leaned down and kissed her deeply.

When he pulled back, she found herself standing in the shadowed back area of the French Market, a few feet from the legendary Café Du Monde.

"Don't worry. No one saw us." He winked at her.

"You do have a motorcycle. I have seen it, right?"

"Yes. But Amanda and Grace said that you wouldn't want to ride with me while you're in a dress."

She looked down at the expensive green velvet. "Come to think of it, I'm not really dressed for beignets, either."

"Don't worry. I can promise you that you won't get a single powder stain on your dress."

"You can do that?"

He gave her a cocky grin. "Baby, there's not much I can't do."

"Then lead on, Sir Wolf."

Vane led her to a small table just to the side of the restaurant. As soon as they sat down a waiter came over to take their orders.

"I'll have an order of beignets and a chocolate milk, please," Bride said.

"Four orders of beignets and a café au lait."

Bride gaped at him. "You're going to eat all that?"

"I told you I was hungry."

She shivered as the waiter left them. "I hope Arcadians don't get diabetes."

"We don't. We're strangely immune to everything

but the common cold and a couple of weird diseases that are unique to my race."

"What kind of diseases?"

"Nothing you need to worry about. The worst is one that takes away our ability to use magic."

She shuddered at that and tried to imagine Vane without his powers. It would most likely kill him. "Is that what's wrong with your mother? She said she couldn't travel through time."

"No, that was my father's doing. After she castrated him and before his own powers dried up, he jerked a lot of her powers from her to make sure she didn't come back to kill him."

Bride closed her eyes in sympathetic pain. "Good grief, they had the relationship, huh?"

"Yeah. But honestly, it's my mother I feel sorriest for. My father had no business hurting her. He got what he deserved as far as I'm concerned. I just wish there was some way to make her whole again."

Bride took his hand into hers and held it tight. "I can't believe you can show compassion to her, considering what she was willing to do to you."

"It's only because I got to you in time, I assure you. Had they harmed one hair on your head, there wouldn't be one of them left standing right now."

A shiver went down her spine at the lethal tone in his voice. He meant that and she had no doubt he could kill someone.

She leaned back as the waiter returned with their order and placed it on the small, round table.

Bride stared at her three pastries warily.

"They won't bite you," Vane teased. "Watch." He

picked up a napkin and held it underneath the powdered beignet, then took a bite. True to his words, the
powdered sugar didn't go flying like it normally did.

Deciding to trust him, she followed suit and quickly
found that so long as Vane was with her, she could actually eat one of these without making a total mess of
herself.

The thought actually made her giggle.

Bride ate two of hers and sipped her milk while
Vane finished all of his.

"Are you not going to eat that?" he asked.

"I'm full." Then at his suspicious look, she added, "I
swear. Valerius fed me a full five-course meal."

"Good for him. He better feed my woman."

Shaking her head at him, she pushed her beignet toward him. "Go ahead, I know you want it."

He didn't argue.

As soon as he had polished it off, he stood and helped
her to her feet. He draped his arm around her shoulders
and held her close as they strolled across the street to
where the carriages were lined up along Decatur.

Vane led her to the first one and helped her up into
the back. Bride settled herself in comfortably while he
paid the female driver, then joined her.

He cradled her against his chest as the driver gently
urged her mule, Caesar, onto the street, toward the
Garden District.

"Are you two newlyweds?" Michaela, the driver,
asked.

Vane looked at her.

"I guess we are," Bride said. Not sure how else to
answer Michaela's question.

"I thought so. You got that happy-in-love look about you. I can always spot it."

Bride closed her eyes as she inhaled the warm, masculine scent of Vane and considered just how much she would love to gobble him up. She could hear his heart pounding underneath her cheek while the mule's hooves clip-clopped through the French Quarter. Music would occasionally drift out of the buildings and cars they passed: jazz, zydeco, rock, and even a country tune every now and again.

The air held just the hint of a chill to it, otherwise the night was extremely pleasant. Her hometown had never looked more lovely to her. And when she passed the street to her shop, she smiled as she remembered seeing Vane there for the first time.

In some ways it seemed like an eternity ago.

Vane leaned his head down so that his cheek rested on the top of her hair while he cupped her face with his hand.

They didn't speak while the driver pointed out landmarks and buildings.

Vane couldn't breathe as he held Bride. Caressing her skin was like stroking satin. She was so precious to him. He felt as if he had been reborn the day he first saw her with that touch of sadness in her eyes at Sunshine's art stand.

He didn't want to think about a future without her.

While visiting Fang, he had told his brother everything about Bride. He'd hoped that it might bring Fang out of his stupor.

It hadn't.

If anything, it seemed to depress his brother more.

How he wished he knew some way to reach Fang. A part of him felt guilty that Bride made him happy while his brother was so miserable.

But he didn't want to go back to the way he'd been before he'd found her. For the first time in his life, he didn't have to hide himself from his lover. It was so incredible to be completely honest about who and what he was.

She didn't judge him or hate him for things that weren't his fault. She accepted him and that was the greatest miracle of all.

All too soon, the carriage returned to Decatur. Vane got out first, then helped Bride down. He tipped the driver, then took her hand and led her toward the St. Louis Cathedral. "Would you like to go dancing?"

Bride bit her lip at his offer. She hadn't gone dancing in years. "I would love to."

"Do you have a favorite club?"

She shook her head.

"Hmmm, I can't take you to Sanctuary, I'm still kind of banished from it for attacking one of my pack mates. Ash and Simi like to go dancing at someplace called the Dungeon, but knowing their taste in music and clubs, I doubt either one of us would be comfortable there. Nick Gautier hangs at Temptations . . . Then again, knowing Nick, I have a feeling it's probably not a good place for you, either."

"No," she said with a laugh at the mention of one of New Orleans's more renowned gentlemen's clubs. "We could try the Tricou House on Bourbon. Tabitha goes there a lot after work. Of course, she's there looking for vampires to stake, but she says they have great music and food."

"Okay, sounds like a destination."

As they walked down Père Antoine Alley, Vane began to slow his pace.

Bride frowned as he pulled away from her and put her behind him.

"What's the . . ." Her voice trailed off as she saw what appeared to be four blond men with an attractive brunette. At first she thought one of the men was making out with the woman in one of the alcoves, until the other three men saw Vane and cursed.

"Back off, Were-Hunter," one of the men snarled. His sinister gaze went to Bride. "You have too much to lose by fighting us."

"Let her go," Vane said in a deadly voice.

They didn't.

"Stay here," Vane ordered her before he threw his hand out and sent two of the vampires flying.

Before he could move, something bright flashed in the alleyway. Bride held her hand up to shield her eyes as Vane made an inhuman cry.

"Grab his mate," someone said.

She was still blinded by the flash. Someone grabbed her roughly. Knowing Vane would never handle her that way, she gave a vicious kick that contacted with flesh.

The vampire crumpled as he cupped himself.

Another one came at her. Just as she was sure he had her, he disintegrated. The other two ran toward a shadow and then they too were gone.

Bride braced herself to fight the approaching shadow until she realized it was Valerius.

"Are you all right?" he asked her.

She nodded as her sight cleared enough so that she could look for Vane. He was a few feet from the woman, who appeared to be unconscious.

Bride froze as she saw him. He was flashing back and forth from a naked human to wolf and back again.

Horrified, she couldn't move.

Valerius ran to him, pulling out his cell phone. "Acheron, I have a Code Red with Vane at Père Antoine Alley. He was hit by something elec—"

Acheron appeared instantly beside her. "You okay, Bride?" he asked.

She nodded.

Ash flashed from her side to Vane's. He took Vane's head into his hands, and with another bright flash, Vane turned human. Arching his back, Vane cried out as if some horrendous pain were ripping through him.

"Easy," Ash said while Valerius checked on the woman.

Bride ran to Vane, who lay on his back, completely naked now. There were tears in his eyes.

Ash ran his hand over him, and a T-shirt and jeans appeared on his body. Still, Vane didn't move.

"It'll take him a few seconds more to get his bearings," Ash explained to her. He looked to the Roman general. "How's the human, Valerius?"

"She's alive. You take care of Vane and I'll get her to a hospital." Valerius picked her up from the street, cradled her in his arms, and headed toward Royal.

Bride sank to her knees and lifted Vane's head into her lap. His birthmark was back on his face, and his entire body was tense and trembling.

"What happened to him?" she asked Ash.

"The Daimons must have had—and I hate to use the stupid word—a phaser."

"Like in *Star Trek*?"

"Sort of. It's a Sentinel weapon that was developed for the Katagaria. Stronger than a taser, it sends a vicious jolt of electricity through the intended victim. Whenever a Were-Hunter from either division gets shocked, their magic goes berserk and they lose all control of themselves. They can't even hold on to a form. If they get hit with a strong enough jolt, they literally fall out of their bodies and become noncorporeal beings like a ghost."

Vane took her hand in his.

Bride stared down at him and offered him a tentative smile.

"You all right, wolf?" Ash asked him.

Vane was still shaking. "What the hell was that thing set for?"

"Kill would be my guess. But luckily it didn't work."

Ash helped him up slowly.

Vane staggered and would have fallen had Ash not caught him.

"Easy, wolf." Ash reached out and touched Bride, then flashed them into their bedroom at Valerius's.

Worried about Vane, Bride stood back while Ash helped him into the bed. Vane collapsed as soon as Ash released him.

"What can I do to help him?" she asked Ash.

"Nothing really. It'll take time for the electricity to stop bouncing around his cells. Don't move him too much since it tends to make them motion sick in this condition."

"Okay." She let out a relieved breath. "I'm just glad his mother didn't have something like this."

"I'm sure they had it. But knowing Vane, I doubt they had time to use it on him. Weres know to expect phasers from their own kind. It's rare that Daimons use them."

He looked back at Vane. "I should have warned you about that. Since there are so many Weres in New Orleans, the Daimons here are a little more savvy than the rest."

"You suck, Ash," Vane said in a ragged tone.

"And on that note, I'll leave the two of you alone and go back to my patrol. Peace."

As soon as Ash vanished, Bride sat on the edge of the bed, beside Vane.

It was rather strange to see him with the birthmark on his face. She touched it with her hand.

"Did I scare you?" he asked.

"A little," she answered honestly. "But those creatures scared me a lot more. Are they always like that?"

He nodded.

"Dear God, Vane, you live in a very scary world."

"I know."

Bride sat there in silence as various scenarios of how this night could have turned out played through her head. After the way Vane had saved her in the past, she had thought he was impervious to anything.

Now she found out he had a very real, and very dangerous, Achilles' heel.

"How bad a shock does it have to be to do this to you?" she asked. "I mean, will static electricity do it?"

"It won't cause me to change forms, but it's not comfortable. The main thing we have to avoid are shocks from outlets, or any other manmade power sources, and lightning. Some batteries have enough power to change us."

"And it renders you incapacitated?"

He nodded.

Bride closed her eyes as a new fear went through her. This was terrifying since the people who were after him knew exactly what it would take to kill him.

And if they bonded, it would kill her, too.

What if she and Vane had kids one day and this happened? What if Valerius hadn't come along when he did?

Or worse, what if the cops or someone else had seen Vane changing forms like that? They would both be arrested and taken who knew where to be studied and cut up. She'd seen enough episodes of *The X-Files* to know the government didn't take kindly to weirdos in their midst.

"I'm sorry we didn't get to go dancing," Vane said quietly.

Bride ran her hand over his arm comfortingly. "Don't think about it."

However, she couldn't help but think about what had happened tonight.

Did she really want to be a part of his world, where people wielded magic as if it were nothing? Where they popped in and out of rooms, buildings, and such? She would be a human surrounded by . . .

She was terrified of the thought. "Vane? Will our children be like you or like me?"

"Were-Hunter genes are stronger and usually dominant. I just don't know if our children will be Katagaria or Arcadian."

That scared her even more. "So you're essentially telling me I might birth puppies?"

He looked away.

Bride got up as that thought went through her mind. Puppies. Not children. Puppies.

Granted, she knew people who thought of their animals as children. Her parents did, but this . . .

This required a lot more thought before she committed herself.

Chapter 12

Days went by as Bride grappled with what she should do. Part of her was desperate to stay with Vane, while another was terrified of it. So far the tessera hadn't shown, but that didn't mean the two of them could or should relax.

It was now Thanksgiving and she stood in her bedroom in Valerius's house with a knot in her stomach. Her parents had invited her, Vane, and Fury over to their place for the annual McTierney throwdown.

She'd told her family about her new "boyfriend" and had no idea how they would react to him. No one in her family had ever cared for Taylor and his air of superiority. In fact, her father had seldom said more than two words to him whenever she brought Taylor over.

What would they say if they ever found out that Vane and his brother were wolves? Granted, they liked animals, but . . .

Just thinking about it made her nauseated.

Taking a deep breath, she headed downstairs to find Fury and Vane waiting in the parlor.

Fury was dressed in blue jeans, a white T-shirt, and a black leather jacket. Vane wore black jeans and a gray and black V-neck sweater with his white T-shirt showing at the tip of the vee.

"Do I need to change?" Fury asked Vane. "I've never eaten a Thanksgiving dinner before, have you?"

"No. I don't know what to wear, either. We'll ask Bride when she comes down."

Fury rubbed the back of his neck. "Maybe this is a bad idea."

"I don't know why you're bitching, Fury. You were at least raised with Arcadians. I have no idea what a 'family' holiday entails. With the exception of the Peltiers, who are friggin' weird, Katagaria don't exactly celebrate holidays."

"You both look fine," Bride said, entering the room. It was somehow sweet and endearing to know they were as nervous as she was. "Just don't plug anything in if someone asks you to."

Fury gave a nervous laugh at that. Vane looked less than amused as he stood up.

"Don't worry," she assured them. "My parents don't bite. Much."

The wolves exchanged a look that said they weren't so sure about that before Vane offered her his arm and led her toward the door.

Bride paused on the steps of Valerius's house as she caught a look at an elegant metallic-black Jaguar XKR coupe. "Whoa!" she breathed. "Whose car?"

"Otto's," Vane said as he led her toward it. "Since he went home to New Jersey for the holiday, he loaned it out to me for the visit with your family."

"I thought he drove a beat-up red Chevy IROC."

Fury laughed out loud. "He does that to piss off Valerius. He keeps the Jag over at Nick's house for the weekends."

"Otto is so evil," she said with a laugh as Vane opened the door for her and let her in while Fury climbed into the back from the driver's side.

One day, Valerius was going to kill his Squire, who couldn't seem to irritate the Dark-Hunter enough.

Once she was in the car, Vane shut the door and walked to his side. Man, he had a gait that would make any woman pant. Really, no one should be so innately masculine.

He slid in the car in one fluid motion and started it. Bride stared at his hands as he gripped the wheel and stick shift. If Fury hadn't been in the back seat, they probably wouldn't make it to her parents' house after all.

Vane gripped the wheel tight as he listened to Bride's instructions on how to get to her parents' house, which was in Kenner, about twenty-five minutes from Valerius's. He'd never been more nervous in his life. Worse, Fury kept fidgeting in the back seat.

In the back of his mind, he kept telling himself that he had to do this. If he were to stay with Bride, she would want her family to know him. He couldn't very well take her away from the people she loved so dearly. But still, this was awkward as hell for him.

What would they talk about?

Hi, my name's Vane and I howl at the moon late at night in the form of a wolf. I sleep with your daughter and don't think I could live without her. Mind if I have a beer? Oh, and while we're at it, let me introduce my brothers. This one here is a deadly wolf known to kill for nothing more than looking at him cross-eyed, and the other one is comatose because some vampires sucked the life out of him after we'd both been sentenced to death by our jealous father.

Yeah, that would go over like a lead balloon.

For that matter, what would Fury say to them? Vane had already threatened the wolf's life if he embarrassed Bride in any way.

Vane only hoped *he* didn't embarrass her.

This was a major fiasco just waiting to happen.

All too soon, they were pulling into the agate driveway of a new Victorian-style house. There were five cars already parked there.

"My brother and sister," she said before she opened the car door.

"Dum dum dum, duuuum." Fury hummed the tune to *Dragnet* from the back seat.

"Shut up, Fury," Vane said as he got out. Although to be honest, he found Fury's humming a bit calming since it reminded him of Fang's offbeat sense of humor.

Fury climbed out last and stayed back by Vane's side while Bride led them toward the front door.

Vane really did feel like he was walking to his execution. Parents. Eeek.

Bride knocked on the door, then turned to give them an encouraging smile.

Vane offered her a wan one back.

The door opened to show a woman about three inches shorter than Bride, who had the same exact build. Her short black hair was liberally laced with gray and she had an older version of Bride's face.

"Baby!" the woman exclaimed before she pulled her daughter into a tight hug. While she hugged Bride, the woman looked up at him.

Vane felt sick and fought the urge to step back. Not that he could with Fury standing on the stairs behind him.

"You must be Vane," Bride's mother said happily. "I've heard so much about you. Please, come in."

Bride entered the house first. Vane stepped inside and turned as Fury, who had his hands in his pockets, joined them.

"You must be Fury," her mother said, holding her hand out to him. "I'm Joyce."

"Hi, Joyce," Fury said, shaking her hand.

Vane expected the same, but instead Joyce pulled him into a tight hug. She patted him on the back and let go. "I know you two are probably nervous. Don't be. Just make yourself at home and—"

A large black rottweiler came running from the back of the house to jump up at Vane.

"Titus!" Joyce snapped.

The dog ignored her as he lay on his back in a submissive pose. Vane reached down and petted him to let the dog know that he acknowledged his rank and to assert his own alpha status.

"Well, isn't that strange?" Joyce said. "Titus usually tries to eat anyone new he meets."

"Vane has a way with animals," Bride said vaguely.

Her mother smiled. "Good then, you'll fit right in here at the McTierney Zoo."

Titus got up and went to Fury to lick his fingers. Fury

patted the dog's head while Vane looked around the cozy house, which was decorated in a country style. The tan couches were stuffed and piled high with cushions.

An empty bird perch stood in one corner and a giant freshwater fish tank was built into the far wall. Vane heard more dogs out in the yard and something that sounded like an entire collection of birds singing from upstairs.

"The men are out back," Joyce said as she led them toward the back of the house, past three aquariums that held one large boa constrictor, a lizard of some sort, and two gerbils. "Your father has a new stray that came in a few days ago that no one can manage. Poor thing won't eat and it tries to mangle anyone who comes near him."

"What's wrong with him?" Bride asked.

"I don't know. Animal control pulled him out of a ditch where they think someone must have dumped him. He's been badly beaten and had worms real bad."

Vane cringed in sympathy.

They entered the kitchen where a slender, tall blond woman was standing over a mixing bowl. "Mom, how much salt—" Her words ended in a shriek as she turned and saw Bride. "Hey, little girl," she said before she seized her into a tight hug.

Bride hugged her close, then stepped back to introduce them. "Deirdre, this Vane and his brother Fury."

Vane tensed as he fell under the scrutiny of Bride's older sister. She didn't like him. The animal in him sensed it immediately.

Even so, she reached her hand out. "Hi," she said with a fake smile.

"Hi," he said, shaking her hand.

She moved on to Fury, who did likewise.

"I couldn't find those diet cakes for you, Bride," her mother said as she went to the oven to check the turkey. "I'm sorry."

"It's okay, Mom," Bride said. "I'd rather eat your pie anyway."

Her mother looked a bit surprised, but didn't say anything. As she stepped back, two cats came running through the kitchen, chasing each other.

"Professor! Marianne!" her mother called, handing her dishtowel to Bride. "Oh, good grief, I better get them before they run into Bart and he eats them." Her mother ran off outside.

"Bart?" Fury asked Bride.

"The gator who lives in the backyard. Dad fixed him up last year after a poacher almost killed him in a trap, and he keeps getting out of his pen."

Fury scratched his cheek. "Man, I wish I'd known your dad when I got caught in a trap, I'm still . . ." Fury's voice trailed off as he realized Deirdre had turned toward him with an arch look. "Never mind."

"Hey, Bride!"

Vane stiffened as an extremely large, muscular man came barreling through the back door to pick Bride up and squeeze her hard.

Bride laughed. "Put me down, Patrick!"

He growled at her as he did so. "Don't get feisty on me, woman. I'll hold you down and frog your arm."

Bride scoffed at that as Vane saw red.

"You better not touch her."

Bride looked up at the growling sincerity she heard in

Vane's tone. By the expression on his face, she actually feared for her brother's safety. "It's okay, Vane," she hastened to assure him. "He's just teasing. He hasn't really hurt me since we were kids and even then it was an accident."

"That's the story I'm sticking to anyway," Patrick said as he offered his hand to Vane. "I'm glad to see my sister's in good hands. Patrick McTierney."

"Vane Kattalakis."

"Nice to meet you, Vane. Don't worry. I'd cut my arm off before I ever hurt one of my sisters."

Vane noticeably relaxed.

"You must be the brother," Patrick said. "Fury?"

"Hi," Fury said, shaking hands. "I know, the names suck."

Patrick laughed. "You guys want a beer?"

Fury looked to Vane for the answer.

"That'd be great," Vane said.

Patrick ducked into the fridge and pulled out two longnecks, then handed them off.

While they opened them, Patrick stuck his finger into the potato salad.

"Get out of that!" Deirdre snapped, popping his hand with a spoon.

"Ow!" he said, jerking his hand back and then sucking his fingers.

"Get out of here, Pat, or I swear I'll feed your portion to the dogs."

"Fine, you cranky PMS avenger." He motioned to Fury and Vane. "Be wise and join me outside where it's safe."

Vane hesitated.

"Call me if you need me to rescue you from Patrick and my father," Bride said before she lifted herself up on her tiptoes and kissed his cheek.

Vane caught an angry look from Deirdre before he followed Fury and Patrick out into the yard, where Bride's mother was wrestling the cats back toward the house.

Vane handed his beer to Fury before he scooped the female cat up. She tensed for an instant, then relaxed. "You want her in the house?"

Joyce nodded gratefully as she cuddled the male.

Vane opened the door and set the cat back inside. "Don't do that again, Marianne," he said.

She nuzzled his hand, then darted off.

"Thanks for the help," Joyce said as she walked past him.

Vane went back to rejoin Fury and Patrick.

"So, Vane, what do you do for a living?" Patrick asked.

Fury gave him an amused look as he passed his beer back to him.

"I live off the interest from my investments."

"Really?" Patrick asked. "Investments pay enough that you can afford a hundred-thousand-dollar Jag?"

Vane could smell the hostility from Patrick. "No," he said sarcastically, "my drug dealing does that. And I make a tidy profit from my pimps down on Bourbon Street."

The look on Bride's brother's face was priceless. "Look, I'm going to be honest with you. You mess with my—"

"Patrick?"

Vane looked past Bride's brother to see a man who appeared to be in his mid-fifties. Fit and trim, he had neatly styled gray hair and a mustache.

"You're not giving Vane the 'Mess with my baby sister and I'll break your neck' speech, are you?"

"I was trying to."

The man laughed. "Don't mind him. I'm Dr. Mc-Tierney," he said, extending his hand to Vane. "You can call me Paul."

"Nice meeting you, Paul."

Paul turned to Fury. "You must be the brother."

"I hope so, I'm wearing his pants."

Paul laughed.

"So, you're the evil neuter king," Fury said. "I wondered what you looked like."

"Fury," Vane said in warning.

Again Paul laughed. "You know anything about dogs, Vane?"

"Yeah. A little."

"Good. I have one I want you to meet."

"Oh jeez, not Cujo, Dad. That's worse than my speech you interrupted."

Paul ignored his son as he headed toward a fenced-in area in the back where Vane could see a number of doghouses.

As Vane and Fury walked past, the dogs, sensing their animal part, came out to either bark or play.

Paul led them to a cage at the end of the row where an angry Lab mix was kept. The dog was filled with rage and hatred.

"We can't do anything with him," Paul said. "My partner thinks we ought to put him down, but I hate to do that. It seems a damn shame to kill an animal who's been hurt."

Fury set his beer down and went to the door. The dog ran out of his house, barking and snarling.

"Shh," Fury said, holding his hand out to the dog so that he could sniff him.

"I wouldn't do that if I were you," Patrick said. "He damn near tore the hand off the animal control officer who captured him."

"Yeah, someone needs to put them in a cage and poke them for a while," Fury said, curling his lip.

The dog continued to attack.

"Stand back," Vane said as he reached for the latch on the door.

Fury stood up and moved while Vane opened it. The dog lunged, then darted back.

Vane shut the door and crouched down. "Come here, boy," he said soothingly, holding his hand out.

The dog ran into his house and barked even louder.

Vane crawled toward the house and slowly reached his hand inside. "Don't be afraid," he said, letting the dog catch his scent.

He could feel it starting to calm. It knew he wasn't entirely human and it was starting to trust the animal that it smelled.

After a few seconds of waiting, the dog licked Vane's fingertips.

"That's it," Vane said, stroking his fur.

He looked back over his shoulder. "Fury? Could you get me something for him to eat?"

"I'll get a bowl," Paul said.

Once Paul returned, he gave the bowl to Fury who brought it inside. Fury crouched outside the house beside Vane and carefully put the food down in front of the dog.

"Man, they screwed you up bad, huh?" Fury said to the dog.

Vane picked up a handful of food and held it out to the dog. It nosed around until it finally trusted him enough and took a bite.

"There you go," he said quietly as he picked up more food and hand-fed the dog.

"Damn, Dad," Patrick said from the other side of the fence. "I've never seen anything like that."

After a few minutes, Vane had the dog fed. He crawled into Vane's lap and lay there, needing comfort. Fury stroked his back while Vane massaged his ears.

Vane felt someone watching him. Looking over his shoulder, he saw Bride beside her father.

"Did you get him to eat?" she asked him.

"Yeah."

She smiled at that. The sight of her there made his heart ache. How could something so simple as a mere smile wreak such havoc with his body?

"I came to tell everyone that dinner was ready. But if you need more time . . ."

Vane stood up. "He'll be okay for a bit."

Fury patted the dog, then rose slowly to his feet.

The two of them left the cage and shut it. The dog came running up to them, howling.

"It's okay," Vane told him. "We'll be back."

"Yeah," Fury added, "with a nice treat for you."

Vane draped his arm over Bride's shoulders as they followed her brother and father into the house. "Is this where you grew up?" he asked Bride.

"No. My parents moved here a few years ago after they sold their small farm."

"I miss the old place," Paul said as he held the door open for them. "There are too many ordinances here. I had to get a special license just so I could keep my patients in the back, and I routinely have to pay fines."

"Why did you move?" Fury asked.

Paul shrugged. "Her mother wanted to be closer to town. What's a man to do when his wife has her heart set on something?"

They entered the dining room where a huge feast waited along with Deirdre, who still looked like she'd rather they leave.

"Come over here and sit by me, Vane," Joyce said, indicating the chair on her right. "And Fury, you can sit on the other side of Bride."

The instant Fury sat down, Titus came running up and tried to climb into his lap.

"Oh, good grief!" Joyce snapped. "Paul, get the dog down."

"It's okay," Fury said, laughing.

Then when Vane sat down, Titus ran for him and licked his face. "Hey boy, watch the dewclaws."

"What has gotten into my dog?" Joyce asked, pulling at Titus's collar. "He's normally standoffish with people."

"Dogs know good people when they see them," Paul said, pulling a piece of stuffing out of the turkey.

"Titus," he said, holding it down for the dog.

Titus ran to get it.

Bride sat down beside Vane. "So Patrick, where's Maggie?"

"Over at her parents'. I'm going over there after I eat here. Since we're sleeping here, she wanted to make sure her mother didn't get jealous."

"Maggie is Patrick's wife," Joyce explained to Vane. "She's going to make me a grandmother in the spring-time."

"Congratulations," Vane said to Patrick.

"Yeah, we'll see. I'm scared as hell. Personally, I don't think I'm ready to be someone's parent."

"Yeah," Bride said with a laugh. "You might have to share your toys."

Patrick grimaced at her before he launched a pea over the table at her head. Vane caught it before it made contact, then zipped it right back at Patrick. It hit him straight between the eyes.

Bride howled with laughter.

"Children!" Joyce snapped. "You behave or I'll make you eat in the corner."

"Nice reflexes, bud," Patrick said, wiping his brow good-naturedly. "I think we should recruit you for the team."

"I don't think so, Pat," Bride said. "I somehow think Vane would balk at wearing a shirt that says 'Snip It and Clip It If You Love It' on his back. He's kind of sensitive about dog neutering."

Vane arched a brow at that, but wisely kept his mouth shut.

Her father laughed hard. "I can appreciate his point of view. Not many men want to play for the Castrators. But we have a lot of female vets who strangely do."

"Ah, we'll work on him," Patrick said. "With those reflexes, we could definitely use him."

Vane noticed the look of sadness on Deirdre's face, but she didn't say anything as she sat there and put her napkin in her lap.

Bride's father said the blessing and then stood up to carve the turkey while her mother began passing the side dishes.

Vane held the bowls while Bride served both him and herself.

"Is there anything you don't like?" Bride asked him.

"Not really."

She smiled at that. "You're so easy."

He impulsively kissed her cheek, until he realized that her family was staring at them. "I'm sorry," he said, afraid he'd done something wrong.

"Don't be," Joyce said. "I'm just glad to see my baby smiling for once."

Vane passed the mashed potatoes across Bride to Fury, who stared at them with a fierce frown. "What are these?" he asked.

"Potatoes," Vane told him.

"What did they do to them?"

"Just eat them, Fury," Vane said. "You'll like them, trust me."

Patrick snorted. "Where are you from that you've never seen mashed potatoes before?"

"Mars," Fury said as he frowned at the way the potatoes clung to the spoon.

He only took a little, then passed them over to Paul. Fury leaned forward a bit and sniffed at the potatoes in a very canine manner.

Bride felt Vane's leg reach over hers to kick at Fury's chair under the table.

Fury snapped upright and looked at Vane, who was giving him a warning stare.

"Really, where are you from?" Deirdre asked again. "Did you guys grow up here?"

"No," Vane answered. "We traveled a lot growing up. We've lived just about everywhere."

Her sister gave him a gimlet stare. "What brings you to New Orleans?"

"Deirdre," Bride said. "Since when is this the Inquisition?"

"Since Mom said you were serious about him. I think we ought to know something more about your new boyfriend than the fact that he looks good in a pair of jeans."

"Deirdre," Paul said in a low but stern tone. "Don't make Bride and Vane pay for the crimes of Josh."

"Fine," Deirdre snapped angrily. "But when he runs off with his secretary and leaves her alone to explain to her kids why Daddy's a jerk, I hope you remember this." She got up and left the room.

"I'm sorry," Joyce said, rising. "Y'all go ahead and eat. I'll be back in a minute."

"Deirdre's husband left her a few months ago," Bride explained to Vane. "Her kids are with him for the holiday and Deirdre's having a hard time with it."

"Why would a hum . . ." Fury stretched the syllable out in a way that let Bride know he was about to say "human." "Humongous jackass do that?" he said, finishing it off.

"I don't know why some men do what they do," Paul said. "I figure though that it's good riddance to bad rubbish."

"I agree," Bride said, looking at Vane, who was playing with her thigh under the table and making her extremely hot. His touch was electrifying.

Joyce returned to get Deirdre's plate, then left the room again.

Paul sighed. "I wish I could make it better for her. There's nothing worse than seeing one of your children in pain and not being able to stop it."

"I could kill him for her," Fury offered.

Vane cleared his throat.

"Well, he could have an accident," Fury tried again. "Humans have those all the time."

Patrick gave an evil laugh. "I have a shovel."

"Screw that," Paul said before he sipped his wine. "I have a gator in the backyard."

They all laughed.

Joyce returned and sat back down. "Sorry about that."

"Is she okay?" Bride asked.

"She will be. It just takes time."

Vane sensed Bride's sadness. He squeezed her thigh comfortingly.

"I probably shouldn't have brought Vane. It was insensitive of me."

"Oh bah!" Joyce snapped. "You didn't do anything wrong, Bride. We wanted to meet him." She smiled at Vane. "This is Deirdre's issue, okay?"

Bride nodded.

They finished their meal in peace while Patrick and Paul bantered back and forth. Then Joyce brought out a pecan pie and a four-layer chocolate cake.

Bride cut a small piece of pie.

"Don't you want any cake?" Vane asked. "I know chocolate's your favorite."

She stared at it longingly. "No, I better not."

Before she could pass it over, Vane set a slice down on her plate.

"Vane!"

"You wanted it. I know that look."

She rolled her eyes at him and picked up her fork. "Thank you."

Vane nodded. He felt her mother watching him. Glancing over, he received a grateful smile from Joyce, who reached over and gently patted his forearm.

It sent the strangest sensation through him. Was that what it was like to have a real mother's touch?

After dinner, Bride decided she had tortured Vane and Fury enough for one day. "We probably should head back," she said.

"What?" her father asked. "No game?"

"You and Patrick can watch the game, Dad."

To her utter shock, her father actually pouted.

Bride gave him a hug for being so kind to Vane and Fury. "I'm going to go say goodbye to Deirdre. Be nice to the guys until I get back."

Bride headed up the stairs to the guest rooms. She found Deirdre in the last room on the hall.

"Hey hon," she said, pushing open the door. "You okay?"

Deirdre's eyes were rimmed in red as she sat on the bed, clutching a pillow to her stomach. Her plate of food was still untouched on the nightstand. "I'm fine. I guess."

Wishing she could do something to help her sister, Bride walked over to the bed. How she sympathized with Deirdre's broken heart. She'd felt the same until Vane had come her way and made her smile. "I'm so sorry."

"Don't be. I'm glad the asshole's gone, but you . . . you should let go of Vane."

It wasn't so much her sister's words that shocked her as the rancor in Deirdre's tone. "Excuse me?"

"C'mon, Bride. Don't be stupid. Look at him. Look at you. The two of you don't belong together."

Bride gaped at her sister. "I beg your pardon?"

"Taylor was a great guy—you should have held on to him with both hands. He was reliable and stable. Most of all, he was well respected in the community. But instead of doing what he wanted, you refused to lose weight and he left you because you're *fat*. Now this guy comes along and you jump all over him like Taylor never existed. Not that I blame you. He is prime, but don't be a fool."

Oh, that was a low blow and, quite honestly, Bride was tired of being the "smart" one while Deirdre was always known as the "pretty" one. "Just because you married a snake doesn't mean that Vane is a dog."

Bride hesitated at that. Actually Vane *was* a dog, kind of. But not like that. "Vane would never cheat on me."

"Yeah, right. Look at me, Bride. I was the first runner-up for Miss Louisiana and would have won had I not been so young at the time. I'm still damn attractive and yet my husband ran off on me. What chance do you stand?"

Angry at her "perfect" sister, Bride refused to look at her. Instead, she moved to the window that faced out onto the backyard where she saw Vane and Fury with her father.

"You married Josh for money, remember?" Bride said as she watched them with the dogs. "You actually told me that the night before the wedding."

"Oh, and I suppose you *love* Vane for his personality? I'm not stupid. You love him for how nice his ass looks."

And yet as Bride watched her mate, she knew the truth. Vane wasn't human. He didn't think or act like a human. Unlike Taylor and Josh, he would never leave her because she wasn't what he wanted her to be.

He loved her just as she was. Not once had Vane tried to change her or alter her in any way. He just accepted her, faults and all.

Vane would never cheat on her. Never lie. But he would kill anyone who hurt her.

And in that moment as she watched him pet a dog that no one had been able to reach, she realized how much she loved him.

Just how much she needed him.

The very idea of living without him killed her.

She couldn't. In the last few weeks, he had become an integral part of her life. Most of all, he was an integral part of her heart.

Her eyes teared as the reality of that thought crashed down on her.

She really, truly loved him in a way she had never known a woman could love a man.

"You have no idea what you're talking about, Dee. Vane is kind and considerate. He takes care of me."

"You've only known him for a couple of weeks on the heels of breaking up with Taylor. It's shameless the way you hang all over him."

Bride looked back at her sister. She felt sorry for Deirdre, but that didn't give her sister the right to try and make her feel bad. "You're just jealous."

"No, Bride, I'm not. I'm a realist. Vane's way out of your league."

Bride glared at her perfect sister, but deep down, she felt so very sorry that Deirdre would most likely never know the love she had with Vane.

If she could, she would give her sister that gift. But it wasn't within her control.

"Whatever, Dee. I'll see you later."

Vane and Fury were outside in the yard with the Lab again.

"You wouldn't want to take him home with you, would you?" Paul asked as Fury played with the dog.

"Valerius would piss his drawers," Fury said. "Can I?"

Vane laughed. "Sure. But Cujo will probably end up at Sanctuary."

"You know," Paul said, "I should have thought of asking the bears about that myself."

Vane gave Paul a suspicious look. "Pardon?"

"But then, since he's just a dog and not a Were, I didn't think about the bears welcoming him in."

Vane couldn't have been more stunned had Paul kicked him.

"Close your mouth, Vane," Paul said in a fatherly tone. "I'm the leading vet in the state. Carson is still learning the practice. Who do you think he calls when there's something he can't deal with?"

Carson was the resident veterinarian at Sanctuary. A Were-Hunter himself, he was only fifty years old, which in their world made him not much more than a child.

"I know all about Fang, too," Paul continued.

Fury came forward to stand before the fence. He put his hand up on the links as he stared in disbelief at Paul. "Why did you let us come here?"

Paul took Vane's hand in his. The mark was hidden. "You didn't have to cover it. I knew the minute Bride told me your name what had happened. And I know how you guys guard your mates. I can't say I'm exactly happy about this, but at least I don't have to fear you will ever hurt her the way Deirdre was hurt."

Vane clenched his fists. "Does Joyce—"

"No. She knows nothing about your world and I want to keep it that way. I've never told anyone about Sanctuary." Paul let go of Vane's hand. "If you're looking for my blessing, you have it. I wasn't sure until I saw you two at dinner. It's been a long time since I've seen my little girl so happy. But remember, if you ever hurt her . . ." He glanced over to where a dog was in a cage with a cone around his head.

"Ah man," Fury breathed. "That's just sick."

"I definitely concur," Vane agreed.

"Yeah well, Bride is my baby and I know how to use a tranq gun and a scalpel."

Vane cringed as Fury cupped himself.

"Vane?"

They turned to see Bride walking toward them.

Paul stepped back. "Let me get you a leash for—"

"We won't need it," Fury said, opening the gate and letting the dog out with him.

"No, I guess not," Paul said. He went to pet the dog, who snapped at him.

"Behave," Fury said, pulling Cujo back.

Bride hesitated as she drew near.

"And you better not nip at Bride," Vane warned. "Or we'll leave you here."

The dog wagged its tail and sat down.

"Is he coming with us?" she asked.

Her father nodded. "They were kind enough to adopt him."

"That was sweet of you," she said to Vane.

Fury scoffed. "Not really. I feel for anyone who gets tossed into a ditch."

Bride reached out and hugged Fury. She felt for the wolf and what he'd been through.

Fury cleared his throat and stepped back. "Don't get mushy on me, Bride, I don't know how to handle it. Much like Cujo, my first instinct is to attack and that would cause Vane to make me look like that poor guy over there."

Bride saw the dog with the cone. "Ouch."

"Exactly."

Vane wrapped his arm around her and together they walked back to the house with her father, Fury, and Cujo following them.

Joyce looked up in surprise to see the dog with them, but didn't say anything as she handed Bride a large sack of Tupperware. "I split the leftovers with everyone."

"Did we get any potatoes?" Fury asked.

Vane cocked a brow. "So now you like them?"

"Yeah, they were good."

Bride kissed her mother on the cheek. "Thanks, Mom."

Patrick met them in the living room. He held his hand out to Vane. "It was good meeting you, even if you are a drug-dealing pimp."

"You, too."

"Excuse me?" Bride asked.

"It's a long story," Fury said with a laugh.

"Y'all be careful going home," Joyce said as she led them out to the car. "Oh wait, let me get a blanket for the dog so he won't scratch the leather seats."

Bride took a few minutes to say goodbye again while her mother fetched the blanket, then put it in the back for Cujo. After she'd hugged and kissed her parents, Bride joined the wolves and dog in the car.

Within no time, they were headed back toward the Garden District.

"You have a nice family, Bride," Vane said.

She looked at him and then Fury. "Yeah, I do. I think you guys are the best."

Vane's heart pounded at what she said. "I meant *your* family."

"You and Fury are part of my family, Vane. You're the best part of it."

"I think you two need some privacy." Fang sat up

and squeezed Bride's hand. "Later, little sister." Then he and the dog vanished out of the back seat.

Vane pulled to the side of the road and stopped the car. "What are you saying to me, Bride?"

She lifted her hand up to play with his hair as she stared into those incredible hazel eyes that held her heart enslaved. "While my sister was yelling at me about how you would one day leave me high and dry, I had an epiphany. I've never in my life known anyone like you, Vane, and I doubt I ever will. I like the way you look at me as if you can already taste me. I like how you worry if I'm too cold or if I've had enough to eat. Most of all, I love the way you feel at night when you're holding me close. The way you touch me as if you're afraid I'm going to break. And how you take care to cradle me in your arms."

She paused and took a deep breath before she continued. "I love you, Vane. I don't think I ever knew what real love was until you came into my life."

She held her marked hand up to him. "I'm ready to mate with you."

He looked startled and uncertain. "Are you sure about this?"

"The mere fact that you're asking me that question when you know what you'll lose if I say no proves to me just how right I am about you. Yes, Vane Kattalakis. I'm sure."

A slow smile spread across his face two seconds before he pulled her into his arms and kissed her breathless. Vane pulled away with a deep, wolfish growl. "I really hate that I had to drive this damned thing. Otherwise I'd have us both in bed right now."

"Can't you poof the car home?"

"No. It's too big and heavy, and if I abandon it, it'll get stolen and Otto will never forgive me. He loves this damned hunk of junk." He released her and settled back in his seat.

And damn near gave her heart failure as he drove home in record time. Richard Petty had nothing on this guy as he weaved in and out of traffic.

They squealed to a stop outside of Valerius's door and Vane flashed them from the car to their bedroom. One second they were standing next to the bed; in the next, they were naked in it.

Bride laughed at his eagerness. "You don't waste time, do you?"

"I don't want you to change your mind."

"I'm not going to."

Vane kissed her deeply. He was already hard for her.

Bride ran her hand over his back, delighting in the feel of him. His skin was so warm and masculine. "Just remember, this doesn't get you off the hook for a big Irish wedding."

He laughed at that. "Whatever it takes to make you happy."

Her smile faded as seriousness set deep in her heart. "That would definitely be you."

He kissed her again, nearly devouring her.

By the time he pulled away, she could barely breathe. "Okay," she said quietly. "What do we need to do?"

Vane rolled over onto his back and stole her breath at the way he looked there. His tanned skin was set off to perfection against the cream sheets. His hair was loose and made him look all the more alluring. "You need to press your marked palm to mine."

Bride laid her palm to his warm and callused one. Vane laced his fingers with hers.

"Now you have to take me into your body without my interference."

"That's kind of strange, but okay."

"Not really. It was set up as a safeguard to protect our females. The Claiming can never be forced on a female. She must complete it by her own free will."

Bride sat up on her knees and carefully straddled his lean waist. She stared down at him, wondering how this would change them.

Would it change them?

How could it not?

After this they would be mated. She would belong to him and, until the day she died, he would belong to her.

Vane took her free hand into his and kissed it gently.

Her heart pounding, Bride shifted her body until he was deep inside her. They both moaned at the sensation.

Vane ground his teeth as his hand started to heat up. It took all his willpower not to thrust against her. But this wasn't his choice, it was hers.

"Now you have to say the following: 'I accept you as you are, and I will always hold you close in my heart. I will walk beside you forever.' "

Bride locked gazes with him as her own palm tickled. "I accept you as you are, and I will always hold you close in my heart. I will walk beside you forever."

Vane's eyes darkened before he repeated the vow

back to her. No sooner had he spoken them than he arched his back as if he were being racked with pain.

Bride squeaked in surprise as his canine teeth grew like something out of a vampire movie.

Vane held her still while he breathed raggedly. His entire body was tense and rigid.

"It's okay, Bride," he growled. "Don't be afraid. It's just our Claiming spell calling out the *thirio* so that we can bond our life forces together. It'll pass in a few minutes."

"You look like you're in pain. Is there anything I can do?"

"Just wait for it to pass," he panted.

"If we bond, will it stop?"

He nodded.

"Then bond with me."

He hissed, then locked gazes with her. "Do you understand what that is, Bride? If I die, you die with me. Instantly. Unless you're pregnant and then you will die as soon as our baby is born."

Her heartrate tripled. But as she stared down at him, it seemed a small price to pay. Did she want to live without him? "What the heck?" she said. "If we're going to do this, let's go all the way with it."

"Are you sure?"

She nodded.

Vane sat up under her. He cradled her to his chest and nuzzled her neck. "After I bite you, you'll have to bite me back in the shoulder."

Before she could respond, he sank his teeth into her.

Bride cried out, but not from pain. An unimaginable

pleasure tore through her as she felt him swelling inside her. She thrust herself against him as a divine orgasm ripped her apart.

Her vision blurred as she felt her own fangs growing in her mouth. Something seemed to possess her until she no longer felt human.

It was . . .

Wonderful. The next thing she knew, she sank her teeth into Vane's shoulder.

Wrapped in ecstasy, they held each other as their heartbeats synchronized and the room spun around. Bride had never felt this close to another being in all her life. It really was as if they were one person, united. Physically.

Spiritually. Perfectly.

Vane couldn't breathe as he tasted her. He should never have bonded with her and yet he was so grateful that she would be with him. For the first time he understood why Anya had bonded with her mate.

He didn't want to lose Bride. Didn't want to even try to imagine a single day without her in it.

Now he wouldn't.

His head swam as his orgasm faded and his teeth receded. Bride pulled away and stared at him as if she were drunk.

"Is it over?" she asked.

He nodded, then kissed her. He kissed her again. "You are mine, Bride McTierney. Now and always."

She smiled.

Vane leaned her back on the bed and laid himself over her. He only wanted to feel her. His mate.

The reality of that encircled his heart and made him fly.

Bride cradled him with her entire body. He felt so good there. She ran her hand through his hair and started to laugh.

"What's so funny?"

"I was just thinking that it's not every woman who gets to have her very own tamed wolf."

His eyes twinkled. "I'm not sure I could call myself tame. Only you have that effect on me."

"That's what I like most of all."

As he dipped his head down to kiss her, his phone rang. Vane pulled back with a grumble. He held his hand out and the phone flew across the room, into his grip.

Bride frowned. "I'm not sure I'll ever get used to you doing that."

He nipped her neck playfully, then answered it.

"Hi, Aimee," he said, then paused. He looked at her and she noted the confusion in his eyes. "Thanks, I really appreciate that. Hang on a sec."

He pressed the mute. "It's one of the bears at Sanctuary who is watching Fang. They're having their own Thanksgiving celebration and have decided to temporarily lift my banishment if I want to visit Fang tonight."

"Okay."

"I was wondering if you'd like to go with me and meet him. I mean, he's not really saying anything, but—"

"I'd love to meet your brother," she said, interrupting him.

He looked relieved before he returned to the phone. "Yeah, we'll be there in a little bit. Thanks."

He hung up the phone and placed it on the nightstand.

Bride lay there quietly, trying to come to grips with what she had done. What had happened to them this afternoon.

"Are you sure I'm not aging? I don't feel any differently."

"You should be joined to me, but since I've never mated before, I don't know what we should feel."

Bride looked at her hand. Her mark was now a vibrant red. "This is different, though. What about yours?"

"Looks like yours."

That was a good sign. "Do I have to keep drinking your blood?"

He shook his head. "Never again."

"Good. The thought of it is really gross."

Vane got up and pulled her out of the bed.

"What are you doing?"

"I'm going to bathe you, Lady Wolf, so that I can take you to Sanctuary and show you off to everyone."

How she wished she were as beautiful as he thought she was. It was so nice to be with someone who looked at her with rose-colored glasses.

Vane led her into the bathroom and turned the shower on. Once he had the water regulated, he opened the curtain and let her enter first.

Bride felt a bit awkward. She'd never bathed with a man before. But as Vane started soaping her body, her awkwardness vanished in a wave of hot desire for him.

He looked really good naked and wet, and his hands were incredible as they slid over every inch of her body.

"You're really talented," she said, her breath catching as he washed between her legs.

He kissed her gently as he dropped the washcloth and used his fingers to caress her.

"You're never satisfied, are you?" Bride asked as she felt him harden again.

"Not where you're concerned." He pressed her back against the cool tile wall. He lifted one of her legs up to wrap around his narrow waist before he slid into her.

Bride cried out in pleasure as he thrust against her. It wasn't until she came that she realized she had wrapped both legs around his waist and that he was supporting her full weight as he continued to thrust.

His hair was wet and dripping as he captured her lips. He buried himself deep inside, then shuddered.

Bride was only vaguely aware of the water's spray against her arms and legs as she watched Vane's face. Her wolf was beautiful when he came for her. He held her effortlessly while his body continued to shudder.

After he finished, she set her legs down as he withdrew from her.

He took a ragged breath, then turned around to face the water.

Bride impulsively pressed her front to his naked back.

Vane hissed at the sensation of his Bride against him. She wrapped her arms around his waist, sliding her hands over his body. "You keep doing that and we'll never leave this shower," he said huskily.

"Sure we will. It won't be much fun in here if the water turns cold."

"True."

Then to his delight she left him and picked up the washcloth to bathe him.

Bride had never done anything like this. It was actually a lot of fun to soap those magnificent muscles and to help rinse his body.

"You are decadent," she breathed.

He answered that with a smile and a kiss.

After they were finished, they left the shower. Bride thought they'd have to dress, but Vane surprised her by re-dressing them in the clothes they'd worn to her parents' house.

"How do you do that?"

Vane shrugged. "It's like breathing. I barely think about it and poof. It's magic."

"I wish you would warn me a bit before you do it. I'm still getting used to all this."

In order to please her he led her through the door and down the hallway to Fury's room.

Vane knocked on the door.

"Yeah?" Fury called from inside.

Vane shouldered it open to find Fury with the dog on his bed. "We were heading over to Sanctuary. I was just wondering if you'd like to join us."

"Sure. Can Cujo come?"

"I guess. We can always put him in one of the cages if he gets nervous."

"Cages?" Bride asked.

Vane turned to face her. "Since Sanctuary has a lot of different kinds of animals in it, they have a whole room of cages in the event someone gets nasty."

Fury and Cujo flashed out of the room.

"How do you want to go?" Vane asked her.

Bride let out a deep breath. "Beam me over, Scotty."

Vane took her hand and flashed them to Sanctuary.

It took Bride a second to get her bearings. She'd been by this bar a million times, but had never been inside it before. There was a sign on the door that said it was closed. However, there was plenty of activity inside. At least fifty "people" were there, including Fury and Cujo, who was sniffing around various occupants.

Several tables had been pulled together to make one really long banquet table that was covered with white tablecloths. Another series of tables held more food than she had ever seen in her life. There were a dozen turkeys, twenty hams, and at least two dozen kinds of cakes and pies with every side item known and a few she couldn't identify.

But what stunned her most was how incredibly attractive everyone there was. Jeez! It looked like a model revue.

Bride felt extremely intimidated.

"Vane," a tall, gorgeous blond man said as he came over to them. "We were wondering if you'd make it."

"Hey, Dev."

Bride noticed two more "Devs" who entered the room, carrying more food.

"We're quadruplets," Dev said with a wicked grin. "You can tell me by this." He pulled his T-shirt sleeve up to show her a bow-and-arrow tattoo, then he pointed out his brothers. "The mean-looking one holding the gumbo is Remi. The bashful one over there with the bear cub in his lap is Quinn, and Cherif is the one holding the platter of crab legs. Don't worry if you can't remember who's who, just yell 'quad' and we'll answer."

He seemed very friendly and open.

"I'm Bride," she said, holding out her hand to him. "Nice meeting you."

As he shook her hand, another attractive blond man appeared behind Vane. He growled low in his throat, reminding her of a wolf.

"Don't even think about it, Sasha," Vane growled back, giving the man a lethal stare. "I'm in no mood for your shit."

"Wolves," Dev said to Bride. "The alphas have to do that dominance crap whenever they see each other. See, me, I'm a bear. We get along with most anyone. Unless you mess with us, then we rip your head off."

Dev inclined his head to Sasha. "Why don't you go help Papa bring out the kegs?"

Sasha came over and sniffed at Bride. He appeared to calm a degree before he looked back at Vane. "Sure, Dev. I wouldn't want to embarrass Vane in front of his mate by defeating him."

Vane took a step toward him until Dev cut him off.

"Go, Sasha," Dev said sternly.

Sasha finally left.

Dev took a deep breath and grinned at her. "You should have tried a bear, Bride. Then you wouldn't have to worry about this."

"It's all right. I'm rather fond of wolves." She watched as Sasha neared Fury.

Fury came instantly to his feet with a snarl so sinister that it actually scared her. Always easygoing and a bit inept, she'd had no idea that Fury could look like that.

He was truly frightening in his wolf persona.

"Wolves apart!" a tall, slender woman said in a

French accent as she came between them. "Or else I shall throw water on you both."

Remi appeared by her side. "Do you need help, *maman*?"

"Not from you, *cher*," she said, patting him kindly on the arm. "Go and help Jose in the kitchen."

Remi gave the wolves a warning glare before he obeyed his mother.

Once Sasha and Fury had some distance between them, the woman came over to her and Vane.

"There you are at last." She kissed Vane on his cheek, then turned to Bride. "I am Nicolette, but most people call me Mama."

"Bride," she said, shaking the bear's hand.

Nicolette smiled up at Vane. "She is beautiful, *mon petit loup*. You have done well for yourself."

"*Merci*, Nicolette."

"Come," she said, gesturing them further into the room. "Vane, introduce your mate to our people while I make sure my sons do not fight. And have no fear if you can't remember our names, Bride. There is but one of you while we are many. You will learn them all in time."

Bride thanked her, then Vane took her around the room and introduced her to lions, tigers, bears, hawks, jackals, and leopards. Even a couple of humans were there.

Nicolette was right. She couldn't keep straight who was who or what. Since there were only a handful of women, most of them mates for the men, they were easier to remember. But the men . . . it was enough to make her head spin.

"Where's Fang?" she asked as Vane finished introducing her to the people in the kitchen.

"He's upstairs. C'mon and I'll introduce you to him next."

Vane led her through a door that opened out into a grand Victorian parlor.

Bride paused at the sight of it. Plush and decorated with antiques, the house was stunning.

"This is Peltier House," Vane explained. "The Were-Hunters live on this side of things where we're safe from discovery."

"It's beautiful."

"Merci," Nicolette said from behind them. "It has been our home for more than a century now. It is our goal to keep it so."

"How can you do that without anyone finding out who and what you are?"

"We have our ways, *chérie,*" she said with a wink. "Magic does have its benefits." She handed Vane a small votive candle.

Vane saw that the glass container had the name "Anya" engraved on it. His heart ached at the sight of it.

"We always remember our loved ones who are gone," Nicolette explained. "Since Fang cannot honor Anya, I thought you might want to."

Vane couldn't speak past the sad lump in his throat as Nicolette led him and Bride into a side room where four candle stands were set. The light from the candles flickered like diamonds against the dark green walls.

"There are so many," Bride said, awed by the number of names.

"We live a long time," Nicolette said. "And we are at

war. The Katagaria against the Arcadians, the Dark-Hunters against the Daimons. The Apollites against everyone. In the end, all we have are memories."

She indicated two candles that were set up on the wall. "Those are for my sons. Bastien and Gilbert." A tear slid down her cheek. "It is in their honor that Sanctuary was founded. I vowed that no mother, no matter if she is human, Apollite, Katagaria, or Arcadian, would ever know my grief so long as her child was housed here underneath my roof."

"I'm so sorry, Nicolette."

The bear sniffed and patted her arm. "I appreciate your words, Bride. It is for you that I am renouncing Vane's banishment."

Vane looked stunned.

"It is my wedding present," Nicolette said. "You have no pack to protect her with and, as Acheron says, you have paid a high enough price for your kindness. You protected Sunshine for the Dark-Hunters and so we protect you and your mate."

"Thank you, Nicolette," Vane said. "Thank you."

Nicolette inclined her head, then excused herself.

Vane lit the candle, then placed it next to the one for Colt's mother. His hand lingered on the glass. By his expression, Bride could tell he was remembering his sister. That he was grieving horribly for her.

His eyes were bright and shiny as he watched the candle flicker. After a moment, he glanced to her.

"Come," he said, taking Bride's hand. "It's time to meet my brother."

Bride followed him out of the room and up the staircase.

As they passed the first room, a man stepped out whom Bride actually recognized. "Carson?"

He looked as shocked by her presence as she felt for his.

"Bride? What are you doing . . ." His voice trailed off as he sniffed the air. His eyes widened. "You're one of us?"

"Us?"

"Carson is a hawk," Vane explained.

"No way!"

Carson nodded. "I'm the resident veterinarian and doctor here at Sanctuary." He opened the door to the room he was leaving to show her a state-of-the-art examination room that was complete with some of the cages Vane had mentioned.

"I can't believe it," Bride said as she stared at Carson. She'd known him for years now.

"Neither can I," he said. He looked at Vane. "I suppose congratulations are in order. You do know what her father does for a living, right?"

"Yes. Neuter King."

Carson drew his breath in between his teeth. "You do have guts, wolf. Lots and lots of them."

"Yeah, I know."

"Well, I suppose you were on your way to Fang's room. I'll see you two downstairs."

Vane took her to the next room, which was a bedroom.

Bride half-expected to see a man on the bed and was a bit surprised to find a brown timber wolf there. There was also another extremely attractive blond woman, who could have been Nicolette's younger sister.

Vane introduced her to Nicolette's daughter, Aimee, who quickly excused herself to leave them alone with Fang.

Vane released Bride's hand as he closed the distance and knelt down on the opposite side of the bed where Fang was facing. "Hey, little brother," he said quietly. "I brought someone here I wanted you to meet. Bride?"

She joined him.

The wolf didn't budge.

"Hi, Fang," Bride said. She looked at Vane. "Can I touch him?"

"If you want."

She placed her hand on his head and rubbed him behind his ears. "It's nice meeting you finally. Vane's told me a lot about you."

Still, he didn't move.

Bride wanted to cry for them both. She could feel how much it hurt Vane that his brother wouldn't acknowledge them.

"I guess I'll take you back downstairs," Vane said sadly.

"It's okay. We can stay for a while. I don't mind."

"You sure?"

She nodded.

"Okay, let me go get us something to drink and I'll be right back."

"Wait," she said before he could poof out on her. "Is there a bathroom around?"

"There's one in Carson's office."

"Good."

Vane flashed out of the room. Bride left to take care of her business.

As she left the bathroom, she noticed that Carson's office had a two-way mirror that looked into Fang's room.

But that wasn't what made her heart stop.

Standing in Fang's room was Bryani.

Chapter 13

Vane was behind the bar getting Cokes for himself and Bride while Colt razzed him.

"Now aren't you glad I sent you back to her?"

"Shut up, Colt."

"C'mon, wolf. I know you hate it. Say 'Thank you, Colt.'"

"I'd rather stick . . ." Vane's voice trailed off as something bright flashed onto the dance floor. At first he thought it was someone else joining the party until he realized the "human" couldn't stay in human form. He kept flashing from human to wolf and back.

He also recognized him.

It was Stefan.

Vane put the drinks down and leaped over the bar. He ran across the room to the wolf.

"Easy," Carson was saying as he laid the injured wolf against the concrete floor. "Can you stay in your base form?"

"Warn . . . Vane."

Vane grabbed Stefan and used his powers to keep him human. "Warn me about what?"

Stefan was a bloodied mess. Someone had beaten him one step away from death. It was amazing the wolf was still alive. "Your . . . mother . . ."

"Don't talk," he told Stefan. "Think it."

Stefan leaned his head back and closed his eyes.

"She and her Sentinels killed Petra and Aloysius," Stefan said in Vane's head. *"I didn't want to die. I made a pact with her that if she let me live, I would bring her here to kill you and Fang."*

Vane ground his teeth at that, but didn't do anything to interrupt.

"She was supposed to let me go. Instead when she learned Fang was in Sanctuary, she turned on me. She's coming, Vane. She may already be here."

"Whoa!" Kyle's voice rang out from the doorway that led to Peltier House. "Everyone, come quick. Vane's little human mate is having a major smack down with some wolf chick upstairs. And she's winning!"

Bride was terrified. Her heart hammered, but even so she wasn't about to just stand there and let Bryani kill Fang.

She probably should have called Vane, but she wanted this over.

And she knew how to end it.

She hoped.

Bride threw open the door to Fang's room.

Bryani turned on her with a snarl. "Stay out of this. It's not your concern."

"Yes it is. You hurt my mate, you hurt me, and I'm not going to let you do it."

"I don't want to hurt you, Bride."

"Then leave."

Bryani threw her hand out and slammed her back into the wall. Bride's back throbbed at the impact, but it did nothing to loosen her resolve.

Bryani turned back to Fang and reached for him.

Bride grabbed the ladder-back chair and brought it down across the other woman's back. Bryani fell to her knees, then tried to blast her with her hand again.

Before she could, Bride shot her with a tranquilizer that she had grabbed in the examination room.

Bryani screamed and rushed her. They went slamming into the dresser.

"I'm really too old to fight," Bride said between clenched teeth. "And so are you!"

Bryani staggered back as the drug began to take effect. She used her powers to hit Bride with the lamp, but it fell to the floor before it could reach her. "What did you do to me?"

"I drugged you."

Three seconds later, Bryani was sprawled out on the floor.

Bride went over to her and rolled her onto her back. Bryani's eyes were wide open and the woman stared up at her. Satisfied she had her tamed for a minute, Bride seized her mother-in-law and dragged her into the next room, where she locked her into a cage. There was a red switch at the top that said "lock." Bride flipped it and hoped that would somehow keep Bryani from using her powers against her.

"There now," she said as she watched Bryani carefully. "I'm going to get Carson in a minute because I'm not sure if I gave you the right dosage. Believe it or not, I don't want to kill you. But please notice that I said I don't *want* to kill you. It doesn't mean I won't."

Bryani's hand moved.

Then again, it was just as likely Bride hadn't given her enough, which is why she'd locked her in the cage.

"Look, Bryani, I'm really sorry for what happened to you. I am, and I understand why you hate Vane's father. You have every right to. But that is between the two of you. It has nothing to do with Vane or Fang or Fury. They are *your* children."

"They need to die," Bryani gasped, letting Bride know she really hadn't used enough tranquilizer. "They're animals."

"Have you looked in the mirror?" she asked her. "Animals eat their young for no reason. Vane didn't try to kill you for taking me. He left you and your village alone. You're the one dancing through time to kill someone who has never done anything to hurt you. My God, you beat Fury, your own flesh and blood, and left him to die. How is that humane? Stop lying to yourself. You're not human, either, Bryani. Or maybe you are. God knows, humans have committed some of the most atrocious crimes imaginable against each other.

"Animals, like Fury said, only kill to protect and to eat. They're loyal to those they love. My heart was ripped out of my chest and stomped into the ground by a human. And it was Vane who came along and made me feel happy again. He picked my heart up and he cradled it carefully in his hands. I know he would never hurt me, not like that."

Bride's eyes teared up as she realized just how much she really did love her mate. "I guess if I have to choose between a human and an animal, I'm going with the animal. So be warned, Bryani. If you *ever* threaten Vane or his brothers again, I'm going to show you just how human I am. I will don my camouflage, hunt you down, and skin you while you scream. Do you understand me?"

A massive cheer rang out from behind Bride, startling her. Turning around, she saw the whole Peltier clan plus some others crowded in and around the doorway.

But it was Vane who held her attention. The proud look on his face made her entire body hot.

"Damn, Vane, you got a hell of a mate there," one of the Peltier quads said.

Bryani lunged at Bride. Her arm reached out from the cage as she tried to grab her. "You can't stop me, *human*."

"No, but I can."

Bride stepped aside as Acheron walked through the crowd to stand before Bryani.

He crouched down near the cage and held her gaze with his. "I'm going to take you home, Bryani, and I'm going to make sure that you can never leave your time frame again. No more piggyback rides with anyone else."

Bryani gave him a sullen look.

"No," Ash said as if he could read her mind. "Alastor won't help again. Your contract is nullified."

"You can't do that," she growled. "He's not free until all of *them* have met their mates."

Ash gave her a taunting half-smile. "You should hang around the gods more often, Bryani. They've tutored me well on loophole laws. You see, all of your sons *have* met their mates. They just don't know it yet."

"Excuse me?" Fury asked.

Ash ignored him. "Alastor is free of you, and for fear of my retribution, he won't enter into any new agreements with you."

"What about *my* retribution?" Bryani shrieked as she rattled the bars of her cage. "Where is *my* justice?"

Ash stood up and sighed wearily. "I'll tell you what. How about this for a bargain? You return to your time period and make sure Dare remains where he is, and I'll give you the one thing you want most in life."

Bryani cocked her head as she contemplated the Atlantean. "You swear it?"

"Yes, I do."

She made a gesture from her heart to her lips. "It's a deal. Now let me out of this cage so that I can enact my revenge."

Ash shook his head. "I'm not going to let you kill your sons, Bryani."

"But you said—"

"Your fondest wish has nothing to do with them. I'm sending you home now, and I promise you, by nightfall you'll be a happy woman."

Bryani vanished out of the cage.

"What are you going to do to her?" Fury asked.

Ash folded his arms over his chest as he turned

around to face them. "What's the one thing your father has always publicly said he'd give anything for?"

Vane's jaw went slack. "To have his mate back. But that was only a lie he told so that the pack would feel sorry for him."

"Well," Ash drawled. "You should be careful what you wish for. You just might get it."

Vane whistled low. "Remind me to never piss you off."

"You're not really going to put the two of them together, are you?" Bride asked.

Ash shrugged. "They were fated to be together and it's time that they dealt with each other. Whatever happens between them though is their business."

"What do I owe you for this favor?" Vane asked.

"It's gratis. When you helped Talon out, you paid a higher price than anyone should ever have to. Consider this a wedding present from me and Simi. Neither your mother nor your father will ever again threaten you or your children."

"Are you predicting the future, Acheron?" Nicolette asked.

"Not exactly. I'm not telling them what will happen. Only what won't."

"Thanks, Ash," Vane said.

"Since you're in a giving mood," Fury said from the doorway, "want to tell me who my mate is?"

Ash gave him a roguish half-smile. "It's up to you to find her."

"Yeah, but—"

"Hang it up, wolf," Colt said, clapping him on the back. "The great Acheron isn't going to answer that."

"Ah man, this is going to drive me crazy. You know I've met thousands of women in my lifetime, right?"

"Yes," Ash said, "but you haven't slept with them all."

Fury looked like he was in pain.

Vane came forward and pulled Bride into his arms. "Thank you," he said, hugging her close. "When Kyle told me my mother was up here with you . . ."

She wrapped her arms around his neck and let the love she felt for him wash over her. "I wasn't about to let her hurt you."

Ash shooed everyone out of the room so that they could kiss in private.

After a few minutes, Vane flashed them from Carson's office, back to Sanctuary. Stefan was sitting up in a chair, looking a bit dazed and still bleeding.

The poor wolf. But he would live.

Someone started playing "Sweet Home Alabama."

"You're too late," Colt shouted. "We already know Ash is here."

"So," Ash said, strolling over to Vane and Bride. "Who are you going to support to take over your pack?"

"Not my concern. I was exiled."

"Yeah, but since Markus will be gone in about, oh, an hour, they'll need someone to lead them."

Vane looked at Stefan, who had wanted the pack for years. Unfortunately, the wolf was an idiot, hence his attempted pact with Vane's mother.

His gaze went to Fury and Cujo.

"Fury?" Vane called out. "How do you feel about leading a pack of wolves?"

A sly smile spread over his face. "I'd love to."

"Bullshit," Stefan snarled as he tried to rise to his

feet. He was still too weak. "He's not strong enough to hold the pack."

Vane looked at his brother, then Stefan. "Yes he is. Because I know my brother is going to relocate the pack back here to New Orleans."

"I'll never stand for it," Stefan snarled.

"You can't stand at all, dickhead," Fury retorted.

Vane ignored Fury's outburst. "Yes you will. If you don't, you and I are going to go the distance." Vane withdrew his spell and let his markings show on his face.

Stefan turned even paler.

"Any questions?"

Stefan turned to Fury and shook his head. "Do you want me to start the move back?"

Fury's grin turned wicked. "I would say yes, but you look like the only thing you can start is bleeding. I'll take care of the pack. Carson, want to help Stefan upstairs before he collapses?"

Carson nodded, then flashed out of the room with Stefan.

Fury came forward. "Thanks, Vane."

"No problem. You've earned it and you definitely deserve it more than any of the others."

Bride couldn't have been prouder of Vane than she was at that moment.

"Food!"

Bride turned at the happy cry from a voice she recognized.

Ash's friend Simi came through the door with a beaming smile. Her long black hair was plaited on each side of her face and she had a shiny pair of red horns on her head. She wore a short black PVC skirt with purple and black striped thigh-high leggings that vanished into a pair of scuffed combat boots. She had on a fishnet shirt and a tight red bodice.

Bride noticed that several members of the bear clan had strained looks on their faces.

"Okay, Vane," she asked quietly. "What is Simi? Animal, vegetable, or mineral?"

"Other," he said with a laugh. "She's a demon. Literally."

"Someone count the cubs," Dev shouted.

"Oh pooh," Simi said to him. "I'm not going to eat no furry food while you gots the good stuff." She opened up the large black tote bag she carried and pulled out an extra large bottle of barbecue sauce.

Simi bobbed her way through the crowd until she saw Bride. She shrieked in happiness. "You play here now too, Bridie? You got any of those great sparklies with you?"

"No, Simi. They're in my shop."

The girl pouted, then turned to Ash. "*Akri?* Can we go visit Bridie's shop again?"

"Sure, Simi. But not today. Bride's here and not there."

"Oh. Okay. Can the Simi buy everything she wants?"

"Of course."

Simi grinned widely, then jumped up and down like a small child. "Okay, everybody dance! You, too, *akri.*"

Suddenly, the Macarena started to play. Everyone in the bar groaned, except Simi, who laughed happily. She grabbed Ash's hand and pulled him to the dance floor.

"Everybody now!" Simi said.

Slowly the rest of the bar's inhabitants made their way to the dance floor.

Bride was stunned when Vane took her hand to lead her to the floor.

"Vane . . ."

"When Simi says dance, everybody dances."

"Like hell," one of the surlier brunette men snarled from his chair at the table beside them. "I dance for no one."

No sooner had he spoken than he jumped up and started patting at his groin as if it were on fire.

"Damn you, Ash," he snarled.

Ash smirked. "The lady says dance, Justin. Get your panther ass out here."

Bride laughed as everyone, including Ash, started doing the Macarena. This had to be the strangest moment of her life.

When it was over, Simi ran with her barbecue sauce to one of the tables and grabbed an entire turkey for herself.

"You're evil the way you spoil that demon, Ash," Justin snarled.

Ash shrugged good-naturedly and strode over to where Simi sat devouring her turkey.

Bride and Vane sat down next to Fury while everyone started a line for the food.

"I'm still stuffed," Bride said.

"Me, too," Vane agreed. So they sat and chatted with the bears while they ate.

Conversations rang out in the room until Bride's

ears buzzed from the happy chatter and music.

All of a sudden everyone grew quiet.

Bride saw Vane's jaw go slack as he stared at the door to the kitchen.

She turned her head to see a gorgeous man approaching them. He was a little taller than Vane and had black, shaggy hair. He had his arms wrapped around himself protectively and wore a long-sleeved black shirt and jeans.

His gaze was focused on her and Vane as he walked slowly through the crowd without speaking to anyone.

He stopped beside them. His eyes were sorrowful and brooding as he held his hand out to Bride.

Her hand shaking, Bride reached out to him.

"She's beautiful, Vane," Fang said, his voice hoarse. "I'm glad you found her."

Vane stood up, but Fang stepped back.

"Fang?" Vane asked.

Fang withdrew from them.

Bride couldn't breathe as she watched him make his way back toward the kitchen where Aimee was waiting. The female bear put her arms around him and, to Bride's amazement, Fang allowed Aimee to hold him as he returned to Peltier House.

"Are you okay?" Bride asked Vane as he took his seat.

A smile played at the edges of his lips. "Yeah. For the first time in a long time, I think I am."

"Good," Fury said. "'Cause if he's messing with Aimee Peltier, Fang is going to need both of us to keep those bears from skinning him."

The band, which was made up of various animals,

took the stage and picked up their instruments.

While they tuned them, a small monkey came running over to Bride and jumped up on her shoulder.

"Hi there," she said to him. "I didn't know there were Were-Monkeys."

"There aren't," a tall, lean blond said as he held his arm out for the monkey. Bride remembered being introduced to him earlier. He was named Wren. "Marvin's the only non-were in the bar." The monkey ran up his arm and perched on his shoulder.

"Oh, sorry."

Wren smiled at her. "It's okay. It took me a long time to get used to the people here, too."

She watched as he walked off.

The band broke into a rendition of wolf songs. Bride felt her face heat up as they sang "Little Red Riding Hood," "Werewolves of London," "Bad Moon Rising," and even "Midnight Special."

"C'mon up here, Vane," Colt said into the mike. "And sing for your supper."

Vane looked a bit sheepish before he left her and joined them on the stage.

"I didn't know he could sing," she said to Fury.

"Neither did I."

She expected Vane to sing some classic rock tune, so when he started singing "The Story of Us," Bride felt tears well up. Vane wasn't singing for his supper.

He was singing for her.

Dev came up to her and pulled her toward the stage.

Bride couldn't breathe as she listened to Vane. He had a beautiful voice, and when he finished his song, he pulled her up on the stage with him. There, in front of all the Were-Hunters, he went down on his knee before her.

"I know we're mated by Were-Hunter custom, but I wanted to make sure and do this right for you, baby." He put the microphone down on the stage and pulled a ring from his pocket.

Bride felt the tears fall down her cheeks as he placed the round diamond solitaire on her finger.

"I love you, Bride McTierney, and I want to spend the rest of my life showing you just how much I need you. Will you marry me?"

She couldn't stop blubbering. Heck, she could barely see him for her tears. All she could do was nod like a hysterical loon.

She thought Vane was smiling, but she couldn't be sure.

"It's okay," Vane said into the microphone. "She cried like this on the day I met her, too. I think it's a good thing for humans."

"Ahhh, I'd cry too if I had to look at you every day for the rest of my life, Vane," Colt said.

Ignoring him, Vane stood up before her and wiped her tears away with his hands. "I'm getting better at this, Bride. I didn't poke your eye out this time."

"No," she said, sniffing back her tears, "you didn't."

He kissed her gently, then led her from the stage.

Ash met them there with Simi, who was also crying. "That was bootiful," she sobbed hysterically at Vane. Then she turned to face Ash. "*Akri*, the Simi wants someone to propose like that to her. Go get that model

Travis Fimmel for me and make him do that, too. Please!"

"I told you, Sim, you can't just take humans away from their lives."

"But Vane took Bride."

"No, Sim. Bride *chose* Vane."

"Then go make Travis choose me."

"I can't do that. It wouldn't be right."

The demon blew him a raspberry before she saw one of the bears bringing a cake from the kitchen. Her tears dried instantly.

"Ooo," Simi breathed, eyeing the cake hungrily. "Chocolate. My favorite. Gotta go now. Bye."

Ash laughed as Simi ran and literally attacked the poor bear who was holding the cake. She grabbed it out of his hands and headed off to a corner to be alone with it.

Shaking his head, Ash turned back to them. "Your father is now out of your hair and I just wanted to say congrats again to both of you."

"Thanks, Ash," Vane said, holding his hand out to him.

Ash nodded as he shook it. "By the way, you don't have to worry."

"About what?" Bride asked.

"You'll have babies and not puppies. And no litters."

Bride was more relieved than she would have thought possible. "Thank you."

"Any time."

Ash left them and picked up a pie from the table which he took to Simi, who looked up at him with her face covered in chocolate. She literally inhaled the pie in less than ten seconds.

Vane draped his arm over Bride's shoulders. As they walked back to her table where Fury and Cujo were sharing a piece of steak, Bride started laughing as she looked around her newfound zoo and family.

"What's wrong?" Vane asked.

"Nothing. I was just thinking that my life has gone completely to the dogs and I wouldn't have it any other way."

Epilogue

Vane shifted himself to the past. It didn't take much effort to find his parents. After all, Acheron hadn't bothered to shield their scent from him and they had only been here together for about an hour.

The Dark-Hunter leader had sequestered the two Were-Hunters on an isolated island during the fifth century. Neither of them had the power to leave either the island or the time period.

It was truly a fate worse than death.

Or at least it was about to be.

Vane flashed to the "arena" where his parents were battling each other with swords drawn. They were both bloody from the fighting, and even though he should be amused, he wasn't.

How could he be? These two people, for all their faults, were his parents, and if not for them he would never have been born.

Even so, some things could not be forgiven.

His father hesitated as he saw Vane. It gave his

mother the opening she needed to run Markus through with her sword.

It should have been a killing blow.

It wasn't.

His mother jerked the sword free, cursed, and stabbed Markus again. Markus only stood there blinking in disbelief as he remained immune from her attacks.

"Give it up, Mother," Vane said as he approached them.

She spun on him with another curse until her eyes focused on his face.

For once Vane didn't bother hiding his facial markings from either one of them. He stared at her blankly as horror filled her expression and she realized the truth about her eldest son.

"I know Acheron probably couldn't care less if you two destroyed each other," he said slowly. "But I couldn't live with myself knowing that he had sentenced one of you to die even though you deserve it."

"What do you mean?" Markus asked.

"I'm altering things a bit. You two can fight and kill each other over and over again, but neither one of you will be able to die by the hand of the other."

"Fine, then," Markus snarled. "I'll kill myself."

"I won't allow that, either."

Bryani cursed him. "You can't stop us."

Vane laughed. "Yeah, Mom. I can. You should have listened to Fury when he tried to tell you about my powers. There are only a small handful of people on this earth whose powers can negate mine. And neither of you are one of them."

Bryani's eyes narrowed. "Why are you doing this?"

"Because you two need to come to terms with each other. What Markus did to you was wrong, but then, I've always been told that two wrongs don't make a right. So here I am trying to do the right thing for once. You two have to deal with each other and settle this hatred." He took a deep breath. "I'll be back in a few decades to see how it's coming."

"You can't leave us here. Not like this!" Bryani screeched.

"Why not, Mom? Dad beat me and Fang and hung us out to die, literally. You beat Fury and left him for dead. Now the two of you can both pummel the one who really pissed you off, and we can live our lives out in peace away from the two of you. Have a nice war."

Vane flashed himself away from them, back to where Bride was busy packing up their things in Valerius's house.

"You know you don't have to do that?"

She jumped and gasped. "I think I need to put a bell on you!"

He laughed.

Bride jumped again as all of their belongings suddenly appeared neatly folded in her suitcases. "Vane . . ."

"What?"

"Never mind," she said with a laugh. She didn't really want to change him, either.

He came up behind her and pulled her to him.

Bride took a moment to savor the feel of him there. To savor the strength of his arms around her waist. "So what are you going to do with the rest of your life now that your parents are taken care of and Fury has control of your pack?"

"Honestly?"

"Yes."

"I don't want to do anything other than spend the rest of my life watching you."

"Yeah, but—"

"No buts, Bride. I've spent the last four hundred years fighting tooth and nail for everything. Hiding who and what I am. Now there's no need. You're safe here in New Orleans and I intend to make sure you stay that way."

She turned in his arms and wrapped her arms around his neck. "And what about my shop?"

"It's all yours."

"Will you help me watch it?"

"No. I'm going to be too busy watching you."

Read on for an excerpt from
Sherrilyn Kenyon's
next book

SEIZE THE NIGHT

Now available from Piatkus.

Valerius pulled at the edge of his right leather Coach glove to straighten it as he walked down the virtually abandoned street. As always, he was impeccably dressed in a long black cashmere coat, a black turtleneck, and black slacks. Unlike most Dark-Hunters, he wasn't a leather-wearing barbarian.

He was the epitome of sophistication. Breeding. Nobility. His family had been descended from one of the oldest and most respected noble families of Rome. As a former Roman general whose father had been a well-respected senator, Valerius would have gladly followed in the man's footsteps had the Parcea or Fates not intervened.

But that was the past and Valerius refused to remember it. Agrippina was the only exception to that rule. She was the only thing he ever remembered from his human life.

She was the only thing *worth* remembering from his human life.

Valerius winced and focused his thoughts on other,

much less painful things. There was a crispness in the air that announced winter would be here soon. Not that New Orleans had a winter compared to what he'd been used to in D.C.

Still, the longer he was here, the more his blood was thinning, and the cool night air was a bit chilly to him.

Valerius paused as his Dark-Hunter senses detected the presence of a Daimon. Tilting his head, he listened with his heightened hearing.

He heard a group of men laughing at their victim.

And then he heard the strangest thing of all.

"Laugh it up, asshole. But she who laughs last, laughs longest, and I intend to belly-roll tonight."

A fight broke out.

Valerius whirled on his heel and headed back in the direction he'd come from.

He skirted through the darkness until he found an opened gate that led to a courtyard.

There in the back were six Daimons fighting a tall human woman.

Valerius was mesmerized by the macabre beauty of the battle. One Daimon came at the woman's back. She flipped him over her shoulder and twirled in one graceful motion to stab him in the chest with a long, black dagger.

She twirled as she rose up to face another one. She tossed the dagger from one hand to the other and held it like a woman well used to defending herself from the undead.

Two Daimons rushed her. She actually did a cartwheel away from them, but the other Daimon had anticipated her action. He grabbed her.

Without panicking, the woman surrendered her weight by picking both of her legs up to her chest. It brought the Daimon to his knees. The woman sprang to her feet and whirled to stab the Daimon in his back.

He evaporated.

Normally the remaining Daimons would flee. The last four didn't. Instead they spoke to each other in a language he hadn't heard in a long time . . . ancient Greek.

"Little chickie la la, isn't dumb enough to fall for that, guys," the woman answered back in flawless Greek.

Valerius was so stunned he couldn't move. In over two thousand years, he'd never seen or heard of anything like this. Not even the Amazons had ever produced a better fighter than the woman who confronted the Daimons.

Suddenly a light appeared behind the woman. It flashed bright and swirling. A chill, cold wind swept through the courtyard before six more Daimons stepped out.

Valerius went rigid at something even rarer than the warrior-woman fighting the Daimons.

Tabitha turned slowly to see the group of new Daimons. Holy shit. She'd only seen this one other time.

The new batch of Daimons looked at her and laughed. "Pitiful human."

"Pitiful this," she said as she tossed her dagger at his chest.

He moved his hand and deflected the dagger before it reached him. Then he slung his arm toward her.

Something invisible and painful slashed through her chest as she went flying head over heels.

Dazed and scared, Tabitha lay on the ground.

Horrible memories ripped through her of the night when her friends had died. The way the Spathi Daimons had torn through them . . .

No, no, no.

They were dead. Kyrian had killed them all.

Her panic tripled as she struggled to right herself.

Her head was dizzy, her vision blurry as she pushed herself to her feet.

Valerius was across the alley in microseconds as he saw the woman fall.

The tallest Daimon, who stood even in height to Valerius, laughed. "How nice of Acheron to send us a playmate."

Valerius pulled his two retractable swords from his coat and extended the blades. "Play is for children and dogs. Now that you have identified which category you fall into, I'll show you what Romans do to rabid dogs."

One of the Daimons smiled. "Romans? My father always told me that all Romans die squealing like pigs."

The Daimon attacked.

Valerius sidestepped and brought his sword down. The Daimon pulled a sword out of nothing and parried his attack with a skill that bespoke a man with years of training.

The Daimons struck at once.

Valerius dropped his swords and swung out with his

arms, releasing the grappling hooks and cords that were attached to his wrists. The hooks went straight into the chest of the tallest Daimon and the one he was fighting.

Unlike most Daimons, they didn't disintegrate instantly. They stared at him with hollow eyes before they burst into golden dust.

But while he was distracted by them, another Daimon retrieved his sword and cut him across his back. Valerius hissed in pain, before he turned and elbowed the Daimon across the face.

The woman was back on her feet. She killed two more Daimons while he killed the one who had wounded him.

Valerius wasn't sure what had happened to the others and in truth he was having a bit of trouble moving from the vicious pain in his back.

"Die, Daimon snot!" the woman snarled at him an instant before she stabbed him straight in the chest.

She pulled the dagger out instantly.

Valerius hissed and staggered back as pain ripped through his heart. He clutched at his chest, unable to think past the agony of it.

Tabitha bit her lip in terror as she saw the man recoil and not explode into dust.

"Oh, shit," she breathed, rushing to his side. "Please tell me you're some screwed-up Dark-Hunter and that I didn't just kill an accountant or lawyer."

The man hit the street hard.

Tabitha rolled him over onto his back and checked his breathing. His eyes were partially opened, but he wasn't speaking. He held his jaw clamped firmly shut as he groaned deep in his throat.

Terrified, she still wasn't sure who she had mistakenly stabbed. Her heart hammering, she pulled up his turtleneck to see the nasty-looking stab wound in the center of his chest.

And then she saw what she had hoped for . . .

He had a bow and arrow brand above his right hipbone.

"Oh, thank God," she breathed as relief poured through her. He was in fact a Dark-Hunter and not some unfortunate human.

She grabbed her phone and called Acheron to let him know one of his men had been hurt, but he didn't answer.

So she started dialing her sister, Amanda, until her common sense returned. There were only four Dark-Hunters in this city. Ash who led them. Janice whom she had met earlier. The former pirate captain, Jean-Luc, and . . .

Valerius Magnus.

He was the only Dark-Hunter she didn't know personally in New Orleans. And he was the mortal enemy of her brother-in-law.

She hit the CANCEL button on her phone. Kyrian would kill this man in a heartbeat and bring down the wrath of Artemis fully on his head. The goddess would kill Kyrian for it and that was the last thing Tabitha wanted to see happen. Her sister would die if anything happened to her husband.

Come to think of it, if half of what Kyrian said about this man and his family were true, she should just leave him here and let him die.

But then Ash would never forgive her if she did that

to one of his men. More than that, she couldn't leave him here. Like it or not, he had saved her life and she was honor-bound to return the favor.

Wincing, she realized she was going to have to get him to safety.

NIGHT PLEASURES

Sherrilyn Kenyon

Amanda Devereaux has a crazy family. Her mother and older siblings are witches and psychics, and her twin sister is a vampire hunter. All Amanda wants is a quiet, normal life. Only when she finds herself the target of an attack meant for her twin, she wakes to find herself handcuffed to a sexy, blonde stranger.

He is Kyrian of Thrace. And while Amanda's first thought is that this might be another of her sister's attempts at extreme match-making, it soon becomes clear that Kyrian is not boyfriend material.

He is a Dark-Hunter: an immortal warrior who has traded his soul for one moment of vengeance upon his enemies. Kyrian spends his eternal days hunting the vampires and daimons that prey upon mankind. He is currently on the hunt for a very old and deadly daimon named Desiderius who has deemed it sport to handcuff Kyrian to a human while he hunts him. Now Kyrian and Amanda must find a way to break their bond before they give their dangerous attraction to one another. Or Desiderius kills them both . . .

978-0-7499-3608-2

NIGHT EMBRACE

Sherrilyn Kenyon

Talon was once a Celt warrior cursed by his ancient gods. Following the murder of his sister, the dying Talon has made a deal with the goddess Artemis. He has been given one act of vengeance against the clan who betrayed him, in exchange for his soul and his eternal service as a Dark-Hunter.

Talon has sworn to fight Daimons and rescue the human souls they've captured. He has never had cause to regret this choice – until he meets Sunshine Runningwolf.

The unconventional Sunshine should be Talon's perfect woman. She is beautiful, sexy and isn't looking for a long-term commitment. But the more time Talon spends in her company the more he starts yearning for dreams of love and family that he buried centuries ago. But loving Sunshine would be dangerous for both of them. Talon is destined never to know peace or happiness while his enemies still seek to destroy him and everyone close to him . . .

978-0-7499-3609-9

DANCE WITH THE DEVIL

Sherrilyn Kenyon

Zarek is the most dangerous of all the Dark-Hunters. He endured a lifetime as a Roman slave and centuries as a Dark-Hunter in exile. Zarek trusts no one. Because of his steadfast denial to follow any orders, he is kept in isolation in Alaska where his activity is seriously limited and closely monitored. There are many who fear he will one day unleash his powers against humans as well as vampires.

Have nine hundred years of exile made Zarek too vicious to be redeemed? The gods want Zarek dead but reluctantly agree to allow justic goddess Astrid to judge him.

Astrid has never yet judged a man innocent, and yet there is something about Zarek that tugs at her heart. He views even the smallest act of kindness with shock and suspicion. But while Astrid struggles to maintain her impartiality in the face of her growing attraction to Zarek, an executioner has already been dispatched . . .

978-0-7499-3610-5

Sherrilyn Kenyon's award-winning paranormal romances have topped the *New York Times* bestseller charts, offering readers a world full of dark and dangerous heroes, feisty heroines and a richly imagined mythology. Sexy, fun and utterly addictive, this series is best described as *Buffy the Vampire Slayer* meets *Sex and the City*.

From the world of the Dark-Hunters comes the most anticipated book to date . . .

ACHERON

Eleven thousand years ago a god was born. Cursed into the body of a human, Acheron endured a lifetime of hatred. His human death unleashed an unspeakable horror that almost destroyed the earth. Brought back against his will, he became the sole defender of mankind. Only it was never that simple . . .

For centuries, he has fought for our survival and hidden a past he never wants revealed. Now his survival, and ours, hinges on the very woman who threatens him. Old enemies reawaken and unite to kill them both. War has never been more deadly . . . or more fun.

Finally, the story of the Dark-Hunter leader, Acheron, is revealed.

978-0-7499-0866-9